Fae

THE SINS OF THE WYRDE

BOOK THREE OF THE RIVEN WYRDE SAGA

BY GRAHAM AUSTIN-KING

THE RIVEN WYRDE SAGA

For Liam, Naomi and Matthew.

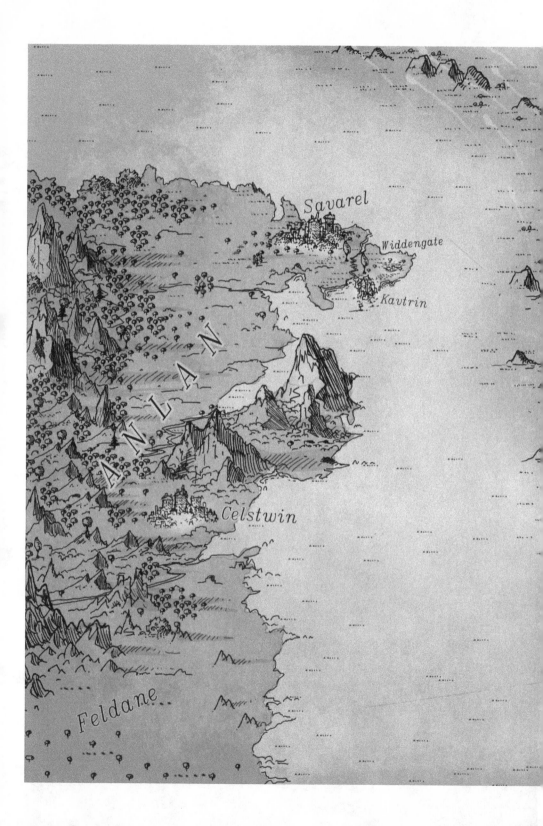

Hesk

The Barren Isles.

The Vorstelv

N

W   E

S

PART ONE

CHAPTER ONE

Miriam moved mechanically, trudging as she pulled a foot free of the sucking mud, and took another step. There had been many times when the smothering touch of the fae's mind had put her into a stupor, but this time her daze was caused by exhaustion. Her feet faltered in the oozing mud created by the passage of hundreds of satyr and the human slaves that followed, and the muscles in her legs burned.

The group of fae, satyr, and fae'reeth had been following Aelthen for days, travelling the ancient trails and paths as they headed away from Tir Rhu'thin, moving southward. They paid little attention to the needs of their human attendants, barely seeming to stop during the day for food, or to rest. The satyr rushed out to hunt after they stopped each day, and the sounds of their feasting and drinking carried on late into the night as she sought what sleep she could.

Miriam stumbled as her foot caught on a rock, her black robes flapping wet around her ankles as she sought to regain her balance. The leather cuff dug painfully into the skin of one wrist as the spun-silver chain grew taut and Ileriel glared back at her as she hurried to catch up with the fae's mount.

Ileriel had always laid only the barest touch of her influence over Miriam. It was as if she wanted Miriam to be fully aware of where she was and the torment she was enduring daily. Even after all these years the fae seemed to delight in her misery and in the bargain Miriam had made, taking pleasure from the fact that Miriam had unwittingly invited this life. Of late, her influence seemed to have been lighter still. Perhaps she simply wasn't worth the exertion of the fae's yoke any longer? Perhaps Ileriel simply no longer cared. After all, she was no longer necessary for the fae to pierce the Wyrde. She was too old now to breed from. What use was she? The thought gave her pause and she stopped in the track without paying attention.

"Keep up, human!" the fae spat back at her, pulling hard on the chain so that Miriam had to struggle to keep from falling.

Miriam flushed and tried to ignore the childish giggles that rose from the satyr around her. More than anything else in this nightmare world, they terrified her. She could cope with the other horrors she had been forced to endure, the half-breed children that had been pulled from her, and the thousand other daily torments. The satyr, however, filled her with dread.

More than once she'd thought of killing herself, ending it all. At once an image flashed into her mind, of her surrounded by a crowd of satyr in the woods as one of them forced himself between her legs. She looked up sharply and met Ileriel's eyes defiantly as the fae looked back at her. The unspoken promise was as clear as it had ever been. Death was hers to choose should she wish it but it would come at the hands of the satyr once they had tired of her, not from her own.

She glanced around, avoiding the scathing eyes of the other humans in the group. The trees were different here. They were clearly getting closer to their destination but, unlike Tir Rhu'thin where the trees were sculpted and shaped by the will of the fae, these were somehow wilder. It was a subtle difference and it had taken Miriam some time to notice it. The sculpting was by no means lesser, it was just less pronounced. As if the design were more in tune with nature, celebrating the wildness of the environment rather than it being twisted for the sculptor's own delight.

The trail led down a gentle slope as they crested the rise, and she enjoyed the respite until the different set of muscles began to burn. Abruptly Ileriel stopped ahead of her and the line slowly drew to a halt. Humans would have questioned it by now, or made some protest at the sudden halt, but the fae simply waited in silence as their human slaves shifted and fidgeted beside them. She could feel Aelthen ahead of them, further along the trail. He was far out of sight around a corner but even from this distance his presence was palpable. The sheer weight of his mind was a sensation pressing against her. It challenged her. Diminishing her as it questioned her right to breathe, to exist, even as it demanded that she wonder at his glory.

The stop was both long and yet somehow still short enough to be cruel. Her muscles protested violently as they began moving again and she hurried along behind the white horse Ileriel rode. It was a glamour, of course. A conceit. No horses existed in the Realm of Twilight, not that she had ever seen. The beast was most likely a shade-cat, concealed beneath the casual magic of the fae's illusion.

The trees parted abruptly with none of the gradual thinning that would be found in Haven, her own world. They passed out onto a lush plain, an island of grasses in the ocean that was the endless forest. For all her years in this world of the fae, this was the first time she had ever been beyond the trees. The place felt suddenly wondrous and alien to her all over again. The empty sky screamed down at her and she fought back a wave of fear and the urge to huddle down like a mouse hiding from a hawk.

It was hours before the city came into sight, though doubtless the fae had been able to see it long before her. It sprawled, spreading out in a ragged circle from the titanic tree at its centre, visible even at this distance. Unlike Tir Rhu'thin the city had clearly been surrounded by a high wall at one point but the buildings had long since spread beyond its protection. Beyond the walls, what seemed to be farmed fields stretched out towards the distant trees on either side of the city.

The differences between this place and Tir Rhu'thin did not stop there. The homes and buildings here were more fashioned stone than the tree homes she was used to and the streets were paved and laid out with a clear structure. Tir Rhu'thin ambled. It reached out from its centre in a languorous stretch with buildings and dwellings laying where they would, with no thought given to order, or at least none that she had ever understood.

Her eyes were wide with wonder as they moved towards this new fae city and her gaze passed along the long line of fae, past Aelthen at its head, and back towards the enormous tree.

The tree was normal enough, save for its massive size. If it weren't for the city surrounding it the sight would have been nothing to raise an eyebrow. As it was the buildings gave her some perspective and the sheer size of it was enough to take her breath away. The uppermost branches and much of the leaves were obscured by a mist, or haze of some kind, and she squinted as she tried to focus on the fog that seemed to swirl and shift slowly about the tree.

The effort made her eyes water and her head ache. She soon gave up and looked down the slight hill, following the line of fae towards Aelthen, far ahead of them. She watched as he approached a small group that had emerged from the city and stood waiting on the path to greet them. They were largely satyr by the looks of things, with only a single fae among them. Her eyes widened in shock as the great creature bent a foreleg to incline his head in a stately bow as he approached the group. Whatever it was that Aelthen wanted here it was clear he didn't hold himself as superior.

"Come, my prize." Ileriel urged her forward, pulling her out of the line so they could move more swiftly. "I'll not sit with the pack whilst Aelthen enters the court."

She ran awkwardly, her old joints working as fast as they could with a lurching, painful, gait. Ileriel glanced down at her, giving her a look of utter disgust at her pace, and then reached out to haul her up, laying her over the horse's rump like a sack of meal. The texture of the beast's skin did not feel like horse. The motion was somehow more sinuous than any horse would ever manage but, in her position, it still jolted and forced the breath from her lungs. She forced herself to try and relax as she gripped at its flanks with her hanging arms as Ileriel rode at a canter to the head of the column.

Miriam was vaguely aware they had passed under a large archway into the city but her position made it difficult to see much beyond the flagstones that made up the path even after Ileriel dropped the horse back into a walk. A buzz filled the city, laying beneath the musical sound of the fae as they spoke. It was a low drone and Miriam had a fleeting mental image of the bees she had once seen kept in hives by a long forgotten uncle. She mentally shook her head at the memory and slid off the horse and down to her feet as they drew to a halt.

The plaza was wide and surrounded by columns with intricate carvings, though all showed signs of age and weathering. Miriam stood in silence and watched curiously as Aelthen followed his escort and stepped forward, accompanied by Ileriel and a handful of his fae. A small group waited for him in the centre of the plaza. Fae with a handful of satyr and fae'reeth that surrounded a tall, pale figure.

Aelthen stopped just short of the group and offered a short bow. The tall figure stepped forward out of the cluster surrounding her, gossamer clothing trailing behind her, and revealing a fae woman of incredible beauty. Miriam stared at her openly as she felt her mouth fall open. It wasn't just at her beauty, albeit a cold alien beauty. The woman filled the plaza, the sheer presence of her was overwhelming. She commanded the eye in much the same way as Aelthen always had, but it went far beyond her appearance. Her mind pressed against all that stood within the plaza, a raging force that touched the edges of Miriam's consciousness and seemed just barely contained.

"After all the long ages the hunters have returned at last," the fae intoned. Her

FAE - THE SINS OF THE WYRDE

FAE - THE SINS OF THE WYRDE

voice was little more than a whisper yet somehow seemed loud enough to shake the leaves from the closest trees. "Among all of those that remain in Tira Scyon I am among only a handful who might have known those old enough to remember the last days of the hunt. I was a babe at the time. You are as tale or song come to life. You are myth made flesh and you will find things much changed in these lands, I think. I would be the first to bid you welcome anyway. I am named Tauntha. Welcome to Tira Scyon, the last home of the fae."

Miriam ignored Aelthen as he made some formal reply and frowned as she looked at the fae woman. There was something not quite right about her. Her eyes refused to entirely accept what they were seeing. There were minute eddies and disturbances in her form, she realised, as if her perfect features were somehow formed of a mist surrounding a hidden truth. She narrowed her eyes as she concentrated, and then, as if she had blown into a fog, the image parted and for the briefest moment, Miriam caught a glimpse of the ancient and wizened creature at its centre. She gaped at the sight and staggered as Ileriel jerked the silver chain, pulling her forward even as the ancient creature paused in what she was saying to look at Miriam curiously.

"...my favoured daughter, Ileriel, the Pathfinder," Aelthen was saying as they drew closer. Miriam ground her teeth as another sharp jerk on the chain forced her down to her knees by Ileriel's feet as the fae gave a short bow. "Be welcome also, Ileriel," the woman greeted her. "And this creature? A manling she? The first I have seen, I will confess."

"A trophy, Revered Elder," Ileriel replied with pride shining in her eyes. "This human is the Wyrde Reaver. Were it not for her we should still be locked away within the Outside." She favoured Miriam with a cruel smile. The old woman shrank away from her expression as thoughts of Devin and her betrayal bombarded her, cutting like jagged glass. She bit back tears as she fought to keep the emotions from showing on her face. So long as Ileriel wished to torment her with these thoughts she must leave Miriam's mind free to react to them and the pain was a price she was willing to pay. Despite that, Miriam would sooner claw out her own eyes before she gave the fae the satisfaction of knowing what effect her words really had.

Across the plaza a fae hissed, a sharp intake of breath to cover her obvious anger as she glared at Ileriel with fury clear on her face. The Elder turned at the sound and beckoned her forward.

7

"My own daughter, Aervern," she said by way of introduction.

Ileriel looked at the newcomer, a frank appraisal clear in her eyes. "Were you admiring my pet, Aervern?" Ileriel asked. "Or was your little squeak intended to mean something more?"

"Your time in the Outside must have blunted your mind as well as your tongue, Ileriel," Aervern spat. "Tauntha rules here. Over fae, fae'reeth, and satyr. She is no mere Elder. You owe her your respect."

"Aervern, be still." Tauntha muttered, her voice was pitched low but the tone was hard and sharp enough to carry.

"There is much that will have changed, much that must still be discussed. Make amends for your rudeness." Aelthen said, half-turning to Ileriel. His words were ostensibly a rebuke but they held none of the harshness that Tauntha's had and Miriam caught the warmth of approval in his tone.

Ileriel bowed her head in acknowledgement and turned to the still-seething fae. "My apologies, Aervern," Ileriel offered. "Perhaps if I present you with a gift to atone for my thoughtless words?"

Aervern's eyes narrowed at that. "What do you offer?"

Ileriel tugged sharply on the chain, pulling Miriam forward on her knees. "I have had little opportunity to amass trinkets but perhaps you would take some small pleasure in my trophy?"

Aervern glanced at Miriam, eyes narrowing as she weighed the value of the gift. "I thank you," she managed to grate, though her eyes told a different tale entirely.

Ileriel passed the silver chain across as Aervern drew closer and, as she did so, a wave of emotion passed through Miriam. She had thought herself relatively free of the crushing influence of the fae but, as Ileriel relinquished her hold, the rush was almost enough to overwhelm her. She stood, half-stunned, as the conversation carried on about her. Tauntha and Aelthen were still speaking. She was dimly aware of plans for a great feast but her mind churned and spun too furiously for her to pay much attention. She walked blindly as she was led to the far side of the plaza and hardly noticed when she was eventually ushered away.

Aervern walked her through the streets to a shining stone courtyard surrounded by columns. Over-hanging archways and trellises, bedecked with ivy and creeping flowers, stood beside a strangely shaped stone building that was almost swallowed by a stand of tall trees. It was as alien a dwelling as any she'd seen, and it was only her years in the world of the fae that allowed her to understand that the trees were as much a part of the building as the stone was.

"You will reside here, as my guest for a time," Aervern spoke softly, eyes still appraising her as she headed towards a corner of the plaza.

"Yes, mistress." Miriam gave a half bow.

Aervern shook her head. "No! I will not be your mistress. I will not *keep* you, human. You will be a guest with me, not a possession."

Miriam blinked. The words were such a foreign concept to her that she almost asked the fae to repeat herself. No, better to be still for now. To watch and learn. Long experience had taught her that one did not question the fae. This was far more likely to be another game than anything else. Daring to hope for anything more would only lead to crushing disappointment and the laughter of this creature as she watched it unfold.

"Seat yourself," the fae prompted as she sank down onto a collection of pillows.

Miriam lowered herself awkwardly down to the cushions with a grimace. Her hips and thighs still protested the march she'd endured tethered to Ileriel's wrist.

"I confess I am unsure just what to do with you. I expect there is much we can learn from each other and much we should speak of." Aervern began. "The returner named you, 'Wyrde Reaver'," Aervern said. Her words were halfway between statement and question, with an odd intonation, and Miriam sat in silence as she waited to see if she would say more. Eventually she gave a small nod.

"I would know the tale." Aervern said formally, placing a strange emphasis on the words.

"I don't remember a lot of it, Blessed One," Miriam hedged.

Aervern laughed, genuinely amused. "Do not call me that. I am no more blessed than you."

Miriam looked at her, careful not to meet her eyes for too long. "In what manner should I address you, mistress?"

"The name I was gifted is Aervern. You may use that." The fae favoured her with a smile as she looked at her curiously. "'Wyrde Reaver' is an awkward title. Do you not have another name?"

"Miriam." The word came too hard to her lips, little more than a whisper as it passed them. She tried again. It was easier the second time. "My name is Miriam."

"A serviceable enough name, I suppose," Aervern said with a snort. Her nose wrinkled as if she smelled something she'd rather not. "And will you tell me your tale Mir' Rhiam?" she asked. "Of how you came to be with the Returned and how you pierced the Wyrde? In exchange I offer you wine and meat and shelter."

She let the odd inflection pass. "I will tell you what I remember, Blessed…" she stopped herself at a sharp look from Aervern that was softened with a small smile. "…Aervern," she finished with a sheepish look.

"Compose your thoughts. A tale such as this should not be recounted unprepared. I shall arrange for your refreshment." She stood in a fluid motion and made her way over to an archway, clapping her hands loudly as she approached. The satyr that appeared was nothing like those Miriam was used to. His features were the same as the others but his demeanour was one of servility rather than that of a barely-restrained hunter. Aervern spoke to him, giving swift instructions in a low voice before she returned to the cushions and looked at Miriam expectantly.

"It's hard to remember too much, it was all such a long time ago. I do remember that I was injured," Miriam began haltingly. "I'd been wounded, an arrow in my leg, and the wound had turned sour. I remember being lost in the woods, feverish, and waking in the night to the sound of flutes. There was something about a ring of stones…" The words came slowly at first as she struggled to remember things that felt more like the tatters of a dream than anything else. Aervern proved to be almost the perfect audience, however. Quiet and attentive yet willing to prompt if Miriam faltered, and she found herself telling the whole story. Of how she'd first been brought to the cold and barren place that held the fae, and then later, onward to this twilight world.

"And what of the Wyrde?" Aervern asked Miriam after a time as she sipped at the wine the satyr had brought. "How did you ever learn to pierce it? How did you learn to travel to the Land of Our Lady?"

Miriam looked at her, the interruption throwing her train of thought for a moment. "I didn't. I mean, I don't know that I did anything myself. They took me with them whenever they needed to cross but I never did anything. It seemed like just my being with her was enough at the time. Now, of course, I am not needed at all. I think Ileriel only brought me here because it amused her."

Aervern fell silent then, a deep frown on her face. "I think that is enough for now. I would ask something of you, however. Though I have no intention of keeping you as Ileriel did, it would be curious if I did not make some use of you. I would have you act as cup-bearer at the coming feast. An easy enough task, and one which will send the correct message to the Returned. If you will consent?" She waited for Miriam's bemused nod before she spoke again. "Take rest. I will have Gannkis take you to a room. I do not imagine that your journey was an easy one. You have some days until the feast, which you may use as you will. Gannkis will provide sustenance as you require it, you need only ask. I would not suggest you leave my dwelling unescorted, however. You are more of a curiosity in this place than you know." She gave a complex short bow, touching her forehead with one hand, and then left Miriam with the odd little satyr.

"If you'll follow me, human?" the creature waved her onward and led her through an archway and into the marble-clad building. The interior was well lit, with numerous windows and polished mirrors positioned to make the most of the natural light. Gannkis led her up a sloped corridor that ran in a spiral until they reached her rooms. A wooden bed, fashioned from a single piece of timber and carved with intricate vines, filled a large portion of the room. Against one wall an odd wooden bowl sat resting upon what appeared to be a tree stump that looked to have sprouted from the wooden floor itself. The window looked out into the courtyard, half obscured by thick leaves that hung from the branches that reached to stroke the window in the breeze.

Miriam sank down onto the bed as the satyr turned to leave. Her hands curled, resting inside each other, as she looked unseeing at the polished stone wall. The world had moved beneath her and, somehow, she was lost without having really taken a step. Eventually she sank down onto the silks and slept. A true sleep, without a touch on her mind or dreams. Perhaps her first in years.

The house seemed different when she woke. The light was little changed and she lay in a tangle of silks as she tried to decide what time of day it might be. It was empty, she decided. A house has a certain feel to it when there is someone else there, something entirely different when it is empty. She stood slowly with no need to hide the aches and pains that vanity normally demanded. With little other option she threw on the tired black robe and decided to explore.

The house seemed huge and rambling with its gently sloping floors that turned in a lazy spiral taking the place of stairs. It wasn't really even a house, not in the conventional sense anyway. The majority of the structure was stone but one turn in a corridor revealed thick bark making up a section of the wall. At some point a tree must have formed the core of the building and had long since been enveloped. Perhaps there was a message to take from that. For all the veneration the fae seemed to have for nature they were quick to discard it when it no longer suited their needs.

Miriam wandered slowly, giving no real thought to her destination. To say the house was odd would not have even touched the edges of it. There was an entire room filled with tiny bells, strung on strands of thread that ran from floor to ceiling and wall to wall. Another room seemed empty aside from a wide band of blue silk that ran from the floor to where it hung suspended by a polished rail strung near the ceiling.

Miriam shook her head and headed in the other direction, down towards the courtyard. She was intercepted before she ever got close. The manservant satyr proved impossibly light on his feet, his cloven hooves seemed to make no sound at all on the polished wooden floors.

"Are you in need of sustenance, human? I was about to wake you." The words were polite enough but the eyes were as hard and angry as Caerl's had ever been. Caerl? Lords and Ladies where had that thought ever come from? She hadn't thought of him in years. But then, had her mind been hers to wonder with? She realised Gannkis was still stood looking expectantly at her and she coughed to cover her embarrassment. "Not at the moment, Gannkis, thank you."

The satyr gave a curt nod and turned to go. "Aervern mentioned you could show me the city?" She called out, stopping him. He paused and looked back at her, his unblinking amber eyes almost making her falter mid-sentence. "If it's not too much trouble that is?" she finished weakly.

"Such was the mistress's instruction." Gannkis replied, his words as flat and expressionless as his eyes.

"If you're too busy..." she trailed off. He was so hard to read. It wasn't quite hostility but closer to some kind of resentment, though even that wasn't the right word.

He shrugged. "It is of no moment, human. We shall leave now if you have no wish to break your fast."

He led her out through the courtyard and into the streets. The morning was among the brightest she'd seen and rare white clouds scudded along in a light breeze. The streets were quiet and Gannkis led her at a brisk pace in the rough direction of the massive tree she had glimpsed at the city's centre.

"Gannkis!" she gasped after only a few minutes. "I can't go as quickly as you, we're going to have to slow down."

He looked at her then, as if only just now seeing her for the first time. A tiny old lady wrapped in a dark robe hobbling along behind him. He bowed his head slightly, tilting it in acquiescence, and then set off at a slower pace.

She gawked like a child at the marble-clad buildings and intricately carved statues. It was so beautiful. So wild. So utterly wrong in so many ways. The realities of this world were suddenly as sharp as any razor's edge and her mind recoiled from both them and the realisation of how much of her life had been lived through a fog. Before Gannkis had led her more than ten minutes from Aervern's home she was pleading with him to take her back, and she fled back to her room to huddle in a ball with the bedsheets held tight between her fists as she sobbed for a life both lost and stolen.

As the days passed Aervern seemed content to let her come and go at will. She had done little more than look in on her since the first night. The second trip came at Gannkis's insistence and lasted far longer, allowing them to make their way to the larger streets. This time it was the staring of the satyr that drove her back to the compound, away from eyes as awestruck as her own.

She was dressed and ready for Gannkis the next day. It had come as a simple realisation as she lay sleepless in the bedsheets. This was her life now. She could either embrace it and take it for her own, or she could hide for as long as Aervern would let her, or until the darkness claimed her.

"Do you mind if I ask some questions as we go?" Her only response was a grunt and a curt nod. It would do, she needed something to distract her from the eyes she could already feel upon her.

"Would you tell me about this place? All I know of this world is Tir Rhu'thin. I didn't even know there were other fae until we travelled here."

"This is Tira Scyon, our home for more years than any of the tales I have learnt will tell. From the age of legends, the time of the hunt, and the search for the Land of Our Lady, we have resided here. Here and the surrounds," he added. "There are those that prefer the wild of the forest to the city."

Miriam was silent for a moment as they walked, admiring the statues that seemed to sit at the centre of every crossroad. "The time of the hunt?" she asked finally.

"Before your kind forged the Wyrde."

"I think there is a lot I am missing here, Gannkis," Miriam admitted.

"Did they not answer your questions at Tir Rhu'thin then, human?" the satyr asked, genuine curiosity in his eyes.

"They keep humans as slaves in Tir Rhu'thin," Miriam said, her voice low. "We're breeding stock and little more."

Gannkis grunted and looked at her as if waiting to see if she would say more. "There is some wisdom in that I suppose." He gave her a wry smile as she gasped at his words. "Look around you, human, do you see many fae? Little ones at play? No." He shook his head. "We are a dying breed. More often than not a coupling leads to one of my kind or to a fae'reeth. A fae child is a rare thing indeed, and one that has been in decline for many years."

"You seem very different to the satyr I have encountered."

"Different?"

"Calmer, somehow more human I suppose. The satyr at Tir Rhu'thin are almost feral."

The satyr snorted and gave a grim smile. "No doubt those at Tir Rhu'thin have not had to adopt the measures we have undertaken here. My kind are creatures of desire, be it for the hunt or for womankind. How well do you think our people and this city would fare were it filled with endless satyr with no hope of release?"

"I suppose I'd never thought about it," Miriam managed through her blush. She inwardly laughed at herself, fancy blushing at her age!

"We are a long-lived people. Eventually urges give way to rage, and rage to destruction. We learnt that lesson long ago. Satyr here are given the choice once they draw close to this point. Either go to the wilds or be gelded."

"Gelded!"

"It is a minor thing, and one that soon heals." Gannkis shrugged. "There are times when I regret my choice but not many."

"What happens to those that go to the wilds?" She asked.

"None could say. They never return," he told her with a strange look.

Silence fell clumsily between them, stumbling over the remnants of the conversation as Miriam followed after him. Gradually she became aware of the eyes upon her. It was a prickling, uncomfortable feeling that made her feel exposed despite the full-length robes she wore. The satyr watched her openly, some peering out from doorways, some gawking at her as she passed by them. The few fae they encountered were little better themselves, though they fell short of actually stopping in the street to stare at her.

She ignored them as best as she could, examining the city around her. The simple fact of her curiosity was overwhelming. It wasn't something as obvious as a blind man regaining their sight. It was closer to regaining a sense of smell that had been fading for years. The freedom of her own mind both delighted and disgusted her as each new sight brought home the reality of just how far under Ileriel's power she had been buried.

The city was beautiful, but gloomy. The dim light from the sky was barely enough to light their path on the narrower streets, once the tall buildings and trees had blocked their share of it. Gannkis walked her around the city, careful to move at her pace but, despite this, she was soon forced to lean on his arm. The very act of taking help from the creature made her skin crawl despite herself, and she fought hard to keep her expression blank.

It was a slow process but she eventually began to notice the city itself. It was ancient, but then any city can be ancient. Kavtrin hadn't been a new settlement. No, it wasn't just that it was old, it was tired. That was a good word for it, she decided as she nodded to herself. The buildings sagged, some falling from the embrace of tree limbs that had decided to grow in different directions than those they had been bidden. More than one dwelling sported the remains of wellpumps outside its doors. The pipes covered in verdigris and lost to time and neglect.

Miriam looked ahead to the tree, more to give herself something to focus on than anything else. The haze she had noticed as they'd approached Tira Scyon was more pronounced now, a purple tinged mist that swirled around the leaves. "What is that around the tree, Gannkis?"

He looked up and smiled at the sight before looking back at her. "The Swarm. It is more impressive once you draw closer. Come." He waved her onward, leading her through the streets past dark windows and sculpted foliage towards the massive tree.

15

The droning grew louder, the sound seeming to split into a harsh fluttering, and then to increase almost to a roar. Gannkis took her hand as she hesitated, drawing back from the noise, and pulled her the last few yards to the end of the street. The square was almost completely filled with the roots of the tree as they thrust through ancient paving slabs and quested down into the earth. The trunk alone was so vast that it would have taken ten broad men linking arms to reach all the way around it. This was not what made her gasp, however. The purple mist that had seemed to surround the foliage of the tree was now clear. The tree was surrounded by a swirling mass of fae'reeth. The tiny winged creatures moving in an endless pattern, shifting in a slow dance around each other and the tree as their wings formed a wind all its own that buffeted at Miriam as she stood with one hand pressed to her mouth.

Their numbers were beyond count, and she found herself almost entranced by the swirl of the pattern before she noticed the figure behind the curtain of tiny bodies. It was a fae'reeth, or at least something similar. Rather than flying with the others, though, it hung almost motionless in the air, its wings holding it still but close to the trunk of the tree as it met her gaze and stared back. There was no animosity in the gaze. It held little more than curiosity, and perhaps an invitation.

"It is… unwise, to remain too long," Gannkis told her as he tugged her back out of the square. "The tree is the place of the fae'reeth. Even Tauntha would hesitate to outstay her welcome here."

She let him lead her away, casting frequent looks back over her shoulder. The sheer number of the fae'reeth had staggered her. There had to have been tens of thousands of them, all as beautiful as they were deadly.

"I would appreciate it if we could return now, human." Gannkis said with a faintly pained expression. "The sun will be rising shortly and I have never cared for its touch."

His words touched a chord with her and the connections fell into a neat order in her mind. The sun would leach his power just as the light would render any exposed glyph powerless. She looked around again, noting the dark windows, the unlit streets. Since she had come to Tira Scyon she had yet to see a single moon-orb or rune plate, even the wellpumps had all been in ruins. There hadn't been a glyph in sight.

CHAPTER TWO

"Gannkis tells me you managed to go as far as to The Swarm?" The voice was soft, but it still made Miriam jump. She bolted upright on the cushions and hurriedly set the tea down on the floor beside her as she looked around.

"I didn't hear you come in," she said with a nervous laugh. The fae stood in the archway leading out towards the city, watching her with an unreadable expression.

"May I join you? I would speak with you," Aervern asked with a strange formality.

Miriam pushed down a shrug. That would have been rude, but then why was Aervern even asking for permission? "Of course," she managed with a watery smile.

Aervern sat cross-legged at the very edge of the pile of cushions, silent for the moment as if wondering how to begin. "How are you finding my home? Do you have everything your kind requires? I confess I am not overly used to humans."

"It's very comfortable…"

"Yet?"

"I'm sorry?" Miriam frowned.

"You had more to say," Aervern explained. "Do not let some odd sense of propriety still your tongue. It is very comfortable yet…?" she left the question hanging.

"I'm not quite sure what I ought to be doing." Miriam let out a noise that could have been a nervous laugh had it just a little more courage.

"It is for this reason that I would speak with you." The fae woman's eyes held her own. It wasn't just that she was staring, it was more that she obviously didn't place any emphasis on it or understand it might be considered rude. The creatures were so very different and it showed in the thousands of tiny little ways far more than it did in the obvious things. "The feast will take place this night and I would have you as my cup-bearer but there is a deeper task I would have you perform." She cocked her head to one side, as if thinking . "Perhaps it would be simpler for me to show you. Are you able to walk for a time?"

Miriam pulled herself to her feet. "Of course, although I walk a lot slower than

I used to."

"I will be mindful of this," Aervern nodded.

They left in silence, taking the same winding route Miriam and Gannkis had followed that meandered towards the city centre, but then branching off towards areas that Miriam had never seen before. They passed through a long-neglected park to a series of low bridges that led them over shallow streams and then through a succession of tiny islands, each with its own marble bench or statue. Even these were marred, however, with the broken ruins of other bridges laying in the waters, the thick roots that had once supported them, twisted and wild.

Miriam looked at her often but the fae appeared content to remain silent for now and seemed oblivious to her companion's curious glances. She gave up. If the woman wanted to walk in silence then so be it. The city was quiet, with only faint strains of music drifting on the light breeze with the faint smell of wood smoke. These fae seemed to have no particular compulsion to live close to each other, or to form neighbourhoods, she noted. Whole districts stood empty between those dwellings that she could see were occupied. The buildings that stood between them were often half-collapsed or fallen from the trees that had once cradled them. Not for the first time Miriam wondered at the place. Half the city seemed to be in ruins yet the fae seemed not to notice as they lived in opulence amongst the rubble.

As they passed over another low bridge the sound of music grew louder. Lights became visible in windows and strung across tree-born platforms. Between one street and the next the feel of the city changed. What had felt like a lifeless ruin suddenly shook itself awake and stirred to life. She glanced at Aervern only to find the fae watching her, gauging her reaction. Within another hundred yards there were fae and satyr everywhere. They wandered the streets in groups of twos and threes, lounging in the gardens as they sipped wine from wooden goblets or listened to the satyr play as fae'reeth circled the musicians in a lazy spiral.

The light from moonorbs spilled out from buildings and the aromas of roasting meat wafted from more than one doorway but without the tell-tale smell of wood smoke. Miriam turned slowly, her eyes tracing the skyline. The chimney pots over the city were scattered but smoke could be seen rising from all areas, all except this district.

"This is the enclave of those come from Tir Rhu'thin," Aervern said in a low voice. "We will not linger here but will pass through swiftly. I would have the use of your eyes. Pay close attention to what you see. I will wish to speak with you on this."

Miriam shot her a confused look but the woman was already moving, striding forward towards the light of the moonorbs. She did not slow but rather led Miriam at a pace through the district. In contrast to the rest of Tira Scyon this area fairly buzzed with life. Fae and satyr were everywhere she looked but far more striking were the fae from Tira Scyon. The look of awe stood out all the more strongly on their faces. That most human of expressions looked out of place on the beautiful features of these fae. Like a fire burning on the water, it did not belong.

Aervern ushered her along at a brisk pace, allowing her only the most cursory of glances as they passed through the throng. Often though, one glance was enough as the fae from Tir Rhu'thin astounded a crowd of fae and satyr by infusing long-dead series of glyphs with a trickle of power. Grime encrusted wellpumps hissed to life, throwing steam and muddy water in all directions amid a burst of laughter and delight from the throng. Moonorbs that had been kept only as a curiosity piece, flared to life after centuries lying dark and dormant. All around the fae delighted in this trinket and that as they were infused, and all about Miriam was that same expression, awe and delight. It was like being surrounded by children opening Midwinter's gifts.

They ventured only the smallest distance into the Tir Rhu'thin enclave, turning the corners so that within five minutes they had stepped back out away from these foreign fae. Foreign fae? Had Tira Scyon become her home? The notion stilled her enough that Aervern shot her a curious look and hurried her along. She slowed her pace as they passed the first of the bridges and turned to her. "Do you understand why I brought you?"

"I don't, mistress," Miriam confessed, using the title before she thought and casting a guilty glance at Aervern's face.

"The day you arrived here in Tira Scyon, when I first saw you chained to the wrist of Ileriel, you did something extraordinary." Aervern met her eyes as her feet slowed. "When you beheld my mother, Tauntha, tell me, what did you see?"

Miriam froze, the question could mean so many things. "I saw a great beauty, mistress."

"I've asked you not to call me that," Aervern snapped. "You are not a cup or a knife. You are not my possession, human." She took a deep breath as she waved away Miriam's attempts at apology. "That Tauntha is beautiful is without question but that is not all you beheld. Tell me."

"I… I saw a beautiful fae woman but, that's not all I saw." Miriam glanced up and Aervern motioned for her to continue. "As I looked at her, I could see that there was something surrounding her, almost like a mist. It seemed to cling to her, cloaking her like a second skin. It seemed so odd to me and I remember trying to make sense of what I was seeing, and then suddenly I could see through it and see the form that stood within."

Aervern nodded, her eyes regarding Miriam intently. "Do you know how many fae could have pierced a glamour created by Tauntha?" She shook her head, her long hair floating in a cloud around her for a moment. "Maybe one in ten score, and then only if she was distracted. Tauntha felt you pierce the glamour. She looked at you, if you remember? For a human could do this…" she frowned, losing the thread as she stared at Miriam. "I almost wonder…" she muttered, shaking her head again.

"This is why I brought you with me today," Aervern began again. "Ileriel's *gift*," she twisted her lips on that last word, "may be far more than she ever imagined. You see what is really there, Miriam. Eyes such as those may prove invaluable."

"I don't understand," Miriam admitted with a shake of the head.

Aervern looked around them suddenly, scanning the empty homes and ruins. "Come, we should not speak of this here and there is much that should be done before the feast." She moved off, leaving Miriam to struggle behind, fighting to keep up as they headed back to Aervern's odd home.

"Attend me whilst I change," she instructed as they entered the house. For all her protests that she would not keep Miriam as a slave she was apparently not opposed to issuing commands. The fae moved swiftly, leading Miriam to her rooms and shedding her clothes with a casual abandon that would have shocked Miriam had she not already spent years with Ileriel. "We were speaking of your piercing of my mother's glamour, were we not," she asked over one shoulder as she plucked at the simple garments hanging in front of her.

Miriam nodded but the fae had already turned away. "I value eyes that can see what is truly there before them. The Returned present a challenge to us, one that has already become evident. Did you perceive this when we entered their enclave?"

"There seemed to be a lot of excitement," Miriam said slowly as her mind raced, replaying the events.

"There is much knowledge that has been lost to us. The working of these glyphs is one of the things my people have forgotten."

Miriam moved to a simple chair, considering Aervern's words before she spoke. "Then surely this reunion is a good thing for your people?"

"You think they will give this knowledge freely?" Her laugh was bitter. "No, there will be a price to pay. Every service has its reward and every gift its cost." She tugged at the shoulder of the diaphanous garment and turned to face Miriam. "Your service this evening will also command its own price. What would you have of me?"

Miriam froze, the thought tearing up from the darkest hidden corner of her mind where she had buried her hopes. Her tongue moved and she spoke without even thinking. "If I am no slave of yours, would you let me return to my world, to my home?"

Aervern smiled then, a small smile touched with regret. "I cannot." She spoke softly, the denial delivered gently and the disappointment was a knife that thrust slowly through her flesh.

Miriam nodded once, and fell silent as her lips pressed together. Better to be still than to provide the response that this creature had clearly been looking for. She let her mouth twitch in the smallest of wry smiles. To think, she had almost begun to let herself believe that this one might have been different.

Aervern seemed oblivious to the silence and continued to preen herself in front of the looking glass. "You will need to leave shortly. Gannkis will take you to the feast. There will be preparations you can busy yourself with until my arrival."

Miriam stood, biting down on the tender flesh inside her lip as she gave a stiff bow and left.

Gannkis was easy enough to locate. He grunted his acknowledgement of her as she entered the long low kitchens. The sight of the satyr bustling about the kitchen was almost enough to lift her mood. Almost.

"You are quite correct." Gannkis replied to her question. The mistress will require you at the feast shortly, and doubtless there will be much that is still to be done. I will escort you now, if you are ready?" Miriam looked down at herself. She was still dressed in the black robe Ileriel had provided for her. Was this fitting for this feast? It wasn't as if she had anything to change into and, at that moment, she couldn't bring herself to care. She shrugged. "I'm as ready as I can be."

Gannkis gave her a look, its meaning lost in his amber eyes. "Shall we depart then?" He led her back out through the courtyard and towards the centre of the city at a brisk pace. Her hips were screaming within the first half a mile but Gannkis either chose to ignore her limping or, perhaps, he simply didn't care.

She heard the noise of the preparations long before the feast came into sight. The central plaza was filled with a series of long, low tables, surrounding a central portion with other tables set into a horseshoe shape. Bright cushions were strewn about where humans would have put chairs, and the tables themselves were set low to the ground. A huge fire had already burnt down to dull coals in the centre of the horseshoe where whole deer were turning on spits, watched by a handful of satyr. Their expressions were serious, and they were clearly concentrating on the task at hand. Gannkis pointed out the long table set to one side of the plaza, filled with wine and platters of food, and left without a word, a dark look burning in his eyes.

Miriam threaded her way through the throng, ignoring the weight of the stares of the satyr around her. They worked mostly in silence with only the briefest of conversations carrying on around her. She was given no direction, and largely ignored, as she carried empty goblets and plates, setting them in place on the table.

The time passed swiftly, and as the first flutes struck up a tune the mood of the place shifted. What had become a comfortable silence for her, as she worked alone against the background of the murmured conversation of the others, suddenly became taut. A bowstring pulled tight to the lips as it strained for release. She turned, knowing what she would see before she looked. Figures were approaching the edges of the square. She watched as they drew closer, frowning as her mind tried to make sense of what she was seeing.

The closest figure seemed wrapped in a thousand cobwebs, and spiders scurried in and out of the web as she walked. Another was wreathed in a storm of fire and frost that spun about him in a tornado that just barely revealed the form standing naked and unconcerned within. Of course, Miriam nodded to herself as it became clear. This banquet could never hope to accommodate all of the fae. Only the highest echelons of fae society could hope for a seat. In her own world the guests would have been dressed in their very finest clothes, gowns that would have bought her father's inn three times over. What need did the fae have of elaborate gowns and clothing? Instead they wrapped themselves in the most spectacular glamours they could fashion.

A fae with a tattered black cloak sank down into the cushions beside the low table and waved her over to him. It was only as she drew closer that she saw the tortured faces that screamed and writhed in the folds of the cloak. It was as if it were woven from the very fabric of nightmares itself. She fought down a shudder and hurried to fill the goblet he waved at her.

Aervern's entrance was subtle and Miriam would have missed her had she not been looking in the right direction as she slipped in just ahead of Tauntha and Aelthen. Her glamour was simple. An elegant gown that reached down to brush against the earth. It was the colour of the true-night sky and, as she looked, she realised that no, it wasn't just the colour of the night sky, it was the sky itself. Dark clouds scudded across it, allowing the stars to shin through for just the barest moment, leaving the beholder to wonder if they'd really seen them at all.

Tauntha was stunning as she rode in beside Aelthen. She wore no glamour save the one she always wove to conceal her real form. Instead, she rode on the back of a massive shade-cat, the largest Miriam had ever seen. The shade-cat seemed docile and utterly under her control. Its green eyes passed over the assembled fae with little interest as it yawned, revealing sabre-like fangs. She drew it to a halt with a word and a hand pressed to its broad neck, and extended her other hand to Aelthen. The horned creature dipped a foreleg in a bow as he took it, assisting her as she slipped off the side of the massive cat. Miriam could see why she had chosen to ride, standing by his side she was dwarfed by Aelthen. He stole the eye and did not share it with the smaller figure.

Tauntha slapped the rump of the shade cat, which came easily to her shoulder, and it darted away in shock, turning to give her a baleful look before running through the streets toward the distant forest.

"An impressive entrance was it not?" Aervern spoke into her ear, her breath hot on Miriam's neck.

She jumped. "Most impressive," Miriam replied, keeping her eyes and voice neutral. Aervern didn't seem to notice, pressing an ornately carved wooden goblet into Miriam's hands. She leaned closer, her lips hardly seeming to move as she spoke in a whisper. "I regret the way I must act this night, Miriam. Know it is a display for the eyes that watch us. Take note of what you see and hear. I would value your thoughts."

"I don't understand, mistress."

"This is the court, Miriam. The remnants of the greatest of the houses gather here at Tauntha's call to welcome those who have returned. There are ten times a thousand tales of treachery and deceit I could tell you of the court but know this, they are watching you and I as intently as you watch them. Take note of what you see and hear, wine and pride have loosened many a lip." She nodded towards the end of one table, to a figure shrouded in mists that seemed to emanate from the horned helmet and heavy plate armour he wore. "This fool here styles himself as the Lord of Mists. Pay special attention to him, feed him wine as often as you are able and have an ear for his conversation." She turned Miriam, steering her with a hand on her shoulder. "The one dancing with the satyr is Dehr'mione. She is skilled at acting the fool but her mind is as sharp as any here. Be wary of her but she is another I would have you pay attention to. Note what she says if you can. If not, then note who it is she speaks with."

With that she directed Miriam to the serving tables set to one side. "Your duties are simple enough and will leave you ample time to observe. You are to serve me before any other. You may pour wine and bring food to other fae but only if I have no need of you. Make sure my cup does not run dry and fetch me some meat once Aelthen has begun to eat. As the night goes on spend less time attending me. Your ears will catch little if they are tied to my table."

Miriam rushed to fill the cup from the pitchers of wine, looking about her as she did. Aelthen's fae had brought other human attendants with them. She could see the lost hopeless expression that she associated with the press of fae minds. They probably were barely even able to function, lost in the fog that filled their heads. She doubted they would even notice the glamours that surrounded them.

The satyr, she noted, could be easily split into two groups. Those who served were much like Gannkis, subservient and somehow less wild than the satyr she was used to. It was nothing obvious, present only in the mannerisms and the way they carried themselves. Those satyr from Tir Rhu'thin lounged at the tables drinking and eating or dancing to the ever-present flutes. They looked at their cousins with clear contempt. Over time disdain gave way to dismissal and finally they ignored them.

The numbers continued to grow until the plaza couldn't possibly hope to contain them. The fae stretched as far as she could see, leaning against decrepit doorways, crouching on rooftops or simply standing in the streets. Those closest to the plaza drank wine that had been passed to them but many simply watched.

They seemed wilder, these fae. Many were dressed in leathers or pelts whilst still others sported glamours that had them entwined in ivy that seemed to sprout from their bare feet. At least she assumed it was a glamour. She paused, thinking about it as Aervern glared at her, holding her empty goblet.

Aelthen sat in the centre of the high table sipping at a cup as his eyes swept over the gathering. He rose slowly to his feet, allowing his movement to still the tongues of those about him rather than calling for silence himself. He stood for a long moment, simply looking at the assembled fae and satyr before he spoke.

"Long years were we trapped in the cold, the Outside. I have dreamt of this return so many times, that all of this scarcely seems real. Yet real it is, and I rejoice that we are able to breathe the sweet air of our homeland once more." A cheer rose up and he held a hand up for silence as he continued.

"The days pass more slowly in the Outside. Long ages have my huntsmen and I lost as the years flitted past here, turning just as the leaves flick in the winds. Now we have finally returned and I find my people are as a shadow of what they once were." One hand gestured to the deer roasting on spits over the coals as he spoke. "Never in my time would we have stooped to burning meat over hateful flame. Never would we have treated our brothers of the hunt in the fashion you now do, gelding them as if they are common beasts."

Miriam could see the faces of those closest to Aervern growing grim and it must have been obvious even to Aelthen as he lifted a hand again to stem the growing whispers and angry mutters.

"I do not hold my children as superior, or claim they are the only true fae. I only say much has changed in the time we were locked away. The treachery of those who were once our servants has taken its toll upon all of our peoples. You are much changed from the people we left behind when we embarked upon that last hunt. There is much that could divide us, but instead I call for unity. Let the court be united in purpose as we recapture the glory of our people. There is much we can teach you, glyph-lore and a thousand uses for the Lady's Gift. In return, I ask only that we join under one banner. I would lead you to the Land of Our Lady. Lead you so that we might remove the infestation that pollutes that place. That land that was truly meant to be our own.

"Since our return I have led my children through the Worldtrails. I have passed through to the Land of Our Lady, and led our people on the Wild Hunt. I have seen what they have become. Those scattered few manlings that ran from us, those that fled from battle and through the Worldtrails rather than face us with honour, they have bred like maggots in rotten meat. They infest our promised land, covering the earth like a blanket of filth. They have bred beyond control and now they must be culled. Our promised land will be reclaimed!"

He fell silent and the silence spread out from him, enveloping the plaza until the only sound was the faint hiss of fat falling from the roasting meat onto the coals. The cheer when, it came, grew all at once. Starting as one voice, and then becoming a roar as the fae stood in concert and cried out their support. Miriam looked in horror at the assembled figures with their fists held high. Among the throng only Aervern and Tauntha remained seated, their faces telling different tales. Aervern's one of horror, whilst Tauntha's face was etched deep with resignation as she beheld a destiny that she had likely long seen coming.

The music was swift to follow the cheers and fae and satyr alike moved out onto the floor to dance to a tune too wild and frenetic for Miriam to really follow. Fae'reeth flitted through the air over the feast, forming their own dance over the heads of the fae below.

"A human!" A deep voice spoke, penetrating the wonder she'd felt for a moment. "An old one at that. Can you be the one they have been speaking of? The Wyrde Reaver?"

She turned to see the figure wreathed in smoke-like fog stood before her. "Blessed One," she acknowledged him with as deep a curtsy as she could manage. "Ha! And versed in our tongue no less. It seems the Returned have trained you well." The voice seemed delighted, but with the face shrouded in the glamour it was hard to tell. As if reading her thoughts the fae reached up to its head, pulling the fog that was formed into the rough shape of a horned helm back over its head until it was reformed as a cowl thrown back on its shoulders.

"I am known as the Lord of Mists," the fae said as he smiled. "I expect many among the Returned will come to know my name before much time has passed. Now, tell me, are you truly this 'Wyrde Reaver' I have been hearing about?"

How to respond to that? "I am, Blessed One." Miriam replied, making sure her head was slightly bowed in submission.

"And now you belong to little Aervern, is that right?"

"My mistress made a gift of me, Blessed One."

"A pity you were not fortunate enough to be placed under a fae of greater stature. Little Aervern has been riding Tauntha's tail for as long as I can remember."

What did this creature want? "Truly, Blessed One. My new mistress spoke of you before attending the feast. I must say meeting you in the flesh far outstrips the tales she told."

The fae were not immune to flattery and Miriam had to stifle a laugh as the creature basked in the compliment, almost seeming to preen in front of her. "Come, dance with me, human. You can tell me more of what little Aervern said of the Lord of Mists."

Miriam glanced past him to the whirling figures and shook her head violently. "I couldn't possibly, Blessed One!" she gasped. "My old bones could never match your pace and I would mar your own perfection with my stumbling."

"Nonsense." He moved in a blur and took her by the wrist, leading her out among the dancers as a father would pull a wayward child. He leaned close, "Only a fool lets the music set the pace. The dance belongs to the dancers." He pulled her into a complicated series of steps that passed through the melody and rhythm of the flutes, coming close enough to brush the beat they set, but then drifting off into its own arrangement before returning to visit once more. They moved slowly, passing both fae and satyr leaping and spinning to a much faster beat yet somehow it did not seem out of place. It was as alien a thing as Miriam had experienced in all her years in their world but yet, on some strange level, it made sense. The dance had a beauty that moved beyond the music and she found herself smiling despite herself.

He quizzed her as they danced. Questions that seemed to bear no relation to each other, ranging from Aervern, to how many cups she'd filled that night, to Tir Rhu'thin and the humans there. Eventually he stopped, leading her out of the dance. "I'll return your pet now, Aervern," he said as he pulled Miriam into the space between them. "She's an entertaining thing, though worthless given she can no longer breed."

"Caraviel," Aervern replied, inclining her head politely. His smile twisted at the sound of what Miriam assumed must be his real name and, giving the briefest of bows, he dropped Miriam's arm and turned on his heel.

The feast went on long into the night and Miriam lost count of the number of times she refilled cups or was pulled out onto the floor by fae or satyr. The fae seemed capable of eating, drinking, and dancing without limit. Aervern finally dismissed her and she fought to make her way through the revelry in search of her bed, slapping away the hands of the satyr who sought to drag her back to dance. She glanced back once at Aervern and the image stayed with her long after the tables were out of sight. Aervern, tearing at a slab of venison with her teeth and bare hands. The meat so rare that it bordered on raw, the blood running freely down her chin as it caught in the firelight.

Chapter Three

Aervern woke her with a gentle shake and Miriam sat up in the bed, rubbing at eyes that didn't want to open. The darkness of true night was gone but it didn't quite feel like the day had started.

"I would not wish to take from your rest," the fae woman apologised. "We have tasks this day and I would speak with you before we need to begin them." She rose from where she perched at the end of the bed. "Dress. I will arrange for food to be made ready."

Miriam pulled herself upright as the fae left. The smooth floors felt odd under bare feet. She was too used to the roughly fashioned hut that Ileriel had kept her in. She shook her head, and then her eyes grew wide as she realised what she was seeing. Where her tattered robe had hung the night before over an ornate rail set against one corner, now a selection awaited her. She ran the fine fabrics over her fingers. Silks, satins, and fabrics she couldn't even name. Robes of every colour and design, dresses she would have blushed to wear when she still had the looks for them. They must have been brought in whilst she was sleeping, but where had they even come from? Since she had arrived in Tira Scyon she had yet to see a single trade being performed. The satyr worked the fields and provided fruit and meat but who made the clothes? Who made the knives and pots she'd seen in the kitchen? In Tir Rhu'thin these things had largely been done by the slaves, but even then there had been some things which were just there. She'd been too fuddled by Ileriel's mind to notice it, but now that she thought of it there were many things that didn't make sense.

She caught herself, suddenly aware of the time that she'd wasted, and picked out a simple white dress with an odd belt that tied at the waist in an elaborate clasp, dressing quickly and heading down to meet Aervern.

The fae sat in the courtyard, a selection of fruits and honeycakes set out before her. "Sit. Eat." She waved a hand at the food set before her and waited as Miriam eased herself down into the cushions.

"I would tell you of some things whilst you eat. Do not interrupt me, I will have questions of my own for you once I am finished." She somehow managed to make the sentence sound like a question and looked at Miriam intently, holding her gaze, until she nodded.

"I spoke of how those that have returned present a challenge for my people? You will have seen some of these things as we entered their enclave here. Even that, my calling it an enclave, is a sign of the problem. There has been no gift to them, no ceding of power or right. This enclave is merely an empty portion of Tira Scyon in which they were allowed to rest during their stay here. Already we speak of it as being theirs, of belonging to them." She waved a hand, brushing the thoughts aside. "It is of little importance now."

Miriam picked up a honeycake and nibbled at it in silence as Aervern leant forward, placing a hand on the low table. "You saw the glyphs at work amongst the Returned when we visited them?" Miriam nodded. "You have seen these things before, at Tir Rhu'thin, of course. Here though, here that knowledge is lost. We have no glyphs and none among us has the knowledge of how to imbue them with what grace we are given." She paused and took a deep breath before she continued. It was a very human act and Miriam caught herself. These creatures were not human, she reminded herself. It would be all too easy to fall into the trap Aervern was obviously setting for her. To allow herself to accept this feigned friendship the creature offered. The only difference between Aervern and Ileriel was the city and their names.

"You see what it is that Aelthen offers, do you not?" Aervern didn't wait for her to answer. "His offer is benevolent on the surface, but like the frozen lakes in the Lightless Steppes it is a trap. The ice is too brittle. The waters, and the creatures that lurk beneath the surface, hunger for anything foolish enough to attempt it. Aelthen's offer is much the same. Likely you did not hear this when you were serving at the feast but, already, names are fashioned for us. *Wildfae* they call us. As if we are some pitiful satyr lost to lust and madness in the woods. Already I have some of my own people look upon them and call them *Trueborn* or *Highfae*. This is how it begins, Miriam. This is how my people will be enslaved."

She snatched up a goblet Miriam hadn't even noticed was there, draining it of the wine it held in long, graceless gulps. "What was the mood of those you served last evening? How did they look upon Aelthen?"

"They were certainly admiring," Miriam hedged

Aervern slammed the goblet down onto the table, the anger coming fast and terrible. "Do not clasp your thoughts so tightly to your breast, human. I could rifle through your memories in moments if I but chose. If I wanted a witless slave such as those from Tir Rhu'thin keep their humans I would have kept you as such." She forced down her anger with a visible effort. "It is your opinions I want. Tell me what those wise eyes of yours saw."

Miriam uncurled slowly from the fetal ball she'd recoiled into. There was a desperation clear in the woman's amber eyes. Despite everything she found herself beginning to hope.

"What do you offer in return?"

Aervern rocked back as if she'd struck her. "You dare?"

Miriam waited, keeping her face impassive as she fought down the rising fear.

"I feed you, give you shelter, and more," Aervern told her in a voice made all the more dreadful for its icy calm. "You are free of the Returned. Free of the Touch. I owe you nothing."

Miriam looked down at her hands, the wrinkles and calluses marking out her years as a slave. "I'm an old woman, Aervern. Most of my life has been spent as a slave to Ileriel. I don't imagine I have many years left to me. If you want my thoughts, my help, you'll have to offer me something in return."

The fae's eyes narrowed in thought as she looked at her, measuring her. "What would you ask of me?"

"Nothing more than I have asked already." Miriam told her. "Return me to my home, to my own world."

Aervern stood, throwing her arms into the air. "Have you not heeded a single word I have spoken to you? That knowledge is lost to us. I could no more pass through the Worldtrails than I could imbue a single moonorb. Your only path to your home lies with the Returned." She fell silent, watching as Miriam collapsed in on herself. "I will make you this oath, however. Should a way present itself I will aid you however I am able." Miriam's eyes shot up at that and Aervern met her gaze with one as stern as hers was hopeful. "You must understand what I offer here risks my life and those of my people. If you betray me, human, singers will refuse to tell the horrors of your ending."

Miriam nodded once, silent, as the fae sank back down to the pillows. "Now, tell me of the feast. Begin with the Lord of Mists."

* * *

Miriam cursed as the hem of her robe caught on another branch. She freed it quickly, stabbing herself on the thorns as she did so. Aervern was already ahead of her, following at a respectful distance from Aelthen and Tauntha. If Miriam didn't hurry she'd lose sight of all of them.

She forced her legs into a slow trot, ignoring the twinge of pain from her hips and knees as she rushed through the forest. Aervern watched her, looking back over one shoulder with a faintly amused expression.

"Like someone watching a new pet," she muttered to herself in briefest of whispers. She regretted it instantly and fought to keep the guilty expression from her face as she gauged the fae's eyes. Had she heard her? It was impossible to tell.

She fell back into a walk beside Aervern. At least the creature didn't insist she walk three paces behind her or some other such nonsense. A glance to the right showed Ileriel, Aelthen's escort, some fifty yards away, as she passed easily through the trees. As if she'd felt Miriam's eyes upon her she glanced at the old woman. Her eyes were flat as she regarded Miriam with cold disinterest, and then turned away.

"How you do propose to proceed?" Tauntha asked as she walked, her voice carrying easily through the trees.

"The humans have grown in numbers, far beyond what we could ever have imagined. Though they are pitiful creatures, even the strongest shade cat could be brought down by enough rats. The full strength of our race will be required if we are to succeed." His look was direct and clearly conveyed a meaning that was lost on Miriam as she listened in silence.

"You do not know what you ask," Tauntha said after a moment. "They were given their choice and they have made their oaths. They have gone to the wilds and owe nothing to Tira Scyon. They will not return. They will not listen."

Aelthen met her eyes and turned to look out through the forest. "I am not of Tira Scyon. I was Lord of the Hunt before your banished were ever born. I am a figure returned from an age of myth and legend. I am as much a tale to them as the Mistress of Shadows or Firla Flameseeker. I am a song made flesh. They *will* listen to me and when the call goes out, they will come."

Tauntha stopped as she considered this. It was a handful of breaths before she spoke again. "Still, it is a risk you propose. I could not say where they reside or guess at their numbers. This is a thornsnake you suggest we snatch up blind, not knowing if we grasp the head or the tail."

"You speak of risks?" Aelthen gave a mirthless chuckle. "Do you know how it is I came to this form? How I came to be satyri? A thousand nights and more I spent basking in the light of Our Lady's full strength. Years spent hoarding her Grace and fleeing from the rays of her jealous brother. I shunned the chase and those who would tempt me to squander this power. I became a mockery of what it means to be a satyr and few were those who would suffer my presence. Do you suppose I received some signal when the time was right? That there was a great light from the heavens or that Our Lady herself spoke to me? No. There was merely the risk of attempting it, and failing, wasting years of effort and endured scorn for naught. Do not speak to me of risks." He led off again, moving through the trees in silence as he looked into the distance.

"Much has changed here. Our numbers are diminished greatly from my time, our people once covered this world. Is this truly all we are now? What of the Carnath? What of Tir Riviel? Of the Singing Woods?"

Tauntha shook her head. "All gone, all fallen."

"All?"

"The Carnath sought to rule. They rejected the Ivy Throne, and the Court, and marched upon the people of the Singing Woods in a bid to claim them. Theirs is a sad tale I do not wish to recount but both are long gone now and Carnath itself is nothing more than a collection of charred stones. Tir Riviel is deserted. Its people left this realm just a handful of centuries after the Wyrde rose. They sought the home of the manlings, though none remembered the ways. Perhaps they found them. Perhaps they wander the Worldtrails still." She lifted her eyes from the trail. "Are the numbers of the humans truly as great as you say?"

Aelthen nodded. "Greater. Their number seems beyond count. As well guess at the number of leaves in the forest."

"You propose a slaughter then?" Her words were light but even from the distance they followed at Miriam could see the anger than played just below the surface of

Aelthen's eyes.

"I propose to reclaim what is rightfully ours. The Land of Our Lady was found using our arts. The humans would never have discovered the power of glyphs had we not taken them to serve us. The knowledge was given to them and they have abused it. Their betrayal is without peer. They turned the grace of Our Lady into a mere tool, an insult to every fae that ever drew breath. They fashioned their devices to harness her like a beast of burden. Then they rebelled, and when it became clear we would not suffer them to live, they fled. Of all the places the might have fled to, why there? It combines insult and betrayal in one act." He snarled out the words, eyes flaring as he spoke.

"No, Tauntha. I will not flinch from your words. I do propose a slaughter. I propose we wade, hip-deep through their blood, until only a manageable number remain. These we will keep in their proper place, in the breeding pens. Our people will rise to greatness once more and we will know revenge." He fell silent and for long minutes the only sounds were the rustle of leaves and the cracking of twigs under Miriam's feet.

"What of the Ivy Throne?" Aelthen asked then. "It is empty?"

"It is," Tauntha sighed. "Empty since before you, yourself, left this land I believe?"

Aelthen nodded, half-listening as he stroked his long beard with one hand. "I should have thought it claimed by one of the houses."

Tauntha laughed then, an ugly, bitter sound at odds with the beauty of her face. "The houses are all but gone, Aelthen. Did you not say it yourself? We are a shadow of what we once were. A fae child is born maybe once in a hundred births. The number of fae'reeth begin to challenge the stars in the skies and I could not tell you how many satyr choose the wilds. My own daughter, Aervern, was one of the last fae born to us. Our numbers dwindle as each fae passes. Though it would pain you to admit it, we need the humans."

Aelthen drew back as if she'd slapped his face. His face grew dark and Miriam felt Aervern stiffen beside her as her hand crept to the small of her back.

"We need them as the flower needs the bee," he said in a dreadful, quiet voice. "They are a means to an end, a tool, and those we choose to keep will be treated as such. Among all who remain among the fae *you* should have learnt these lessons. You have lived long enough to know how far we have fallen."

He shook his head then, as if shaking off the conversation. "What of you? Why have you not claimed the throne yourself? Your daughter herself called you ruler here."

Tauntha glanced back at Aervern and shook her head, an odd expression playing over her features. "I do not truly rule. I lack the support to mount a successful bid for the throne. The rule of Tira Scyon, of what fae remain, is a tenuous thing lying between myself and Variska, the Light of the 'Reeth."

Aelthen raised an eyebrow at that, genuine surprise on his face "A Fae'reeth? Truly? I would not have thought one of them capable."

Tauntha nodded. "She is ancient, far older than I, though she seldom leaves the tree and her swarm now. There are a score or more of self-styled lords who would reach for the throne but their game, of houses long-fallen, is little more than petty squabbles. They have not the influence or the numbers to make a true claim."

Aelthen waved the response away. "Enough of this. Our Lady will be full and glorious as she fills the skies no longer than a handful of nights from now. I will take my children, and all that choose to come, on The Hunt. Will you come and see for yourself of what I speak? Of what the manlings have become?"

Tauntha shook her head with a laugh. "You flatter me, Huntmaster, but these bones are too old for the Worldtrails. My daughter perhaps?" She looked back at Aervern with a raised eyebrow. Aervern fell still under their attention and nodded once. Beside her, Miriam kept her face impassive but within her a desperate hope took shape.

* * *

Aervern stepped out into the courtyard behind Gannkis as he carried the tray of honeycakes and fruits to Miriam's small table. It had become a morning ritual of sorts, Aervern would join her for breakfast and question her on the events of the previous day. Half the time, in fact, most of the time, Miriam didn't understand what it was Aervern was looking for. She seemed to focus on the most unlikely of events but, as the night of the full moon drew closer, she seemed increasingly anxious.

Aervern sat down into the cushions with a fluid elegance that would have made a dancer weep while Gannkis set down the tray. A human would have sunk down or simply collapsed into the cushions. Miriam herself struggled to sit in the cushions and retain any shred of dignity. She smiled a greeting as she reached for one of the honeycakes.

"Did you sleep well?" Miriam asked, prodding a gentle smile out onto her face even as it fought to run and hide. She couldn't really care less if the fae had slept well or not. What she wanted was to understand what this creature really wanted from her.

"We do not truly sleep," Aervern was saying. "Not as your kind do. To say we take rest would be closer. It is hard to explain."

Miriam nodded.

Aervern picked at a cake, breaking off small pieces barely larger than crumbs. "I would know your thoughts of Aelthen's intentions."

Miriam coughed on the honey cake, the seeds and nuts spraying from her lips and bouncing against her raised hand. The fae woman looked at her, her amber eyes intent, clearly waiting for her to begin. "You want to know what I think of Aelthen's plans? His plans to travel to my world and slaughter my people?"

"That was my question, yes."

Miriam stared at the woman for a moment and shook her head in wonder. "I think—" she began but cut off as Aervern sprang to her feet and looked about wildly. She clapped a hand over her mouth and sprinted across the small courtyard. Miriam stared after her as Aervern ran to a tall clay urn and bent over it, retching and heaving.

"Aervern!" she struggled to her feet and hobbled after her on legs gone stiff from sitting.

The fae was pale and shaking. She shrugged off Miriam's hands as she reached for her and wiped at her mouth with one trembling hand.

"Are you sick?" Miriam asked.

Aervern sneered at the notion. "We fae do not get, 'sick'." She went back to the table and snatched up a goblet of wine. "I do not understand this. It has been the same most mornings for days now."

Miriam's eyes widened. "Days?"

Aervern nodded. "Always the same. I catch the scent of these cakes and then I am…as you saw. I do not understand this. The aroma is not unpleasant."

Miriam looked at the fae curiously. "Aervern, could you be pregnant?"

"What would this retching have to do with that?"

"Women often find that they become sick in the early stages," Miriam said with a shrug. "For most it's something that passes."

"Fae females do not suffer from this." Her voice was firm but her eyes darted about under a tight frown. She was hiding something.

"Ileriel would sometimes have me serve those fae who'd visited the breeding pens in Tir Rhu'thin," Miriam said, the words coming slow and cautious. "Morning sickness was not unknown amongst them."

"Fae do not get sick." Aervern glared at her, biting off the words.

Miriam ignored her. "Those carrying a human child did." She fell silent as Aervern's head sank down into her hands.

"What is it for then, this sickness?"

"I'm sorry?"

"What purpose does it serve?" Aervern asked her.

"Purpose?" Miriam shook her head.

"All things have a purpose when birthing a child," Aervern stated, brooking no argument. "The urge to eat increases, providing food for the babe. The teats grow, and ready themselves for milk. What purpose does this retching serve?"

Miriam laughed but stifled it at Aervern's expression. "I don't think it works like that, Aervern." Her smile faded. "Really? Fae women don't get morning sickness? Ever?"

The woman shook her head firmly. "Never."

Miriam fell silent. If Aervern was pregnant it was by a human. She thought back, had the fae ever told her she had never met humans? If what she'd told her of the Wyrde and the Returned was true, she couldn't have. But then how could she be pregnant? The thoughts tumbled over themselves inside her until her common sense gave way and she spoke without thinking. "I thought I was the first human you'd met?"

Aervern's eyes flashed as she caught the slip and she sipped at her goblet before she spoke again. "I did not feel the need to speak of it."

The words were mild enough but there was a heat behind them, warning Miriam off. She ignored it. Life was short enough and she'd lived a life she'd despised. "Yet you expect me to tell you everything about Tir Rhu'thin, about how the fae here react to the changes Aelthen brings. You've made me your spy, Aervern. Don't you think you owe me this news about my own kind?"

Aervern started to speak, the tone hot and angry, but then bit it back and Miriam relaxed out of the flinch that had only half-started. "You are right. I do have truths I should tell." She met Miriam's eyes and her expression was both haughty and ashamed, like a child forced to admit a lie. When did childhood end for fae? Miriam wondered. She pushed the thoughts away as Aervern began to speak.

"Far from here, closer to Tir Rhu'thin, lay the ruins of a city, Tir Riviel. It is ancient, older than many parts of Tira Scyon, and it is a place of mysteries. Humans dwelt there, ages past, when fae and human lived as one. I travel there sometimes, to wander its empty squares and lost gardens. I met two humans there, not long before you arrived here with the Returned."

"Humans!" Miriam blurted. "From where? What happened to them?"

"From Tir Rhu'thin," Aervern replied. "They had escaped the camps there and fled. They came upon that place by chance."

"When was this?" Miriam demanded, excitement filling her.

"Ten or twelve weeks past."

"I thought you said it wasn't long before I got here?" Miriam protested, biting her tongue as Aervern shrugged, unconcerned. "So where did they go? What happened to them?"

Aervern drank deeply from her cup, draining it and reaching for the jug to refill it. "They stayed for a time, long enough for the male and I to grow close enough to couple anyway. Eventually I left them."

Miriam let that one pass, focusing on the rest. "So they could still be there?"

"No, Miriam." Her voice was soft, almost gentle.

"Why not? They could be!"

Aervern shook her head. "They had escaped from Tir Rhu'thin. Satyr were already hunting them."

"What are you saying?"

She looked down into her cup as she spoke. "They were hunted, Miriam. You must know what happened to them?"

Miriam nodded as tears pricked at her eyes.

"Say it," Aervern insisted.

Miriam lifted her head to glare at the fae. There was no reason behind this. This was purely spite and she would die before she allowed another of this race to take pleasure in her misery. "They're dead," she said, her voice flat and cold.

"I would have saved them if I could," Aervern said. "The Returned had not yet made contact with Tira Scyon, though we knew of their presence. I could not have our first contact be overshadowed by tales of us aiding their escaped slaves."

"No, that would be terrible," Miriam said, drawing out the words until the sarcasm fairly dribbled from them.

"You forget yourself!" Aervern snapped.

"No, Fae." Miriam snapped back, slamming a hand down onto the table. "I remember myself. For the first time in thirty years or more, I am not buried under Ileriel's influence. My mind is free to see things as they really are. I see you are not the same as Ileriel but you are still fae. You, and all your kind will always see us as beneath you, less than you. We are barely a step above animals to you and you will always use us as you will!"

"Yes, we will." Aervern agreed, calm despite Miriam's outburst. "The difference will lie in how we treat you. How those at Tira Scyon might treat humans need not be the same as how those from Tir Rhu'thin have. Aelthen will soon make his bid for the ivy throne. Already the Returned hold themselves as superior. Already fae here accept the name Wildfae." She stood abruptly. "Walk with me. I wish for you to see something. It is something you have seen before but clearly you did not get the message."

She led Miriam out into the streets of Tira Scyon and towards the enclave they had visited before. She did not speak, ignoring Miriam's attempts as she hurried her along. The streets were crowded as they entered the enclave. It seemed that most of the fae in Tira Scyon had packed themselves into the district. Aervern still did not speak. Instead she would touch Miriam's hand and subtly indicate things she wished her to see.

A tall fae made her way along the path, her bearing imperious and she looked through Miriam rather than at her as her eyes swept over them both. Behind her three fae followed, bearing baskets. On the wrist of each of them was a black leather cuff, embossed with red markings. Miriam raised an eyebrow at Aervern in question but the fae shook her head and led her onwards.

The leather cuffs were suddenly everywhere she looked, on both fae and satyr alike. Fae wore haughty expressions as they paraded along the winding paths or lounged on the stone benches.

"Aervern, are you taking your pet for a walk?" Aervern spun in place to face Ileriel as she made her way towards them. A satyr and male fae stood to one side of her, eyes downcast as they waited.

"As are you, it would seem," Aervern replied, unruffled.

Ileriel gave her companions a glance and shrugged. "These two? They serve in exchange for knowledge. I could accommodate one more, should you wish to learn of glyph-lore yourself?"

The hiss was soft but Miriam was close enough to hear it as Aervern fought down her rising anger. "An interesting offer but I must decline. I was under the impression that glyph-lore was to be shared freely?"

"As it is," Ileriel forced frost into the shape of smile. "These two just wish to acquire the knowledge more swiftly than other wildfae."

Aervern shrugged, looking bored.

"And what of your new pet? Will you be bringing her along this night as Our Lady rises? Will she ride along behind you on The Hunt? There is little point in possessing a trophy if none can see it, now is there?"

Aervern studied Miriam as if seeing her for the first time. "She would be of little use I expect."

"A banner is of little use if not flown," Ileriel countered. "Bring her. She can be the living flag of the wildfae as they taste the sweetness of the hunt."

Aervern's eyes flickered to meet Miriam's, carrying an apology in that briefest of looks. "Perhaps I will, at that."

Ileriel flicked a glance at Miriam, laughter in her eyes though no smile touched her lips. "Excellent. I look forward to seeing you as we muster at your great tree."

"At the tree?" Aervern asked.

"Had you not heard?" Ileriel looked honestly surprised. "Variska herself will join us on The Hunt. The Swarm will rise."

Aervern gasped. "The Swarm has not left that tree in my lifetime."

"And how long has it been since any wildfae joined the hunt?" Ileriel laughed. "When we reclaim that land that is truly ours the fae'reeth will have their place. Of course the Swarm rises! As soon as Aelthen find the satyr you sent into the wild they will rise also."

"Until the Lady rises then." Aervern nodded her farewell and pulled Miriam after

40

her. She dragged Miriam along by the wrist until they passed beyond the enclave and into the empty pathways of Tira Scyon. "The Swarm," Aervern breathed. "I had not thought Variska would leave her tree again."

She looked over to Miriam. The mask had shattered and for the first time Miriam could see true fear in her amber eyes. She looked lost.

As a very young child Miriam thought of her father as perfect. His deep voice was rarely raised in anger and his strong hands were always there guiding her. They had often wandered the woods close to the inn, harvesting the wild mushrooms her mother was so fond of. It was just a scratch really, but when the knife slipped in his hands, slicing into the delicate skin of her leg, the real wound was her sudden realisation he was human. He too could make mistakes. He wasn't all-knowing. The thought had shocked her so much she hadn't shed a tear or uttered a sound as her father fussed about her, binding the wound and carrying her in his arms all the way home. The look on Aervern's face was the same as she'd worn then. The world had shifted under her feet. Something about the fae'reeth joining the hunt had shocked her to the core of her being.

"I must leave you for a time." Aervern spoked suddenly as she collected herself and looked at the old woman. "I will return in good time to collect you for the hunt. I will have to bring you on this. I wish it were not so but Ileriel gives us little choice." She gave a short bow of farewell, apparently forgetting herself so thoroughly that she bowed to an almost-slave. Miriam stared after her in silence before turning to make her way back to Aervern's home.

CHAPTER FOUR

The moon climbed into the cloudless sky, cresting the trees slowly, and ignorant of the dread it brought along with it. It spilled out over Miriam, carried along by the silvery light, and then it gnawed at her. The courtyard was silent as she waited and the windows of the house watched her, dark and soulless.

She waited. Aervern had not returned even as the twilight faded into true night, but still she waited. She knew it could not be long. The moon was still rising but the horns did not wait. The first call, long and mournful, sounded as soon as the lowest edge of the fae's silvery goddess no longer reached down to touch the trees. Other horns rose to join with the first. To them it probably sounded glorious and jubilant but to Miriam it sounded a death knell. A call to butchery.

Aervern appeared without ceremony, passing through the archway into the courtyard and reaching out to take Miriam's arm as she drew close. The silvery cord that she fashioned was just a glamour, Miriam knew this, but it was identical to the one Ileriel had chained her with. She raised an eyebrow at Aervern and lifted her arm experimentally, testing the weight though there was nothing to feel but a cool, mist-like touch on her skin.

"Ileriel has me bound by her expectation but she cannot force me to become her, no matter how much she forces me to appear as if she has. So long as we two know the difference, that is enough." The fae ignored Miriam's questioning look. "It is a glamour only. Do not stray far from my side or we will be undone."

Miriam followed as the fae began the walk towards the distant tree at the centre of the city. The chain hung between them, weightless but yet heavy with implication. She ran a hand through it, the silvery links of the chain passed through the flesh of her fingers as if they were no more than fog themselves. Aervern glanced back at her, perhaps feeling her actions. She was intent on not treating Miriam as a slave, as less than her, yet they walked together towards a hunt that would see the fae chasing down humans like rabbits. The notion was ridiculous and the long bone knives strapped to Aervern's back muddied the waters further still. Miriam was close to giving up on her attempts to understand her but the questions refused to still in her mind, and she worried at them as they drew closer to the tree.

The central square was packed, fae creatures of every colour and size were pressed in. Miriam shivered under the weight of the eyes that fell upon her. Free of Ileriel's influence she realised for the first time that she truly was a trophy. She shifted closer to Aervern and looked down at her feet, avoiding the eyes around her.

Those closest to Aelthen sat astride pale white horses, waiting in silence. Aelthen stood at the tree itself, a hand pressed to the trunk as fae'reeth beyond count swirled around the branches above him. The moonlight played over him as he stepped out from the shadows, his fae and satyr parting to make way for him.

A human would have spoken. He would have given a speech or said some words to mark the event. Even as she realised that Aelthen had no intention of speaking she recognised what a human thing it was to do. They all knew why they had gathered. Why speak about it?

He stopped, raising his face to the moonlight as he drank in the power, and then lifted a hand, palm upraised, as the Lady's Grace rushed out of him. It began as more of a sensation than a spectacle. A chill swirled around her feet as if a cold tide had rushed in. Miriam looked down between the press of feet and saw the first tendrils become thick coils as the mist began to form, motes of light dancing inside the shifting grey mass. He lifted his palm upwards and then stepped up onto the ever-thickening blanket of mist. With one hand he beckoned, calling the fae to follow as he charged upwards into the sky.

Miriam kept close to Aervern as the packed fae surged forward. *Huntmaster*, Tauntha had called him and, as he led the pack, he did, indeed, look glorious. His antlers shone in the light and his powerful form was a challenge to all that beheld him. Miriam pinched herself and muttered a curse at the pain. It wasn't that she was falling under the fae's influence at all. He simply was just a magnificent sight.

Those on horseback easily outpaced the others until they stepped up onto the mist. It swept them along behind Aelthen and Miriam found that she easily kept up with those in front. On an impulse she stopped moving altogether and yet somehow was still beside Aervern. It didn't matter if she ran or not. She laughed out loud at the pure vanity of the creatures. The shining armour, the galloping horses, all of it was fuel for their incredible egotism.

The host rose above the trees, turning in a broad spiral as they climbed. Miriam looked back and watched as the Swarm rose from their tree, Variska shining at their centre as if they'd somehow stolen a piece of the moon. The fae'reeth needed no help from Aelthen to take flight and they flew to one side of the trailing mist, keeping level with the head of the column as they flew towards the farthest edges of the city.

They swept out over the fields, empty now of the satyr that tended them, and passed over the forests, leaving the city far behind. Aervern's eyes were wide with shock and wonder as she looked behind them, and then up to the head of the column and the antlered figure that led them. Miriam followed her gaze. Thousands of fae and satyr were running in this hunt. Did the creature know no limits? How much power and effort was this taking? He certainly showed no sign of strain. Another facade, she realised. If he could have lifted the fae so easily why would they have trekked all the way from Tir Rhu'thin? No, Aelthen was not without limits. He was expending the power he'd hoarded during their journey to Tira Scyon. This jaunt was designed to gather fae to his banner but it was not without its cost.

She looked down at the trees beneath them. The sight was dizzying but her stomach was already roiling and focusing on something solid seemed to help for a little while. The moonlight was bright enough for her to see down into the forest clearly and dark shadows moved and shifted with them, seeming to course after the host as it flew.

They were not headed for Tir Rhu'thin, that much she was certain of. After spending so much time with Aervern it was easy to forget that the Returned were not strangers to this land, just to the land it had become.

After a time the trees began to thin and, as she looked down again, she saw the shadows moving once more. The moonlight caught on something, and then again, and as the thin clouds parted the bright light was reflected on something with numbers beyond counting. The host surged overhead as she stared down at them and suddenly she realised they were eyes she was seeing. Endless pairs of amber eyes, glaring up at them in the moonlight. She caught at Aervern's sleeve but the look on her face showed she'd already seen.

"This is where they flee to." Aervern explained sadly as she leaned close to Miriam's ear. "When we drive the satyr from Tira Scyon this must be where they gather."

"Lords and Ladies, there must be tens of thousands of them." Miriam gasped. The forest parted ahead of them and as they drew closer Miriam finally realised the sheer scope of the numbers. The clearing was packed to overflowing with satyr, pressed shoulder to shoulder as they glared up at the fae. The laughter of the fae fell silent as more and more of the host saw what lay beneath them, and then knives were bared and thrust skyward as the satyr screamed out, hurling their hate at the sky and the fae that had rejected them.

Aelthen did not spare them a glance but urged them onward, galloping at the head of the host. He charged ahead, outdistancing the others and reared suddenly, stabbing a hand down towards the earth. The stone ring was smaller than the others Miriam had seen but Aelthen raced down towards it, green mist already rising from his arms as he reached for the central monoliths.

The cold was as bitter as she remembered it as they moved through the stones into the darkness. It clawed at her, scouring her skin as her lungs threatened to burst. To breathe in here would bring unending agony. Ileriel had warned her of that. Only the living could pass through the stones. Those who fell in here were too close to death to escape or to pass on. They would remain, lost in the darkness with only their agony for company but denied the final release.

They charged through the featureless darkness, passing into another place and touching onto an expanse of lifeless grey stone before moving into the darkness again. She had almost convinced herself that this place existed only in her nightmares. Tangled memories twisted in her head as recoiled from them. And then they were out, pushing through the stone into the warmth of the night as the same moon looked down onto a different world.

Miriam sagged, and would have fallen, if Aervern hadn't caught her. It was all very well being able to walk on her own but when she had been brought through on Ileriel's horse at least she had been able to collapse over the animal.

Around her, wildfae shook off the frost and ice that clung to clothing and hair as they recovered. Most ignored it, their elation too bright to be dulled by mere ice. A blast of a horn called them onwards and Aelthen lifted them into the air once more, his skin sparking with fresh power under the light of the moon. The night was chill but Miriam barely noticed. The differences were slight in the darkness but looking up she could see the stars. This was her world. This was Haven. She was home.

The fae climbed until it seemed they must reach the clouds and the vista opened up beneath them. Lights in the distance drew closer as they skirted a fishing village and Miriam marvelled at the sight of the moonlight dancing on the waves. A small town was next as they traversed the skies. As, what must surely be a city, grew before them Aelthen's voice sounded in her ears, clear despite the rush of wind and the clamour of the fae. "See how our wayward servants have spread? How their rude settlements litter this land as they themselves spawn and defile it? This was to be our land. The Lady herself promised it to us and yet these manlings have stolen it away. All this shall be reclaimed. All this we shall purge!"

He turned sharply, banking away from the lights of the city on the horizon and driving the host down towards a farming village Miriam hadn't even noticed was there until the last moment. Fields spread out around the walls and the buildings were dark save for a smattering of oil lamps in windows.

Aelthen's hoof pushed down through the mist and hit the packed dirt of the road like a thunderclap and, as the fae charged, a dog inside the village began to bark a desperate warning. The village gates shattered, hunks of splintered wood flying in all directions as he shouldered them aside, and then the hunt began.

Miriam looked in horror at Aervern as the slaughter began but her eyes were locked on the spectacle. Fae and satyr crashed through doors and windows, and the screams that followed told a sickening tale of what happened thereafter. They were the lucky ones. Others were driven out into the streets for the satyr to torment. Aervern's eyes gave nothing away of what she might be feeling but she made no move to join the others.

Miriam looked around at those closest to her, and then took an experimental step. The mist had reduced to a thin ribbon running along the road, no longer pulling them along but still keeping them a few inches above the ground itself. She reached out with a foot, past the edge of the ribbon and touched down onto the hard earth. A wild glance back at Aervern, distracted by the gory spectacle, and she slipped away into the night.

She had done it. Fear and hysterical laughter fought for control of her voice as she slipped between two buildings, and then she ran. She went as fast as she was able down a small back-street. Screams were rising over the shrieks of delight and the laughter of the satyr. A desperate wail turned her head and she glimpsed a man being carried aloft by the Swarm as the fae'reeth tore him to bloody shreds.

Doors opened around her as heads poked out into the streets before slamming shut far faster than they had creaked open, curiosity replaced with terror. She didn't look back, just running took all she had. The village wasn't a large one. She would need somewhere to hide. Running for any length of time would be futile, she knew. Her feet splashed through the muddy puddles, soaking her robes and feet.

A scream, closer than the others, forced her under an over-hanging roof and tight against a large doorway. The smell of straw and manure filled her nostrils and she fumbled with the door until the latch gave and she stumbled inside.

The sound of animals shifting nervously filled her ears as she eased the door shut and moved forward, one hand thrust out awkwardly in front of her in the darkness. Faint shafts of light filtered through the cracks in the stable's door and walls. As her eyes adjusted she could make out a series of stalls and what she hoped was a ladder leading up. A pail clanged loudly as she kicked it over and she fumbled on the floor to right it, looking back at the faint outline of the door before she shuffled deeper into the stable.

Flailing hands found the ladder and she pulled herself up into the hayloft on her hands and knees, clambering over the straw. A hand touched flesh and she jerked away as the foot kicked out and a young voice cried out, "Who's there!"

"Hush, lad," she said in a hoarse whisper. "I'll not hurt you."

A scraping accompanied a burst of sparks, and then soft lantern light filled the stable. "Who are you?" the boy asked as she flinched back from the light. His head turned before she could answer as the sound of screams reached him.

"Lords and Ladies, child, put that out!" she hissed.

He snuffed the lantern quickly and she pulled him down to the hay. "What's going on? Who's out there?" he asked in a tight whisper.

"No one you want to meet," she muttered and winced as another scream sounded, seeming to come from directly above the roof. A wet spattering on the shingles was followed by a series of thuds and she reached for the boy's hand without thinking, squeezing tight.

The door creaked and then slammed a moment later, catching in the night breeze. "You're not from here. Are you with them?" The question was barely louder than her own breath.

"I'm not with anyone. I ran from them," she replied. "Be still now, child. I'll tell you anything you want to know later but for now, shush."

As she said the last word she realised just how quiet the stables had become, the animals still and silent. She inched closer to the edge of the hayloft, lifting her head to peer over the edge. The eyes were calm as they locked on her, glowing gently in the darkness of the stable.

"You cannot run from me, Miriam. Not now." Aervern's said in a small voice "I might wish it were otherwise, but for now you must be bound to my purpose."

Miriam sighed as hope left her and she reached for the ladder. "Why can't you just let me be free? I'm of no use to you."

"You are of more use that you know. It is more than that though, Miriam. I do not expect you have been missed but your absence would be noted when we return to the Realm," Aervern said softly, every word an apology. She needn't have bothered. Nothing she could say would ever be enough for this.

The anger came all at once, hot and fierce and bringing a bitter tang to her tongue. "I am not your tool to use, *fae!*" she spat. "I won't go back. You'll have to kill me."

Aervern gave her a cool look. "I am sorry for this, Miriam. I never would have wished this."

Miriam looked down as she felt the cool touch of the glamour as the chain formed around her wrist once more, and then the full weight of Aervern's mind fell upon her, crushing her, and sense and reason left her.

Another scream sounded close to the stable doors and Aervern glanced up at the hayloft. "Be still now, manling," she whispered to the child. "They come!"

* * *

Miriam stood on the crumbling balcony. The building stood close to the edge of Tira Scyon, in an area none of the fae seemed to bother with. She took an experimental step towards the low wall and felt the presence grow inside her head. It grew more alert, watching for her next move. She was close, only six feet from the edge where the wall had broken and tumbled away. Two quick steps were all it would take. She could hurl herself into the air and end it all.

It didn't take much, just a slight shifting of her weight in preparation to throw herself forward. The presence moved faster than she would have thought possible, smothering her, draining away her will, her anger, until she sighed and stepped back, numb.

Aervern had tried to speak with her several times in the days since they'd come back to Tira Scyon. She'd removed 'the Touch' as Aervern had described it, as soon as they reached her home but Miriam had refused to speak to her since. A small part of her had thought she was being childish but then, what more could she do? The hunt had demonstrated one thing, however. Despite all that Aervern claimed she was as much a captive under her as she had ever been with Ileriel. Aervern's plans, whatever they were, required her cooperation.

Her attempts at suicide were not truly serious, not that she wouldn't have welcomed death if the opportunity presented itself. It was more an effort to show the fae that she was the one in control, not her. However much Aervern might be able to smother her attempts Miriam was the one triggering the fae's actions. Aervern may have made her into a puppet but the strings ran in both directions. She could tug on them too. Her lips curved into a perverse smile at the thought.

Movement on the disused street caught her eye and she stepped forward again, leaning on the remains of the wall for support as she craned her neck out. They moved furtively, the cautious movement itself somehow drawing more attention than moving normally would have. It was a satyr, though one far more wild than any she'd seen before. Its clothing was little more than rags, a tattered length of cloth flung over one shoulder and tied around the waist. A flicker turned her head and she caught sight of another, then three more.

She was halfway down the stone steps before it came to her. These satyr must be coming in response to Aelthen's call. These were the ones who had taken the other path to Gannkis. These were the satyr that had chosen to be exiled from Tira Scyon rather than accept gelding.

The thought gave her pause. The satyr she had encountered in this city were more like servants than anything else. The barely contained wildness and cruelty she'd know from those at Tir Rhu'thin had been cut away. These satyr she had glimpsed from the balcony seemed somehow worse than those serving Aelthen.

She forced herself onwards, suddenly wishing that she hadn't sought out this deserted quarter. The street was still and empty by the time she reached it but distant shouts made her head for the city centre. The cries attracted others and she soon found herself following a growing crowd of fae and satyr.

Aervern's voice was clear long before Miriam was close enough to see her or make out the words. She stood in the centre of the square railing at Ileriel as Aelthen watched on impassively.

"What right do you have to violate our law and custom? These have made their choice. They chose exile and yet you invite them to return? You, who are not even of Tira Scyon? You send missives to this beast and his pack and you bring him here? *Here*, of all places?"

"Aervern!" the voice was somehow all the more penetrating for its gentle tone as Tauntha made her way through the throng. "It is not your place to do this, child."

Aelthen nodded in a polite acknowledgement as Tauntha turned to face him. "The question is not hers to ask," she said in even tones. "Yet it stands unanswered. By what right do you violate our laws? By what right do you invite this creature here?"

"This *creature* is Riahl, Lord of the Great Revel. He is owed your respect, Tauntha, for he is as much an elder as you yourself. He answered my summons as Lord of the Hunt and he comes to bear witness."

"Bear witness?" Tauntha echoed him with a frown and shook her head. "You do not answer the question. By what right do you violate our law and custom?"

"By right of challenge." Aelthen's voice rolled out over the assembled fae like a wave. It broke over Tauntha's words and sent them tumbling to the surf. "I summon your exiled satyr, my brothers in the hunt, to bear witness. I am Aelthen. Huntmaster, Worldwalker. I stand as leader of the Returned and I would lead all fae. I would claim the Ivy Throne. Are there any among you who dispute my right or contest my claim?"

Even from the back of the square Miriam could see the impact of the words. It was almost funny. The shock stripped the fae of their arrogance and, for just one moment, many looked almost human.

"I contest." The call came from the back of the square and heads turned to see the fae Miriam had been forced to dance with, once again wrapped his glamour of mists. The crowd parted as he approached and Aelthen regarded him evenly.

"How are you called?" he asked after a long silence.

The mists sank down, curling about the fae's shoulders and revealing the proud face "I am Caraviel, Lord of Mists."

Aelthen studied him, measuring his worth. "You pose no threat to me, faeling," he told the fae. "Withdraw your challenge. I will not hold you to words spoken with no thought or reason."

Caraviel's nostrils flared as he glared at Aelthen and spoke through clenched teeth. "I will not withdraw."

Aelthen sighed, waving a dismissive hand at his challenger. "I will not waste time on this. You cannot best me."

"The dance of blades." Caraviel roared in anger as he tore curved daggers from within the mists that clung to his body. "My challenge will be by blade."

Aelthen sighed again and looked at the fae with contempt. "You foolish child. You challenge, knowing little or nothing of me and yet you place no limits on your challenge." He extended an arm in a lazy fashion and stones erupted skyward as thick roots flew out of the ground beneath, wrapping around Caraviel's limbs and dragging him spread-eagled to the stones.

Aelthen ignored the struggles of the fae as he fought the grip of the roots. "Let all take note that I offered this faeling the chance to withdraw." He looked back to his challenger and the smile left his face. Caraviel's shouts became cries for help, and then screams of pain as Aelthen gestured and the roots began to pull. The screams grew louder and more frantic until, with a wet tearing sound, Caraviel's arms and legs were ripped from his body and he exploded in a shower of gore. Aelthen smiled then, a thin smile devoid of mirth or compassion as he ignored the roots as they feasted and turned his eyes back to the crowd.

"Does any other contest my right?"

"I contest, Worldwalker." The call was soft, almost regretful, but the words carried anyway. Aelthen turned to regard Tauntha and smiled. She made her way to his side with no hurry, nodding thanks at those who murmured support as she passed.

He bowed with genuine respect as she approached. The gesture stood in stark contrast to the contempt with which he had treated Caraviel and, as Miriam looked on, the square fell silent.

"What form would you choose?"

"I choose the Grace of Our Lady. The art of glamours," Tauntha replied and, for the briefest moment, Miriam saw a flicker of doubt cross Aelthen's face. "Strip me of my glamour, if you can. The challenge is by Grace alone." Tauntha spoke formally and turned to face the watching crowd as she closed her eyes.

Without really thinking about what she was doing Miriam moved through the throng until she reached Aervern's side. The fae nodded to her once in greeting but said nothing.

The attack came without preamble. No foolish posturing, no wasted words. Aelthen extended one hand towards Tauntha and the power began to flow out of him. The green mist came from his hands, rising up above Tauntha, and then crashing over her in a wave that continued to curl under and around her until she was surrounded in the eye of its storm.

In the centre of it all she stood, silent and unmoving, unruffled by the power that raged around her. The contest carried on in silence, each of them focused on their efforts. Motes of light swarmed around Tauntha like maddened fireflies and her form rippled for a heartbeat, before solidifying once more. Aelthen muttered in obvious frustration and thrust another hand out, bearing down with his teeth clenched in a grimace.

Miriam glanced once at Aervern's face but the fear and worry was enough to turn her gaze away. Aelthen roared out in frustration as the torrent of power flowing from him began to wane. He glanced out once into the throng before reaching a hand out towards the crowd.

An anguished gasp passed through the crowd as the first tendrils of power rose from them, leeched away by the force of Aelthen's will, and passing swiftly into his outstretched fingers. He became a conduit, draining power from the fae only to send it blasting into Tauntha's form.

The gasp became more pronounced, overlaid with thin, reedy, wails of pain as some of the weakest collapsed to the ground. Aelthen drew himself up, shoulders bunching as the power infused him and his eyes flared with a bight amber light. A torrent of power burst from him, slamming into Tauntha and tearing around her, shredding the layers from her glamour as she screamed in the centre of the cyclone of mist that surrounded her.

As the power raged Miriam became aware of another current. A flow of mist trailing back out of the torrent surrounding Tauntha. Aelthen wasn't just destroying her glamour, he was tearing the power from her.

Tauntha shook as the torrent rocked her, her image wavering as chunks of it were torn away, revealing the truth concealed beneath. She began to shine brightly, the light blasting out from her to be greedily absorbed by her adversary as her glamour was destroyed. A final roar of triumph from Aelthen and, at last, Tauntha's voice rose to join his in an agonised scream, pain twisting her face before she fell silent and collapsed to the dirt.

Miriam looked from the horror on Aervern's face to the scene that was unfolding before them. The creature she had only ever before glimpsed for the briefest moment lay in the dirt, exposed and unmasked for any to see. She lay gasping, naked in the truest sense of the word, as those closest gaped at her frail, wizened form. Her chest rose and fell in painful, laboured breaths as Aervern made her way forward and knelt beside her. She bent low, perhaps to catch one whispered sentence, and then Tauntha was still.

Aervern stood then, striding forward toward Aelthen. Fae and satyr rushed from her path and from the dreadful silence she seemed to carry with her.

"The challenge was to strip Tauntha of her glamour," she snarled.

Aelthen looked down at her. "She placed poor limits on her challenge."

"It was to be by the Grace of our Lady alone," Aervern grated.

"And as it was."

"That is not so." Aervern snapped. "All here saw how you drew upon the Grace of those present."

Aelthen frowned in mock confusion. "Is that not the Lady's Grace?"

"None from Tira Scyon could draw the grace from another," Aervern persisted.

"Should I have limited myself then?" Aelthen asked in mock concern. "Been less than I am? If this challenge had been by blades ought I to have fought with less skill? This was my right to the Ivy Throne contested. I would bring to bear any and all of my skills to win, as would any other here. You do no honour to the fallen with this display."

Aervern stopped cold and looked around at the eyes upon her. She drew herself up then and gave a curt nod of acceptance before stalking into the crowd.

"Is there any other among you who would contest my claim?" Aelthen called out across the square. He waited in silence for five long breaths before turning to the great tree. "Variska," he called. "Speak for the fae'reeth. Is the claim accepted?"

The only answer was silence and the ever present sound of the wings as the fae'reeth circled the branches in their endless dance. Aelthen smothered a look of frustration that was not lost on Miriam as he turned to face the crowd once more.

"Riahl, will you kneel to the throne? Will your Revel return to make the fae as we should be once more?"

"We will, Satyri. Our people should be as one." The voice was soft, urbane, and not at all what Miriam had expected.

"My children," Aelthen spoke up as he lifted his arms high. "My lost brethren of Tira Scyon, Brothers of the Hunt, I would make our people great once more. I would reclaim the Land of Our Lady and purge the maggots that infest her body. I claim the Ivy Throne by Grace and blade. Join with me so that we might summon the throne to us."

The roar that followed his words seemed all the louder for Aervern's silence as Aelthen smiled his acceptance. He turned to the Great Tree and held a hand out, as if beckoning. Stood to one side of the square Miriam could see his eyes close. The first rumbles were so slight she barely noticed them but soon there could be no doubt as the earth heaved and boiled before him. The stones moved first, buckling and being forced aside as the first of the thick roots thrust up through the earth. More soon joined it, twisting and weaving around each other as they formed together. Smaller tendrils worked around the larger roots, whipping around in a fury as they wove themselves into a tight lattice.

"What is he doing?" Miriam whispered to Aervern.

She did not look at her and her words were thick with emotion. "He summons the throne. Not seen in the days of my life or those of my sires."

The roots formed into a broad dais with thick columns rising up to support the latticework roof the tendrils had formed. In the centre of the dais the throne itself sat, roots and vines still writhing under his will. Aelthen nodded once in satisfaction as the vines burst into bud, and then sprouted, surmounting the back of the throne in a crest of ivy.

The square fell silent, doubly silent Miriam realised as the fae'reeth stilled their flight, landing lightly on the boughs of the great tree. All eyes were on Variska as she took flight alone, glowing brightly as she flew across to the House of the Throne. Though no sound was spoken something must have passed between them, Miriam realised, as the Swarm itself descended upon the House of the Throne, touching down lightly on the roof until the fae'reeth filled it entirely. Those that could not land began a new spiral, flicking around in their complex dance above the throne in a whirling column that extended up toward the sky.

Aervern spun abruptly, pushing through the crowd of awestruck fae and satyr as she fled the square, leaving Miriam struggling to keep up as she followed.

CHAPTER FIVE

Torna reached back into the sack at her waist and flung the handful of rye seed onto the broken field. The sun was already starting to think about giving the day up but she'd made a good effort on the field at least. It was just too big. The farming they'd done on Bresda was no different but the land here seemed to go on forever. She could sow a field in Bresda in a day. She'd been working on this one for two full days already.

"Daft man," she muttered. "If he listened to anything except what's between his legs once or twice…" she trailed off. She told the bloody fool there was no need to start so big. Their farm of Bresda hadn't been a tenth of the size of what he'd plotted out.

Torna sighed and tossed another handful of rye. She'd have her moment to laugh when it came time to reap this lot. It made sense to plant winter rye, she knew. There was already a huge demand for fodder for the horses and livestock. Kornik's plan would see them in good stead, and with a healthy pile of coin if they could manage the crop.

She looked up at a half-heard sound in the trees. Some animal or other, she decided. This land was different in so many ways. Wilder in some ways too. Man had left such an imprint on Bresda that it was hard to find a spot where the land had been left to do as it pleased. Almost every inch was given over to farming, if it was green enough, or mining and fishing if it wasn't. Here, though, there was so much untouched. It was like stepping into a fable. You could walk through the trees and wonder if they'd ever known the touch of man.

Her ears pricked again and she looked up at the sun, just visible through the gathering clouds. It had already found the horizon and was almost half-gone. Time she was getting back, she decided. It looked like rain and Kornik should be heading in soon anyway. She pulled the drawstring tight on the seed bag and hushed at her growling stomach as she thought of that evening's meal. They had chickens but it seemed senseless to kill a bird when the woods were teeming with game.

Kornik rushed out of the trees in the distance in a crash of bushes. It was too far to make out his face but the way he'd stumbled out of the woods and his frantic, staggering, stirred her. He shouted at her, something too garbled to make out as he flapped his arms in her direction and her tentative steps towards him became a run.

"What is it?" she cried as she drew closer.

"Get away woman, run!" he gasped between ragged breaths. He glanced back over one shoulder and froze as he saw the empty field, the still trees. "They were behind me, scores of them. Chasing me and laughing." He fell silent, shaking his head.

"What were?" Torna asked. She'd never seen the man like this. He was actually shaking.

"Monsters," the word seemed to slip out before he could stop them. "Some kind of beasts." He pushed past her, walking instead of his frantic run but still moving swiftly.

"What do you mean beasts?" She demanded as she hurried to keep up. "There's nothing in those woods worse than a bear. You told me that yourself."

"I was wrong," he muttered and kept walking.

"Damn it, Kornik. You dragged me halfway around the world to this place. If you go soft in the head on me now…"

He whirled around on her, moving so fast that he staggered to keep from falling. "I know what I saw, Torna. They were right behind me!"

She let him go. His face had been twisted with anger as he'd spoken but she'd still seen the fear hiding behind it. The trees on the far side of the field were still as the last rays of the sun fell upon them. "Monsters or not, I'll not stand in a field in the night." She snorted and hurried after his distant figure.

The rain began before she made it back to their cottage. It was light but the dark clouds made it clear that this was a rain with plans and ambition. The cottage wasn't much but at least it was their own, and she cursed under her breath as she saw the door left open and the rain blowing in.

"Kornik where are you? You left the door wide open!" She fell silent as he came out of the small bedroom, travel-sack in hand.

"Where are you going?"

He met her eyes. The panic had abated and he looked at her with a calm resolve. "We're going to the village. I want stouter walls around me tonight."

"The village?" she protested. "But you said you hated it there. Crammed into those little huts they've thrown up. It's why we moved out here in the first place."

"There's guards there. There's people there, Torna," he said in a soft voice.

She shook her head. "Are you still on that? You got spooked by a shadow or boar or something. It happens to everyone now and then."

"No, Torna. It wasn't a boar, it wasn't a shadow. My nanna used to tell me tales about what it was. We've all heard those tales. There's trels, or something like them, in those woods and I'll not sleep out here. You stay if you won't believe me but I know what I saw."

"Trels!" she snorted, stifling it quickly at the look on his face. "The Keepers would never have shipped us all over here if there was something like that."

"Do you see any Keepers here?" He asked, waving his arms around the room. "They're all back in Hesk getting fat on the coin they make off us while we scrape by on farthings! Do you really think they have any idea what might be in these woods? What do we really know about this place?" He didn't wait for her to answer. "Nothing! Everything we know, they've told us. Well this time I'm the one telling you something." He stepped closer to her, jabbing a finger at her as he spoke. "I saw something in those woods. I saw a horde of those damned things and they near ran the life out of me, chasing me through the trees. I'm going to the village. You come or you stay but I'm gone."

She watched him go, clumping through the cottage in his heavy field-boots and leaving mud with every step. It was only as he looked back at her on the threshold that she saw the size of the travel-sack. She glanced around the cottage, at the things that were missing, and she could see it in his eyes. He didn't expect to be coming back.

It was almost fully dark by the time they reached the walls of the village. Flaming torches burned on the walls and out amongst the sharpened stakes that surrounded them. Torna huddled deeper into her cloak as Kornik shivered through a brief conversation with the wall guards.

The village only had the one street and rain and feet had already worked to turn it to a thick sludge that oozed and sucked at her boots. There was no chance of getting into an empty farmer's cottage this late in the day and Kornik wasted no time in heading for the inn. It was rude by Bresda's standards but it was still warm and dry. A fiddler was sawing out a tune in the corner, close to the fire, and the laughter and conversation, coupled with the smell of hot food, was almost enough to make her forgive Kornik for dragging her out through the wet.

She took a small table in the corner and held it with her wet cloak before going to the bar to order food and drinks whilst Kornik haggled over the price of a room. It wouldn't be cheap. He was soaked through and it was late. It was a seller's market.

He stumped back over to the table just as the food arrived. A turnip soup with a thick crust of bread. Not the best meal by a long stretch but better than nothing. At least it was hot.

He still hadn't relaxed. She could see him throwing furtive looks at the window between mouthfuls of soup. She leaned over the table. "Do you want to talk about it?"

He grunted around his spoon and avoided talking for a moment by sticking his nose into the mug of ale. "I saw one before the rest," he said finally, speaking softly. "Just stood there in the shadows of the trees, staring at me." He shook his head and avoided her eyes, speaking to the wall beside them more than to her. "I thought I was seeing things until it moved. It pulled a knife, slow-like, and licked the blade. I ran then, charging through the woods like a spooked sow. I could hear it behind me. Even over all the noise I was making I could hear it laughing, like it was soft in the head or something." He met her eyes finally and the fear was plain for her to see, all fresh and sharp edges.

"I thought I was just running blind but it was herding me or something. I remember falling in the stream, and when I looked back there were hundreds of them, maybe thousands. They just stood there, waiting for me to start running again, like it was all a game of chase."

He looked down at the soup, poking at it with the carved wooden spoon, and opened his mouth to speak. The horn was low and mournful, it cut through the room leaving only a shocked silence in its wake as eyes shot to the door and windows. Silence fled as the chairs scraped and clattered to the floor. Kornik reached for Torna's hand and pushed through the press of bodies as he pulled her from the inn.

The muddy street surged with villagers as they raced to their defence stations. Torna snatched her hand away from Kornik as the horn blasted again. "What are you doing? You should be going to the walls?"

"Those walls won't stop that lot," he told her. "We need to get out of here."

She shook her head at him, fear warring with a strange sense of betrayal. "No!

Barad, Kevet, and all the others are going to the walls. We only need to hold long enough for help to come. They're depending on us!"

He gave her a long look. "Fine, we'll go to the bloody walls. Then you'll see."

He half-dragged her between two buildings to a quieter section of the wall and up the rough ladder lashed in place.

"There!" He stabbed a finger out to the darkness lurking between the flare of torches. "Do you see them?"

She looked at him in shock for a second, and then followed his finger out into the murk. It was hard to see anything past the torchlight but something was moving. It was as if the darkness itself moved, shifting and restless, and then she saw the eyes.

Her fingers clutched at his arm as the image came together. Amber eyes stretched out like an ocean of fireflies. The smallest were just pinpricks in the dark but the closest shone clearly, glaring out of the faces of nightmares. She looked back at him and the single nod was all the answer he needed.

The first screams were already turning to echoes by the time they reached the rear gates. They were already abandoned. There weren't enough men in the village to man the walls properly, let alone keep men to guard gates that were on the wrong side from the fight.

Kornik threw the bar down into the dirt and shoved the heavy gate open, and then they ran. They ran until their sides heaved and their eyes burned with tears and, behind them, in the darkness, a village screamed in fear and agony.

* * *

Klöss made a mark on the chart and looked up at the messenger as he hovered in the doorway. "What is it?"

"A message for Seamaster Kurikson," the messenger said.

Klöss muttered something vile under his breath and glanced down at the chart again. "So why bring it here? Do I look like Frostbeard?"

The messenger fiddled with a torn corner of his leathers. "No, my lord."

"Do I look like a lord?" Klöss grated up at the man. He was possibly enjoying this a little too much but the man was irritating him.

"No, Shipmaster."

"Am I going to have to drag this out of you, man? I'm a little bit busy. Why are you here?"

The messenger squirmed as he shifted his weight from foot to foot. "I did try, sir. The Seamaster, he isn't answering his door and, well, I didn't like to just barge in. But the message, sir, well it's supposed to be urgent." He let it hang.

"Oh, for the love of… Give it here, man!" Klöss snatched the paper from his hand, breaking the seal and reading quickly. He frowned and read the message again before tossing it aside and reaching for the chart. Skelf was a tiny village, one of the most recently constructed, but in an area to the north and far behind their front lines. How had they even managed to reach it let alone attack it?

He grabbed up the message and pushed his way past the messenger, rushing through the halls. Whoever Frostbeard was with would just need to cope with the interruption. This was more important. If they had found a way past the front this could upset their whole effort. It could ruin them. A large enough force could cut to the heart of the lands they'd taken. Supply lines would be severed, dispatches waylaid. It could spell disaster for everything they'd achieved so far. If it was the Anlish, that was.

He'd expected to hear voices through the door but Frostbeard's study may as well have been empty for all the sound that escaped it. His knocking was met only with silence.

"He is in there isn't he?" he asked the guard stood at the door, receiving a confused nod in response.

He tried again, louder this time and tried the door. Aiden was sat at his desk with a preoccupied, pained expression on his face as he rubbed absently at his arm.

"What is it?" he snapped as Klöss came in.

"A message came for you. There's been an attack behind our lines." Klöss frowned at the old man. "You don't look so great. Are you sick?"

"Don't be ridiculous," Aiden snapped, reaching for the paper in Klöss's hand. His eyes widened as he read and he headed to the wall and the large map that hung there.

Klöss followed him. "You see my point? If it's the Anlish then they've somehow passed through three districts and who knows how many patrol lines to get to there."

"And why bother?" Frostbeard grunted. His voice sounded tight, strained. "It's a small village of no real strategic value. They didn't even bother to burn it. We could take it back and repopulate it in days. Why attack here?" He turned back to Klöss,

THE SINS OF THE WYRDE

the thought occurring to him obvious on his face. "You said *if* it's the Anlish. You think it's this other group? The ones that attacked during your Reaping?"

"I think that would make more sense." Klöss shrugged. "More sense than the Anlish making it through our entire territory and passing who knows how many patrol routes without being noticed, anyway."

Frostbeard raised an eyebrow. "You think they're a third player in all this?"

"I think it's time we stopped fooling ourselves," Klöss replied, throwing his arms in the air. "The men have been talking about it for months. These things, whatever they are, they're not human. Call them keiju, or trels, or just something weird they have in this place. We need to deal with it. Enough of the men saw the way Verig was killed to set tongues wagging. Even Tristan has spoken to me about it."

Aiden waved a dismissive hand, bending oddly at the waist. "He's from the Far Isles though, and they've always been a superstitious bunch."

"He hit one of these things in the face with an axe. It didn't even draw blood." Klöss pressed. "Lords of Blood, Sea, and Stone, Uncle, what is it going to take? You've seen them yourself. Do you really think it was the Anlish who managed to smash down our gates and ride through the streets of Rimeheld?"

Aiden grunted and staggered back to the chair. "Damn it!" he gasped.

Klöss had no time to respond as Frostbeard clutched at his chest and pitched forward. He grabbed for the arm of the chair with one flailing hand even as he sank to the floor, his face the colour of fresh ashes, pulling the chair crashing to the ground beside him.

"Aiden!" Klöss dropped down to his knees beside the man, and then rushed to the door, ripping it open. "Get a healer in here," he screamed at the shocked guard.

Frostbeard lay half-curled on one side, his breath coming in short, pained gasps. Klöss sank down beside him. "Hold on, old man. You can't leave me with this mess now, can you?"

His Uncle managed a watery smile. "You'd be fine you know?" he gasped out between breaths. "You don't give yourself enough credit."

"Just hold on," Klöss pled in a whisper but his Uncle wasn't listening.

He sat in the chair as people rushed around him. The healers fussed and wasted time with a body they could do nothing to help. Messengers, and those too nosey to listen to their own good sense, came and went. He was vaguely aware that Tristan was somewhere in the mix, pushing people out with his gentle voice, and then with a harsher one when that didn't work.

The room was awash with good intentions. They would do little. Frostbeard was already dead. Klöss stayed, even after they had carried the old man away, sitting at the desk staring at nothing, until a sound made him turn.

Larren stood in the doorway watching him. He tried a smile but gave up on it as he came in. "I thought we ought to talk."

"Of course, Sealord." Klöss, stood and righted the chair his uncle had toppled.

"Don't fuss with that, lad. We can forget the silly titles for the moment as well." He turned and shut the door firmly. "This probably isn't the best time for this but we need to be pragmatic. Your uncle was the driving force behind this campaign. If we let it falter now there are whole sections of the Chamber just waiting to pull it apart."

Klöss nodded but made no move to speak.

"What we need now is continuity," Larren told him. "Someone has to run things here and I can't spare the time away from Hesk to do that. I have my own duties that are already being neglected."

The penny finally dropped. "You can't mean me?" Klöss blurted.

"Who better?" the Sealord said as he smiled. "You've been involved since the beginning. You know the plans, the factions within your own men, which of the Keeper's demands we can fulfil and which must wait."

"Yes but—"

"But nothing." Larren cut him off. "The timing is bad, I understand that, but I need you. These men need you. Do your duty, son. Make your uncle proud."

Klöss sighed. He'd lost this before he'd even spoken. "What do you want from me?"

The older man smiled at that. "Not much more than you were already doing," he said. "The thane would have to sanction an appointment like this anyway but, for now at least, I need you to act as Lord of Rimeheld."

"Lord?" Klöss protested. "It never had a lord!"

"Don't be absurd." Larren snorted. "Aiden never liked the title but everyone knew what he was."

Klöss fell silent. The man was obviously serious but could he really do the job? As he asked himself he realised he already knew the answer. He also knew that no matter how Larren dressed it up he'd never really had a choice.

"Good lad!" Larren clapped him on the shoulder as he nodded. "You'll have a bit more oversight and input from me than Aiden did but I think we can both see why. For now, I believe you have a village that's been attacked. And I have a ship to catch. Keep things moving along and don't dwell on Aiden. He lived well. I'll be in touch." He clapped Klöss on the shoulder again and left. It wasn't until his footsteps faded around the distant corner that Klöss thought to wonder how he could have known about the village.

* * *

Tristan stood, scraping his chair back, and gave a deep bow as Klöss walked in. He smiled at the dark scowl Klöss shot him, unruffled.

Klöss looked from Tristan to Gavin and back. "You've heard already then?"

"News like this moves with haste," the large man said as he shrugged. "I am sorry about your uncle," he added, his dark eyes serious for once. "He was a good man, I think."

Klöss sank down in a chair at the table opposite Tristan. "He was, and thank you."

"Is it not too soon for you to be commanding this vessel?"

Klöss gave him a long look before he spoke "He's dead, Tristan. It's been three days and right now it's not going to get much better. I'll not disgrace myself by falling apart or letting this campaign do the same."

Tristan nodded, though he looked far from convinced. He jerked his head at Gavin who sat sprawled in a chair at the end of the table with his feet up, toying with a knife. "Your message said for me to bring this one along?"

Klöss nodded. "There was an attack, a village called Skelf. It's way behind our lines. I want you to take some men and find out what happened."

Tristan grunted with a frown. "How far behind our lines?"

"Far enough that it makes me question if it was the Anlish," Klöss admitted. He pinched at the bridge of his nose and ran his hand back over his head as he sighed. "I don't know who it was but I can't see how the Anlish could have made it past our lines and penetrated that deeply. The report we received says the village wasn't burned, at least not that the farmers saw while they were running. If I were the Anlish I'd have burnt it to the ground."

"So what are you suggesting?" Gavin spoke up.

"We all know what we saw at the reaping," Klöss told him. "Whether these things are the trels and keiju from nursery rhymes, or whether they're something else, it doesn't matter. If they're a threat to us we need to deal with it. Right now I need information, and fast." He looked back to Tristan. "Take some men and scout the area. See just how good this one is on the way." He gave Gavin a pointed look. "If he's half as good as he makes out then we'll have a talk when you get back." He frowned, looking at the knife in the thief's hand. "What is that, iron?"

Gavin glanced at the blade and nodded. "Had it made a few days after the reaping."

"Iron's no good for a blade," Klöss scoffed. "It'll be no use against someone with steel."

"It's just something I remembered, things from stories." Gavin shrugged to cover the flush on his cheeks. "I figured it couldn't hurt."

Klöss raised an eyebrow. "I think I'd have some steel on me as well."

Gavin snorted and stood to reveal the four daggers strapped to his back. "I'm not short on steel."

Klöss gave a short barking laugh. "Very nice, but they won't be much use against a good swordsman."

"Swords are slow." Gavin muttered.

Tristan sighed loudly. "If you are finished seeing whose one is bigger we have hunting to do, yes?"

Klöss and Gavin shared a look before glaring at Tristan but the big man was already headed for the door. He stopped in the doorway and looked back at Klöss. "What will you do while we are gone?"

Klöss gave a twisted smile. "I expect this place will find a way to keep me busy."

Tristan shook his head. "That is not good. You will mope. Papers do not clear a man's head or stir his blood. You need more."

Klöss raised an eyebrow. "What did you have in mind?"

"Why not come and view this village yourself?"

"Are you mad?" Klöss burst into laughter at the thought. "The sealord would have a merry fit! I'm supposed to be leading this campaign now not running around the woods."

"And you will be of how much use with your uncle inside your head?" Tristan asked.

Klöss rose, scraping the heavy chair over the stone floor. "And what if something happens?" he pressed. "What if we're killed or captured? What then?"

"These are not new risks to us, Klöss," Tristan reminded him. "Who would the task fall to if you fell?"

That was something he hadn't really considered. Klöss thought about it for a moment. "Lek, I suppose. He's more at home with reports than a sword these days but he knows what's important."

"Then leave this paper to Lek." Tristan shrugged.

"I can't do that Tristan. The sealord—"

"Did he not just leave by ship?" Tristan interrupted.

"Well, yes but—"

"Then I do not see this problem."

Klöss stared at him for almost a minute before his smile grew. He turned to Gavin who stood watching the exchange. "Let me have another look at that dagger. Maybe it's not such a bad idea."

* * *

They travelled north in bands of twenty. It made sense to keep the parties small and working independently of each other. The sun had been with them for the past three days but now the rains had swept in and Klöss glared at the back of Tristan's head as they walked. The road was not much more than a mud track but it made sense to follow it while they could. They were far behind their own lines and speed was more important than stealth for the moment.

He'd thought of Anlan as lush when they'd first caught sight of it on that training raid all those years ago. The trees here were broader and more numerous than the thin pines of Bresda, but for the last day or so they'd made their way through a featureless plain and the rain had lashed at them driven by winds that seemed intent on reaching every last dry patch of skin that remained.

"Remind me why I'm here again?" he called over the winds.

Tristan didn't turn. "You need more fun in your life."

Gavin snorted at that, earning his own black look, but he seemed as impervious as Tristan. Klöss glanced around at the others, noting more than one barely suppressed smile.

The days dragged, and what had begun as an escape from the monotony of dealing with administrators and dealing with petty issues soon became its own chore. The rains pushed them on, refusing to let up and their nights were as bad as the days as they huddled in tents and tried to ignore the pounding of the rain on the treated canvas.

The trees came as a blessed relief when they reached them and by the second day under the canopy Klöss was close to forgiving Tristan. He glanced at the map again and thrust it back into his pack. "We're probably another three or four days away from Skelf," he said to Tristan. "Form the men up in scouting pairs in clusters of four."

Tristan nodded and began passing the word. Each pair would act independently of the group as a whole but keeping within reach of one other. If they were forced into combat the pairs would form up into groups of four as they fell back and reformed into the company. If truly pressed the company itself would fall back and try to meet up with another of the scouting parties. He'd planned this well and the men were used to this procedure. Hopefully it wouldn't be necessary. They were here to scout and gather information, not to fight.

He moved through the trees and undergrowth as silently as he could. Though he'd never make a tracker himself the time he'd spent in Anlan had made him stealthier than he'd once been. Tristan walked beside him, oddly silent despite his huge size. Ahead of them the grey-green ghost that was Gavin drifted through the trees, making less noise than a passing breeze as he scouted ahead from the noisier pair.

It was slow going but Klöss was glad for it. If the force that had attacked Skelf were still close it wouldn't do to blunder into them. If the force that attacked Skelf wasn't human it *definitely* wouldn't do to blunder into them.

He found that the tension moved in cycles. He'd been an oarsman three years before he was trusted with a crew, working his way through oarsmaster to shipmaster in short order. He'd seen more than his share of blood and raids gone badly and he was well used to the fear that all men find in the silence of themselves before a battle. That was nothing to this. The things he'd seen on the reaping both fascinated and terrified him and the fear of blundering into them made him overcautious as he moved through the trees.

What started as caution gradually built into a fearful walk as his eyes darted about, trying to watch everything at once. No man can maintain that level of anxiety for long though, and he soon drifted through calm and into complacency until a cracked twig underfoot brought the cycle back around again.

Sleeping in watches in a cold camp made for poor sleep and stiff muscles. By the third morning it was beginning to show on the men, which Klöss knew meant it would be twice as bad as it looked, and he found himself almost hoping they'd encounter Anlish troops.

It was late afternoon when the call of a moonthrush sounded ahead of them. A runner emerged from the trees slowly. The moonthrush was rare, even in the Barren Isles, and so made a good signal, but a wise man moved out slowly. Rash scouts didn't tend to live long.

"You have news?" Tristan asked, not lowering his handbow. Identical to the larger arbelest in every way but its size. Klöss had arranged for every man on the mission to carry one.

The scout answered to Klöss though he hadn't asked the question. "We've reached the village, my lord,"

"I'm not a lord..." Klöss began but Tristan waved him to silence.

"It's abandoned," the man said. "It's..." He glanced at Tristan and swallowed. "You'd be best seeing it for yourself, I think."

Tristan and Klöss exchange a look before waving the man on. The village proved to be only be an hour away from them, a distance they covered all the more swiftly knowing the way was clear. The other scouting parties rejoined them as they walked, until they were at half their company strength by time the walls came into sight.

Skelf was not much of a village. A single street housing the inn and a smithy, and then cottages packed tight to fit within what had been the wooden palisade. It was the standard first-stage village for Bjornmen settlers.

Klöss made his way to the wreckage of the gates. He sank down to one knee and picked at the splinters as he examined the scene. "What do you think?" he asked Tristan over one shoulder.

"Odd," the man muttered. He looked to Gavin and the scout who'd led them in. "Give me your hands for this?"

Together they hauled one side of the gate out of the mud and back up against the edge of the palisade. He looked closely at the muddy poles. "No marks."

The other gate hung loose, sagging on one remaining hinge. Klöss examined it quickly and turned to shrug at Tristan.

"It's obvious isn't it?" Gavin spoke up, looking from one to the other. The gates weren't bashed in. They were forced open from the inside. If it hadn't been raining so much you'd be able to see the footprints. As it is all that's left is this." He pointed out the large depression in the mud just behind where the gates would have met.

"If they wanted out why not just lift the crossbar?" Klöss asked the thief.

"I don't know. They obviously didn't, or maybe it was more that they couldn't." He shrugged. "The only thing I can think is that they were pressed so tight to the gates that there just wasn't room."

An uncomfortable silence fell between them as they each imagined the panic and fear it must have taken to push enough people against the eight foot wooden gate to force it open. The crossbar hadn't moved, instead the hinges had given way.

"What else?" Klöss said as he walked into the village itself. "Survivors?"

"None, Shipmaster," the scout told him. "Some fouled tracks heading north is all we've found. Aside from the bodies that is."

There was a tone in his voice that made Klöss ask, "Bodies?"

The scout avoided his eyes and looked vaguely sick as he motioned them through the village to the wreckage of the other gates. They had been pulled from their hinges and torn apart. Thick posts from the gate were stacked to one side, their intended use was obvious.

The corpses were piled high, impaled on thick posts taken from the ruined gates. Men and women had been stripped naked and then rammed down over the spiked end of the posts that had been driven deep into the earth. Flies were already thick around the grisly scene and the stench was rising in the late afternoon sun.

Klöss took it all in with a stony expression. He was no innocent but this was sick. The tortured faces of the bodies showed that some, at least, had still been alive when they'd been impaled. It wasn't just that it was barbaric, it was senseless. These people weren't warriors, they were simple farmers. He was honest enough with himself to admit that, if he'd attacked this village, then they probably wouldn't all have survived. He'd have burnt the place to the ground, but if they'd chosen to flee he'd have let them. He glared at the line of posts whilst, behind him, Gavin retched noisily against the ruined palisade.

CHAPTER SIX

Skelf lay a day and night behind them. Klöss had to fight against the temptation to have it burned to the ground. The villagers deserved something better than they'd been given but there was no sense in announcing their presence to everything within thirty miles. In the end they'd left the dead where they were. They hadn't the time or the tools to dig the posts out, and cutting them down wasn't an option. There is little noise that carries better than the sound of men chopping wood. The dead wouldn't complain. They seldom did. It is the living that worry about the dead, and there was nobody left in Skelf to care.

The scouting parties fanned out again, forming into a rough arc with Klöss and his group at the centre though he'd halved their number by doubling their size. The sight of the corpses of Skelf had stuck with the men and his order for the scouting parties to stay closer together had been received with more than one satisfied nod. They were here to scout he'd reminded them, not to fight. If it came to it he'd rather run than get bogged down in a meaningless skirmish.

Gavin led again, with two others working to each side of him. The man had an ability with tracks that was almost uncanny. Considering his life had been spent on the streets of Hesk it had taken him little time to adjust to the woods of Anlan. He moved quickly, eyes down at the leaves and bushes as he followed the trail.

Rather than take the roads the villagers seemed to have headed into the woods, breaking their own trail through the brush. Though he'd lost it a few times even Klöss could spot the occasional footprint.

The woods were quiet. There was an occasional burst of birdsong but most of the time it was just the sound of the wind in the treetops or simply silence lurking behind the slight noise of their own passage. Klöss glanced up to try and catch sight of the sun and gauge the time but the thick canopy made it all but impossible.

He'd been enamoured with these thick leafy trees when he'd first seen them. There was a world of difference between seeing them and being between them, however.

The woods seemed dark and oppressive, with thick stands of nameless bushes that seemed to have grown up in any space large enough to hold them. The rare sound of a small creature in amongst the leaves was enough to make him jump almost every time. Frankly, he'd have given a lot for an honest fight on a beach or in an open field.

Gavin's hand shot up, warning them to still their feet but Klöss had already heard the noise, a sharp rustling as something darted through the leaves in the bushes ahead of them and off to their right. He looked to both Tristan and Gavin, motioning for them to spread out and approach from the left whilst the others took the right. Drawing his sword felt good, the stress bleeding away in expectation of something more honest than skulking through the trees.

Tristan was already moving, crouched low and with feet more sure and quiet than Klöss had ever managed. He pointed into the bush and waved them forward, breaking into a run and crunching through the dry leaves underfoot as he crashed through the thin branches that sought to stop him.

It was the sound that stopped him. A thin mewl of terror that a wounded animal or a terrified child might make. A flash of brown scrabbled back away from him, deeper into the bush, and then Gavin was there, appearing from nowhere to grab a pale arm and yank hard.

The woman he dragged howling from the bush was filthy. Mud streaked her long, dark hair that hung lank and heavy where it wasn't stuck to her face. She screamed and twisted weakly in Gavin's grip, reaching to claw at his wrist until Tristan took her other hand.

"Damn woman, calm it down," Gavin told her as she howled and screamed. "We're not going to hurt you!"

Then Klöss saw the blood. Her dress had probably once been a dull green or grey colour at one point but the mud covered it so thoroughly that now it was hard to tell. A dark stain he had first taken for more mud spread from her waist, streaking down past her knees and blooming up over her belly.

"Let her go," he said, repeating himself as they gave him odd looks. She didn't wait for them but instead wrenched her arms out of their grip and lay on the ground with her chest heaving.

"Were you from Skelf?" he asked, crouching down to her level.

She looked at him then, pure misery and anguish on her face.

"Were you?" Gavin persisted. She glanced at him but stayed silent.

"Answer the bloody question, woman." Klöss snapped. They didn't have time for this. He needed answers.

"She cannot, Klöss." Tristan murmured.

Klöss looked at him in irritation. "What?

He spoke with a pained look. "It is not that she keeps silent. She cannot speak, look." Klöss looked back to her as she opened her mouth in an anguished wail and what remained of her tongue glistened wet and angry in a mouth stained with blood from where it had been crudely hacked out.

"Lord of Midnight!" Gavin breathed.

Klöss tried a different approach. "Can you understand us?"

She nodded once and wiped the tears from her face with the sleeve of her dress. It didn't help and streaked the mud and dirt on her face.

"You were at Skelf?"

She nodded once.

"The attack, was it the Anlish?"

She shook her head and buried her face in her hands as sobs overtook her. Gavin moved to take her into his arms then, letting her sob into his neck as the other two looked on awkwardly. "I think I know what it was," he said to her, his voice barely above a whisper. "I've seen them too. Was it the monsters?"

She pulled back away from him, her face was incredulous as she looked at Gavin like he'd just sprouted wings, but then nodded.

Klöss motioned Tristan aside as Gavin continued to question her and the two of them stepped back away from her. "What are we going to do with her?"

Tristan winced, and then shrugged.

"That's not much help," Klöss muttered. "We can't very well take her with us and there's nothing to send her back to."

"They took about thirty of the villagers," Gavin said, interrupting them. "I can't get much more out of her with nothing to write with but I get the impression it was mostly young women, though there were a couple of men too. She made it pretty clear they've been making free with the women every time one of them can't keep up."

"Making free?" Tristan asked, confused, and then held a hand up to stop him. "No, I understand now."

"We can't take her with us, Gavin," Klöss said.

He nodded, looking back at her. "I know. We can't just leave her here like this though."

Tristan sighed and made his way back to her. "It is dangerous where we travel to," he explained. "We will follow these creatures and seek out where it is they come from. You cannot come with us. Can we leave you with anything? Is there anything you need? Some food?"

She shook her head, as her eyes filled with tears, and pointed to his belt. Tristan looked down, "You want a belt?"

She shook her head again. "Iyfff!" she said in little more than a whimper, pointing at the belt again.

He looked at the others helplessly.

"She wants the dagger." Klöss said.

"No," Gavin said as the woman shook her head. "She wants to die."

They looked at her then, raped and bloody, tongue ripped out by something so far removed from humanity that it was closer to monster than man.

Gavin pulled out his own knife. "Nobody wants to die alone. I'll stay with her. Go on ahead and I'll find you."

She looked at him gratefully and he settled down beside her, speaking in low comforting tones. Klöss met his eyes and gave a grim nod as he waved the trackers ahead.

It was three hours before he caught them. His eyes were flat and hard. They did not speak of it.

They came across others on the trail, broken bloody things that had been discarded. None were still living and Gavin's eyes flashed at every body they found.

* * *

They moved at what felt like a snail's pace for the next few hours. Gavin was visible, not much more than twenty yards ahead, picking his way through the ferns as he moved from trunk to trunk.

The faint sound tore through the trees like a scream at a wedding, echoes of an agonised howl that cut off with a silence that was as savage as the scream had been.

Tristan met Klöss's eyes. They were close. Possibly too close now. He shifted towards Klöss, whispering directly into his ear. "We should wait now, wait for darkness."

Klöss considered it briefly. The scream couldn't have been that far away though it was hard to judge how far it might have echoed. Normally he'd have agreed. Night was the perfect time to scout an enemy's territory. The guard relaxed, no matter how well disciplined the men. Those on watch soon became bored and spent more time longing for hot food and a warm bed than keeping an eye on the darkness beyond the camp.

The battle where Verig fell though, that had taught him a lot. These creatures clearly had no problems seeing in the darkness. He shook his head and moved his lips to Tristan's ear. "No. They are not blind in the dark like us. I'd rather we could both see than just them. Let's send Gavin in. He's the quietest anyway. Send Kest and what's-his-name to pass the word to the other groups as best they can. Scout the perimeter and try to get an idea of their numbers. I want only our quietest out there."

"Kahrlson, Klöss," Tristan said, shaking his head. "His name is Kahrlson."

Klöss waved the reproach away and waited. It was funny. He'd grown accustomed to the blood. He'd even become used to the fear that sometimes struck in battle but he'd never found a way to cope with the waiting. Though this was a scouting mission, the waiting was just as interminable, possibly worse.

He hunched down behind a tree, toying idly with a dagger. A wild, savage part of him wanted to just charge in, numbers be damned. The beast wanted battle and the feel of steel in his hands. He forced it down. It was hungry for bloody vengeance against these things, these creatures that had stolen his child and his wife in all but name. He could feel it rising the more he thought about it and found his hand clenched so tight around the dagger's hilt that it cramped.

Tristan gave a soft whistle and then Gavin was there, breathing hard. He sank down quick beside the tree and pulled out a skin, drinking water in short gasping gulps before he spoke. "It is the trels. There must be thousands of them. The land dips a bit up ahead, almost into a little valley. From what I could see they're filling most of it, though there's some kind of mist blocking a lot of the view."

"They've made camp there then?"

Gavin shook his head. "Not that I could see. They just seem to be milling around, waiting for something I'd guess. There's some kind of old standing stones in the centre but I couldn't get close enough to see much of it."

"What about the villagers?" Klöss asked.

"I couldn't see any of them..." His voice made it clear there was more.

"But?"

"There's something else. I thought they were men until they walked into the shade. Their eyes are like the ones we saw in the reaping except these are blue."

"Blue?"

Gavin shrugged. "They shine bright as any lantern's flame, except for the colour."

"Fine," Klöss said. "I'm not taking on thousands of them, villagers or no. We'll wait for Kest and Kahrlson, and then we'll move out. I don't mind admitting I don't like being this close to the bastards."

Tristan snorted at that but Gavin was silent, looking out through the trees. The hiss of his daggers as they came from their sheaths was almost buried in the explosion of leaves as Kest burst from the trees.

"They're coming," he managed as he turned and held the arm of his small handbow against the earth with his foot whilst he levered the wire back over the hook.

"Shit!" Klöss said as he drew his sword and long dagger, moving away from the tree he had rested against to give himself room.

The first of the creatures tore through the woods, coming at them at a dead run and pulling knives as it ran. Gavin moved like a snake, shifting to meet the attack and throwing himself into a roll only to come up with daggers extended and thrusting at the trel's chest. It batted the daggers away as if they were nothing, slashing with its own blades and forcing the thief back.

Tristan hacked at the creature's legs as they passed his position, but though his blade staggered it the monster suffered no injury and continued on in amongst them.

The daggers flashed as both thief and trel slashed at each other, the blades meeting with a dull rasping ring with every block and parry. Klöss stood ready, waiting for an opening but the two spun and wove as they battled, making any swing risky at best.

Between one slash and the next Gavin dumped his dagger, his hand flashing to the small of his back to grab another. He swung hard with his left, leaving his arms open wide, an invitation the creature couldn't resist as it darted in with blades extended. Rather than simply stand there though, Gavin had never stopped moving. He spun against the attack and thrust the knife deep into the side of the beast's neck as it passed him, its blades missing him by less than a finger's breadth.

Blue fire flared around the blade of the dagger and Gavin swore, flapping his hand and darting away as the trel burst into flame, screaming and clawing at the blade buried in its neck as it fell writhing to the leaf-strewn dirt.

Klöss shut his gaping mouth with an audible clack of teeth and plucked the dagger free from the still smouldering corpse, handing it back to Gavin. "I guess you were right about the iron then," he said. "Next time though, let's try one of these first?" He hefted the handbow and grinned at the little thief as he sucked at his burnt fingers.

The smiles soon faded as the sounds of combat drifted through the trees and they moved out at a trot. They headed in the rough direction of Skelf, covering each other with the handbows as they moved in two groups, leapfrogging each other's position and turning to cover each other's withdrawal. Their numbers grew slowly as other scouts found their way back to them. First individuals, and then small groups of two and three, all with wild eyes and small wounds.

Attacks came sporadically and seemingly spontaneously. The trels came individually at first, rushing at them through the trees until an iron bolt brought them down. The handbow bolts were well made and were largely recoverable, if the men moved quickly enough. Blue fire had ruined several and they were too valuable to lose.

Then the attacks began in earnest and it seemed that they barely had time to recover what bolts they could before the next group of trels ran at them.

"We cannot keep at this, Klöss," Tristan managed between heaving breaths.

"I'm not exactly having fun myself." Klöss replied, looking over the man as they ran. "If you've got ideas I'd love to hear them."

Tristan stopped and ducked behind a broad oak, covering the second group as they ran past them. "The road." Tristan pointed vaguely through the trees. "It should be in that direction. We would move faster on the road with less chance of being surprised."

"Less chance of concealment too," Klöss muttered beside him.

"I do not think concealment is a worry at this point, do you?"

Klöss looked back behind him at the retreating men, waiting until they were in position. "Fine," he said to Tristan. "You lead off then. You've got a better idea of where you're going."

"Lost again?" Tristan sighed. He flashed a grin at Klöss's darkening face and, with a last look in the direction the trels had come from, started off at a run.

The sounds of fighting still dogged them as the light began to fade. It was too distant to risk calling out and trying to gather the men to them. There might be safety in numbers but the noise would draw the trels. Klöss knew the information they carried was more important than individual lives but it was poor comfort each time the sound of blade on blade fell silent and the screaming began.

Their numbers had grown to over thirty and they moved in three groups of ten in an almost continuous motion. It grew into a rhythm, cover a retreat, turn and run past those covering them, then cover their retreat. Again and again. And again. It did mean they were covering more ground but the attacks were wearing.

A snarl of rage announced the satyrs at the last second as they attacked, tearing into the right side of them. Bolts flew wildly into the trees as shocked men turned to meet the attack, and for long minutes chaos reigned. The steel weapons they carried were largely useless. They clearly caused pain to the beasts but did little or no damage. Five men were down before the handful of iron daggers among them could be brought to bear. A trel went down with an iron bolt slammed into its face and, as the blue fire flared, men snatched up the bolts, using them as improvised daggers. In moments, silence fell.

"Shit!" Klöss spat as he surveyed the mess. Ten men were down, a full third of his force. He examined a shallow cut to his forearm, a slash that had gone through his leathers as if they weren't there.

"Three are dead," Tristan reported after a few minutes. "Five can probably run but will be poor use when fighting. The last two we will need to carry."

Klöss swore again. "Let's get moving as soon as we can. I think we're still ahead of most of them. I really don't want to tangle with a large force do you?"

Tristan grunted and went to hurry men along as wounds were examined and rough bandages tied.

The two that were worst were men Klöss barely recognised. He felt a brief pang of guilt about that but shoved it aside. Now was not the time. Tristan took one over his shoulder whilst two others carried the other man. Both were pale, with teeth clenched tight as they fought to keep the groans inside their mouths. With a grim expression, Klöss waved them forward and the group set off at a slow jog.

The first man died before it became fully dark. They'd stopped to catch their breath and Tristan let loose a long string of curses as he bent to look at the man he carried. He glanced at Klöss and shook his head. There was no time to mourn. The man was stripped of anything the others could use and wrapped in his cloak. It wouldn't be the first man Klöss had left in the woods of this land but it didn't make it any easier.

The road caught them all unawares as they passed through a thick stand of holly and then out onto the broad, packed earth. They were all of them exhausted and Klöss ordered a staggered run. Five minutes jogging would be followed by two minutes walking, and then back to the run. It didn't work as well as he'd hoped and they were forced to abandon it and drop into a walk as men started falling behind.

"We will need to find somewhere to stop, Klöss," Tristan observed in low tones.

"Where do you suggest, Tristan?" Klöss snapped. "Is there a handy fort around that I don't know about?" He regretted it instantly but didn't make apologies. They needed leadership right now not coddling. He looked around and up at the dark, clouded sky. "We push on until while we can still see. I want to cover as much ground as we can."

They moved on in silence, the only sound the pounding of boots on the hard earth and the occasional rattle of a loose weapon. The pace slowed. Slipping from a jog to a trot, then from a trot to a walk. They'd had no signs of the things that stalked them for over an hour when Klöss finally called a halt but he knew they were out there.

He looked around at the road. The path itself was little more than twenty feet wide but the trees and brush were cut back to either side, presumably to help deal with bandits and the like. He motioned the men closer and sank down in the centre of the group.

"All right, normally I'd say we'd lost the bastards but I trust them like I'd trust a new oarsman with an itchy arse to row to the drum. If we're going to fight I want to bloody well see what I'm doing and they can see just fine in the dark already. Build me some fires, boys. Make it so I can see what I'm shooting at."

The scouts set to work gathering up what wood they could without having to range too far into the trees. The fires surrounded them, arranged in rough rings that expanded out and away from them. Klöss looked out over the flames and into the darkness beyond.

"You think this enough?" Tristan asked as he came up behind one shoulder.

"I don't know," Klöss confessed. "They'd have to be blind to miss us but we can't risk going without the light. If even one of those damned hell-beasts got in here among us in the dark it could do for us all. At least this way we have a chance to see them coming."

"Go and sleep," the man told him. "I will sort the watches."

Klöss thought about protesting for half a second, and then nodded. He settled down in the centre of the circle of men. Half were already snoring. The other half stared out past the fires with handbows held ready. The tiny sliver that was all remained of the moon peered down through gaps in the cloud at them. Duty fought with fatigue. Duty lost.

He woke with a grunt as Tristan kicked at him gently. "I think they are coming."

The words were all he needed to bring him fully awake. He rolled to his feet, taking up the handbow as he rose.

"There have been shadows about the farthest fires," Tristan advised quietly. "Nothing worth a shot but they are increasing. They test us, I think."

Klöss peered past the fires, into the darkness. The farthest had burnt down to coals that glowed sullenly against the black of the forest. "Has it all been from the same direction?" he wondered as he glanced around to either side of them.

"This far," Tristan grunted.

"That won't last unless they truly are stupid. Have you got them in quads?" Klöss nodded at the men closest to them. They'd worked out the idea of the quads on the retreat through the woods. Once the trels began to close, and they could no longer rely on handbows alone, then the men would work together in groups of four, one with a steel blade to engage the trel whilst the second struck with an iron dagger or a handbow bolt and the third fired handbows with his partner reloading.

"They're ready."

They waited. Sparks flew up as men darted out to throw wood onto the fires closest to dying. The shadows beyond the furthest fires grew, shifting in the darkness as the number grew. Firelight obscured the eyes that Klöss knew would be glowing in the darkness but there was no doubting they were out there.

They came in tentative pushes at first. Small groups of four or five that flinched past the first of the fires and came charging at the waiting Bjornmen. Blue sparks exploded in amongst the fires as the trels fell writhing to the dirt.

As if the first few had burst a dam the trels charged, a flood of dark bodies howling hate as they poured past the farthest fires. The Bjornmen fired in pairs, with one shooting a handbow whilst the other worked frantically to reload for him. The explosions of blue fire were all but blinding as the bolts tore into the seething mass.

Klöss called out orders to fire, and then pass back the handbows to be reloaded in a calm voice that fell into a steady chanting rhythm. The keiju were advancing on them but the toll was horrific, and the stench of burning flesh and fur carried easily to them in the soft night breeze.

They formed into the quads as the keiju grew closer, and Klöss abandoned his chant to draw weapons and take his place in the line.

The keiju threw themselves into the fight with a savage abandon, seeming almost to relish the danger even as the steel swords left them open to the thrust of an iron dagger.

The quads worked almost perfectly and blue fire flared along the line as the trel fell. Then the first man fell as the creatures adjusted to the tactic. Another screamed as a bone knife took his eyes and the line staggered as the Bjornmen were pushed slowly backward.

There is a moment in a battle just before the panic takes hold, when the realisation that this is the fight that you cannot win slowly sets home. Klöss had seen it half a dozen times, on raids gone badly and in fights aboard ship against Dernish in their Broadscows. It began in the eyes, and by the time it had reached a man's courage it was already too late.

He could see it now in the men closest to him. There were simply too many of these damned things. Another two men fell, far along the line to his left, but their screams carried and he couldn't help but look as they pitched forward and fell to the dirt.

"Hold the line!" he growled, his order taken up by those closest and shouted on.

Men on the right staggered back another five feet, forcing the rest to move with them or be left exposed. "Hold the fucking line!" Klöss roared.

Tristan's axe drove a creature to its knees and Klöss darted in with the knife before it could rise. He rammed the blade home, wrenching it free and backing away from the blue flames that gushed from its throat as dark blood boiled and hissed in the fire.

Still they came. When one of his men fell the others only knew if they heard the scream or if they were close enough to see. These creatures though, with the fire that erupted whenever iron pierced them, the others couldn't help but see it. Despite this, despite seeing every death, they came on.

The line broke. A man fell, and then another, leaving a hole in the line as men staggered back away from the raging trels. It only took one to turn and run before the others followed.

"We cannot hold, Klöss," Tristan shouted at him, his voice barely audible over the screams of the creatures.

He was right. It was the choice between turning and running, risking a knife in the back, or staying and knowing he'd eventually get one to the throat.

"Ready handbows and fire!" he roared, shrugging the weapon from his back and loosing the bolt without really bothering to aim. It would have been more work for him to miss at this range.

The line exploded in fire and sparks again and Klöss was already turning as he shouted "Now run, you bastards!"

He led off in a sprint, throwing the bow onto his back. Tristan ran beside him, his heavy axe in one hand. Already men were screaming as the monsters pulled them down one by one. Bursts of blue fire flared as men turned to loose a bolt into the horde that followed. A glance over one shoulder revealed an image that belonged in a nightmare. The fires were all but obscured by the creatures as they surged forward, dark against the failing flames. Their eyes though, burnt as bright as any flame. Glowing bright in the growing darkness, lit by strange magic or just by hate, it didn't matter.

Men fell around him. Some screamed as the clawed hands pulled them down, some gasped as the knife took them. He fought against the desire to rip his sword and dagger free and turn to fight. His own hot rage warring with the knowledge that he had to get the news back to Rimeheld. Death was a luxury he couldn't afford to indulge in.

His anger was bitter in his mouth as he ran. He'd failed. These deaths were his fault and his own death, another failure, would soon follow. A hand fell on his wrist and he glanced in shock at Gavin as the thief pulled him and Tristan off to one side of the road and into the trees.

Gavin stopped them almost immediately, pressing his hands to their mouths to call for silence. He used his hands alone to push at them gently, making them crouch low and move no faster than a crawl through undergrowth that they could barely see. All the time, the sound of the pursuing trels thundered in their ears, punctuated with the screams of his men as they were dragged down, one by one, and butchered.

Gavin stopped them with another hand in the darkness, pulling them down. He pushed and hissed curses at them as they reluctantly wormed under the edge of a half-rotten log. The ground was slick with mud and what could have been moss or perhaps some manner of mould. Either way it stank, and the damp worked its way through clothes and leathers until the icy touch of the stuff found skin.

The night fell silent eventually as the sounds of the chase faded away. They did not speak. The trels might still be close enough to hear them and none amongst them had words for what had happened. They lay in the filth, each with their thoughts tormenting them as they drifted in and out of a fitful sleep until dawn eventually found them.

CHAPTER SEVEN

Klöss walked on silence. The trip had been grim from the start, even after they'd sacrificed the stealth of moving through the woods for the speed of travelling on the road. They'd passed body after body, torn and broken on the packed earth. They were scattered in groups of two or three, never more than five. The signs of their battles lay in the dirt around them. Blood sprayed wide on the road next to the scorched earth where a trel had fallen.

There had been too many to even consider burying or burning. The creatures might still have been close enough to find the smoke and each body he abandoned was another betrayal, each pair of sightless eyes hurling its own accusation. *Coward. You hid!*

They had been his men, his responsibility. His mood had grown darker with each man they came across, and they had walked in silence long after they had finally stopped checking for any signs of life in those they passed.

Some had made it farther than others and the trail had lasted for miles. The sun had shone happily down on the bodies and the flies and birds had wasted little time settling on the corpses. The image of the crows pecking out gobbets of flesh, or an eye, only for the flies to settle in the oozing holes they left, stayed with him as they walked. Even now, days later, the sight was there whenever he closed his eyes.

He ached, bruises contending with sore muscles. They'd been on the move for over a week, and their journey was nearly over. The minor cuts and bruises he'd suffered had mostly gone but the worst of his wounds were still healing. Every step brought an aching pain that did nothing to improve his temper. He spent his time alternating between thinking about what he could have done differently and wondering where the beasts had vanished to.

"No signs?" He shot over to Gavin, walking on the other side of Tristan.

His head whipped round, startled after hours walking in silence. "What?" he asked with a confused look. Then, "Oh, no, Nothing. Not for days now. I've stopped really looking to be honest."

Klöss grunted and caught Tristan staring at him with an appraising eye. "What?" he demanded.

"Are you ready to speak about this?"

Klöss scowled at him and took a moment to kick a loose stone off the path, sending it bouncing down the rocky slope towards the river far below them on their left. "What do you mean?"

"You do this, you know?" Tristan explained. "You are a good man to follow. You have a mind for tactics and you never allow greed or anger to steer your course. My thought is that it is because of this that you have not lost many battles, or many men, in the years I have fought with you. When you do though, it is like an insult to you, a personal attack. We do not have time for you to sulk, Klöss."

Gavin gave a snort which conveniently transformed into a cough as Klöss shot his head round to glare at him.

"I do not sulk." He bit off each word.

Tristan shrugged. "*Brood* then. The word is not important. Are you ready to speak about it?"

"What about it?"

"This is not your fault," Tristan told him, his voice brooking no argument. "There was no way to know there would be so many of them. We did not blunder in there. We took every care. They do not act like a normal enemy though. I do not understand this."

Klöss frowned. "How do you mean?"

"You have never been stupid, Klöss," Tristan chided. "Do not start now."

Klöss bit back a retort as he caught the sly grin. "Go on…"

"These creatures, name them trels, name them what you will. They were massed in numbers higher than the largest reaving. Where were their supplies, their tents? They are not mindless animals. We all heard their speech as they fought, calling out to each other. For that matter, where have they now gone? We must have faced over a hundred as they gave chase. Who knows how many more passed us once we were hidden. There were easily a score of thousand in the valley." He glanced over at Gavin for confirmation.

"Don't ask me," the thief said as with a shrug. "More than I could count, that's for sure."

"So where are they now?" Tristan waved his hands around at the silent trees.

Klöss glanced around him as he chewed on his lip. "We're too close to Rimeheld now, they wouldn't be here anyway."

Tristan grabbed Klöss suddenly, grasping his shoulders and forcing him to face him. "They broke through the gates at Rimeheld," he reminded him. "They came down from the sky to attack the Anlish during the reaping. Now they destroy this village, Skelf. They could be anywhere. They could be in Hesk tomorrow."

"They're in Hesk already," Gavin added in a soft voice.

Tristan glanced at the younger man and gave a nod of approval. "It is time we faced this threat, Klöss. We need for our eyes to be open. Hiding from this will not help."

Klöss nodded and pulled away from the man to begin walking again.

"That was not my meaning anyway." Tristan said, looking down at the rocks and the water that dashed itself to a white froth against them. "Those that chased down our men, where did they go? They did not pass us and we have seen no sign that they continued on. The tracks from their feet simply end."

"Maybe they went back through the woods?" Gavin offered.

Tristan looked to the trees. "I think not. They could have, but why? There is no threat to them here, why take a slower passage for no reason?"

"So, what? They simply vanished?" Klöss snorted.

"I do not know. We know nothing of these trels." He jerked his head at Gavin. "This one took the idea of using iron for his dagger from old tales. How much more is true?"

Klöss stooped and picked up a stone, turning it over in his hands as he thought. "So what do you suggest?" he asked after several minutes.

"Perhaps it is time we talk to the Anlish," Tristan offered.

"The Anlish? Why?"

"We both saw them being attacked during the reaping, Klöss. These trels are no allies of theirs. Could it be the Anlish know something of them?"

Klöss sighed and sent the stone flying, following the path of the one he'd kicked. "I can't see them really being open to a friendly chat, Tristan."

"So offer them something," Tristan muttered with a shrug.

"Yeah, the sealord's going to *love* that!" Gavin snorted.

"It's not the time to start peace talks, Tristan," Klöss told him. "Only a fool negotiates before he's tried his full strength, and whatever else these Anlish are, they're not fools."

Tristan grunted and fell silent. The sun was already sinking and the shafts of light stabbed at their eyes as they fought through gaps in the trees. "It would not need to be peace talks. Just talks would be enough."

Klöss grunted. "I'll think about it. Gavin's right though, I can't see the sealord going for it." He looked around. "I'd hoped we'd make it back today but it doesn't look likely now and I don't see much point in stumbling along in the dark. Let's find somewhere to make camp."

"That is another thing," Tristan said as they left the road and picked their way into the trees. "You risk too much with the way you act here."

"What do you mean?"

"The sealord, he is like the tide lapping at a beached boat. He will take what he can if nothing is done to stop him.

Klöss nodded, letting the conversation end as he brooded. They set up a crude camp only a few hundred yards from the edge of the trees. A broad oak provided their shelter, standing at the edge of a small gully. The leaves would keep them mostly dry if it decided to rain and the steep bank would be enough to conceal a fire. After days on the road, and only just missing the warmth of a real bed, Klöss was not prepared to suffer a cold camp. He sank down and let the others worry and light the fire, avoiding attempts at conversation. Despite being bone weary he found he couldn't sleep and stared into the dying coals of the fire long after the other two had dropped into deep breathing slumber.

They set off at almost first light. The camp was cold when they woke and there was little point in staying any longer than it took to chew down some dried fruit and a ship's biscuit.

The day wore on and the sun seemed to sense his mood and hid behind the thick clouds for most of the morning. The path veered gently away from the river, passing beyond the trees and snaking between the low hills as they drew closer to Rimeheld. The closest of the farms and small villages were visible as soon as the three of them left the trees and the sight alone was enough to lift his mood. Despite the failure that dogged his thoughts they'd made it back.

It appeared, all at once, grim and forbidding in the distance as they rounded a small rise. The sight brought a sense of relief and despite everything that had happened he couldn't help but give in to a small smile.

The path brought them close to the cliff's edge, giving a view of the harbour. He looked over to Tristan breaking the silence. "You're probably right about the sealord." He admitted, eliciting raised eyebrows in response. "Frostbeard was worried that the fact he sent the Black Fleet meant he was going to try and take more control here."

"He told you this?" Tristan asked in surprise. "I would not think he was ever a man to express doubts."

"Not in public perhaps, but yes," Klöss replied, nodding.

"What did you tell him?" Gavin asked with a curious look.

A smile grew on his dirty face. "I told him that Rimeheld was his. Everything else? It was all politics, appearances. The Ssalord could do what he liked, bringing in ships and calling it the Black Fleet but it was still Aiden the men had named the city after."

"That doesn't mean anything now though," Gavin said. "Now it's just a name."

Klöss turned to the thief with a questioning look. "What makes you think that?"

Gavin shrugged. Then, seeing Klöss waiting for more, "I don't know anything about politics but I know cities and I know power. Hesk has the thane and its stupid lords but they only rule what they can see. Hesk's underbelly is ruled by the Six and they know more about power than any council member wrapped up in his fur and robes."

"The Six?" Tristan asked with genuine interest.

"The leaders of the six major gangs in Hesk," Gavin explained. "They run everything from the pawnbrokers that pretend they aren't fences on the side, to the whores that stand by the docks."

"This is all very interesting, Gavin," Klöss broke in. "But what does it have to do with the sealord and Rimeheld?"

"Let me finish and you might just learn something," Gavin snapped, and then carried on quickly as Klöss's face darkened. "The Six rule in Hesk as much as the thane and his council does, but it's a balancing act. If any one of the gangs were to grow too powerful it would pick off the others or they'd all work together to destroy it. It's the same inside them. One man leads each gang, more by strength and fear than by brains, though I've known that to happen too." He held up a hand to stop Klöss before he interrupted. "I'm getting to the point, just hold on.

"The leader of the Fishers died a few years ago. Nothing so exciting as being killed or taken down. He choked on a bone. Probably the first time one of the Six died of something that didn't involve poison or blood. Anyway, his second thought he'd be able to just take over. That leading the Fishers would just pass on to him. He was wrong. The others fell on him like rats on a wounded cat. The Fishers rule the streets and warehouses around the docks. After dark the docklands of Hesk were nothing but knives and blood for weeks. Power belongs to those that take it, it doesn't pass naturally. It needs to be seized."

"What are you saying?" Klöss asked with a frown.

"I'm saying that Rimeheld won't pass to you unless you reach out and take it. The sealord is probably testing you at the moment, seeing if he can use you. If he decides against it then he'll try and take that power for himself. You're sitting, nice and cosy and letting him make that decision for you. If you want this you need to act. The sealord can name you Lord of Rimeheld. Hell, he could call you King of Anlan if he likes. Until you take that power for yourself it's just words."

"What do you think?" Klöss said, but Tristan walked in silence, eyes on the harbour and a faint frown on his face.

"Tristan?" Klöss tried again.

"Hmm? I was not listening." He looked back to the harbour. "Klöss, where are the reavers?"

"What?" Klöss shaded his eyes and looked down to the water.

"I see the fishing fleet and some of the smaller ships your uncle had built here but the galley reavers, the defence fleet, they are gone."

Klöss stared, stupidly, as if just looking could make the view change. Tristan was right. The harbour stood almost bare and the briefest glance at the horizon told the same tale. The ships were gone.

* * *

They moved as fast as aching legs would allow. The urgency drove him but three weeks of travelling, fighting, and hiding in the dirt had taken its toll. Klöss was experienced enough to listen to his body when it spoke to him. He was definitely not going to ignore it when it screamed at him. That said, Lek had been left in command of a secure city and the task shouldn't have been enough to move him beyond his precious papers. The fact the fleet had sailed both frustrated and worried him and his irritation at not having the answers he wanted grew with every passing step.

Chains clanked in the distance as the heavy gates swung ponderously open and a double rank of men rushed out, forming up around them as escort.

Klöss recognised their leader, though he couldn't put a name to the man. He nodded an acknowledgement in place of voicing thanks. Conversation was not something he was looking for at the moment.

The whispers followed them through the streets. They'd began as whispers at the gates when the shocked guards stood at attention as they let them through. By the time they had passed the central market the whispers had grown beyond mutters, and the staring and pointing was beginning to get on his nerves. He dismissed the escort as they approached the keep and let his irritation show on his face.

"Where's Lek?" he barked at the closest guardsman as he strode through the doors to the keep.

"Lord Klöss, you're alive!" the man blurted.

"Obviously." Klöss growled, ignoring the title for once. "Now, where is he?"

"It's just, we'd heard your party was attacked."

Klöss didn't bother to reply. Instead his hand lashed out, grabbing the shocked man by the throat and lifting him up against the stone wall. "Listen, it's been a really long week," he grated. "I've got blood and dirt in places I can't even put names to and I really don't have the patience right now. So how about you just tell me where Lek is?"

Tristan pulled Klöss's arm down gently as the guard made frantic noises. "Put him down, Klöss. The blame is not his."

"I really would advise just answering the question," Gavin suggested with a grin as Klöss let the man slide down the wall.

"Seamaster's office," the guard managed in a breathless gasp.

"Thanks." Klöss growled and left the others as he headed through the halls for the closest stairs. The wide eyes and whispers followed him through the halls as he passed servants and guards and they did nothing for his temper.

The men standing guard outside Frostbeard's office were smart enough not to voice an objection as Klöss opened the door without knocking.

Lek was an older man whose once formidable bulk seemed to have been drained from him as he'd grown older, falling away like sand through some twisted form of hourglass. He jumped up as Klöss entered and stepped out from behind a small desk that had been set to one side of Frostbeard's. It looked ridiculous and somehow managed to make the large room feel small and cramped.

Klöss stopped with the words still in his throat as he looked at the small desk set beside the larger one. Reports and papers were still strewn about the surface of Frostbeard's desk, just as they had been when its owner had last sat there.

"Why in the world aren't you using the desk?" Klöss demanded.

Lek glanced behind him and turned back with an embarrassed smile. "It…just didn't feel right somehow." He laughed nervously, a weak and tremulous sound.

"Lords of Blood and Frost." Klöss exploded. "It's only a desk, man. You've set it up as a bloody shrine!"

"It's not important," he said, waving away the apology before Lek really had time to voice it. "Where is the fleet?"

Lek glanced out of the window at the empty docks. "The sealord gave orders for it to move south."

"He did what?" Klöss demanded. "When? He was on a ship for Hesk only three weeks ago. He shouldn't have even landed there yet!"

Lek spread his hands. "He returned to Rimeheld barely four days after he left, a day after the reports came in."

The response stopped him cold. "What reports?"

Lek turned and pulled a handful of papers from his small desk, handing them to Klöss without a word.

"Kellik, Seros, Halfjur… These places are nowhere near each other!" He eased past Lek and went to the map on the wall. The villages were on opposite sides of Rimeheld, and all far closer than Skelf. "We have a fort between these two. How did they slip past us?"

"I only know what the report says, my lord," Lek said with a wince.

Klöss ground his teeth. "I'm not a…" he began, but stopped. Tristan and Gavin's words coming back to him. The power was there, waiting to be taken.

He waved the papers at Lek. "You've read these?" It wasn't really a question. "What condition were they left in?"

Lek frowned at that. "I'm not sure I—"

"The villages, man!" Kloss burst out. Was the man an idiot? "What condition were they left in after the attacks? Were they razed? What happened to the villagers?"

Lek grimaced for a moment before he spoke. "The villages were left almost entirely intact, my lord. The villagers though…" Lek glanced out the window at nothing before looking back. "They were slaughtered to a man. Not just killed either. There were things done to them that—"

Klöss held a hand up to stop him. "It was the same at Skelf." He looked to the far wall beside the desk. "Show me where he sent the fleet."

Lek moved to the map and traced a finger down along the known coastline and off the bottom of the chart.

Klöss grunted as he gnawed at one knuckle. "He sent…how many ships?"

"We have two small fleets out patrolling the waters close to Rimeheld, and the normal escorts for the supply route through the Vorstelv. The balance of the ships, however, have been taken south."

"That's upwards of three hundred ships!" Klöss stepped away from the map, sinking into the heavy chair behind Frostbeard's desk. This was too much. Was the man insane? He met Lek's eyes. "Why?"

Lek blinked in surprise at the question. "These attacks, Klöss. He couldn't just let them stand."

"He thinks this was the Anlish?" Klöss laughed, an ugly, bitter sound. "Bloody fool! How fast does he think those horses of theirs can carry them? No, don't bother. What was the fleet supposed to do?"

Lek sank down behind the desk and looked at him. The years were suddenly clear on his face, the lines etched deeper by the stress. "You need to understand, Klöss. He was furious when he returned. He expected you to be here, taking care of things, not investigating Skelf yourself. Then, when these reports came in, he snapped. He's right though, in my opinion. We need to play to our strengths. If these Anlish can move past our lines this quickly, if they can attack like this, then we need to strike. We're not meant for fighting in muddy fields. We are, and have always been, the wolves that come from the sea. He sent the ships south to burn. To find every fishing village and coastal city that they can and raze them to the ground."

Klöss moved to a cabinet against the wall and rummaged around inside until he stood with a bottle. The neck clinked against the metal goblet as he poured the amber liquid and tossed it back with a grimace. "That's just the thing, Lek. The attacks weren't from the Anlish. Frostbeard knew this. Larren damned well *should* have known this. The things that destroyed Skelf, that killed my scouts almost to a man, they're nothing to do with the Anlish. The sealord has just sent ships south to destroy the cities of the very people we need to be talking to!"

Lek stood silent for a long moment, absorbing that before speaking again. "He's going to want to see you."

"He's here?" Klöss said in surprise. "I'd have thought he'd be with the fleet."

"No, he stayed behind. Said he wanted to take a closer look at things until you returned, or until... Well, you know?"

Klöss filled the glass again. "Well I suppose I'd better go and find him. It's not going to get any better if he finds out that I'm here." He looked at the glass, almost surprised to find it full again, and set it down on the desk, leaving without another word.

The sealord had been given rooms in the keep. They were nothing opulent. Nothing in the keep was. The building had been constructed for defence, the finer touches would come later. He had been given another room to use as an office, however, and as Klöss rounded the corner and saw the guard at the door he knew his guess as to where the man would be was right. There is little point in guarding an empty room, after all.

The guard nodded at him. He didn't quite meet his eyes, Klöss noticed. The man's gaze slid from his face like slipping on ice. Probably not a good sign. He knocked and took a deep breath before entering. The room was small, almost too small for the desk that filled one end of it. The Sealord sat, writing in a neat but tiny script in the glow from a single candle that sat on the desk despite the light from the window behind him.

"Klöss," the Sealord said. His voice was dry, emotionless. Nothing more than an acknowledgement of his presence. "You're back, I see."

"Larren." Klöss nodded politely.

The Sealord pursed his lips in thought, looking up at a spot on the ceiling. "I think, on this occasion, 'sealord' is probably best, don't you?"

This was not going to go well. "As you wish, Sealord."

"Yes, I rather think that's the crux of it, isn't it? As *I* wish." The Sealord stood and stepped out from his desk, picking a speck of lint from his velvet robes. They were midnight blue, almost black, and served to make his hair seem all the whiter, the grey almost invisible.

"I'm disappointed, Klöss," Larren told him, glancing at the floor as if unsure of his path. He looked up at him and the threat of his fury was clear in his gaze. He was just barely holding it in check. It was a weight held by a fraying rope.

"When I decided to return," he grated, "to offer support whilst you came to grips with things here I did not expect to find you'd gone off for a little jaunt in the country."

"The attack needed to be investigated, my lord," Klöss said.

"Yes," Larren agreed. "Yes, it did, but not by the would-be Lord of bloody Rimeheld. Any band of scouts could have gone to that village. Your job is too important."

"I understand that, my lord," Kloss managed. "I serve only at the thane's pleasure."

"No." Larren let his voice drop, and it floated above a dangerous whisper. "*I* serve the thane. You serve me."

Klöss gripped the back of the chair set in front of the desk. "This expedition began as a private venture."

Larren gave him a scathing look. "Don't be so stupid, boy! This began when Aiden came to me with the idea. Do you think I am fool enough to risk my own influence in the Chamber? I sponsored this from the shadows when you were still learning which end of the sword is the sharp one."

He moved closer until Klöss could feel the air from his breath with each word he spat out. "You risked too much with your little stunt. Four villages were razed whilst you were playing soldier in the woods. That has a cost. In supplies, in man-hours, in blood!"

"I know, and I left Lek—"

"Lek?" Larren turned his face to spit on the rug. "If I'd wanted fucking Lek running things I'd have fucking left him in command! He barely knows what a damned sword is for anymore. If it had been left up to him he'd have sent a strongly worded letter to the Anlish in response."

"Instead of which *you* sent my fleet," Klöss said, meeting the man's gaze. "South, to where we have no charts, no knowledge of what we might be facing. You stripped the walls and left us with men less skilled than boys I've sailed with to defend this city."

Larren laughed and perched on the corner of the desk, shaking his head. "You have some more growing up to do, boy. You think that because you sat in a camp watching men build boats that the fleet belongs to you? Or even that it belonged to Aiden?" He lifted his head and his true anger was revealed, burning hot and bright in his face. "If it touches the water it is mine. From a galley reaver, to a fucking cork tossed into the harbour. I am sealord, the sword of the thane. If it floats or carries a blade, then it answers to me!"

"And what if I told you the attacks on these villages had nothing to do with the Anlish?" Klöss asked in a spiteful hiss.

That stopped Larren cold and he cocked his head to one side, eyes narrowed in thought before he stepped back away from him, turning to pick up a paper on the corner of the desk. "Go on…"

"There is a third player in all this," Klöss explained through his temper. "Frostbeard knew it, the men know it."

"These tales of trels in the woods?" Larren scoffed.

Klöss clenched his teeth until they matched his grip on the chair. "I saw them myself. I fought them. I only made it back with Tristan and one other. As far as I know the rest of the men were cut down as they ran. You've seen these things yourself, the attack on the night of the banquet."

"I saw a city attacked because it wasn't secure," Larren said. "I saw no trels. I don't recall seeing any laka's hiding sweets inside anyone's shoes either."

"I—" Klöss began.

Larren cut him off. "I believe I have heard enough, Shipmaster. I am sure there's some minor paperwork you can be doing. Lek will direct you to it, I'm sure. I have more pressing matters to deal with than your children's tales. In time, if you prove trustworthy, I believe there are haulers that need shipmasters. If I need your presence before then I'll be sure to send for you."

Klöss bit back half a dozen responses and made his way to the door, the words burning in his throat.

* * *

The place was as grimy as Gavin remembered it. It had only been a matter of months since he'd first stepped foot in the Golden Goose but it felt far longer. He stepped inside and went quickly to the bar. The place was deserted for the moment and the innkeeper peered up as the door opened. A look that came close to recognition flickered over his face, then was gone.

"What can I get you?" the grubby man asked.

Gavin looked carefully around the small taproom. The windows were dirty enough that a man would need to press his face to the glass to see through. The place was as perfect as he'd thought it would be.

"Drink?" the barman pressed.

"No." Gavin dropped a heavy purse of coin on the bar, noting the look on the man's face as it struck. It takes a particular kind of man to gauge the contents of a purse by the sound of it landing. Gavin knew all about that kind of man.

"I need you to close, Rolant," he said casually.

Rolant cocked an eyebrow on a face that was otherwise devoid of expression. "Do I know you?"

"I just have a good memory for names. You don't need to remember me," Gavin told him.

"Fair enough." Rolant shrugged. "Close?"

"Close," Gavin confirmed with a nod of his head. "I need the use of this room for a few hours.

"I don't rent rooms," Rolant said flatly. "This isn't that kind of inn."

Gavin glanced around and snorted. "This is barely any kind of inn!"

"I don't ha—"

"Look," Gavin said, leaning forward on the bar. "You're not busy. You're not going to miss out on business. Just take the money and piss off for a few hours while I talk to some people."

The man glanced at the purse and back to Gavin's eyes. "I don't want any trouble in here."

"Talking is all," Gavin said through a smile. "There won't be any trouble, I just want some privacy."

Rolant met his eyes, grimy cogs whirring behind conniving little eyes. When his hand reached for the purse, Gavin knew he had him. He smiled again as the man peered into the purse and noted the silver amongst the copper.

"Two hours and you'll pay for any damage," Rolant stated

Gavin stifled the laugh and nodded. "Of course, but I'll want four hours."

The man grunted sourly, and then snatched up the purse.

Gavin waited while the man fussed around the taproom. Then waited some more while he vanished into the back before returning in a cloak that had seen better days.

Once he'd finally gone Gavin made a quick search of the building, making sure there were no back entrances left open. Satisfied, he moved the tables around until one sat deep in the shadows of the corner, at an awkward angle to anyone trying to peer through the windows.

A quick look behind the bar produced three mugs. He sniffed into one and briefly considered giving it a quick wipe. Then he looked at the cloth laying on the bar, and thought better of it.

The ale was as bad as he'd remembered. Rolant was accommodating but, as innkeepers went, he had a long way to go. Gavin sipped at the ale, waiting for his tongue to adjust to the bitterness or just to give up and dissolve.

It was dusk by the time the door creaked open and two men in hooded cloaks entered. They stepped in quickly, closing the door fast behind them.

"And that was your idea of inconspicuous was it?" Gavin asked. "Look at the two of you. Hooded cloaks? Arriving together? You may as well have rung a bell as you walked." He waved a hand in disgust and went behind the bar.

Klöss scowled as he shrugged his way out of the cloak, tossing it over the back of a chair. "See any mead back there?"

"No, but the ale's not bad," Gavin's muffled voice replied. He stood and carried the drinks to the table, setting the tankards down with the edges of a smile on his lips.

"What is this about, Klöss?" Tristan asked as he reached for his drink, sipping at the ale and raising an eyebrow at Gavin's intent expression.

"I needed somewhere to talk privately." He shrugged and looked around at the empty taproom. "So I asked Gavin to sort it."

Tristan frowned. "What is so private that it needs," he paused to peer into his ale, "this?"

"The sealord is making his move," Klöss said. "He's removed me from command and plans on sending me out on a hauler just as soon as he can."

Tristan gave a long, low whistle. "That seems harsh punishment. What is the reason?"

"Skelf," Klöss spat.

Tristan's face fell but Klöss stopped him quickly. "I know what you're going to say, that my going was your idea. I don't blame you. This really has nothing to do with Skelf. I think it's more about my not being willing to be his puppet."

"What are you going to do?" Gavin asked.

"There were four other villages attacked while we were at Skelf," Klöss went on. "All were left in a similar state. Larren refuses to listen to me about the trels. He won't even entertain the notion of there being a third player in this game. If we don't work to counter them we stand to lose everything."

"You didn't answer the question," Gavin said, lifting his tankard to drink deeply.

Klöss looked at the faces across the table. "I'm tired." He sighed. "I've only been in his shoes a month and already I'm tired of the politics, of the games. I don't know how Frostbeard did it. Most of all I'm tired of fighting blind."

He sipped the ale and gasped at the taste, wincing and giving Gavin a black look. "I've been so busy that I've never really taken the time to stop and think. Things have changed for me now. This wasn't how things were supposed to be." He drank again, grimacing only slightly this time. "Ylsriss was supposed to have been living here with me by now. We said we'd wait until Rimeheld was secure and the baby was old enough to pass through the Vorstelv, but she should have been here."

He leant forward, hunching over the drink and stared at the table as he spoke. "Everything has shifted on me. These damned trels have changed everything. We'd beaten the Anlish back. They were probably going to come at us in force at some point but we'd be too entrenched by the time that ever happened. We own the seas, our farms have started producing." He shook his head. "These creatures have changed everything. We can't fight them effectively and we have no idea how they can move around so damned fast."

He looked up at Gavin, "You told me it was one of these trels that you saw take Ylsriss in Hesk?"

Gavin nodded.

"Tell me again what it was you saw?" Klöss asked in a low voice.

"Just as we saw in the reaping," Gavin said slowly, picking his words as he thought back. "They were the same creatures, though when I first saw them they were dressed like priests, all in black. You remember the park in Hesk? The kissing stones there?" He waited for the nod before he carried on. "They killed Tessa. So fast it was effortless for them. As easy as breathing. One of them must have followed me from there when I ran. I had nowhere else to go, no one else to go to. Ylsriss was like a big sister to me when I lived with the Wretched. Lord of Blood, Klöss, I must have led it right to her!"

The muscles worked in his face as Klöss clenched his teeth together tight to match the grip he had on his drink. "What did it look like?"

"Tall," Gavin said, his voice was a whisper stolen from confession. "Pale, but the skin had a kind of greenish cast to it too. It was the eyes that got me though, burning like a winter's sunset."

He drained his drink and went behind the bar. "She could have let it go. She could have taken the coward's way. She didn't though, she fought it. She fought for your son."

Klöss's hands were trembling around his cup, and the ale threatened to spill out, but his voice was level, cold. "You've told me all of this before. I just needed to hear it again." He looked over at Tristan. "I don't think I'm going to play the sealord's game. It's time I did something for me. I want to know what the Anlish know about these creatures."

Tristan looked at him, taking that in. "They seemed as shocked as our men during the reaping," he said. "It is hard to know if they have any knowledge we lack."

Klöss nodded slowly. "I know, and that's why someone has to talk to them."

Tristan sucked air in through his teeth and sat back in the chair. "Without sanction? This will be taken as treason, you know this."

"I know." Klöss shook his head. "I've been thinking about it all night," he admitted. "Always before this there was a reason not to. Another attack to plan. Men depending on me. Even my uncle, needing my help. Now... Well, now I have nothing, do I?"

"This does not sound like you have thought things through," Tristan muttered.

Klöss slammed his fist down on the table, shaking the tankards and slopping ale. "Damn it, Tristan! I've done nothing but think. My uncle is dead. My wife, in all but name, is missing with my son. My men have been taken from me. What do I have here for me?

Tristan watched the ale run across the table top and trickle down to the floor. "What is it you plan?"

"Just to leave. Head for their lines as quickly as possible," Klöss said. "I need to know there's someone here that I can still trust though. Someone with half an ounce of common sense."

"Ha!" Tristan snorted. "You would need to look hard to find one like this, I think."

"Not so hard as you would think," Klöss said as he smiled.

"No," Tristan said, standing to fetch the rag from the bar. "I see what it is you dance around and, no, I will not do this."

Klöss frowned and the chair creaked as he sat back. "Why not?"

"You will need people at your back on this journey."

"He won't be going alone, Tristan," Gavin said, ignoring Klöss's startled look. "The reason I came here in the first place was to try and help Ylsriss."

"And you will be a good help to him," Tristan replied. "But he will need another sword arm I think."

Klöss looked back and forth between them. "I'm right here, you know?"

"So you are." Gavin grinned.

Tristan shook his head as he mopped up the ale. "No, I think I will be coming with you. He will only foul things up if he is not watched."

Klöss threw his hands in the air. "Do I have any say in this?"

"Not really," Tristan said, with a shrug. "No."

PART TWO

CHAPTER EIGHT

Erinn swept. The room was dark and there was barely enough light to properly see the dirt. What little light there was came in from the small windows and the open door behind her and most of that was blocked by her own body. The room was always a mess. Ten women and girls sleeping in one room would make mess at the best of times but it seemed the floor was always dirty. The building opened onto the packed earth of the camp and mud was always being walked in. She couldn't often see it, even with all the lamps and candles lit, but every time she stood in bare feet she felt the grains of dirt shifting under her feet.

They'd been lumped together when they first arrived, with families and friends sharing tents. That hadn't lasted long though. Some busybody complaining about it being indecent with strangers and young women in the same tents soon put pay to it. Never mind the fact there were four or five to a tent. It was a shame really. It had been cramped but at least it had been family and friends. Now they slept in these bunkhouses, crammed together until something better could be arranged.

Feet clumped on the two wooden steps leading up into the bunkhouse and she turned her head as she bent to sweep under the edge of a bunk. The broom reached under as the boots thumped into the short hallway leading in.

"Don't walk in here, I'm sweeping!" she snapped as she turned to the door, pulling the broom out behind her. The head caught the chamberpot as she pulled, sending it spinning across the floor to crash into the stone slab set under the woodstove.

"Damn it!" she swore as the pot smashed and the contents pooled out over the wooden floor she'd just swept.

"Erinn, are you?" Rhia stopped as it hit her. "Gah! What is that stink?"

Erinn pointed wordlessly and sank down on the edge of the nearest bunk. Just like that she was crying. It was just all too much. The tears fell as Rhia looked at her, stricken.

"I'm sorry Erinn," Rhia said, sitting down beside her. "Look, I'll clean it up. It's not that bad."

Erinn stiffened as the girl put her arms around her, attempting to pull her into a hug. "It's not the mess, Rhia," she managed. "It's this place… It's everything!"

"This place?" Rhia asked, looking around the hut. "It's not so bad. It's a bit crowded I know but it's cosy. We've got this nice room and we're warm." She shrugged. "It's a chance for a new home."

Erinn pulled away from her, incredulous. "It's not a home, Rhia," she snapped. "It's a hut. And before we lived in a hut we shivered in a tent."

Rhia gave her a long look. "You've been in here too long. Why don't you get some air. I can finish the rest of this for you."

"It's my turn," Erinn protested, though not too strenuously.

Rhia gave her a knowing look. "It's fine. You were almost done anyway until I interrupted you." Erinn didn't need to be told again and, mouthing her thanks, she left.

Carik's Fort was a sprawling mess. It was a fairly new structure to begin with and this had brought its own advantages and challenges. The fort was, almost entirely, a military complex. It hadn't been around long enough for a large village to spring up around it. This gave it some flexibility when the mass of refugees from Widdengate, and farther east, flooded in. There weren't streets full of buildings in the way, there was space to pitch tents and then, later on, build shelters. The walls, though built of good, strong stone, could be supplemented with a wooden palisade encircling the camp farther out from the centre of the fort.

The disadvantages were almost entirely due to the fact that it was purely a military camp. There were had been few women in Carik's Fort, a handful of wives, and certainly no children. Now the place groaned.

Rhenkin had stayed barely long enough to order the fort expanded before he left. Sarenson seemed to be a capable enough man to Erinn but he was slow. He was very clearly one of those men who needed to plan everything meticulously, examining every issue that might arise before beginning a project. As such, the refugees had huddled in tents, squeezed inside the walls for the best part of a month before any work began on more permanent shelters.

The village of refugees, that had once been a sea of tents, had begun as a well ordered construction. As more refugees flocked to Carik's Fort the plans had suffered, and now the original fort was dwarfed many times over by the village that surrounded it.

Noise assaulted her from every direction as she made her way away from the hut she shared. The ever present sounds of sawing and hammering were overlaid with the cries of babies and small children, mingled with the laughter of yet others. Buried beneath all of this, almost overwhelmed, was the barely noticeable bark of command as Sarenson's men drilled and did whatever it was that soldiers do when they aren't fighting.

Sarenson had refused to move on that one point. Carik's Fort was a fort, a military camp, and it would remain so. Though he'd had no issue setting men to work on building shelters, and then encircling these within the palisade that had become the outer wall, he would allow nothing that might have encroached on the fort itself. None of the wooden shelters stood within the original walls and the tents had been moved out as soon as the palisade was erected.

Erinn picked her way through the throng, lifting her skirts high to avoid the mud. It had been three days since it had rained with any real effort but the constant tread of feet had churned the mud into an oozing muck. She walked as close to the edge of the buildings as she could to avoid the worst of the mess but she'd have wet feet no matter what she did.

She didn't really have any destination in mind, letting her feet pick their own direction more than anything else. Before long she found herself climbing the steps to the stone walls of the fort. Once constantly manned it was now largely deserted as men guarded the palisade instead. She leaned back against the stone wall, her eyes drifting over the camp, unconsciously seeking out the smoke and sparks of her father's forge.

"Can I help you, miss?"

She jerked around to face the solider, and then blushed at her own reaction. How had he moved so quietly in all that armour? "Sorry, I was just...I mean...no. Thank you, I'm fine."

He frowned at her slightly, reminding her of Kainen for some reason, though he had to be at least ten years older. "You shouldn't really be up here, you know?"

She smiled. "It's not all that important is it? Just for a few minutes?"

He grunted as the hint of a smile flitted over his lips. "I suppose not. You're the smith's girl aren't you?"

"I do have a name," she grated.

If her temper bothered him he didn't show it. Instead he nodded calmly. "You probably do, I don't know it yet though."

She flushed. "Erinn," she supplied, feeling stupid.

He grunted. "Thought I recognized you. That hair. You're like a spark from your da's forge."

That brought a smile from her. "Aren't you quite the poet?"

"Just because I carry a sword doesn't mean I don't have a brain." He turned away from her, looking out into the distance.

"I'm sorry," she said, the words tripping out in an awkward mess as she tried to cover her embarrassment. "I didn't mean…" She stopped as she caught his smile. "You're making fun of me!"

"Just a little," he admitted with a shrug.

"You haven't even introduced yourself and you're making fun of me, how outrageously rude," she said, smiling despite herself.

He grinned back. "Mayden," he said.

"Maiden?"

"Mayden. With a Y," he said again, in a tone which made it clear he'd already heard all the jokes he was willing to about this.

She looked out between the merlons, suddenly at a loss for words.

"What was it like?" he asked her.

She didn't turn. "What was what like?"

"Widdengate."

"Oh, it was lovely, peaceful." She smiled at him. "I'd never known anywhere else until they came and burned us out."

"The Bjornmen?" he asked.

She nodded, her smile a memory.

"Don't worry," he told her, giving her a look he probably thought was comforting. "It won't happen here. Widdengate was a village. No matter what they did it was never built to be defended. This is a fort. They'd have a shock if they tried anything here. I can't turn back the past but me and the boys can make sure it doesn't happen to you again."

She looked at him, nodding again, but she couldn't make herself believe him. "Have you always been here then? This place?"

"No," he told her. "Just this last year. Soldiering's a funny job. You tend to move about a lot."

"Where are you from then?" she asked, curiosity getting the better of her manners. "Originally, I mean."

"Reylan," he replied. "You've probably never heard of it."

She shook her head and reached to brush her hair from her face, tucking it behind an ear. "No, where is it?"

"West of here." He shrugged, pulling his cloak tighter against a sudden chill from the wind. "Far west of Savarel... West, of anywhere really."

He was actually quite good looking, she decided. In a gruff sort of way. Not that she was interested, of course. It was just interesting the way that it wasn't immediately apparent. Some people wear their beauty on the surface, clouding what lurks beneath. Artor had been like that. She bit her lip at the thought. Artor, she'd barely spared him a thought since they'd fled Widdengate.

"Well," she said, pulling her own cloak around her in a businesslike fashion, "I suppose I should get on. I'm sure you have better things to do than talk to some silly girl."

He looked confused at that, sensing the shift in her mood but unsure what had happened to cause it. "Hardly silly, but you're probably right. Maybe we can talk again?"

She lowered her chin, looking up at him artfully. "You never know your luck," she teased.

His laugh was bigger than both of them. "You're a dangerous one. Lords and Ladies, with a father as big as yours a man needs to be careful around you."

"I don't know what you mean," she replied, all wide-eyed and faux innocence. She couldn't hold it in and laughed at herself and his reaction. "Besides, he's all talk really."

"Well if he doesn't get me the captain will if I stand around here much longer." He gave a mocking little bow. "I'll look for you."

"Maybe you'll find me." She threw a grin over one shoulder and skipped past him and made her way down the steps. Maybe Carik's Fort wasn't so bad after all.

* * *

Her arms ached from working the bellows. The pain ran up her shoulders and down to the small of her back. She'd stopped hearing the rush of air and the roar of the coals. Even the ringing of metal on metal had dulled in her ears as Harlen worked the swords, forcing the iron into shape with deft blows of the hammer.

She looked over at him as he set the hammer down. "Are we nearly done?"

He paused to wipe he grime from his forehead with the back of one thick arm. "Nowhere close to it, girl. You take a break for a few minutes, get a drink, and shake those arms out."

She looked out of the newly converted building that now housed the forge, at the people passing by on the newly formed street. "I don't see why Domant couldn't have stayed on as your apprentice."

Harlen pressed his lips tight as he took a deep breath and let it out, sighing through his nose. "You know full well they chose to go on to Kavtrin with the Taplock's. Can't hold a lad to an apprenticeship in times like this."

"Why don't you just take a new one then?" she asked, rubbing the backs of her arms.

"Don't you take that tone with me, young lady," he shot back at her. His voice softened as he went on, "I don't have the time to train someone, Erinn. It'd take me the best part of a month to teach them how to tend the fire right and work the bellows without me having to stop every two minutes."

She gave him a look that said clearly she believed none of it.

"I'm behind as it is, child," he said with a sigh. "It won't hurt you to help out now and then."

"I don't see why you need to be the one to produce all this anyway," she said, waving at the stacks of swords and crates of arrowheads.

Harlen gave her a penetrating look. "What's this really about, Erinn? You're too smart to be objecting. You know full well why I'm making iron weapons, just as you know why I can't take an apprentice right now."

"I was supposed to meet Mayden," she admitted.

"That sergeant who's been chasing you around?" Harlen grunted. "I don't know I like the amount of time you've been spending together."

"I'm sure you don't," she laughed. "It's my life though, Father. I'm a grown woman after all. I can't spend it all pumping bellows."

"You're not as grown as all that," Harlen muttered and bent to examine the blade he'd been shaping. "Besides, I don't like the way he looks at you."

"Oh?" She folded her arms and looked at him pointedly. "And how exactly is he looking at me?"

Harlen glanced at her and flushed behind his spark-singed beard. "You know what I mean. He's too old for you anyways. He must have fifteen summers on you."

"He's nowhere near as old as all that!" Erinn protested. "And how much older than mother were you?" Erinn threw back. "For that matter, how old was she at the time? Fourteen when you first started walking out wasn't it?"

He ignored that, going to the other side of the forge and busying himself with a polishing cloth set on the bench. "You were a lot more pleasant before you developed this clever mouth, Erinn."

She grinned at his back. "You didn't really answer the question though, father."

"Which one was that?" He glanced back at her.

"How much longer will you need me for today?"

"That's because you never really came out and asked it, Erinn." He went to her, placing his hands on her shoulders. His hands engulfed her. He always made her feel like a child's toy when he did this. "I suppose I can manage for now. You be careful with him though, Erinn. I don't want you getting hurt."

She swallowed hard and turned her face away, blinking back the pricking in her eyes. He always did this. One moment he was overprotective and completely unreasonable, the next he was like this. She buried herself in his chest, pressing her face into the thick leather apron and hugging him tight for a moment.

"You just make sure you're home when it's still light," he told her as she left. She smiled back at him. A smile was as good as an answer sometimes.

The day was dull and wet but warm enough, and she barely shivered from coming out of the forge. Normally it took her a good few minutes to get used to the fresh air. She rushed back to the bunkhouse, nodding at Mira who was sweeping it out, and quickly changed into the yellow dress she'd been saving for a day worthy of it. She was lucky. Harlen had packed properly before they'd fled and she had a selection. Some of the men had only the clothes on their backs.

Though she was in no real hurry she moved swiftly through the fort. Shops, after a fashion, were springing up already. Some of the refugees sheltering in the fort had little in the way of money and even less of a way of earning more. A life spent farming or making barrels is not something that lends itself well to doing nothing though, and those that could work were doing what they could.

Mayden had said he'd meet her by the stream. It wasn't far from the front gates of the palisade and she passed through the stone wall and the streets of the refugee village to the palisade's open gates with a small smile on her lips. She ignored the knowing grin on the faces of the men standing guard there. Word had clearly got around and they'd been doing it for weeks now. It was funny, once she'd moved beyond the ditches and spiked stakes, the country was truly beautiful here. She made her way through the long grasses, heading for the edge of the woods and the stream that lay just inside.

"I didn't think you were coming?"

His voice made her jump and she spun around in a shock that ended in a girlish squeal as he caught her up in his arms. She turned her head, allowing his kiss to find her cheek but not what he'd sought.

"I said I would try," she said, brushing down her dress with both hands.

"I know you did." He laughed. "I just didn't expect that bear of a father of yours to let you out of his sight." He walked her over to the stream and threw himself down onto the carpet of soft moss, patting the ground beside him.

She looked down at him for a moment. "That *bear*, as you call him, is my father. I don't like it when you talk like that."

"Ah, you know I didn't mean anything by it, lass." He laughed.

She sat down on her knees, spreading her dress out in front of her. He hadn't even complimented her on it yet. Had he even noticed it? So far this wasn't going the way she'd expected it to. "Tell me about the places you've been?" she asked, more to give him something to talk about than from any real interest.

"Again?" he sighed in mock exasperation. "What do you want to hear about this time? Reylan? The time I went as a caravan guard to Feldane?"

"Tell me about Celstwin," she urged, playing with the end of her plait. He'd not noticed her hair either, so far as she could tell. If she were ever to settle with this man he would need some of the edges worn off him. Now where had *that* thought come from?

She sat and listened to his talk of the capital, with its marble-clad buildings and soaring spires. Of the merchant fleet that sailed from there, bringing fine wines and spices back from Surama and islands she's never heard of.

After a time she moved closer, settling down beside him. He smelled good. Not like the smoke and coal smell of her father. This was more leather and oil and a faint smell of horses. An outside smell.

They talked as they snacked on the bread and bottle of elderberry wine he'd brought.

"How did you end up in Carik's Fort?" she asked. "You make travelling sound much more fun that being cooped up in a fort for years."

"It is, for the most part," he admitted. "There's a freedom to being on the road, even if you are guarding merchants and travellers. It's not as dangerous as most would think. Bandits value their own skin more than they do a cartload of wool or turnips. It does have its downsides though."

"Winter?" she guessed.

"Winter's no fun, no," he admitted. "Once or twice I'd saved enough up to not have to work, and I managed to hole up for the winter. Other times I wasn't so lucky. I guess that's probably how I ended up here. It's not much of a life but signing on for a three year stint means three warm winters instead of sleeping under a wagon, trying to stay warm."

He propped himself up on one arm and moved in, kissing her neck. Erinn froze. It was so fast she hadn't had time to move, let alone protest. He carried on, taking her silence for encouragement somehow. His weight came down on her, pressing her into the moss even though more than half his weight was on the ground or his other arm. His lips sought and found hers, kissing hungrily and she let out a moan that could have meant anything. His lips were soft for a man, though the stubble scratched at her. Her leg came up, seemingly of its own volition and then his hands were running over her, touching, then pawing.

"Artor, stop!" she gasped. He didn't listen but she stiffened as she realised what she'd said. It was the same all over again, even the damned stream was the same!

"Stop," she whispered. Then again, louder this time. "Stop!"

Her knee came up, sharp and hard and he stiffened with a gasp that swiftly became a groan as he rolled off her. She picked herself up, eyes streaming with tears, and ran.

Branches and thorns clawed at her, scratching and drawing blood even as they ripped at her dress. She was past caring or feeling. She was a wild thing, running on instinct, her mind a mess of shame and hurt. They were right. They'd all been right. She was a tease. She led men on and said no when it started getting serious. Artor had known. He'd told her right. Now Mayden, a grown man! She'd ruined everything again. Even now she could hear the whispers and the laughing following her through the trees.

The ground dipped unexpectedly and she stumbled, rolling down the steep bank and tumbling into the stream. A rock found her head as she pitched into the water and her vision tilted around her. Ironically it was the water that probably saved her. It was icy cold and the shock of it hitting her face was enough to stop her passing out. She pushed down with one hand, finding the bottom and lifting her face above the surface as she coughed and spat. The blood ran down her face, cutting a path down her nose and dripping into the water. Tiny red clouds bloomed in the stream, born in an instant, and then torn away by the current.

She crawled to the far bank, not quite trusting herself to stand yet, and huddled on the ground as the water streamed from her dress. "Stupid girl." The first words she'd spoken since she fled, and the truest to pass her lips.

She'd led him on. That's why he'd been all over her, pawing at her, tearing at her clothes. If she hadn't screamed…

Her stomach heaved and she gagged, lurching forward onto her hands as knees as she vomited onto the moss. Her stomach lurching over and over until she had to gasp down snatches of breath between each heave. Finally it stopped and she crawled backwards a couple of feet before collapsing onto the moss. His hands, everywhere. The thought filled her with so much shame and bitterness. Except, they hadn't been had they? He'd kissed her. But then, she'd been kissing back. His hands had just stroked her face and her neck. He'd laid down with her, laid on her a little but he hadn't pinned her. Lords and Ladies, she hadn't screamed at all! That had been Artor, not Mayden. What had she done?

She cried then. Tears of shame. Tears of anger at herself. The trees caught her sobs and threw them back at her, echoes twisting them into a thousand tiny laughs. The sound shook her and she scrubbed the tears from her face with the back of one hand. Sulking in the woods would do her no good.

She nearly fell twice until she had the presence of mind to use the tree roots in the bank to help her stand. It was so much darker than she remembered it being. How long had she huddled on the bank of the stream? A fallen branch made a useful crutch and she hobbled across the stream, discovering new aches and pains as she went.

"Mayden?" she called out. Not that the man would ever want to speak to her again. She tried again, louder this time. "Mayden!"

It took a ridiculously short time for him to find her. They must have been almost on top of each other. She stepped around a large oak, leaning on the trunk with one hand, and there he was.

"Erinn! Oh hells, Erinn!" He rushed to her, easing her down to the ground so he could get a look at her forehead.

"I'm so sorry," she whispered, her voice too scared to project.

"Shhh, none of that matters." He pulled her arm around his shoulders, helping her stand. "Let's get you back to the fort. We can talk when you're all cleaned up. Bloody Droos, you're soaked. Here, take my cloak."

"What's that?" she asked, looking past him into the distance.

He turned and peered into the deepening murk. "I don't see anything."

"No." She shook her head. "It sounded like…like laughing."

Mayden stood silent, listening. Finally he shook his head and gave her a worried look. "I don't hear anything. Come on, let's get you home."

They moved slowly. Despite her protests that she was fine, he seemed to think she was made of fine glass and stopped every time she made the faintest whimper.

They were still half a mile from the gates when the horns came. The sound seemed to come from everywhere and yet no particular direction. They both froze as the haunting notes sounded again, discordant and wild. Erinn looked at him, an unasked question sharing her eyes with the fear that was plain to see.

"I've no idea, Erinn," he said as he looked around. "It's not from our men, that's for sure."

They moved faster, the sound of the horns urging them on, though their source remained a mystery. The gates were shut fast against the darkness and Mayden pounded hard on the tar-smeared wood until the peep slid open. "Harkis, open the damned gates, you fool!" he hissed as the horns sounded again.

"Be bloody quick about it then," the man said through the grate. One side of the gates creaked open just wide enough for them to squeeze through, and then slammed shut, the heavy crossbar falling back into place.

Mayden turned to Harkis as soon as the crossbar fell "What in the hells are those horns?"

"Caltus's bloody balls, girl! What happened to you?"The guard looked Erinn up and down and shot a suspicious look at Mayden.

"It's a long story," Mayden muttered and helped Erinn away from the accusing eyes.

Harlen found them before they were even close to her bunkhouse. He came down the narrow street like an angry bear, roaring his rage and frustration.

One burn-scarred paw took her from Mayden's side, pulling her close. "Lords and Ladies, Erinn. What happened?"

"It's a long story, Da," she managed, stealing Mayden's line. "Let me tell it once I'm cleaned up?"

He held her at arm's length, searching her eyes for something for a moment before he gave a non-committal grunt.

He put an arm around her and started towards the bunkhouse, making sure she was still moving before he turned back to Mayden. Harlen's fist lashed out so fast Mayden didn't even have time to flinch and he was lifted off his feet as the smith clenched his fist tight around his shirt. "If I find you've harmed one single hair," he said, the threat hanging heavy from each syllable as the soldier's feet dangled helplessly.

Erinn tugged at his arm. "It wasn't him, Da. Stop it. Put him down!"

The horns sounded again, low and mournful, and the sound rolled through the fort like a wave. Harlen lowered Mayden to the ground as he looked first to the walls and then up at the rising moon. Trumpets were calling out on the walls and the sound of running feet and jangling armour filled the night. In seconds the evening had gone from still to frantic and Harlen was wide eyed despite his calm, serious voice as he looked to his daughter.

"The fae," he said. "Get to the forge, Erin. Get some iron around you," he said, his voice little louder than the wind that had picked up and was tossing leaves along the street.

"What's going on? Where are those horns coming from?" Mayden asked.

"It's the fae," Harlen said again, face grim.

Mayden looked at him like he was an idiot. "The fae? What, fairies?"

Erinn wheeled on him in shock. "You don't know? They didn't tell you?"

"Get to the forge, Erinn," Harlen repeated. "I've got to find that idiot commander."

"I'll take her," Mayden told him, the threats forgotten in the face of the huge smith's urgency. "Sarenson will probably be in the officer's mess at this hour. Head for the barracks. Anyone can take you from there."

Harlen gave the man a look, and then a curt nod of approval before he turned and ran towards the stone wall of the fort.

"Let's go," Mayden said, reaching to pull her arm about his shoulders again.

They did not speak. The fort was alive with the shouts of men rushing to their posts and the slamming of doors. The wind grew stronger still, whipping loose leaves at them and tugging at Erinn's tattered dress.

"Where are you going?" Erinn cried, looking about her in dismay. "The forge is the other way!"

"I wasn't thinking," Mayden admitted. "Let's get you to the bunkhouse. You can get cleaned up there and get out of this wind at least."

A horn sang out so close it drove both their hands to their ears. Erinn matched Mayden's look of shock and confusion as they both searched for the source of the noise, and then the night turned to horrors. Between one breath and the next the leaves that flew so close to them transformed, seeming almost to shimmer in the light of the moon as they became tiny winged creatures that hurtled through the streets. They both stared in wonder at the creatures passing them on all sides. A scream of incredible agony carried to Erinn's ears, and then the spell was broken.

The swarm of fae'reeth tore through the fort like a vengeful storm, tiny knives clutched in their hands as they spun and wove around those fool enough to be out in the night. Erinn ran, half-dragging Mayden along with her as he stared, mouth agape, at the creatures. The bunkhouse was just ahead of them, door swinging in the wind whipped up by wings beyond counting.

A group of soldiers staggered around the corner ahead of them, flailing at the creatures spinning around them in a blade-filled whirlwind of wings and flitting purple bodies. Blood already oozed from a thousand tiny cuts and, as the other two staggered onward, the third was suddenly lifted into the air. Small hands buried in his hair or clutched at his clothing as he twisted and screamed. The cuts and slashes increased, matching the tempo of his cries until his throat was opened and the blood fountained as he fell, crashing to the dirt.

Mayden grabbed her, stirred from inaction by the scene. He sprinted to the side of the bunkhouse, pushing down on her shoulders and urging her into the air gap under the hut, where it rested on thick timber beams. Designed to keep the base of the shelters from rotting, the space was narrow, barely a foot high, but it was enough.

Erinn clambered under quickly, in a motion halfway between a crawl and a slither. She moved as fast as she dared whilst trying to be quiet. Her life might depend on her silence. She shifted back, making room for Mayden. Instead, a girl was shoved under the hut, shaking and making muffled squeals as she strove to hold in the screams that sought to escape. Erinn wormed closer to her, inching forward on her belly until she could whisper soothing noises into the girl's ear.

The footsteps pounding on the floorboards above their heads were soon replaced by screams, the sound somehow all the more awful for being muffled. A drip landed on one cheek and Erinn reached to wipe it away. It wasn't water. She shifted back in shock as her fingers found the thicker texture of it. As the blood began to drip down between the gaps in the floor Erinn bit down on the back of her hand to keep her screams from joining the chorus above. Pressed close beside her the other girl's body shook with silent sobs.

The sounds of battle reached under the hut for them. Swords clashing and yelled orders mingling with the sounds of panicked screams. Blue flashes of light flickered at the edges of her vision and twice deafening crashes sounded but Mayden never joined them. They huddled, too terrified to let each other cry or make a sound louder than a breathy whisper as, all around them, the fort reeled under the onslaught.

CHAPTER NINE

Erinn lay in the darkness, listening. The shouting and screams had finished hours ago. They'd been followed by laughter and strains of a strange music but even that had gone now, cut short by harsh words in a language she couldn't understand. Now she just listened to the silence, trying hard not to accept what that meant as she watched the darkness under the bunkhouse slowly turn into the dim light of dawn.

Survivors of the attack that had any real numbers would have been out searching for others by now. Sarenson's soldiers would have been making their own noise if they'd lived. The silence fit. Carik's Fort was empty. It was an oversized tomb.

She was struck with the need to know. To put the fears to rest one way or another. Almost everyone in the world she knew and loved was in Carik's Fort. She couldn't just sit in the darkness and hide. They might be wounded. They might need help.

And yet she didn't move, she couldn't. She lay in the mud cursing herself silently for a coward as hot tears ran down her nose and dripped onto her hands.

Tears turned to frustration and that, in turn, was shouldered aside by hot anger. She wormed her way forward. If the fae were still out there they were welcome to her craven soul.

"Don't go out there!" The words were hissed in a voice just edging past a whisper but the desperation and the fear spoke more clearly in their own, far louder, voice.

Erinn looked back at the girl, just visible in the dim light from the edge of the bunkhouse. "It's been quiet for hours. We can't stay under here forever."

The girl reached for her and clutched at her dress. "What if those things are still out there?"

"Then they're still out there." Erinn shrugged, surprising herself with her sudden calm, but then a person can only maintain anger or terror for so long. "Look…" She broke off. "I was going to say something then, but I've just realised I don't even know your name."

"Kel," the girl whispered, still holding the fold of fabric in her fist.

"Look, Kel," Erinn began again. "If those things are still out there they'll come for us sooner or later. If I'm going to die I want it to be with the sun on my face not hiding here in the dirt."

She took Kel's wrist and pulled her dress gently from the girl's grasp. Kel didn't resist but watched her with huge eyes. The ground was damp as she wormed her way to the edge of the bunkhouse. Not wet, but a dampness that was easily confused with simply being cold. It seeped into her dress and leeched away at the warmth she'd worked so hard to hold on to as she'd clung to Kel in the night.

The edge of the bunkhouse scraped at her back as she pulled herself out into the light but she didn't let it slow her. The village was silent. She turned, still in her crouch, and recoiled as she saw the first body only a few feet from her. It was torn and broken, covered in blood and hundreds of slashes. The glimpse before she turned her face away was enough. The uniform and the dark hair. She didn't need to look closer to know it was Mayden.

Her scrapes on her back stung as she pressed against the side of the bunkhouse. She would allow herself this one moment, with Kel still under the floor of the building, when she could be human. After this she would be iron, hard and unfeeling.

A single sob broke from her lips, muffled as she clapped her hands over her mouth. She sniffed and rubbed her eyes with her sleeve before edging her way to the corner of the hut and peering around it.

The fort and the refugee camp that surrounded it were utterly still, the silence so total it was surreal. Bodies littered the ground in every direction, the blood staining the streets around them. A flutter of wings sent her scurrying back behind the cover of the bunkhouse but it was just a crow, landing on one of the bodies and pecking at the gore. The bird proved to be the first of many as she looked on, and the silence was broken by their caws.

Erinn stood in silence, trying to listen past the sound of the crows for long minutes until Kel called her.

"Erinn?" She turned towards the small voice and caught Kel's face just as it withdrew back into the shadows under the bunkhouse.

"It's safe enough," she told her. "At least, I can't see anything. Come on out but…" she grimaced, there was no other way to put it. "There are a lot of bodies out here, Kel. Try not to look, okay?"

Now that she could see her properly in the light she realised the girl was far younger than she'd imagined, no more than twelve at most. Her dress was in better condition than Erinn's own, being thick wool. Looking at her, and then down at herself, Erinn realised just what a state they were in. She reached for the girl's hand. "First thing's first then, let's see if we can get some dry clothes, eh?"

Kel nodded, her eyes were wide and frightened and she gripped tight to Erinn's hand as if scared it might slip away from her. Erinn moved slowly, barely making a sound as she listened for any sign of life. The crows were making too much noise to hear and she worked hard to listen past their incessant cawing. She froze again at the corner of the bunkhouse, pressing her ear to the wooden wall before she dared to peer around the corner. Kel was a silent ghost by her side. She'd have forgotten she was there if it weren't for the hand that clung so desperately to her own.

They darted through the open door of the bunkhouse and into the dimly lit room. It was still as Erinn had last seen it, aside from the blood. Where the bodies might be was anyone's guess but there was blood enough staining the floor for three men.

"Wait here," she told Kel, turning her so she faced into the corner.

She fetched a sack and began stuffing clothes into it, taking others that she hoped might fit the girl.

With the bag filled with more clothes than they probably needed she looked around, suddenly at a loss. She headed out to the street and looked at Kel who stood watching her with expectant eyes. What was she supposed to do now? A loud rumble came from her stomach. "I suppose that answers that question," she muttered.

"What?" Kel asked.

"I was wondering what we should do next," Erinn explained. "I suppose we should find some food."

They made their way around the village, slowly at first as they darted from building to building, and then more confidently as it became obvious that there was no sign of life. The bodies were everywhere and Erinn had to make a conscious effort not to look at them. Most were too torn and shredded to recognise anyway, but there were others where she thought knew the clothing.

The soldiers were clustered together. They'd died in groups. The villagers though, seemed scattered as if they'd been tossed by a careless child.

A heel of stale bread from an empty bunkhouse went some way to silencing her stomach, though Kel grimaced and refused to try to eat. The packed earth of the village streets was riddled with tracks. Erinn was no hunter but the cloven hoof prints were hard to miss.

The forge was empty. Somehow she knew before she even stepped inside that she wouldn't find her father there. Bodies were scattered in a wide arc around the entrance, crumpled into a tableau of pain on the scorched earth. She picked up an iron sword and, just as quickly, dropped it again. The blade was far too heavy for her to swing let alone defend herself.

The swords were mostly where Harlen had left them, stacked to one side of the workshop next to barrels of arrowheads and the sheaves of iron arrows that had come back from the fort's fletcher. She plucked an arrow out, holding it like a dagger. It probably wouldn't do her any good if it came down to it but it made her feel slightly less helpless.

"Erinn," a small voice said behind her.

She turned. "Yes?"

"I want my mother." The plea was simple and heartfelt and Erinn glanced out at the bodies on the street before she could stop herself. She knelt and put her hands on the girl's shoulders. "I know you do, Kel. I want my Da, too. Let's go, shall we?"

Kel was the first to call out, shouting for her mother as they made their way towards the fort. The sound shocked Erinn and she reached out to silence the girl before she realised there was no point. If the fae were still in Carik's Fort they'd have found them by now.

They passed the silent buildings, shouting out on every corner. The streets took their words and swallowed them, not even replying with an echo.

The cottage was almost complete. Kel's family had clearly been one of the first to begin construction. She stopped as they approached, standing half a step ahead of Erinn as she looked at the door.

It hung just ajar. Wide enough to let a draft through but not so wide that anyone could enter. Erinn looked down at Kel and grimaced. "Do you want me to go and look?"

The girl turned to look up at her and the tears hung heavy in her eyes as she nodded. "I'm scared." The admission carried the first of her tears with it and she threw herself at Erinn, clinging on with her thin arms.

Erinn held her, drawing comfort from the embrace even as she tried not to think about what she might find and what this might mean for the chances of finding her own father alive. She stepped back away from Kel. The girl's arms parted and fell to her sides as she looked at Erinn, hopeless and lost

Obligation is a heavy thing. It can weigh down to crush the very breath from you, but no matter the burden it is never as great as the guilt that follows if it is shrugged aside.

Erinn touched her fingertips to the door, glancing back over her shoulder at Kel's expectant face. She smiled at her, a false smile filled with hopeful lies, and pushed the door open.

The smell hit her immediately, the air was thick with the metallic scent. She should have stopped then. There was nothing her eyes could tell her that her nose hadn't already screamed. The first body was barely three paces from the door, face-down in a pool of blood. His pose was testament enough to the struggle. A woman lay across the table, her shredded dress and the blood on her thighs leaving no doubt as to how she'd died.

Erinn clapped a hand to her mouth and managed three steps before throwing up violently. She gripped the back of a wooden chair with one hand as her stomach heaved, over and over until she was left spitting and gasping. She made her way to the door, leaning against the wall beside it until she could trust her legs, and then she went to face Kel.

The girl knew. As soon as Erinn stepped out of the little cottage she knew, and the tears began again. She ran towards the door but Erinn caught her easily with one arm, pulling her back. "No, sweetheart. You don't want to go in there. Keep the memories you have."

She took her into her arms, holding her tight until the crying subsided from the wracking sobs to something softer, and somehow more grief-stricken, and then she led her away.

In a strange way having to care for the girl gave Erinn something to focus on and allowed her not to think about her own father. It was time for practicalities, she'd decided. They couldn't stay in Carik's Fort. Even if the fae didn't return the bodies littering the streets would soon create enough problems of their own.

She glanced at the girl beside her. The tears had stopped for now but they had simply been replaced by a deeper hurt. Grief is a dangerous thing, she'd been once told. It can burrow down into a person, out of the sight of others where it will fester and spread. It hides there, in the core of who we are, gorging itself on all the joy and light it can find until misery is all that remains.

"How long have you been here, Kel?" Erinn asked for want of something better to ask.

"I don't know," Kel replied in a mutter.

"A month?" Erinn persisted. "Do you remember more than one full moon?"

"Maybe." she shrugged. "I don't know."

"Where had you come from?"

"Selene. It was new, we made it." The girl couldn't help let a sliver of pride slip into her voice.

Erinn smiled at that. "Did you have other family there? A Nanna or anyone like that?"

The reply was slow to come. When it did it was a whisper of wind in the tall grass. "A sister, Clarissa."

Erinn felt a spark of hope at that. "She didn't come here with you?"

Kel rounded on her then, her mouth twisted as she shouted the words up into Erinn's face. "No, she's dead! They're all dead!"

There was nothing she could think of to say to that and they walked in a silence broken only by Kel's sniffing.

"How do you feel about heading west?" Erinn asked eventually.

"Don't you want to look for your Da?" came the soft reply.

Erinn stopped, realising she'd been avoiding making that decision. "No, I don't think so. I mean, I think we should keep calling out, just in case. But no, I don't want to see."

Kel gave a shrug. The crying had stopped and been replaced with a numb ambivalence. She followed Erinn along without seeming to care where she went or what they did, even the bodies in the streets seemed to no longer bother her.

The entrance to the fort itself had been torn apart. Massive blocks of stone lay scattered around the crumbling entryway. Thick roots were mixed in amongst the rubble that had thrust out from the earth and grown towards the gatehouse. Erinn realised they must have wormed in between the stones of the wall, tearing them apart as they grew. The sight was as shocking as the realisation and she was silent as she climbed up onto the stones and looked into the fort.

Bodies lay thick beyond the gates, many pierced by long, pale arrows. The ground around them was scorched and burn-scarred. They may have fallen but at least they'd taken some of the fae with them, she realised. The thought gave her a bitter satisfaction, and she found herself gripping the iron arrow tightly in her clenched fist as she climbed over the fallen stones and into the square that lay beyond.

She glanced back at Kel, thinking to warn her not to follow, but the girl showed no signs of moving. "I just need to look about, okay? I won't be long."

Kel gave no response but sat down on the large stone, her feet kicking idly. The image of the girl sitting, seemingly unconcerned by the bodies only yards away, disturbed Erinn in ways she couldn't explain.

The square had clearly served as a training ground and the straw targets lined up against one wall still sported arrows. Erinn walked around slowly, looking into the stables and farriers. They were both silent but she didn't need to look to know the horses had not been spared. Bodies were thick in the entry to the main building of the fort itself. She picked her way through until she could shout through the doorway.

"Hello?" she called out. Her voice sounded weak and reedy in the silence. She cleared her throat and tried again. "Da!"

A faint sound had her spin in place. It was quiet, so slight she wasn't sure she'd really heard anything. "Hello?" she called again.

She shouted until her throat grew hoarse. Her only reply was the silence she'd broken, but then what else had she expected? She looked around the training ground of the ruined fort, trying not to see the bodies, trying not to see anything. A small hand crept into hers and led her gently away.

They spent the night in the forge. She'd dumped scraps of iron over the ground inside and tossed a fair littering out onto the street as well. Erinn built the fire high and worked the bellows until the coals fairly roared before tossing small iron scraps into the fire and pumping the bellows again until the air stank. Finally, surrounded by the iron weapons her father had forged, they slept.

The belch was long and heartfelt and Erinn jerked from her sleep, bashing her head against the barrel closest to her. "Damn!" she swore, clutching her head with one hand as she rose to her feet. The sunlight streamed in through the open entry to the forge and Erinn blinked against the light as she peered out.

An old man sat propped against the building opposite, a large wineskin in one hand. He tore a chunk from the loaf of bread he held in the other with his teeth and raised the skin in greeting.

"Samen?" She said, moving closer and shading her eyes with one hand. "Is that you? What are you doing here?"

"Eating breakfast," the old man muttered. "Listening to girls snore."

"I do not snore..." Erinn began, but looked back into the forge as Kel let out a great rasping sound.

Samen smiled at her expression. "You're louder," he observed, and took a deep drink from the skin.

Erinn shook her head and took in a slow breath. "Where did you come from?"

He raised an eyebrow. "Widdengate. Same as you, girl." Then, seeing her expression. "All right, don't get into a snit. I hid, same as you, I expect. I found an old storage cellar and hid in a pile of mouldy sacks."

"I didn't even know you were here," Erinn confessed.

"Where else would I go? Most of Widdengate was here." He scratched at his filthy beard and pulled himself up. "What were you planning on doing?"

She frowned. "Doing?"

"Well, I don't expect you were going to stay here, enjoying the smell of a few thousand bodies in the sun." He gave her a nasty smile.

"We were going to go west," she told him, still trying to catch up.

"Obviously," he snorted. "East is into the arms of the Bjornmen. West where?"

"I don't know, maybe to find Rhenkin," she managed. The old man was flustering her. Why was he putting her on the spot like this?

Samen grimaced. "Ah yes, Rhenkin. The illustrious commander who's managed to protect us twice now. Oh, no, he hasn't, has he?"

She shot him a look that he'd earned twice over for the sarcasm and turned at a light step behind her.

"Who's that?" Kel asked, peering around Erinn's body as she reached for her arm.

"This is Samen," Erinn said in a gentle tone. "He's a bit old and smelly but he does tell wonderful stories." She looked over at the old man, pleading with her eyes for him to be gentle.

"Don't know any stories," the old man grunted and stooped to retrieve the wine. "And I don't like little girls."

"Well that's just great, Samen," Erinn snapped as Kel pressed herself closer to her. "Nice going."

The old man gave another nasty smile, and then looked down the street. "When were you fixing to leave?"

"As soon as we get some supplies together, I suppose," Erinn replied. She rubbed Kel's shoulder absently as she looked down the street. "Do you think there might be others?"

"Other what? Survivors?" Samen asked, following her gaze. "I suppose there could be. They'll find their way to us. Or not." He shrugged.

She glanced at the bread he still held in one hand. "Do you think we could have some of that?"

He looked down at his hand. "There's a pile of it still in the mess. Get your own," he replied with a smile and took another bite.

* * *

The new stores had been built close to the palisade. Probably to make it easier to unload the carts as they arrived rather than have them wind their way through the streets to the fort itself.

As Erinn and Kel drew closer it became clear that the sharpened wooden posts of the palisade had suffered much the same fate as the gatehouse. Large sections had twisted away, tearing open portions of the defensive wall. Fresh leaves grew from branches that had somehow sprouted from some of the posts and thick roots could now be seen reaching down into the earth. Erinn shook her head at the sight and glanced down at Kel but the girl seemed unmoved.

The store was nothing more than a large warehouse. A small office adjoined the much larger room that was stacked with sacks of grain and barrels of salted meat. A row of meat hooks hung from a beam, ready for fresh meat.

"I suppose we'd better get started," Erinn said to Kel, dusting her hands off and making her voice brighter than she felt. "Why don't you see if you can find some apples or carrots? If they're stored properly they'll last well."

She watched as the girl headed away slowly. It was probably a good idea to keep her active, force her to do things on her own. If left to her own devices she'd just sit and stare into space. "What about you then, Erinn?" she muttered to herself. "You're as bad as she is, you just hide it better."

She shook her head against a welter of feelings and reached for the closest sack of grain. One tug told her she'd never be able to carry it, and if she tried to drag it over the floor she risked it splitting. Erinn muttered choice words and looked around as she thought.

A stack of crates stood close to the wall. Splintered and cracked they were probably waiting to be broken down into kindling. She looked from the sack back to the crates and smiled as an idea took form. If she could get one side of the crate loose she might be able to push the sack over onto it. With luck it would slide over the floor easily.

She kicked and tugged at a likely crate until a long split carried down one corner. A good hard tug should have it coming loose, she reasoned. Laying it on its side allowed her to stand on the inside of the wall of the crate. She heaved upwards and was rewarded with a loud crack as the crate came apart in her hands.

The sack fell down onto the section of wood with ease, it even landed square which would make life easier. She leaned down and gave an experimental shove, cracking a smile as the board shifted a few inches.

"Work through your troubles, Erinn," she whispered, quoting her father. It applied equally in both meanings, apparently. She shoved the sack out to the loading dock and rolled it off the board, before heading back for more supplies.

Within an hour they had a large pile of supplies stacked at the loading dock. They were also hot, sweaty and filthy. As Erinn lay back against a sack she wished she'd had the sense to bring some water with her.

"Still, we did it, didn't we?" she said to Kel, smiling brightly, this time without forcing it.

The girl gave a small smile back. It was a weak, watery thing, but it was a start.

Erinn reached into a barrel and pulled out a couple of apples, handing one to the girl as she took a large bite. They were still crisp and, at that moment, one of the most delicious things she had ever tasted. She munched happily, closing her eyes and enjoying the sun on her face.

"An' just where do you think you're taking that lot?" The voice was harsh and accusing and Erinn's eyes flew open as the apple fell from her fingers into the dirt.

The speaker was a dark haired man with an angry cut running from eyebrow to cheek around his eye. He stood slightly ahead of two smaller men and held an improvised cudgel in one hand.

"I…err…" Erinn sputtered.

"You what?"

She took a breath and tried again. "We're going to head west, get away here. You'd be welcome to join us."

He gave her a scathing look. "Are you soft in the head? The land out there is crawling with those Bjornmen, an' who knows when those monsters might come back. No we're stayin' right here. An' so is that lot."

Erinn climbed to her feet. "You can't be serious. I mean, stay if you like but there's enough in there for everyone!"

"Everyone that matters is stood over here by me, Darlin'," the man said with an ugly smile.

"Look…" she looked at him expectantly.

"Stett," he supplied.

"Look, Stett," she tried again. "There's food in there that will spoil before it ever gets eaten. Can't we be reasonable about this?"

"What's in there belongs to this fort. As there's only us left I say it belongs to us." He stopped, looking at her again as something obviously occurred to him. "For that matter, what makes you think you can just leave? It's going to get cold pretty soon. A nice bit like you shouldn't be out on the roads by herself."

A clatter brought him up short and they all turned to see the cart coming down the street, drawn by a brown horse than had definitely seen better days. "Found some more friends then," Samen said, eyeing the men and he eased the cart to a halt.

"They say they're not going to let us leave," Erinn explained.

"Is that so?" Samen replied, turning to look at the dark-haired man. "It's going to smell pretty ripe here in a week or so."

"I didn't say anything about you, old man," Stett said with sneer. "You can clear out now."

"Very kind of you," Samen muttered and reached for the reins he'd let fall to his lap.

"Samen!" Erinn blurted, unable to stop herself.

"He glanced at her and reached down. "Then again, maybe I think they're better off with me?" he said, settling the crossbow into his shoulder. "Now I'm no expert with these things so I might hit any one of you, or I might just make a nice hole in the wall over there. Thing is, I know enough about this thing to know that you're on the wrong end of it."

"You can't get us all, old man," Stett said, hefting his cudgel.

"No." Samen nodded agreeably. "No, you're right but I can get one of you. Have you ever seen what happens to someone who gets shot with one of these things close up? This bolt here will go right through you. Your boys over there are thinking really hard about that right now."

Stett glanced over one shoulder at the worried expressions of the two men with him, and then turned to face them. "We can take him, you idiots. Look at his hands shaking."

It was true, Samen's hands shook gently and the point of the crossbow bolt wove back and forth between the three of them.

"Yer right, Stett," one of them said, kicking at the dirt. "It's just, I don't fancy getting myself shot through. A few knocks with a stick is one thing but…" he shrugged.

Stett glared at him, and then looked from him to the other and back again. "You yellow bloody bastards," he spat and then turned to run down the street.

"Not going with your friend?" Samen asked, lowering the crossbow a little.

"Nah, I reckon you're right." The man shrugged. "This place is going to be crawling with rats an' flies before long. I'll…" he glanced at his companion. "We'll tag along with you, if you'll have us?"

"Don't look to me, boy." Samen snorted. "It's the smith's girl here who's in charge. I'm just along for the wine."

Erinn gaped at him for a moment before remembering herself. She looked the men over. Could they be trusted? Probably not, she decided. But then, if she left them here they might just follow along behind her anyway.

"What are your names?" she asked.

"I'm Fornn, that's Jarik." He jerked a thumb at his companion.

Erinn sighed. "Fine, come with us but Samen will put that bolt through you if you try anything else."

His dirty face split into a relieved smile. "That's kind, lady. More'n we deserve I reckon. You've a good heart."

Erinn felt the beginnings of a blush at that and nodded at the cart. "Yes well, you can start by helping to load this lot."

"Right away, lady." Fornn hefted a sack of grain onto one shoulder and loaded it with an ease that made her mutter to herself.

They ended up with three carts. Samen insisted on putting Fornn and Jarik on their own, though neither were comfortable with horses, and taking another one for himself. "Might as well keep all the trouble in one place," he'd muttered.

It took longer than she'd expected and it was already past midday by the time they had the carts loaded. Jarik made his way over to her as Samen checked over the horses.

"I wanted to thank you," he said. He was a short man and he shifted from foot to foot as he spoke. "Most would have sent us after Stett or just left us behind."

"Yes, well, I suppose I'm not most people," she replied and looked away, fussing with the end of one of the ropes holding the load in place. She wished they'd just let it drop. This was embarrassing and Samen's sly grin wasn't helping.

"No, I reckon you're not." He nodded. "You've something of your Da in you."

She looked back at him then. "You know my father?"

"No." Jarik shook his head. "I knew him by sight. I saw him though, at the end. He took down twenty or more of those bastards with a hammer trying get through to two of Sarenson's men. Most men would have left them, turned an' run. Not your da. He got himself right in there, monsters or no. When they took him down, that was the end of it, I reckon. That's when we started to break."

She felt her face crumble as the tears started. Dimly she was aware of Samen swearing at the man and bundling him away before putting a clumsy arm around her. It was nothing she hadn't known already but she'd worked so hard to avoid confirming it, letting that little spark of hope remain. Now Jarik had dashed that away and the cold reality was all that remained.

Chapter Ten

The cart creaked and rattled, every bump seemed to be working hard to rattle Erinn's teeth from her skull. The roads had been wet from the rains and they'd huddled under cloaks and tarpaulins through the first few days. After that they'd dried out faster than she'd have thought possible and the dust seemed to hang in the air, coating her lips and flying into her mouth with any opportunity.

She arched her back and reached behind her to knuckle the aching muscles. Lords and Ladies but she was tired. Who would ever have thought simply sitting on a cart could be so tiring? The nights were no better. They clustered tight together around a fire they were too cold to be without and too frightened of to take any comfort from. The darkness was almost total out here. The clouds stole the light of the moon and stars and kept them for their own. Every noise had one of them jumping or reaching for a bow. After three days of this she almost wished she'd never crawled under the bunkhouse.

Kel snored loudly behind her, curled up in amongst the sacks of supplies and Erinn found herself giving the girl envious glances, not that she could have slept with the rattling anyway.

She pulled back gently on the reins as the first of the buildings came into sight. It wasn't much of a village. It would probably be exaggerating to call it a hamlet. A farmstead with a handful of other cottages keeping it company beside the road was all it really was. Still, it would give her someone else to talk to. Kel slept a lot of the time, and when she wasn't sleeping she barely spoke. It was the girl's way of coping, Erinn supposed.

Samen was just as quiet. His mood had soured further by the day and he barely spoke to anyone unless it was absolutely necessary, riding alone on a cart just behind her own. Jarik and Fornn were both friendly enough but kept to themselves unless she made the effort to approach them. There are some things that will always taint a relationship. Threats of rape or murder sit fairly high on the list.

She eased the cart around the turn in the road and pulled the horse to a halt as she looked at the farmstead. It was a tidy place, with a small, but orderly, vegetable plot and what appeared be a herb garden growing close to the house.

The stillness hit her and she sank down with a heavy sigh. A place like this should never be still, not at this time of the day. She listened carefully for any sign she might be wrong as her eyes swept over the covered walkway surrounding the farmstead but all she could hear was the hushed conversation of Jarik and his friend on the rear-most cart.

With a look behind her at Samen she eased herself down from the wagon and made her way towards the farmstead. "Hello?" she called. The silence took the sound and swallowed it down, savouring the taste.

Slow steps took her to the wooden steps leading up to the deck. She was about to call out again when she saw the door hanging from a single hinge. A stain on the wood of the deck was fading to a greyish colour but enough of the red-rust remained to leave little doubt what it was. It trailed towards the door and the hand-print removed any doubts that remained.

"What is it?" Samen called out.

She stood from where she'd crouched to look. "Blood." Her face must have said more than her voice because he climbed down quickly and made to join her.

"Go on back to the cart, I'll have a look," he told her, his sour face softening just a fraction. She nodded and gave him a weak smile of thanks.

Kel hadn't roused herself. A small blessing, Erinn told herself. If what she suspected was true then the last thing the girl needed was to hear about this. The door swung closed with a bang and Samen stumped down the three steps to the dirt. His face said all there needed to be said.

"Bjornmen?" she asked, though she knew the answer before he spoke.

"I don't think so." He shook his head and glanced back at the deck. "They'd have looted or burnt this place. They wouldn't have done…" he paused and spat into the dirt. "Done that."

A brief inspection of the other cottages revealed nothing that Erinn wanted to see and she waited on the cart while Jarik and Fornn checked the last of the cottages. Kel had stirred herself and watched the search with a dull curiosity.

"Nothing," Jarik reported. "Nothing moving anyway." He snorted a laugh but his smile faded as the joke fell flat.

"There's a well around the back of the farm. We may as well fill the skins and water the horses while we're here," Samen suggested, ignoring Jarik.

Erinn nodded, not really listening. She wandered away, heading for the other end of the small hamlet. The breeze stroked the heads of the wild-flowers growing in the long grass to the south of the road. This must have been a pleasant place to live. The ground looked to be good and fertile if the grasses and wild-flowers were anything to judge by. A hill, dotted with sheep, rose up beyond the fields behind the farm and the sun caught and glinted on a small stream than ran down and passed into the woods.

She was suddenly struck by a wave of homesickness as she looked around at the tiny hamlet. Widdengate wasn't just a place she missed, it was a home that had been taken from her. It was somewhere she would never be able to return to no matter what happened with the Bjornmen or the fae. Even if some returned to rebuild the village could never be the same place she'd been forced from.

A scuffing made her turn towards the closest cottage. It was the last one on the row and set slightly apart from the others. She looked over the building trying to see the source of the noise. Thinking back, it had been more of a grating than a scuff. There had been a definite grinding quality to it.

The cottage was a low affair with a dark, thatched roof. Small windows stared blankly out at the daylight, hinting at the dark interior. Erinn circled the cottage. The door was torn free and had been propped up against the wall by Jarik or Fornn, whichever one it was that had searched this home. An outbuilding, little more than a cupboard built up against the side of the house, stood on one corner. Erinn pulled gently on the door, wondering if the wind had blown it. It caught after an inch or two, grinding on small stones in the dirt.

That was it. Excited, she pushed the door shut again and yanked, forcing it over the pebbles that had caught it the first time. Cobwebs hung from the roof, straining as they reached down for hoes and garden forks.

Confused, she took a turn around the cottage again. She hadn't imagined it, there had definitely been a noise. "Hello?" she called, low enough for her voice not to carry past the cottage.

She turned again and she saw it. A window, peering out of a bush that had grown up against the wall. Once it had probably provided light to a cellar room but the bush had spread and almost covered it now. She'd passed it three times without even seeing it.

The scrape in the dirt and slight scratching on the flat stones were visible before she even really got close. Erinn knelt down to peer through the dusty pane and a flash of movement fled backwards into the gloom. A pale face seeking to hide in the darkness.

Erinn screamed and fell back into the dirt. Samen, despite his age, was the first to reach her. She stood dusting her dress off, caught halfway between cursing and laughing at herself.

Samen stopped with the question on his lips and looked around. "What are you squawking for, girl?" He scowled.

She pointed to the half-concealed window. "There's someone in there."

"Looks like root cellar or something," Fornn suggested, overhearing. "There'll be a trap in the cottage someplace."

Samen scowled at him, seemingly for no reason other than his suggestion.

The trap door was easy to find, laying under a rug at one end of the cottage. "Just lift it a crack," Erinn instructed Fornn as he held onto the iron ring. He nodded as she knelt down close to the edge.

"Hello," she called down as Fornn pulled up the trap. "It's okay, we're not going to hurt you. It's safe now."

Urgent whispers argued at the limits of her hearing before a voice hissed. "No, don't!"

Another voice. It sounded younger. "Who are you? What do you want?"

"We're from Carik's Fort," Erinn called through the crack. "It was attacked too. We..." She sat up. "I've had enough of this," she announced and reached out to pull the trap the rest of the way open. A boy, not more than twelve, blinked in the sudden light as he looked up at her.

"Come on up," Erinn told him. "This is silly and we can talk much more easily up here."

He turned to look behind him. "She's right, Marjoie. Let's just go up."

Erinn couldn't hear the response but the tone was clear enough and she glanced at Samen with a wry smile.

"What?" he snapped.

"Oh, nothing."

The boy was followed by a younger girl. They clambered up the wooden steps and hovered close to the cellar entrance as an old woman stood at the bottom of the steps.

She scowled up into the light as she tried to grip both railing and stick at the same time. "Have all you men lost your manners then? Or did your mothers never teach you to offer a hand?"

Fornn moved first, reaching down to offer his help. The woman grabbed at him and clung to his arm awkwardly, fingers gripping tight as she made her way up the steps. From the look on Fornn's face either she was heavier than she looked or her fingers were digging into his flesh.

"Move back out of the way," she snapped, waving her arms to shoo them faster. "Well then," she said, planting the stick in front of her and folding her hands over the end. "Now that you've pulled us from safety, what do you want with us?"

Erinn blinked. "*With* you? We don't want anything with you. We're trying to help."

"The Lord helps those as helps themselves," the old woman told her, jabbing a finger towards her with each word.

Samen gave a snort that hadn't quite decided whether to be a laugh or a sound of derision. "The lord? What lord is that then?"

"The Lord of New Days, old man," she told him.

Samen scowled, though whether it was from her tone or being spoken to like a child Erinn couldn't tell. "I doubt your lord did you much good when the fae came screaming through," he muttered.

"Fae?" She curled her lip at the notion. "We're all here too old for that nonsense. It was a scourge that passed through this town. A scourge sent by the Lord to punish those who would not heed his message!"

Lords and Ladies," Samen muttered. "Put her back in the hole, Erinn." He ignored the look he received and turned away in disgust.

"Fae or scourge it doesn't matter, they're gone for now," Erinn said, trying to salvage the situation.

"They will return." The woman stated it as a matter of fact. She seemed oddly satisfied in her certainty.

"Perhaps." Erinn nodded, then sighed. This was not the way she'd thought this would go. "Look, let's start again. My name is Erinn. This is Fornn and Jerrik, the girl is Kel, and my old friend over there is Samen."

The woman pinched her lips together as if she were trying to find something wrong with the statement. "Marjoie," she said, the word clipped and harsh. "This here's Tern and the pretty one is Silla." The girl pulled her face from the old woman's skirt long enough for a smile to flash over her face, then she met Erinn's eyes and turned her head away again.

"Shhh girl," Marjoie said, stroking Silla's hair. "They don't mean you no harm. You're safe with Old Marjoie."

"That's one of the reasons we're going to Druel," Erinn said in a softer voice. "We'll be safe there," she explained.

"To Druel?" the boy burst in. "What's Druel?"

"It's the home of the Duke. It's miles away," Marjoie replied, though she looked at Erinn as she spoke. "Too far for old bones, or young ones."

"We have wagons and supplies," Erinn said. Why was she being forced to sell this idea?

"Hmmph." Clearly it would take more than supplies and carts to convince the woman.

"Can we, Marjoie?" Tern asked, eyes eager as he looked up at her. "I bet it has a castle and soldiers too!"

"Foolish boy," she muttered but there was no force to the words and her eyes had narrowed in thought. "We're not traipsing across hill and dale just so you can see a pile of stones. We're perfectly fine as we are."

Erinn pinched at the bridge of her nose and held in a sigh. The woman was making her wish she'd listened to Samen. "I wish you would come along," she said, struck by inspiration. "I'd feel better with another woman around. Samen looks over me but it's not right, two young girls alone with just these men."

Marjoie looked at Jerrik and Fornn like they'd just confessed to murder. "I see," she muttered.

It took an hour to get the three of them onto the carts. Finding clothes for the children and settling them in was accomplished in minutes but the old woman was another matter. She spent the best part of half an hour directing the men to fetch this and that, and then another half hour going from cart to cart until she found a suitable place.

As they set off Erinn found herself wondering if Samen hadn't been right.

* * *

Tern and Silla took to Kel almost immediately. Though Samen shot them looks when they giggled and spoke too loudly, even from where Erinn was she could see he was pleased at the change in Kel. Despite all the effort Erinn had made trying to bring the girl back to herself five minutes with the children had done more than she'd ever achieved.

The carts moved slowly under the weight of the supplies and, with the extra people, they took to taking turns walking beside them as the carts creaked along. Even with dry roads and easy terrain they would be lucky to make more than thirty miles a day. Marjoie decided her cart was the most comfortable and had hollowed out a space in the sacks and crates of supplies for herself.

"Had you lived there long?" Erinn asked, shifting so she was sat almost sideways to be able see the woman.

"Where, Lunsford?" Marjoie replied. "All my life, girl. I pulled babes from birthing women and put some of them in the ground, too, when the pox hit us." There was a quiet dignity in her words. The thorns and rough bark had slipped aside for the moment, letting the person hiding beneath show her face.

"You're a healer then?" Erinn asked, trying to hide her pleasure at their good fortune.

"No," Marjoie laughed. "Nothing so grand. I know a trick or two is all. That's all healing is really. The right herbs and a bit of common sense." She rummaged around underneath her and produced a long-stemmed pipe and a small pouch, speaking as she thumbed stourweed into the bowl and scratched sparks into the tiny square of charcloth she set on top. "Hedge-witch is what they called the one who taught me."

"They call them hedge doctors where I'm from," Erinn said, catching the growl in the old woman's voice.

Marjoie grunted around the pipe as she puffed it into life. "No one was going to call me a witch, stuff and nonsense. Not that there wasn't a fair amount of nonsense in what Liska taught me anyway. Putting herbs out in the moonlight and using only fresh rainwater in her remedies. Foolishness!"

"So you looked after everyone in Lunsford?" Erinn asked, trying to move on.

"And Roarke's farm," Marjoie told her, nodding. "And all the little places on the way down to Erisbrook. It's not been the easiest life, but once old Liska was gone someone had to do it. I never found a man I wanted, not that I didn't have a few offers." She flashed a wistful smile. "I never had my own babes, Lunsford and all the farms around here were my children. Every man, woman, and child in them. Like most children they didn't listen when I warned them. I told them the Lord would punish them if they kept on with their foolish midwinter festivals and spring-turn dances. They laughed at me, told me the Lord of New Days was just stuffy priests spoiling their fun."

"And then the fae came," Erinn said quietly.

"Then the *scourge* came," Marjoie corrected. "Fae are just a silly superstition. That's the type of talk that brought down the Lord's wrath in the first place."

Erinn bit her lip and let the conversation die where it lay. Marjoie was like Trallen had been in many ways. The unquestioning faith, the certainty of being right. Many in Widdengate had accepted the faith wholesale but it never really taken hold with Erinn. There was something about it that was a little too convenient, and a faith built on stamping out old traditions didn't seem to offer much. Religion aside, Marjoie was wrong about the fae.

The days passed slowly. The way the carts were loaded down meant they couldn't go much faster than a walking pace unless they really pushed the horses. Survivors had begun to find them within five days of leaving Lunsford. Most were refugees from the scattered farmsteads. Some hid until the caravan of wagons had almost passed them. Others simply waited for the carts to catch up with them, and then joined those walking behind.

Erinn looked back. The line of carts and people stretched back until a curve in the road took it from her sight. The survivors of two more villages had joined them in the past few days. Any cart moving with supplies was a beacon of hope to these people. The fae had struck here like a winter storm, pushing past their defences and killing all they could find. Those that survived had fled, running from the mere possibility that the fae might return.

The first two villages they'd passed through had held only a handful of survivors. They'd still been huddled close to the forge, clutching horseshoes in their fists. The third had fared better and Erinn's group had swelled past fifty. More carts and wagons had come with them but the walkers far outnumbered those who rode.

Marjoie, naturally, did not walk, and her blunt refusal seemed to spur Samen into always being one of the first to volunteer to take a turn. There was something about her that seemed to grate at the man. Erinn would be the first to admit Marjoie could be hard work but to Samen she seemed to be an endless source of annoyance. She was the itch he couldn't reach, the mosquito he couldn't swat. Yet he never seemed to be able to resist trying.

They'd been bickering since the first day. It usually began over some minor slight and escalated until either Samen stalked away or Erinn was forced to step in. It was like dealing with small children and Erinn was growing tired of it.

They stopped early each night, making sure there was plenty of time to set up the camp. Though full moon was over a week away she found herself watching every time it rose and grew that little bit fuller.

She shook her head at the sound of a squealing pig and turned around in her seat to face the road ahead. "I'm sick of trees." She sighed.

"How's that?" Samen cocked an eyebrow at her.

I don't know." She gave a lopsided shrug. "I feel penned in, trapped. Is it too much to be able to see for more than half a mile at a time?"

"Maybe not," he replied. "Right now though, these trees and the hunting we get from them are just about all that's feeding your collection of needy mouths. Our supplies are all but gone and we'd get through that little piggy back there in short order."

She frowned at him, trying to look disapproving but the smile slipped through anyway. He'd been complaining about the squeals of the piglet for two weeks now, ever since it had joined them in the arms of the young girl who refused to leave it. He was exaggerating though. The supplies were dwindling but at a manageable rate. The fae had no interest in the contents of the villages they devastated and they'd been able to replenish their stocks at each village they'd passed.

Most of the men carried bows now, though some would be more likely to sink the iron-headed arrow into a tree than anything else. She'd insisted on taking the iron weapons when they left Carik's Fort. It was more on a whim than anything else and Samen had argued against the weight, but in the end he agreed they were too valuable to leave behind. She glanced at the old man as the thought occurred to her and so didn't see the figures as they stepped out from the trees.

Samen reined in gently, raising his arm to warn those behind. She followed his gaze to the small group of men that stepped out onto the road. They were dressed as hunters. *Perhaps they were something more than that,* she thought as she caught sight of the short sword belted at the lead man's waist.

He raised a hand in greeting as he approached. "What is this? Where have you all come from?"

"Carik's Fort," Erinn called back.

He paused, digesting that as his gaze passed back along the line of carts and wagons drawing to a halt behind them. "You've quite a collection of folk with you, what is this? What's happened?"

Samen put a hand on her arm, stopping her as she started to speak. "You ask a lot of questions for a stranger."

The man smiled then, an easy smile that bled the tension from the situation. "You've good sense, old man. My name's Riddal, I'm a scout attached to Major Rhenkin's men out of Druel. Now, what's happened to the fort? Bjornmen?"

Erinn shook her head, trying to think how to handle this, but Samen didn't wait. "No, not Bjornmen. We could have handled them better, I think. This was something different. The fae."

The reaction wasn't what she'd expected. She'd braced herself for the scoffing and ridicule but the man nodded with a grimace before he spoke again.

"How bad?"

"It's gone, lad," Samen told him.

That shocked him. "The entire fort?" the scout breathed.

"Oh, the buildings are all still there," Samen said with a bitter twist to his mouth. "They didn't hardly touch those, unless it was to force their way through. No, the folks that were there is what I meant. They killed 'em all. Us two, an' three others, are all I know managed to make it to morning."

"Blood-swilling Droos," Riddal whispered. "What about these others?" He nodded at the line of carts behind them.

"There's a dozen small farms and a handful of villages between here and the fort," Samen told the scout. "These are all that's left of 'em." He seemed to be taking a perverse pleasure in the impact of the news, Erinn noticed.

"We were heading back to the fort with dispatches," Riddal told them. "I suppose there's not much point now. You'll travel back with us to Druel. The major will want a first-hand report."

"Now just a minute!" Samen bristled, sitting up in the seat. "What makes you think we were heading for Rhenkin? His record stands for itself when it comes to keeping folks safe."

"Samen," Erinn touched his arm. "Let me handle this." She turned back to Riddal. "Don't you think these people have been through enough without being dragged across the country?"

If her tone bothered him he didn't show it. "Druel's the only place close enough that's of any real size, outside of Kavtrin anyway. What were you planning on doing with this lot?"

That silenced her. She'd been running mostly on instinct since Carik's Fort and hadn't made a plan beyond reaching the closest town. She glanced back at the line of carts and people.

"Fine," she gave in. "We'll head for Druel."

He gave her a look that was wandering somewhere between him being slightly amused and downright patronising. "Why don't you let me and this fellow sort this out, all right, darling?" He ignored her expression, nodding at Samen. "I'm guessing you're leading this group?"

Samen shook his head with a smile and pointed at Erinn.

"You can't be serious?" Riddal scoffed as the men behind him grinned.

Erinn bristled for a moment. She wouldn't rise to it, that would just play into what they were already painting her as, an indulged child.

"We've managed well enough so far," she replied. "You and your men are welcome to join us. We could use both the extra bows and men who are skilled at hunting. We've supplies but they'll only go so far."

Riddal smirked as he gave a mocking bow. "At your service, my lady." His words were almost lost in the poorly muffled snickers from behind him.

* * *

"You can't be stopping again!" Riddal didn't bother to speak softly or hide his frustration.

Erinn closed her eyes as she turned her head away with a sigh. "Look, Riddal, we've been through this. The children can only walk for so long before they need a break. The horses too."

He glanced at the horse leading the cart behind her. "They look fine to me. It's going to take all month to get to Druel if you keep stopping every five minutes."

"It'll take even longer if we have animals go down lame because we're pushing them too hard," she replied just as loudly but he was already turning away. He did this. It was infuriating. He wasn't a stupid man, not by any means, but he couldn't see past the fact she was a woman. As if her not having something swinging between her legs made her incapable of making decisions.

They'd been butting heads since the day he and his scouts had joined them. Little things and nothing that was of any consequence. He'd made it clear he wasn't about to take command himself yet he managed to find fault with her at least twice a day.

Erinn shook her head and glanced up at the sky, the light was already fading. She'd have pushed on for another couple of hours normally but the full moon had come around quicker than she'd have liked.

"Get them watered quickly," she told Samen. "I want to find somewhere better than this to stop for the night."

His face soured. "You want me to hold the buckets for them myself, your worship?" it was more a bad habit than anything else, she knew, but he couldn't resist being difficult.

"Just do what you can to speed things along, Samen." Her voice was weary and she knew it. His face softened and he nodded before stumping away.

She went ahead of the line, passing the first wagon and walking until the voices began to fade. The woods seemed endless, though she knew they'd soon pass out onto the plains. Would that be any better than here? If they had to face the fae it would be better to be able to see farther than the closest trees, that was something. It would mean they'd be unable to hide though. The campfires would be seen for miles. There were just too many little things that could make all the difference and she couldn't shake the feeling that she was missing at least some of them. She turned back to the carts. It was time to get people moving again.

The campsite wasn't much but it was the best she'd seen. The treeline had moved back away from the edges of the road until it seemed they were passing through a clearing. Riddal had rolled his eyes as she called a stop for the night but moved fast enough when she started giving directions.

Four large fires were set, two in what would become the camp, and then two more, further down the road to either side of them. If the fae were to come at them there would be little chance of hiding her people anyway. Better that they could see them coming.

The carts and wagons formed a rough circle around them. It would provide no protection from the fae but it would create the illusion of safety, and the longer she could keep people from panic the better.

She set them to getting the camp ready before she went to find Riddal. He sat on a wagon, looking out at the trees as he puffed on a pipe.

"Can we talk?" she asked.

He looked her way and shrugged before patting the wooden bed of the cart beside him. She chose to stand instead and thought how to begin as she pulled the shawl tighter around her. "You saw the fae at Widdengate?"

He nodded, meeting her eyes for a moment before looking away again. That was fine by her. She'd rather not see his eyes when she said this.

"You know what we'll face if they come then." She spoke to the ground, voice low for fear of it carrying. "If they're like the few that attacked Widdengate they'll cut through us before we really even know they're there. Unless it's a smaller group. We have a slight advantage there."

He looked at her then, appraising, weighing. "How so?"

"Well we don't have so much area to defend for one," she said, waving an arm at the camp. "There's far less chance of them getting close before we see them."

"That's true," he admitted. "But when they *get* close…"

"When they get close," she agreed. "Come with me, I want to show you something."

She led him across the camp and climbed up into the back of a wagon, pulling aside a well-oiled tarpaulin. "I haven't let anyone use these until now, we don't have enough to waste on pigeons or rabbits."

Curiosity won and he climbed up beside her.

"I couldn't just leave them there," she said, waving a hand vaguely at the crates

FAE - THE SINS OF THE WYRDE

of swords and arrows.

"Where?" Riddal breathed, still taking in the sight.

"Carik's Fort. Rhenkin set my father to making them." She spat over the side of the cart. "Sarenson never even sent a man to collect them. I think he thought Rhenkin cracked or something."

Riddal took an arrow and examined the fletching. "It's not as clean as I'd like but it'll fly."

"I'm out of practice," Erinn admitted.

"You made these?" Riddal said.

"The fletching's mine on most of them," she told him. "It gave me something to do in the evenings." Erinn shrugged. "I've heard all of Samen's stories before."

"How many?" he asked, eyes on the barrels.

Erinn followed his gaze. "Arrows? I've not really kept a count. Not enough to waste anyway."

"What's in here?" he asked, looking at a sealed barrel.

She smiled, an expression that was cold and vengeful. "An idea, something I'd like to try out if the opportunity presents itself. For now I'd like you hand out these weapons to those you think will get the most use from them."

* * *

The first night passed uncomfortably. Though the fires were warm and everyone ate the waiting dragged on. As the moon rose men fingered their weapons, hefting the unfamiliar weight of the iron swords or setting arrows to strings.

And the wait went on. The fires still burned high but none took comfort from their warmth now. Eyes swept the darkness between the trees, or searched the skies, watching for any movement or sign. The anticipation built, growing until an attack by the fae would actually have been preferable to the tension.

Erinn walked, picking her way through the camp and the legs that threatened to trip her from those seeking sleep. Whenever she passed someone awake she stopped, handing over a small pouch from the sack she carried.

"What's this?" Marjoie asked. Erinn hadn't even registered who she was when she'd pressed the pouch into her hands.

"Something to protect you if they come," Erinn told her.

"If who come? The scourge?" Marjoie curled her lip. "If the Lord seeks to send me from his world for the sins of my past there's nothing you can put in a pouch that will help me."

"Unless it isn't a scourge," Erinn said. "What if it is the fae and nothing to do with the Lord? For that matter, what if the fae are the scourge?"

Marjoie pulled herself upright, face tight as he lips pressed thin together. "I told you, girl. The fae are nothing but superstition."

Erinn thought, brushing her hair out of her face with one hand. "But if they are the Lord's scourge, well, wasn't it you who told me that the Lord helps those who help themselves?"

A faint smile of satisfaction hovered around her lips. "That's right. The Lord holds no truck with those that sit around wallowing in their own misfortune."

Erinn smiled then. "Well then, isn't this just helping ourselves?"

Marjoie grunted, a noncommittal sound that made it clear that even though she might agree with Erinn she'd never admit to it. As she walked away Erinn saw her working the drawstrings back. "Huh," the old woman muttered as she peered inside, poking at the contents with a gnarled finger. "Clever."

Erinn paced. She worked a path into the dirt as she made her way past the children and those who managed to snatch moments of sleep. Pacing worked so long as she kept moving. Twice, when she'd stopped, people had tried to draw her into frightened conversations. She didn't want to talk. Talking led to dwelling and speculation. It just fed the fear she'd worked hard to ignore. And so she walked, back and forth through the cramped camp, picking her way through the legs of those laying on the ground until they took the hint and shuffled back out of her way.

A single weary cheer rose to meet the first light of the sun. Weak and lonely it stopped as quickly as it had begun. Cheers meant a victory. This battle hadn't begun yet.

The second night was better but for all the wrong reasons. They'd made poor progress, with a late start, and too many took turns at snatching an hour or two of sleep on the carts. It didn't seem to help much and most of the refugees looked exhausted by the time night fell. She set them in watches, at Riddal's insistence, and the camp slept in shifts hoping for the dawn.

Erinn sat, curled into a corner of the camp up against a cart's wheel. The fires and the rough blanket were warm enough but sleep would not come. She stared into the coals of the closest fire worrying. If the fae came now most of these people would be too tired to be of any use.

She flashed Samen a tired smile as he sank down beside her. "You should be sleeping," she told him.

"I could say the same of you, girl," he replied with a scowl.

"I'm hardly a girl at this point, Samen," she scoffed. "I've known mothers younger than I am."

He shrugged, indifferent. "In my head you're still that little red haired girl pestering me for stories."

"I haven't been that girl for a long time." She hadn't meant it to sound miserable but as the words left her lips she realised it was probably true and her mood fell still further. "Do you think they'll come tonight?"

"The fae?" He scratched at an armpit, ignoring her pointed look. "What makes you think they'll come at all?"

"The old man at Widdengate, Obair. He said the Hunt comes on the third night after full moon."

"You should know better than to believe every tale an old man tells you," Samen said. He managed to keep his face straight for two or three heartbeats, and then snorted at himself.

Erinn felt her face relax as the smile faded. "Seriously, do you think they will?"

"If they do, then they do. One thing I know, this is no way to live." His look was serious, his customary dour expression suddenly stripped from him. "I'm not a young man, Erinn. I've not many years left to me but I'd rather be meat for the droos before I choose to live like this. These creatures, whether they're fae or the scourge that mad old hag, Marjoie, keeps harping on about. Whatever you call them, they've beaten us without even a fight. We're worse than mice, cowering in the night from the hoot of an owl. I'm done with it."

She pushed herself upright from where she'd been slouched against the wheel. "We *were* defeated, Samen. You were there at Carik's Fort, the same as me. You know what they did."

"Yes I was. And yes, they ran the streets red with our blood." His face grew fierce as he spoke, irritation growing before giving way to something with more heat. "They came and cut us down like they were reaping wheat. I'll tell you this for free though, girl, I'm not dead yet. If I'm still breathing I mean to live and piss on anyone who does less!"

He stopped then, chest heaving, and she knew from his expression that he'd had no idea he'd stood and been shouting at the last. A clap was joined by others and Samen flushed at the applause at first before he recovered himself and turned to give a florid bow.

"You've got the right of it, old man," Marjoie said as she picked her way through the sudden press of people. "Those as live like they're already dead, they get their wish soon enough."

His face darkened but she spoke again before he could get a word in edgeways. "Life is for living, an' I say enough hidin' in the dark. Do you think you could saw out a tune on that fiddle I see you lugging about? A bit of music might remind these folks they're not dead just yet."

A smile climbed out of the shock on his face. "I just might at that."

She leaned closer, lowering her voice. "I may be a mad old hag but I still know how to live." She winked at him, laughing again at the look on his face.

The change as Samen's first notes drifted through the camp was pronounced. While musicians were nothing out of the ordinary it was a sad home that didn't own a pipe or flute. A fiddle though? Well, a fiddle was a rare and wondrous thing.

He started out slow, coaxing out a soothing melody as faces turned towards him from around the camp. Soon though, he shifted to a livelier tune, moving around the fire and unconsciously falling into a hopping, bouncing gait that was a lot closer to a dance than he would probably have ever admitted.

Soon the children were following him around, giggling and clapping along to the beat as the night breezes tossed leaves through the camp. A wineskin appeared from somewhere and was joined by others that were passed around in the light of the fires. Though Erinn would have sworn there was no drink to be had in the camp she was glad of it. There was barely enough for a mouthful each but the impact it had was priceless. All around her, people who'd been ready to give up, to roll over and die as soon as the fae appeared, were getting up to dance with a new life shining in their eyes.

She laughed as a farmhand took her hands and pulled her to her feet, brushing away her half-hearted protests. Soon she was spinning and whirling in a dance she'd known long before any boy had ever been permitted to lead her out onto the floor.

The moon was high and full in the sky but for the first time in months she ignored it, allowing herself a moment of pleasure. The music swelled around her, lifting her, filling her senses as it took her away from the horrors of the past days and weeks. Pipes had joined with the music from Samen's fiddle and the song soared, roaring in her ears as her heart raced to keep up with her spirit. The farmhand passed her off to another, and then yet another until the faces were a blur. The numbers in the camp seemed larger, or maybe it was just the enclosed space. Her mind drifted as her feet moved without her really thinking about it and, with a shock of pleasure, she realised the man who held her was Devin.

He'd grown since the last time she saw him, becoming thicker of body and more muscular in the arms and shoulders, but there was no doubting it was him. The music made it too loud to talk and words would have been wasted now anyway. He moved her expertly around the floor, strong hands roaming unchecked over her back and hips. She laughed wickedly as he pulled her in close, chancing a kiss that she stole away from him at the last second, presenting her cheek.

Her laugh turned into a gasp, and then a moan as he ignored the offered cheek and kissed at her throat instead. Dimly she heard a sound that might have been screams, but none of that mattered now. Her heart was pounding as Devin took her by the hand, leading her between two wagons and out away from the dance and into the darkness.

The arrow took him in the throat and as he clutched at the shaft, blue fire erupted from the wound. The glamour shattered and her vision swam as her ears were filled with screams and the crash of weapons. The satyr dropped to the dirt, dark blood hissing as blue fire spurted from the wound.

Erinn swallowed down the scream that threatened to come out. There was no time for that. The camp was in chaos. Men who'd never held a sword swung at satyrs who danced lightly away from their clumsy strokes. The air above them was thick with tiny purple-skinned creatures, darting about on gossamer wings and looking like the faeries of legend. She grabbed at the pouch around her neck, tearing it free and pouring half the contents out into one hand as she ran towards the closest satyr.

The filings were fine, the dust from fifty or more swords sharpened on the grinding wheel and gathered up from the floor. Erinn put a hand on the farmer's shoulder, hurling the dust past him and full into the satyr's face. The creature blinked, gasping and breathing the dust in even as it reached to wipe it from its eyes. It stood frozen for a heartbeat, and then it screamed. It was a shockingly human sound as tiny blue sparks burst into life on the surface of its skin and eyes. The sparks grew, fanned into flames that seared the skin and burned it blind. Fire gouted from its mouth and nose and, within seconds, the monster was wreathed in flames.

Erinn staggered back, amazed at the effect, and glanced about the camp. Riddal and his scouts were stood atop a wagon, sending shaft after shaft into the mess. Despite their efforts though, Erinn's numbers were dropping. In moments they would be overwhelmed.

"Pouches," Erinn shouted, her voice almost lost in the noise. "Throw the dust!"

Enough people heard and hands were soon tossing the iron filings into the air. When the cloud of filings touched the satyrs they were wreathed in a thousand tiny sparks. It seemed to have little effect unless they breathed it in or it blew into their eyes. It was enough though, enough to freeze them for a moment, and Harlen's iron blades thrust deep.

Where the dust hit the faeries however, the effect was profound. They crashed to the ground with wings burning in hot, blue flames. The dust was light enough to carry a short distance and clouds of it caught in the night wind, drifting through the camp. Erinn grabbed up a fallen sword, wielding it with two hands as she stabbed at a satyr stood rooted to the spot as it clawed at its eyes.

"Come on!" she screamed at the men around her. She drove them through the camp, dealing death and flame to the fae that, moments ago, had been close to killing them all.

It was over in a shockingly short time and she let the sword's tip drop to the ground, her chest heaving as she looked around to see if it was really over. Bodies lay everywhere, villagers mixed in with the fae that still burned fitfully. She caught sight of Riddal, staring at her in shock, and then she sank to her knees, triumph shrouded by exhaustion.

CHAPTER ELEVEN

Selena sipped at the spoon and pulled a face at the soup. Cold…again. It would have been easy enough to have it warmed but she'd had that done once already and twice would seem foolish. "It's you that left it to go cold again, foolish woman," she chided herself. She glanced at the bread roll sat on its small plate beside the soup and grimaced. Fresh bread had always been her favourite food. Warm from the oven and still hot enough to steam as you tore it open. Slathered in butter there was nothing better. Of course that was before she'd fallen pregnant. Now a single taste would have had her stomach churning and her racing for a pot to retch into.

A gentle tap on the door preceded the servant with a letter resting on a silver tray. *Heavens forbid it was simply carried,* she thought.

"A letter, your grace." The servant somehow managed to offer her the tray whilst bowing and yet not look ridiculous. Where did they learn these things?

"So it is, and isn't it so pretty on its shiny tray too?" She kept her face straight. It was much more fun when they couldn't tell you were poking fun at them. "Who is it from?"

"I would never presume to read your grace's correspondence, your grace," he replied.

She looked at the ceiling as she pondered aloud. "Did the letter fly here? Or perhaps it appeared in a puff of smoke?"

"I believe it was delivered by a messenger from Druel, your grace," he admitted. "Though I am given to understand it originated from the Browntree estates."

"Aunt Evelyn!" Selena snatched the letter from the tray. "Why didn't you just say so?"

She waved him to silence as she cracked the seal and started to read. Dimly she was aware he'd bowed and made his way out, but by then the words had taken hold and her vision was already blurred.

"Your grace?" an older voice, motherly.

"Hmm?"

"Are you all right, your grace?"

Selena looked past the letter and into the gloom. How had it grown so dark in here already? "I'm fine, Catherine. Why?"

The woman raised an eyebrow at her. "You're sitting in the dark." She stepped out to the hallway and returned with a taper, moving around the room and lighting the lamps.

"You didn't eat again, your grace," the woman chided her.

Selena glanced at the bowl. "It went cold. We're alone, Catherine, you can drop the grace."

Catherine peered at the tray. "Even the bread? Went cold, I mean?"

Selena pulled a face. "I can't eat bread. It makes the morning sickness worse."

Catherine tutted. "Then why don't you tell the kitchens not to send any up?"

"I can't afford to show any weakness, Catherine," Selena said, ignoring the disbelieving expression. "I'm a woman, holding power in a world that men believe they have a right to rule. Half the men in this very villa think I ought to be doing needlepoint or cleaning something. The fact I'm pregnant only makes it worse. The very notion that a woman is capable of doing more than producing squalling brats has never occurred to most men. If I start sending food back because it makes me feel ill I might as well start swooning and waiting for someone to catch me."

The servant gave her a faintly amused expression. "Is it still really that bad?"

"Oh, don't!" Selena sighed. "I've had a good twelve people tell me that the sickness has usually passed for most women by now. Yes, it's still that bad. Pass me the bread and I'll demonstrate." She cracked a smile at herself and cocked her head as a thought occurred to her. "It can't be that different for you. Practically nobody here even knows your name. They speak in whispers about the 'Mistress of the House.' If you threw up every time you smelled baking bread they'd soon stop worrying about working fast enough and be snickering up their sleeves as you passed."

"You may be right," Catherine conceded. "Why were the lamps unlit?"

"I lost track of time. I was thinking." Selena waved the message. "A death in the family, my Aunt Evelyn."

"The Lady Browntree?" The servant allowed a note of dismay into her voice. "Oh, that is terrible news."

"I haven't seen her in too long, now it's too late." Selena shook herself and cleared her throat, pulling herself erect in the chair. "What did you want, Catherine? I'm sure you didn't come in here just to light the lamps."

"No, your grace." She shook her head. "Sanderson has an…individual with him that you had requested a meeting with. I thought it might be best to advise you myself."

"An individual?" Selena asked, perplexed.

"You had requested he located a personage of somewhat less than savoury character?" Catherine reminded her with a pained expression.

Selena laughed. "Oh, you mean the thief!"

"Yes, your grace." Catherine nodded.

Selena let the grace pass. It was probably the woman's coping mechanism. She'd invited a thief into what she probably thought of as her own home, after all. It must be a little like asking a shepherd to find a wolf to bring back to the paddock. "Why don't you ask Sanderson to bring him… I'm assuming it's a man?" Catherine nodded. "Very well, have him bring him in."

"Very good, your grace." Catherine bobbed a curtsy and left.

The man Sanderson escorted in was nondescript. He was average in every sense of the word. So normal that the eyes slipped off him in search of something more interesting. He stood still as Sanderson introduced him but his gaze darted around the room like a minnow startled from the shallows and seeking a place to hide.

"Sturgeon?" Selena asked. "That's an odd name. Isn't that a kind of fish?"

Sturgeon's eyes flashed back to her. "Might be." He shrugged. "What's a Freyton?"

"A drunk," Selena said with a twitch of her lips.

The man grunted, eyes narrowing as he looked for the joke and apparently decided it wasn't worth finding. "Your boy said you have a job you want doing?" he said, jerking his head towards Sanderson.

"Would you like a drink before we get started?" Selena asked. "Perhaps some tea?"

"No," the man said flatly. "Let's not pretend we're friends or that we're making friends. This is business."

"Indeed." She glanced at the servant who fought to conceal a mildly outraged expression. "I believe that will be all for now, Sanderson."

He bowed and looked back and forth between the two of them, discomfort clear on his face.

"It's fine, Sanderson," Selena told the man. "I'm sure Sturgeon will be a perfect gentleman and, let's face it, I'm far too heavy to steal." She looked down at her swelling waist.

"Very good, your grace." Sanderson's bow was ignored as she turned back to the thief.

"I have a somewhat delicate problem, Sturgeon," Selena began. "Something I value rather highly has gone missing and I'd like you to locate it and return it to me."

Sturgeon made his way over to a divan and fell into it. "Why me? Why not just send some of your men to get it back?"

She paused, re-evaluating the man. He'd not bothered wasting time asking if she knew where the item was. He knew he wouldn't be here if she didn't.

"I could do that," she admitted, "but that would create some complications I'd rather not deal with right now. I was rather hoping for something a little more discrete."

Sturgeon sat up, clasping his hands between his knees as he leant towards her. "Tell you what? Why don't we stop dancing around it and you just tell me what you want done?"

"Direct, aren't you?" Selena murmured.

"I've not often found much benefit in beating around the bush." Sturgeon grinned.

She leant forward, unconsciously mimicking his posture. "Fine then. The king has abducted a friend of mine. A man named Raysh. I want you to locate him and return him to me."

That caught him. She suppressed a smile as he sat back and gave a low whistle. "When you say...abducted?" he said.

"I mean taken by force from his home in the middle of the night. Do you have another definition I'm not aware of?" Selena asked, raising her eyebrows to give him a pointed look.

He shook his head. "I just wanted to be clear. And you want me to get him out of the palace for you?"

"No." She stood, kneading the small of her back. "No I don't think he's in the palace or any official cell. The king would never be so foolish as to try and arrest a lord like that. No, I think he's being held somewhere in the Warrens."

He glanced up at her at the last word, his own eyes narrowing as he adjusted his own assessment of her. "There's not many gentry use that word for the slums."

"I make it a habit to know something of what I am speaking, Sturgeon. Now do you think you can find him?"

"Find him, yes. Get him out alive and back to you..." he left it hanging.

"Well that's the trick isn't it?" She said as she smiled. "Now, shall we discuss your fee?"

* * *

Raysh sat in the darkness of the cellar. His arms hung limp, bound in manacles that stretched up above his head to where the chains were fixed to the walls. It was an awkward, uncomfortable position, but at least they hadn't had his whole body hanging. He shifted, kicking feet out spasmodically into the damp straw as he tried to scratch his back on the stones of the wall behind him. It was a futile effort. The stone was slick with moisture and covered with a slimy mould that robbed him of any rough surface to grind against.

He coughed into the blackness. A tearing, hacking cough that brought up something vile. He shuddered at the feel of it on his tongue and spat it out into the unseen straw.

They didn't need to bother killing him. Leaving him here would do the job soon enough. The air was thick with the smell of rotting straw and mould. Who could say how much of it he'd already breathed in. He could feel the fluid rattling in his chest with every breath he took.

A muffled creak was followed by the clump of boots on stone steps. It would be the bald one. The one with the smiles had a lighter step. The bald one was mean but his cruelty lay on the surface. It was as wide and deep as a street puddle, easy to spot and not so terrible to endure. His was a cruelty that grew out of a love of holding power over others. He was simply a bully in the perfect job.

The Smiler was something else entirely. His cruelty lay concealed, hidden beneath a gentile manner and a veneer of regret at what he must do. His smile told another story however, the truth gleamed between the cracks, a horror that was glimpsed before it was felt. It was like the frigid depths that lay beneath the thin surface of an icy lake. At any moment his smiles might crack, the veneer shatter, and then there was nothing but the fall, down into the cold darkness. His was a cruelty that had yet to find its limits and he terrified Raysh beyond all measure.

The flicker of lantern light reached underneath the wooden door and metal scraped in the lock before they entered.

"And how are we this morning, my lord?" The thin-faced man asked with a sad smile as Baldy stumped into the cell and fiddled with the chains behind him. Raysh had been wrong, it had been both of them. Baldy's heavy feet had covered the sound of the other's passage.

Raysh whispered and croaked something in response but the sound barely made it past his lips.

"He asked you a fuckin' question!" Baldy snapped, planting a boot into Raysh's side that threw him sideways. The chains snapped taught, manacles biting into his wrists as they stopped him short of pitching into the straw.

"Now, now!" the Smiler chided gently. "There's really no need for anyone to get uncivil, now is there?"

Baldy glowered, though he was careful to keep it fleeting and with his face turned away from the Smiler.

"Now then, my lord, shall we continue the little chat we began yesterday?" The smile was the same as always: small, sad, and self-mocking beneath the icy eyes. Pale blue, as untouched by warmth as the harshest winter frost.

"I've told you, I don't know anything!" Raysh managed to croak. His voice gave at the end, breaking into something like the pitiful sound of a beaten child.

"Now that's simply not true, is it?" the Smiler said, pursing his lips in reproach. "You've told us so much already. You know so many things. Surely you can think of some more, hmm?"

"I don't!" Raysh shouted, and then in a softer voice wearing tears on the edges. "I don't."

"That is a great pity, my lord." That same sad smile again.

Raysh's anger fought through, burning past the threat of tears. "Why? You're never going to let me go anyway. Pieter can go and fuck himself!"

"Now that's just rude." The Smiler tutted and shook his head in disapproval. Baldy just looked on, silent and grinning. "You are probably correct, however. You're an intelligent man, Lord Raysh, I won't insult you by telling you we're going to let you go. I don't know for certain, of course. That decision will be made by someone else so there is always the chance, I suppose, if you prove useful." He shrugged, indifferent. "Otherwise, as I expect you realise, there are only two ways out of here and both of them involve a blade. It could be my good friend here," he gestured and Baldy pulled out his rusted dagger. "Or it could be my little toys." That smile again. "There are so many that I've never even had opportunity to try."

He nodded to Baldy. "Bring him."

The thick-set man moved forward and grabbed his arm, working the key in the manacle until it came free of Raysh's wrist, and then rattled the chain through the iron ring set in the wall. Raysh struggled but it was a weak flailing, the final struggles of a landed fish.

Baldy bundled him through the door and down a short corridor to the other room. The one with the chair. Raysh screamed as they drew closer, struggling more violently but he might as well have been raging against the wind for all the good it did him.

He was shoved down into the chair and held down whilst the wide leather straps were made fast around his chest and legs. Through it all the Smiler looked on, pacing idly around the room. "It's a strange thing this art of persuasion," he remarked. "In many ways it's so much more about what you think than what you feel. Now," he rubbed his hands together, "where were we up to? Let's have that left boot off shall we?"

Raysh screamed as it came off, leather pulling against half-healed wounds. The Smiler went to the table in the corner, selecting something that shone brightly from his velvet-lined case before coming over to crouch by Raysh's bare feet.

"They've healed quite nicely, all things considered." His fingertips brushed against the cauterised and blackened flesh in a sick parody of a lover's caress and Raysh jerked away spasmodically.

The Smiler crouched down, holding Raysh's ankle lightly as he stroked the healthy skin on the top of his foot. "As I was saying, My Lord. This art is so much more about you than it is me. It's about expectation. It's about hope. Deep down you hold a secret hope that you will be freed. It doesn't matter that you're far too intelligent a man to really believe that to be true, the hope remains." He stood with a shrug and tapped the flat of the blade against his lips. "If I'm honest I don't know if you will ever be freed. The order could come to kill you tomorrow, or not. It is hope that this art deals in. Hope that you might know enough to make me stop, or at least give me pause. Hope is stronger than faith, more powerful than love. Hope is the lever that can move worlds."

He'd begun pacing again as he spoke and he turned to meet Raysh's eyes as his head lolled back against the chair.

"Your toes, whilst they proved educational for you, can always be covered, can they not? I could remove two, three, perhaps all of them, and it would affect you little." He allowed a small smile at his captive's blank expression. "The right pair of boots, perhaps with something wadded into the toes, and none would be the wiser would they, hmm? Fingers though, that's something different entirely."

The knife was small, closer to a surgeon's implement than a knife really. A tiny sliver of blade held fast in a curving ivory handle. It was closer to a pen than a weapon but still Raysh began to scream as the Smiler drew closer.

"Now that won't do at all," the man said, almost to himself. "Let's do something about the noise, shall we?"

"I'll stop, I promise," Raysh blurted. "Let me talk, please?"

Baldy grunted and worked a knotted cloth into Raysh's mouth. Dragging it roughly back and forth over his lips until he forced it in.

"You still don't understand, do you?" the Smiler said, for once his face looking genuinely sad. "This isn't about you talking right now, this is about education. The talking, if there is anything you know which might interest me, that will come later." He nodded at Baldy who took Raysh's hand, forcing the fingers out of the protection of their fist as he held the hand down on the arm of the chair. It was wider and longer than on a normal chair, providing a small table on which to work.

"Let's start with the smallest one. I don't think it really works with the rhyme, I'm afraid. For some reason I've always imagined it starting with the thumb," he admitted. "I'm sure you'll forgive me if we work backwards though, won't you?" The smile was encouraging, the look you'd give a small child. He looked down at the outstretched hand, held palm-up by Baldy, and began to slice into the pad of the finger. "This little piggy went to market…"

* * *

156

It was barely a scuff, lighter than the sound of cloth brushing stone, but Raysh had come to fear sound. Sound meant smiles, and smiles led to pain. He leant forward against the reach of the chains, straining his ears to catch the sound again. Pain uncurled from the corner he had forced it into and throbbed through his fingers and hands in time with his pulse.

A whisper came at the door. A breath of something metallic and wet that grew into clicks followed by a gentle grinding. The door was silent as it swung open. Raysh knew the creaks of the doors and grates as well as he knew his own voice and the silent movement was enough to make him wonder if he was dreaming again.

A spot of light bloomed on the straw and shifted around the cell to find his face. Raysh blinked against the sudden brightness, pressing his face into his shoulder and squinting away from the light. "Go away." The whisper was more plea than order.

The light vanished and a hand found his mouth in the darkness. "Stay quiet and I might be able to help you. Is your name Jonas?"

Raysh froze, wondering if he could get away with lying.

"Is it Raysh?"

He nodded against the hand, glad he hadn't bitten down when the urge came to him.

"You've some interesting friends who seem to think you've wandered astray long enough. My name's Sturgeon. I've been sent to retrieve you."

The voice fell silent as its owner busied himself with the locks on Raysh's manacles, laying them gently in the straw as they came loose.

"How many guards have you seen?" it asked.

Raysh looked at the man's face in the dim light. "No guards. There are two men that…" his voice faltered. "…That question me but no, no guards."

"Can you stand?" the man breathed, close enough for Raysh to feel the words on his cheek.

"I think I kind of have to." Raysh whispered. "Just don't expect me to run." He accepted the hand gratefully and without thinking. Pain flooded through him as the man heaved him upwards. He made it halfway to his feet before his knee buckled, pitching him sideways and pulling them both down to the filthy straw.

The darkness hid the expression but Raysh could feel the anger in the look anyway. "Don't feed me shit. If you can't stand then say so. Lying will only get us both killed."

"I'll be fine," Raysh gasped. "It's my hands and feet, not my legs. Just help me up."

Strong hands pulled him to his feet and a head ducked under his arm, supporting him as they headed for the door. A sliding grate on the side of the lantern allowed for a tiny beam of light to shine out onto the stone floor, transforming the utter blackness into mere gloom as they followed a narrow stone passage.

The ladder was iron and rusted. Raysh glanced back at the shadowy figure behind him but said nothing. His feet were less of a problem than his hands, he could set his feet with the rungs far back, close to his heel. Gripping the rungs, however, was an excursion through pain. He gave up on his right hand almost immediately, reaching through the rungs awkwardly with his arm and using the inside of his elbow to pull himself upwards. His left hand was little better, with only a three fingered loose grip to draw on. The result was a slow, lurching climb and, though he couldn't hear the sighs behind him, he knew they were there.

A wooden trapdoor gave way to a darkness that smelled familiar though Raysh couldn't place it. He slumped onto the floor, rolling to the side to make room for Sturgeon. The thin shaft of light exposed tall wooden shelves lined with curved wooden slots.

"A wine cellar?" Raysh wondered. "Where in the hells are we?"

"A rundown villa on the edge of the Warrens, near the river," the figure whispered. "And keep your voice down." He pushed past Raysh, taking the lead.

Sturgeon moved slowly, walking in an odd half-crouched position and never really letting his heels touch the floor. For the first time Raysh allowed himself to wonder just who this man was and where he was taking him. It didn't matter, he supposed. Anywhere that was not here would be just fine.

Stone steps led up to a simple wooden door. Raysh watched as Sturgeon pressed an ear to the panels for the length of five ragged breaths, and then eased the door open. Pain was making his heart pound. When he was in his cell he could curl up as much as the chains would allow and hide away from it. Now though, pain had found him and the claws of it raked through him every time he stubbed his boot on the uneven floor or had to use his arms.

Misery fought with reason as he shied away from the thoughts of what kind of ruin his body might be. Darkness had denied him the ability to tell with any certainty, and as they moved closer to the street a small part of him clung to the shadows. There was a comfort in ignorance.

The door led through to kitchens, with just one small corner showing any signs of recent use, and out into once-grand hallways. Footprints had carved a channel through the dust, forcing it to the sides where it mingled with walked-in leaves and the ruins of long-dead spider civilizations.

A lantern sat burning in the middle of what had once probably been a lavish parlour. Its owner lay on the floor beside it, blood pooled out from the savage cut to his neck.

"Baldy," Raysh breathed as he looked in through the doorway. The man looked smaller now, somehow less than he had been. He looked to Sturgeon, "Did you find the other one?"

A small shake of the head. "No, this one was the only person here. I kept expecting to find more but..." he shrugged. "I suppose it's easier to hide with a small operation."

"Who *are* you?" Raysh asked.

"Later," Sturgeon told him with another shake of the head. "We're not out yet."

A small window led them into an alleyway leading to the street and, despite what Sturgeon had told him, Raysh began to relax. He was out. They might be in a part of Celstwin he'd never seen but he was free. He could feel it bubbling up inside him and, despite the pain, a grin found its way to his lips.

The skies were dark and overcast, giving no real hint of what the time might be and the streets Sturgeon led him through were almost as dark as the cell had been. After a moment he realised the man was still moving in the same fashion as he had in the cellar, slow and silent, pausing often to listen.

The grin left Raysh's lips as he looked around himself properly. This really was a part of Celstwin he'd never seen. The buildings were rough and closer to wattle and daub than to the marble-clad mansions and villas he was used to. The streets were in dire need of repair and filth lined the gutters.

What really struck him was the darkness. Celstwin, as he knew it, never really grew dark. Torches and lamps were always hung outside of the taverns and hostelries and the broader avenues were lit with large lanterns at regular intervals. Here though, the streets were dark and shadowed.

It was quiet too. Celstwin was a lively city full of taverns and dining houses for the rich, and louder, more brash places for the rest. Some of the brothels and gambling clubs had been known to carry on until the first blush of dawn. Here though, the silence lay heavy and oppressive. A silence that carried knives and lurked in dark corners.

He hurried close behind Sturgeon and looked about them as they walked. They stayed in the back alleys most of the time, crossing broader streets only to step back into the network of rubbish-strewn passages. As time went on the silence of the slums gave way to faint sounds of life, the darkness split by raucous laughter and the distant shouts of a drunken argument.

Once, a man's scream, filled with pain and outrage, erupted from an alley as they passed. Raysh, jumped and looked to Sturgeon. "Shouldn't we?" he let the question hang in the air between them. The cloaked man shrugged and shook his head. "Not my business," he said simply.

Another filthy passageway led them out onto a broad avenue and, just like that, Celstwin was revealed. Lamplight shone on the surface of the river and the marble buildings had never looked so grand. Raysh sighed and smiled his thanks at Sturgeon but the man ignored him, frowning as he looked at the bridge closest to them.

Raysh followed his gaze, noting the men clustered in the shadows.

"Come on," Sturgeon said. "We'll find another way." He reached for Raysh's shoulder as he turned, urging more speed as more figures stepped out into the street, watching them.

"Can you run?" Sturgeon asked in a low voice.

"I can hobble faster," Raysh managed between clenched teeth.

"Then let's do that." Sturgeon told him, looking behind them. "Follow me and tell me if you can't keep up."

The streets vanished again as Sturgeon led them back into alleys and the even smaller passages that ran between buildings. Raysh gave up on being quiet and put his energies into speed as he shifted into a lurching hobble that would have looked comical at any other time.

Dark doorways flashed past them until he gasped out for help. Sturgeon was there in moments, ducking his head under Raysh's arm and urging him out into the small courtyard.

"Master Sturgeon." The voice caught them both in surprise and their heads whipped toward the dark doorway on their left, and the figure that lounged in the shadows. Man-shapes peeled out of the darkness, edging towards them.

Sturgeon lowered Raysh down, hands flashing under his cloak and returning with daggers before he looked back at the speaker. "Who's asking?"

"I wasn't asking." The voice was faintly amused. "It wasn't a question. I was telling you that you I know who you are."

Sturgeon shrugged. "Didn't answer my question though. Who are you?"

"It doesn't matter who I am," the figure said as he stepped out of the doorway. "The question you should be asking is who sent me? Who would know that you'd be here, on this night, with Lord Raysh?"

"I can think of at least three people," Sturgeon said, tossing the words aside.

"You've never been a stupid man, Sturgeon," the man told him. "Don't start now. Tenebris Gatun has taken an interest in this man, and in your employer. He is most eager to speak with her. I suggest you let her know of his invitation and that Lord Raysh will be our guest for a time."

"What's going on?" Raysh hissed.

"I can't help you," Sturgeon said, stepping to one side and sheathing his knives. "I'm sorry, Raysh, these men will take you from here. You belong to the Hidden King now."

CHAPTER TWELVE

The square smelled. It wasn't quite a strong enough an odour to say it stank, Selena decided, but there was a definite aroma about the place. She wrinkled her nose again and shifted on the carriage seat.

"Fragrant, isn't it, your grace?" Hanris said with a small smile.

Selena nodded. "It puts me in mind of cats. Auntie Evelyn kept cats. Old, incontinent things that were more cushions than pets. Some are just dog people, Hanris. I've never been able to abide cats."

He smiled a servant's smile and looked out of the carriage window as a movement caught his eye. She caught the motion and leaned forward to follow his gaze. A small group of men had entered the square, Sturgeon among them.

"It looks as though this is their delegation," Hanris said as he reached for the door.

"Your grace," Sturgeon called as she and Hanris climbed out to meet them.

"Sturgeon," she nodded at him, then looked around at the men with him. "And is this all of you? Where is this Tenebris Gatun of yours?"

"This is Crabber," Sturgeon said, gesturing to the man next to him.

"Master Crabber." Selena inclined her head politely.

"Your Ladyship," Crabber rumbled. It would have been a deep, rich voice had it not been lost in a rasp born from years of harsh spirits and stourweed smoke.

"The man you're wanting to meet is waiting in there." He jerked his head towards the low building on the far side of the square.

Selena raised an eyebrow. "And I'm expected to go to him, I assume?"

Crabber spread his hands. "Gatun values his privacy. We're all to wait out here. He'll meet you alone."

"If I may, your grace" Hanris said before looking at the old thief. "How are we to know her grace's safety is assured?"

Crabber gave a nasty grin. "She goes in alone to see 'im. If she don't come out then we can all cut each other to bits. Sound fair?"

Selena touched reached for Hanris' arm and gave him a small smile. "I'm sure it will be fine, Hanris. As Sturgeon said, if the man wanted to do me harm he could have done so already."

"Indeed, your grace." Hanris did not look convinced.

She walked across the courtyard, picking her way through puddles and inexplicable piles of mud. The door hung slightly open and she took a deep breath as she reached for it. "Don't look back at them, Selena," she told herself. "A duchess does not lean on the staff."

It was dark inside. A darkness that was somehow intensified by the shafts of light that shone through the gaps and cracks in the wooden walls. Dust hung heavy in the air and the light picked out the floating motes, giving her eyes no chance to adjust to the darkness in the shadows. She moved forward, trailing her hand on the wall as she looked for any sign of life.

Enough of this, she thought. Floundering along in the darkness only serves to reinforce their position. "All right, I'm here," she called out. "Now what."

"We talk." The voice was shockingly close and she spun before she could stop herself.

"You're an interesting woman, Selena Freyton. Or do you prefer Browntree these days?"

"I prefer, your grace," she replied, perhaps a bit too tartly.

The man gave a dry chuckle at that. "No you don't. Titles are irritating, cumbersome things. They're like being stuck with a heavy cloak, nice when it's cold but suffocating if it's not."

Selena said nothing, waiting for him to continue.

The voice came again but from further around to her left. He'd moved and she hadn't heard a step. "You've made quite an impact in the short time you've been here. Enough that even I've heard about it."

"Interesting," she replied. "Do you suppose we could stop this production though? This dramatic little scene here, with you prowling around me in the dark? It's worse than a cheap mummers play."

He chuckled again. It was an easy, well-practised laugh, and Selena knew just by listening that it was not even a nodding acquaintance of genuine humour. "A touch abrupt, don't you think?"

"What I think, sir, is that I have better things to do with my time than loiter in abandoned warehouses," Selena replied. She'd given up trying to locate him but her eyes were finally beginning to adjust and, as he shifted again, she caught the edges of his movement, turning so she'd be facing him when he spoke again.

"To business then," he said, "You are aware, through Sturgeon I don't doubt, that I have a certain position in our fair city."

Was that a faint note of disappointment in his voice? Irritation? Had she spoilt his little game? "I am," she replied.

"You've not been here long enough to understand how Celstwin really works. There are two cities within Celstwin's walls, not one. Our illustrious King Pieter rules over his gleaming marble. I rule something far more real."

Selena sighed. "I fail to see what this has to do with me, and frankly this is growing tiresome. I'm given to understand you hold Raysh captive. What is it you want with him?"

Flint struck steel and a burst of sparks resulted in a glowing wisp of rope, and then a lamp's gentle light. The man stood only twenty feet from her, beside a table set with two chairs.

"Come. Sit with me." The lamplight and his voluminous hooded cloak served to hide his face as effectively as the darkness had.

Selena sighed "A hooded cloak? Really?"

"I have my reasons for remaining anonymous, lady," he replied stiffly.

"Anonymity has its uses, I suppose, though it does make it rather difficult to have a real conversation. What am I to call you? Tenebris Gatun? I think we both know that's not actually your name. The Hidden King?" She shook her head and gave a mock shudder.

He studied her in silence for a moment, and then barked a rough laugh. "You're an interesting one, Freyton. Call me Gatun for now. You're right, it's not my real name, of course, but it'll serve."

"Master Gatun then." She nodded in greeting and moved to sit in the closest chair, toying with the wooden cup as she watched him in silence.

"Captive isn't really the right word anyway. About Raysh, I mean." The man picked up a bottle. "Wine?" Selena shook her head. "I hope you don't mind if I do then." He carried on speaking as he worked the cork loose. "Raysh is more along the lines of an unwilling guest, though I realise that's more or less the same thing. Aside from anything else he's been treated far too well to have been a captive. As for what I want with him? Nothing. He was simply a means of arranging this meeting. In fact he's already on the way back to your villa."

She picked at the tips of her glove, pulling the fabric loose around her fingers as he sat and sipped at the cup. "I see, so then what is it you want with me?"

"Pieter is a simple enough man to understand," he said, turning the cup slowly on the table. "He wants power and is jealous of the power he already holds. I understand that. It's a sensible enough thing. In his own way, he's not a stupid man either. He recognises things for what they are, recognises Celstwin for what it is and, for the most part, we've been able to work around each other. There have been occasions when he's crossed the line and I've dealt with that. By the same token there have been times when I've probably gone a bit too far and he's been quick to let me know that too."

"So you have an accord then?"

"No," he said dismissing it quickly. "Nothing so formal. He is aware that there is an organisation controlling the Warrens and that there are forces that work to maintain a level of order and restraint here and throughout Celstwin. That's about as far as it goes."

Selena tugged the glove off and made a circle of her finger and thumb around it, pulling it through with the other hand. "A gentlemen's agreement then. He leaves you alone, in return you leave him alone."

Gatun snorted a laugh at that, genuine this time and as different from the earlier chuckle as a laugh could be. "A gentlemen's agreement. I like that. I suppose it could be, though I don't think I could be described as a gentleman."

"I don't know, the standard seems to have been slipping of late," Selena replied with a wry smile.

He took a deep drink and wiped his mouth with the back of the hand that held the cup. "There are a lot of rumours about you, Freyton. You've stirred up a remarkable amount of trouble in a very short space of time. Now don't get me wrong, turmoil can be good for business but that all depends on how far it goes."

"Doesn't everything?"

He ignored that. "You're going to topple Pieter, that's clear enough. What I want to know is what happens next."

Selena drew in a breath before she could stop herself. "I didn't come here to dethrone a king."

"That's a wonderful attempt to dodge the question, girl." Gatun growled. "I thought we were done with playing games?"

She frowned at that. This wasn't going the way she'd intended. "I came to petition the king for aid—"

"I know what you've asked Pieter for," he interrupted. "I also know he told you to run along and make needlepoint or croquet or whatever it is you highborn ladies do."

"I suspect you mean crochet," Selena murmured through a smile.

"Whatever." He shrugged. "I also know about your plan for this council of nobles or whatever it is you're calling it. This plan of yours may amount to nothing more than a big mess next to the headsman's block for someone to clean up, or it might go much further. This puts me in an interesting position. From my perspective Pieter isn't a bad man to have on the throne. He's easily distracted and not overly concerned with the lives of the common folk. This makes him good for business. A few well-placed words would put an end to your plans."

Selena nodded and motioned for him to continue.

"On the other hand," Gatun said, "I have interests in Kavtrin as well as Celstwin. Bjornmen burning down the harbour is not going make for reasonable profits."

He drained his cup and tilted the neck of the bottle at her again. Selena started to shake her head, then thought better of it. "Why not?" she muttered.

"You're remarkably well informed," Selena said taking the cup from him. "The truth of the matter is I'm not entirely sure what happens next. You want to know what happens if Pieter falls? What happens to you and the status quo? I suppose that would rather depend on who takes the throne, though I don't imagine there would be too much upheaval. If it were me, which of course it won't be, I would leave things largely as they are."

"Largely?" Gatun scoffed. "There's enough scope in there for just about anything."

Selena smiled over the rim of her cup. The wine really was rather good. "Well, you seem to be administering a significant portion section of this city, and doing it rather well. I see no reason for that to change. There is the issue of contribution of course."

"Contribution?" he blurted with a laugh.

Selena ignored that. "You've also just hinted rather loudly about business interests stretching as far as Kavtrin and I don't doubt you have fingers in pies in Savarel as well. Even if we just look at your operation here in Celstwin the Warrens still use the sewers, the waterways. One thief can be a parasite and have little impact, entire districts of three cities cannot."

"Taxation then," Gatun said. "You want to tax the thieves and whores?"

She shrugged. "Why not? I'm pragmatic enough to recognise that stopping thievery in any city this size is next to impossible, not to mention expensive. I'd suggest we simply look the other way provided the activities remain within acceptable limits."

"You've a lot to learn about bargaining, your grace." The smirk was clear despite the shadows from his hood hiding his face. "You've just told me it would be impossible to stop the thieves and now you want to charge them a tax? Why should I pay?"

"I said next to impossible," Selena said with a grim smile. "That doesn't mean things couldn't be made uncomfortable for you. A city-wide surplus tax dedicated to funding a larger constabulary would make things rather difficult for you I'd imagine? How would your profits fare if every street were patrolled every hour? If every brothel without a licence were shut down? And what if this were expanded out to Kavtrin and Savarel as well?"

"You're threatening me?" Gatun growled, incredulous.

"Weren't you just threatening me?" Selena asked lightly. "No. It's not a threat, this is all conjecture after all. If I had my way I'd leave you in place. There are sections of society that the crown never touches. Much better to have it administered by someone the crown chooses to work with and keep it centralised than the alternative. It's just so much easier to deal with one person than a hundred little ambitions with legs.

"Besides, as I already said, it would never be me on the throne. That said, I think it could be agreed that if the outcome of the Council of Lords results in Pieter being removed your position would remain unchanged."

"Results in him being removed." Gatun laughed. "You high-born folk are too delicate. In the Warrens a man in the way just gets a length of steel in his belly."

"Unfortunately for us Pieter doesn't live in the Warrens." Selena smiled.

"No, he doesn't," Gatun agreed. "You're ten times a fool if you think he's just going to sit back and watch you decide his fate though."

"I don't see that he really has much choice," Selena retorted. "Not if the Council decides otherwise."

"Now, don't go ruining the good impression you've made by talking shit," Gatun warned her. "Pieter has his own reasons for letting things get this far but he's not going to sit back and let you depose him. At some point you're going to have to get some steel involved."

Selena winced. "If I'd wanted open insurrection I'd never have called for a Council. We can't afford to get bogged down in a pointless civil war right now."

Gatun sat back and, for a moment, Selena caught a glimpse of his mouth. He was younger than she would have guessed. "Pieter might disagree with you. If his plans go badly then he'll send men to fix them. I assume you have the men to deal with it when he sends the troops out?"

"We're not unprotected, no," Selena admitted. "But then that just takes us back to civil war. We can't afford to have our men fighting Pieter's."

Gatun emptied his cup and reached for the wine to refill it. "Then it seems to me you need to remove the threat."

"An interesting notion. What do you suggest?" Selena asked.

"I have a few knives at my disposal," Gatun shrugged. "They could be made available, for a price."

"You can't simply cut their throats, Gatun." Selena gasped. "We're not talking about twenty men here. Pieter probably has a good few thousand men garrisoned here in Celstwin. And even if you could we're going to need those men."

"Six thousand," Gatun told her flatly. "He has six thousand men, plus another ten in forts around the city that could be called in. That's enough to quash your little rebellion in about five minutes I'd say."

She sat back, eyes narrowing, and then leaned again, resting her arms on the table. "So what do you suggest?"

"You don't want those men dead," Gatun told her. "Even if it was possible it's not a good idea with the Bjornmen marching towards Kavtrin. What you need is for them to be neutralised for a time."

"True," Selena agreed. "And how exactly does one achieve this?"

"Soldiers are a pretty predictable lot. Not a lot of initiative, by and large." Gatun swirled the wine in his cup, and then drank, sighing appreciatively. "Take away their orders and they tend to do a lot of milling about. The trick," he said, raising a finger as he held his cup, "would be to make sure those orders never arrive. A few knives on the right necks, a few whispered conversations, and I think you'll find a whole host of captains and the like completely forget how to do their jobs."

Selena shook her head. "These are soldiers, Gatun. They're not going to be cowed by threats or a few rusty knives. I expect they're more than capable of looking after themselves. All you'd achieve would be getting your own men killed."

Gatun nodded. "You're probably right. But then I didn't say which necks I was talking about. Wives and children can make much more compelling arguments."

"That's…a bit contemptible isn't it?" she asked him.

He pointed a finger at her. "No, it's getting things done. It's not as if anyone is going to come to any real harm provided they do as they're told."

She frowned. "What about those officers who don't have children or wives, or those who just ignore you?"

"There won't be many," he told her. "Besides their response will be uncoordinated and confused."

Selena pondered this and looked at him, narrowing her eyes. "And you're willing to do this out of the goodness of your heart are you?"

Gatun laughed. "I like you, Freyton, but not that much. Me and mine will provide this service for the sum of twenty thousand crowns."

Selena blinked. It was a ridiculous figure. "Out of the question. That number is outrageous."

The hooded figure nodded. "I thought you might say that. I would, however, be willing to waive that fee if you were to agree not to implement the taxes you mentioned for five years."

"I'm not sure that twenty thousand would cover the taxes, Gatun," Selena said with a smile.

Gatun laughed and raised his cup in salute. "But then, without my help, I doubt you'll be in a position to collect those taxes anyway."

Selena had to laugh at that. "You may have a point. Agreed then, Master Gatun."

"It's been a pleasure doing business with you, your grace," he said as he raised his cup in salute.

* * *

"This really is rather good, Salisbourne," Jantson said, raising the crystal tumbler of whiskey.

"I'm surprised you can still tell." Selena cast a downwards look at the man over one shoulder. "You've been swilling it down since we arrived."

"I'm nervous," Jantson began. "No, scrap that. I'm damned well scared, as well you should be! Pieter simply pulled Raysh out of his house and had him tortured for days. The man has no limits. We could all be next."

"Oh, pull yourself together, man," Selena snapped. "Raysh has been back for a week now. If Pieter was going to have a knee-jerk reaction he'd have done it already. Besides, he has no idea where Raysh is. Only that he's gone." She looked over at the older man at the sideboard as he poured another drink. "Uncle Thomas, has there been any word?"

"Word, my dear?" he asked, not taking his eyes from the drink he was pouring.

"About the Council, Uncle." Honestly, was there no help to be had here?

"Oh, that." Salisbourne sipped at the tumbler. "Yes, a number have arrived already. Curiosity if nothing else, I suppose. Another day or so and I expect we'll have enough to get started."

"Enough?" Jantson raised an eyebrow.

"The numbers are a bit fuzzy on this," Selena admitted. "With the expansion east there have been a number of lordships created. Not only that, but the duchies, earldoms, and what-have-you that existed in Abaram's time have all but vanished. They've been merged, split, and then pushed back together again so many times that the original notion of the Council just wouldn't work. There are far more than the original twelve duchies now and who know how many baronies they are now."

"A hundred and thirty-eight," Jantson said, and then flushed as the eyes fell on him. "It's always good to keep up, you know?" He shrugged.

"Regardless," Selena said. "We're going to have to work on a two thirds majority. The Pact worked on the same basis anyway, it just dressed it up differently."

"And you think this can be achieved, do you?" Jantson asked.

Selena raised an eyebrow. What was going on here? The man was suddenly very formal. "Don't you?"

"I don't know." Jantson sighed and sank down into a chair. "You know, Selena, there's something about this whole process that unsettles me. Voting. Numbers and scraps of paper. That's no way to remove a king or to choose a new one. Whatever happened to divine right?"

Selena swallowed hard to keep from spitting the water out. "Divine right? Don't be absurd, Janton. Before this New Days nonsense there hadn't been a religion in Anlan since before Caltus. Nodding at the Lord of Midwinter hardly counts either. It's closer to wishing winter would hurry along and finish than anything else.

As for choosing a new king I'd much rather use scraps of paper than the traditional method. We've Bjornmen settling whole counties of Anlan. We can't really afford a civil war at the moment."

Jantson tilted his head in a motion that was probably an approximation of a shrug and took another drink. "What is keeping them anyway?"

"Rentrew's with him," Salisbourne told him. "He can't move very fast at the moment, that's all. He probably shouldn't be moving at all, to my mind. From what you told me, Selena, Pieter's butcher fairly did him in."

"And you say we've no reason to be nervous," Jantson said from the bottom of his glass.

Selena gave him a look and then rose to her feet, knuckling the small of her back with a sigh. "Where's Agatha? I thought you said she'd be back?"

Salisbourne grimaced. "I was rather hoping you wouldn't ask that."

Selena cocked her head with a frown, the question unspoken.

"She's at some function at the palace," Salisbourne admitted. "A garden party or some nonsense."

She blinked, thrown for a second. "At the palace? Are you sure that's entirely wise?"

"I don't govern her affairs, Selena," Salisbourne snapped.

"Don't be so peevish, Uncle," she chided with a smile. "I'm the one supposed to be prone to mood swings remember?"

Salisbourne nodded with a pained expression. "You're right, and I apologise. She downright refused not to go actually. Told me to mind my own bloody business, as I recall."

Jantson snorted into the bottom of his glass. He was well on the way to being drunk, Selena decided. She opened her mouth to speak, but then glanced at the door at the sound of distant voices, raised in anger and protest.

"Uncle?" she asked, looking to Salisbourne.

He frowned, setting his glass down and heading towards the door as the commotion grew louder.

"Just what is going on here?" he demanded as he wrenched the door open. Selena followed to find men in golden armour and crimson uniforms stood holding back a cluster of servants as another man, an officer by the looks of things, addressed Salisbourne.

"I tried to stop them, my lord—" a servant began but fell silent at a raised hand as the officer gave a curt bow and spoke.

"Lord Salisbourne, I apologise that I must do this in your home. I am charged by his majesty to take you into custody under charges of treason and sedition."

Selena ignored the gasps and whispers of the servants. "The Kingsworn does not normally conduct arrests. I assume you have a King's Warrant and this has been signed by the Lords High Justice and the Lord Chancery, Major…?" she asked with a glance at the braiding on the man's shoulder.

"Gomen," he replied. "I am charged by the word of the king himself, madam, and I know of no such people."

"Your grace," Selena grated.

That stopped him and his eyes passed over her, taking in her gown and finery. "My apologies, your grace. Would I be correct in assuming you are the Duchess Freyton?"

She inclined her head. "You would."

He nodded. "Then I am afraid to inform you, your grace, that I am under orders to detain you also."

"You are aware that the arrest of a duke or duchess on charges of treason cannot be ordered simply on the king's whim?" Selena told him, icy calm in the face of it all. "The Pact itself lays down this limitation on the king's power."

"I am oath-bound to fulfil the king's wishes, your grace," Gomen said with a small shrug. "I have no great knowledge of law, or of ancient pacts, but I would carry out the king's wishes regardless."

"Your oath is to the office, Major, not to Pieter. Don't lose sight of that." She paused then, peering past him as if confused. "This isn't really all the men you've brought with you is it?"

The glance was involuntary but it told her everything she needed to know. "Really? You came to charge us with treason and sedition and brought only, what? Ten men with you?"

"The remainder of my company waits in the courtyard, your grace," Gomen replied stiffly as he drew himself up.

"Isn't that where your guard's barracks are, Uncle?" Selena asked, throwing the words over one shoulder.

Gomen's eyes narrowed and Selena felt the warning touch of Salisbourne's hand on her arm. "I do not accept your charges, Major Gomen," she told him. "Or the authority of Pieter to levy them. I will, however, accept you as our escort to the palace where I shall speak to the king."

"My orders were to escort you to Chaldragne, your grace." Gomen almost managed to hide the wince as he spoke.

"The prisons? With the rapists and murderers? I hardly think so," Selena replied, her voice thick with indignation and disdain. "No, you will escort myself and Earl Salisbourne to the palace to speak with the king. I will accept nothing less. We really don't want to get the household guard involved in this now do we? I'm sure your Kingsworn are far superior troops but how many do you really have with you?"

"I can easily return with a superior force, your grace," Gomen warned her quietly.

"Only if we let you leave, my dear," she said as she smiled sweetly. "Now, isn't it going to be much better if you take us to the palace to speak to Pieter than if we take *you* to the palace to speak to Pieter?"

His eyes met hers for the space of three breaths before they fell.

"Shall we then?" she reached for Salisbourne's arm and met Jantson's eyes where he stood grey-faced in the doorway. "Council," she mouthed. "Now."

Chapter Thirteen

The carriage was cramped with Gomen and the soldier he'd insisted cram in with them. Selena sat in silence, looking out of the window as it wound its way through the streets. Gomen's Kingsworn rode proud on their chargers to either side of the carriage, forcing the crowds back out of the way. It was largely a futile effort and the throng pressed close, moving out of the way only when it became clear it was a case of move or be trampled. A full troop of Kingsworn was a rare and impressive sight and the gawkers slowed their progress to a slow walking pace.

Salisbourne's own guards followed behind the carriage in a column with almost double the numbers of Gomen's men. It was obvious to all of them that they were there mostly for show. Her threats had been empty and it had shocked her that they hadn't rung hollow as she'd uttered them. Regardless of the numbers, Gomen's Kingsworn would have cut through the household guard like a knife through wet paper.

Salisbourne's estate was on the outskirts of the city and they'd wound through the narrow streets at a crawl, impeded by the press of people. It had been so fast she'd almost missed it. A glimpse of a face in a passing carriage as they'd pushed out towards the centre of Celstwin. The face wore a look of surprise and frustration, and was gone in an instant, but she was sure it had been Raysh.

Now though, they'd reached the broader avenues and the carriage clattered over the cobbles towards the palace. Salisbourne had tried to catch her eyes more than once, a worried frown on his face, but she'd ignored him.

Despite the delays the trip to the palace was over too soon. It was too short a time to think things through and just long enough to allow for worry. The wheels crunched over the fine gravel as they passed through the gates and came to a stop.

"Your grace?" Gomen said from the doorway, a touch of annoyance creeping into his voice.

"Hmm?" She glanced down at him from where she'd been making a show of examining her fingernails.

"I'm going to have to ask you to step down from the carriage, your grace," he told her, a hint of annoyance creeping into his voice.

"Of course," she said as she smiled at him. "Mustn't keep the king waiting now must we?"

She made her own way inside, moving just slightly faster than Gomen and his men to make sure it was they who followed her and not the other way around. She glanced back once and noted that Salisbourne's guards had been smoothly diverted. They were on their own from this point.

Pieter leaned to one side on the throne as they entered, listening as a red-robed attendant read from a sheaf of papers. He glanced up at the doorway as they paused inside the doorway and his eyes widened. One hand waved the attendant away as he leaned forward on the throne, eyes glittering in the light.

"Gomen, I'm assuming you have an explanation for this?" he asked in a quiet voice.

"My apologies, your majesty," Gomen replied from the depths of a bow. "The duchess insisted on being taken to the palace."

Pieter shook his head slightly and curled his lip. "And are you in the habit of taking orders from women, Gomen?"

"She threatened her household guard, your majesty," Gomen explained.

"Then you should have died, Gomen," Pieter snapped. "Fulfilled your oath." He turned his gaze away from the major. "You, woman. What have you to say for yourself?"

Selena glanced at Salisbourne, and then met the king's eyes coolly. "Your majesty?"

"Don't play games with me, woman. You haven't the wit for it." He fairly threw the words at her, contempt heavy in every one. "You plot treason and sedition in my own city, setting my own nobles against me? Explain yourself or you'll swing this very hour!"

Anger flared within her, unexpected and as dangerous as lightning in dry grass. "What do I have to say for myself, my king? What do you have to say for yourself? You have ignored calls for aid against the Bjornmen incursion from myself, Rentrew, and who knows how many other lords and nobles. You ignore the plight of the peasants as entire villages are burnt to the ground. You dare send men to arrest your nobles with no thought to form or process, violating the most central tenants of the

Pact. You, sir, are no king. I declare you unfit to rule and call for a Council of Lords to fill the throne you squat in. By law and tradition I can commit no treason until the Council is complete."

Pieter pulled himself up out of the throne, visibly shaking in his anger. "Pact!" he spat, flecks of spittle flying from his lips as he stalked down the three steps from the dais. "What pact holds power over me? I rule here, I am king. Abaram's Pact is nothing more than the dusty memory of a bygone age. It holds no sway with me."

"With no Pact then there is no crown," Selena stated flatly.

"Bah, empty words." Pieter waved a disgusted hand to sweep away her statement. "Who are you to dictate to me? Your only claim to your lands is the child in your belly. Your family sold you to Freyton, hoping the title would rub off on you. Women should never be nobles, they lack the intelligence for statecraft and the only thing you did to become a duchess was to promise to open your legs. You stupid woman! I declare the Pact abolished, now where does that leave you?"

The chamber fell quiet for a moment with nothing but the furious scratchings of the pens at work behind Pieter to break the silence.

Pieter let his words sink in for a few breaths, smiling down at Selena. "Gomen," he snapped. "Take these traitors to Chaldragne. Let them sit in the darkness and listen to the howls of the lost for a time."

Gomen snapped his heels together and gave a curt bow before turning to Selena and Salisbourne and his men. "Take them."

Salisbourne shook off the kingsworn that grasped his arm. "Take your hands off me, man," he snapped, outraged.

Selena stood cold and silent, reality sitting bitter in her mouth as the men surrounded them. The double doors swung open at their approach and then Gomen froze. Troops in an array of colours flooded into the throne room. Reds, greens and greys, mixed in with Salisbourne's blues, and her own blue and green. Behind them Jantson and Rhenkin stood with others she couldn't name.

Protect the king!" Gomen shouted out as he drew his sword and rushed back towards the throne. Papers flew as the scribes rushed from their long benches and fled towards the doors at the other end of the chamber. It hung there as both groups watched each other warily, then a sword lashed out and the room descended into chaos.

Selena found herself bundled across the room and behind the lines as swords crashed through steel and flesh and the floor ran with blood.

She wrestled free of Salisbourne's grip. "No!" she cried out, spotting Captain Coulson amongst the men. "Coulson, stand your men down." She looked about wildly and forced her way through to Jantson and Rhenkin, "Stop this. Stop it now." They looked at her blankly. "This is the moment, right now, don't you see? We can either do this according to law and the Pact and hold this country together or we can sink into years of civil war and the Bjornmen will sit back and watch as we destroy ourselves. Call your men back!"

The doors the scribes had fled through at the far end of the throne room crashed open and more kingsworn flooded in, surrounding the king and forming a line of gold and steel that stretched across the room.

"Major Gomen," Selena called out into the silence that hung between them. "King Pieter has violated Abaram's Pact by ignoring calls for aid against the Bjornmen invasion. I have called a Council of Lords, the first in centuries, to hold him to account for his actions. It was knowing this that he ordered you to arrest us. Our men will stand down. I call upon you to honour your oath. Protect Anlan. Protect the crown as I call the king to account."

Gomen glanced at Pieter, and then back to Selena.

"Bjornmen." Pieter's mouth twisted in disdain. "There are no Bjornmen. Your attempts to have me send forces east, to leave lands here defenceless against your treason, they end here." He looked left and right along the line of household guards facing his kingsworn. "You are all good men. Loyalty is a fine thing but you have been taken in by these traitors. A pardon to any man who lays down his sword, the gallows for those who do not."

The first sword clattered loud upon the stones and with it Selena's hopes died.

"Get her out of here," she heard someone saying, Salisbourne perhaps? It didn't matter. She stumbled along as her own men bundled her through the palace, forming up tight around her and Salisbourne. Dimly she was aware of Jantson further behind her and the crash of fighting. Not all of their men had laid down their weapons apparently. It didn't matter though, they were outmatched. They were done.

The steps to the palace bristled with spears and swords held ready as she passed through. The bulk of their forces had yet to enter the palace and as Raysh passed through the grand entrance she frowned. The kingsworn were an elite force, even outnumbered they should have torn through her men. How was it they had managed to escape, much less form up on the steps? Why weren't they pursuing? For that matter where were Pieter's regular troops. The order should have been given by now.

She pulled free of Salisbourne's hand, standing taller and looking around them.

"Selena, really, my dear, we must move," Salisbourne told her but she shook her head. Something was wrong here. Either that or something was terribly right. She looked towards the entrance to the palace, and then behind her to the palace gates. Kingsworn and regular troops should have been flooding through both by now.

A flutter of movement caught her eye as she backed away from the steps and she looked up to the roof of the palace. The king's standard twisted in the breeze as it fell, cut free from the flagpole that now stood empty. A section of ragged black cloth was hoisted up the pole as she watched, unfurling as the wind tugged at it and set it to flapping in the wind. The cloth would have been almost impossible to see in the darkness of night. The answer came to her unbidden. It was the flag of the Hidden King.

She closed her eyes tight against the sight, and then the sound of a horn rang. It was deep, so deep as to rumble rather than sound brassy, and the sound spread across Celstwin, leaving a shocked silence in its wake. The horn had not sounded in a hundred years. Celstwin was under attack.

* * *

The ships pushed their way through the early morning fog, the slow steady strokes of the oars driving them onward as they followed the wake of the smaller boats running ahead of them and sounding the channel.

Fires from the ruined forts lit the skies behind them, the flames lending an orange glow to the fog. Keiron pressed his knuckles to the wooden rail and looked to his left at the water as it was split by the prow of the galley reaver. The channel had been plotted three times already but it never hurt to be sure. Even knowing this he chafed at the delay.

A quiet voice came from behind him. "We should be coming up on the last of their forts in another few minutes, Shipmaster."

He grunted and then spoke without turning. "Good, make sure the weaponsmaster knows and is standing ready. I want them dealt with as quickly as possible. We're too bunched up here for my liking." He listened to the receding footsteps before shaking his head. "Damn you, Klöss. This should be your expedition. I'm too old for this."

"Set them to burn, Keiron. Make them pay," the sealord had told him. It sounded easy enough at the time, made sense, too, in a vengeful way. War is all about perception. The Anlish needed to know that they weren't going to let them come in and wipe out their villages without some kind of payback.

"There's names for those that talk to themselves," came the voice from behind him.

Keiron glanced back at the oarsmaster with a smile. "I've been called lots of things in my time, Harald."

The old man joined him at the rail. "I don't doubt it. You've earned most of those names twice over too."

"You're no innocent virgin yourself," Keiron grunted. He pulled his helm free and scratched at his scalp through the thick grey hair.

Harald gave him a sidelong glance and stared back down at the water before turning to face him. "What are you thinking?"

Keiron snorted a laugh. "That I'm too old for this. This whole plan of Frostbeard's, it's a young man's game."

Harald smiled. "You're probably right but we're here now. The last gasp of old men and you're younger than me. I can't let you feel your age, not while I still have oarsmen to shout at."

The grizzled old man grunted at that and looked around at the sky behind them. "Sun's thinking about coming up. We're going to be backlit."

"By the time they see us it'll be too late." Harald said, undecided whether he was reassuring the oarsmaster or himself. "I still can't believe these little forts are all they've got defending the river."

"You heard the sealord the same as I did," Keiron grunted. "These people, they don't ride the waves. If it doesn't come over land they don't worry about it."

Harald shook his head. "It's a strange thing."

Keiron looked to the catapult perched high in the prow, and then to the others on their platforms either side of the deck. Everything seemed to be in order. The weaponsmaster knew his craft, but then Keiron would never have made shipmaster if he'd left everyone to do their jobs.

"You're right," he admitted, looking back to Harald. "It's a strange thing but no stranger than turning horses into beasts of war. You might as well use a bull or a cow."

Harald nodded, missing the humour. "I'd better get back. Relgan will have them all rowing backwards if I leave him too long."

Kieron nodded and grasped the man's wrist tight. He didn't say the word, wishing luck before a battle was as good as calling for your own death. He turned without a word and made his way forward to the prow.

The fort was just becoming visible as he arrived, emerging from the bend on the river with torches burning bright against the remaining tendrils of fog.

"Take them as soon as you're ready," he told the weaponsmaster who stood bent low and speaking to the men at the carefully tended fire. "The others will follow us."

"As you say, Shipmaster." The old man nodded up at him.

Another old one, Keiron thought. I've filled this boat with grandfathers who've never sired sons. He stepped to the side, giving the men room to do their work, and watched as the long pole bearing the red flag was raised high. Moments later the catapult lurched, throwing itself forward against the thick ropes holding it in position. A trail of smoke streaked across the sky, joined by two others as the crews on the weapons platforms joined in. Two missed, one into the river itself and another exploding on the bank, spreading a pool of fire that belched black smoke high. The last firepot flew true and exploded at the entrance to the stone fort. Even from this distance Kieron could hear the screams, and as the reavers behind and to either side of his vessel began their own attack he knew the fort was doomed. A single horseman managed to escape, dragging the terrified creature from its stable and somehow calming it enough to let him mount before he galloped away from the fleet. The warning wouldn't help them. These people were like baby birds fallen from the nest. Against the galley reavers they were helpless and exposed. He nodded once at the weaponsmaster, thanks for a job well done, and quickly.

The fleet had been split into three parties long ago, with the other two raiding towns on the coast to both the north and south of this river. Keiron's own fleet now numbered sixty vessels, spread out behind him and arranged into groups of three that sailed in a V formation.

The muffled drumbeat drove the oarsmen onwards. Spray flew up from the prow as the wind picked up, driving the waves of the river against them. Keiron climbed up onto the catapult platform, grabbing a line that led up to the mast and the furled sails as he planted a foot on the rail itself and leant forward, eyeing the horizon hungrily.

The city was huge. He'd been told by the men from the scout boats who'd sounded the channel that it was massive but it was one thing to hear and another thing to see it. It filled the valley in a way that Hesk never could. Where Hesk was cramped and clung to every available surface this city sprawled, stretching out with languorous abandon away from the river.

Bridges spanned the river that ran through the centre of the city. Some were high, arched affairs, resting on thick stone supports that thrust down through the water. Others were low, simple stone structures. He'd been warned but, again, it was another thing to see it. They'd never penetrate to the city centre unless they destroyed the low bridges that blocked their path.

"Signal the fleet," he said to the man behind him. He nodded to the weaponsmaster. From this point on the man would be largely in control of the reaver.

The fleet spread out, the gaps between the groupings growing larger still. As the first buildings inside the walls came within range the catapults lurched, hurling the smoking pots into the buildings close to the banks. Flames were already belching high from some of them by the time the second group of ships came into range and began their own barrage.

The fleet pushed deeper into the city, bringing destruction with it. As they passed under the first high bridge a deep, brassy horn sounded again and again, the sound mixing with the screams of panic and the Bjornmen set the place to burn.

Keiron hunched low behind the wall of shields clustered around the prow as they approached the first bridge. The defenders had been slow to gather themselves and the river was too wide for arrows to reach them from the banks with any accuracy unless the ships came close to the shore. The high bridge was a perfect platform for them and the arrows were flying in volleys, arcing high into the air before falling in a deadly hail. He swore to himself and shouted over to the weaponsmaster. "Give them something to worry about."

The bridge was an easy target and the three firepots exploded within seconds of each other, engulfing the stone bridge in flames. The archers had scattered as soon as they saw them launch but the screams were enough to tell Keiron it had worked well enough.

Warehouses and docks waited beyond the bridge and the fleet rushed in like wolves among sheep. The air was thick with smoke and the almost constant sound of the catapult's barrage.

A number of small boats, filled with Anlish archers firing flaming arrows, had been launched but they were quickly destroyed or driven off. As they came within range of the next bridge Keiron called for the catapults to be loaded with stone. Where the last bridge had been tall and graceful, this was a low, squat structure.

Flaming arrows arced high from the bridge and the bank as the reaver drifted too close to the shore and Keiron swore as he watched them come, crouching low behind the shields. A shout, too late to be any use, was the only warning Keiron had as a catapult on the bank hurled a hail of rocks from the edge of the bridge. The stones, none larger than a man's fist, churned the water to foam beside the reaver. They'd missed but the next shot would have them, Keiron knew. The speed with which the catapult had been moved into position and the shot calculated told him enough. These men were not without skill.

A shout back at the oarsmaster had the galley reaver moving backwards sluggishly as the men struggled with the awkward stroke. If not for the current of the river helping them it would have been a futile effort. The galley reaver was simply too large to be moved on a simple stern stroke. The massive stone crashed into the water, sending it skyward only to patter down onto the deck. Keiron opened his mouth to give the order but the weapons crews were already moving, turning the catapults on their platforms to line up the shot. Fire exploded on the bank, too far away to cause the enemy weapon any damage but close enough to force the men to abandon their shot and try and move the engine.

Screams and a crash turned his head and Keiron saw the reaver on their left engulfed in flames. Another barrage of rocks smashed into it as he watched, and tore through wood and flesh alike. The boat was doomed and Keiron silently praised their steersman for edging it to the side of the river, as much as he fought the guilty relief it had been them and not his reaver.

He glanced behind them at the galley reavers drawing closer and swore. If they bunched up here they were as good as dead.

"Weaponsmaster, get that bridge down," he roared and within minutes the first barrage of stone began. The rocks had been gathered from the mouth of the river and carefully hoarded. The barrage increased as other reavers came within range and the bridge began to crumble under the onslaught.

A section of the bridge crashed down, sending spray skyward but Keiron already knew this was no good. The gap was nowhere near wide enough and who knew how the stones now lay beneath the waterline.

A trail of smoke from the firepot coursed across the sky, joined by others, and all going the wrong direction. Screams from the reavers behind him told him all he needed to know and, as he looked around at the flames belching from the city on both sides of the river, he nodded. "Enough," he said to himself.

"Oarsmaster, get the men ready." He called, turning to the flagman before the oarsmaster started bellowing orders. "Signal the withdrawal, get those reavers moving."

The signal passed down from ship to ship and the ungainly vessels began to turn, moving sluggishly in the close quarters. The Anlish catapults hurled flagstones, that had been lifted from the streets, out at the turning ships as their archers raked those close enough with flaming arrows. Keiron saw first one reaver, then two more, slow and drift aimlessly as the onslaught took its toll.

There was little he could do but huddle behind the shields and watch as the oarsmen bent to their task. The steersman knew his business and picked a delicate path between the burning wrecks. Injured men, too badly wounded to reach the water, still writhed in the embrace of the flames on the decks and the howls of agony cut deeper than any blade.

* * *

"The price was rather high but I dare say his Majesty will be forced to change his tune about the Bjornmen now, eh?" Rentrew smiled at Selena but the grin faded in the face of her icy stare.

"Rather high?" she said. "Look around you,. Look at the smoke and ashes. If you listen closely you can still hear them clearing the wreckage! Celstwin was in flames, Rentrew. Oh, not the marble clad villas, or not many of them anyway. No, the only people in Celstwin who live in wooden homes are those in the warrens. The poor, the unsightly. The price of changing *his majesty's tune* has been paid in blood. Again."

"Now, Selena," Salisbourne began gently. "I'm sure Rentrew didn't mean it like that."

"I'm sure he didn't." She sighed. "I'm sure it didn't even occur to him that the wood behind that smoke was somebody's home or the body smouldering in the ashes was somebody's mother." She looked up at both of them but the concern in their eyes reached no further than her.

"Are you sure you're ready for this, my dear?" Salisbourne asked. It was funny how she'd never noticed how fatherly he acted around her until now.

She smiled grimly. "I rather think I have to be, Uncle."

"Shall we then?" He extended an arm for her.

The palace had a different feel to it. Nothing substantial had changed but the oppressive air had left. They were met by footmen who took up a position flanking them, with one more ahead and another behind them. *Take away a servant's pomp and they would be forced to admit that they were one step above the cleaning staff,* she thought wryly. No matter that there hadn't been a Council of Lords for well over two centuries, somebody somewhere had thrown together enough pomp to make it seem ceremonious. She smirked at the thought, and then quickly set her lips. It wouldn't do to seem smug, now of all times.

The amused surprise she'd felt at the pomp of the footmen was nothing to the shock she felt as they passed the men guarding the doors and stepping into the throne room. The room was packed with the lords of Anlan and their attendants and was almost unrecognisable. Sections had been marked out with each noble sat surrounded by their servants and staff. All wore their traditional scarlet cloaks and robes of office, trimmed in white fur, and more than one chain glittered around their necks. A broad path had been left leading to the throne itself, which sat silent and empty on its dais. Selena looked to Salisbourne and then pointedly down at their clothes, plain by comparison. "I think we're a little under-dressed."

"It's been taken care of." He smiled with a wink. "Hanris, I'm afraid." He shook his head in mock despair and led her to the waiting herald.

"Lord Salisbourne, the Earl of Westermark," the herald boomed from slightly behind them. Selena winced and forced a small smile onto her lips as Salisbourne was escorted inside by a footman. The crowd of nobles, for the most part, paid no attention. Even pomp grows commonplace eventually, Selena decided.

"Her Grace, the Duchess Freyton of Druel, the Wash and the Eastern Reaches!"

the herald boomed again and her smile turned slightly pained. Heads turned at the announcement and the low rumble of quiet conversation ceased as they turned to look at her. For a moment she felt exposed under the scrutiny. What must they think? An old family forced to sell its daughter into eastern nobility. She must be everything they despised. No wonder they gawked.

She raised her chin, refusing to crawl down inside of herself, and followed the footman to her seat. Hanris stood waiting and smiled as she approached. Another fatherly smile, she noted.

"Your grace." He greeted her with a deep and formal bow.

"Hanris."

She stood still so he could drape the formal cloak around her, fastening the ornate brooch at her neck. He stepped back, allowing her to take her seat before sitting in his own, far plainer chair behind.

The procession dragged on with noble after noble entering the chamber. Though some turned heads the majority were ignored. The heavy robes and the heat of the chamber from so many bodies combined to make the place impossibly stuffy and Selena found herself almost dozing by the end of the procession.

A brassy fanfare preceded the herald, though how the man could still manage to shout was beyond Selena. "His Majesty, King Pieter the Seventh. King of Anlan and Liege of the realm."

The assemblage stood and Selena buried a sigh as she hauled herself to her feet. Standing was becoming more difficult. In fact *everything* was becoming more difficult. Frankly, the birds had the right idea with eggs and nests, as far as she was concerned.

Pieter made his way to the throne at a slow pace that was probably intended to be stately. As it was it looked awkward and, rather than giving the assembled nobles the chance to be cowed by his majesty and presence, it made him look petulant. He glared at those that met his gaze, dark eyes bright with anger as he looked from side to side. Here and there a noble gave their respects, which were met with a barely perceptible nod of acknowledgement.

Pieter climbed up on the dais and sat in the throne, arranging his robes and cloak around himself. Movement from the side of the chamber caught her eye and she raised her eyebrows as Salisbourne came to take up a position facing the assembled nobles with his back to the king.

"My lords," he began. "Allow me to be the first to formally welcome you to this, the first Council of Lords in over two centuries." A round of applause drowned his next statement and he stood in silence as he waited for the noise to subside. As he began again Selena realised with dismay that he was actually going to make a formal speech. She groaned to herself and bit the inside of her lip, using the pain to keep herself alert.

She dimly became aware that he was gesturing in her direction as he spoke. "... call our esteemed monarch to account. To that end I will surrender the floor to her grace, the Duchess Selena Freyton."

She stood, answering Salisbourne's bow with a polite nod of her own and made her way to meet him. "The floor is yours, Selena. Now is the hour," he whispered as they met.

"My Lords," she said, lifting her voice to fill the chamber. It wasn't as hard as she'd imagined, acoustics did a lot of the work for her. "I come to Celstwin fresh from the Bjornmen invasion of our land, of my duchy. The Bjornmen have plagued the coasts of the Eastern Reaches and its neighbours for decades, raiding villages and pillaging what they can. This time, my lords, they have come not to raid but to conquer. Their forces have pushed past defences designed to repel raiders not hold back an army, and they have set entire villages to the flame, driving the peasants west out of their districts and their homes."

She had them now, she knew. A whisper could have been heard in the chamber whenever she paused to draw breath. She turned and waved at the king. "This man, your king, has ignored all of our requests, all of our pleas for aid. Our forces are outmatched. Only the king's armies could hope to repel these invaders yet not one man has been sent. Our king denies the very existence of this invasion even as the Bjornmen push westwards, establishing their own farms and villages upon Anlish soil."

She allowed a hint of anger to enter into her voice, just enough to flavour the performance. "You sit upon your throne, your majesty, passing down decrees and lapping up the adoration of your sycophants. Yet it seems you forget that the throne has an obligation to the lords of Anlan, to the people of Anlan. An obligation enshrined by Abaram's Pact itself, one that you have so casually ignored. You go so far as to claim that the Bjornmen threat was nothing more than my own imaginings. Celstwin lies in ashes, my king. Tell me now that this is the result of my imaginings."

She'd probably gone further than she ought to have and the gasps she'd heard from behind her as she spoke had highlighted this, but the result was clear on his face. Pieter seethed as he glared down at her and, as he stormed to his feet, she thought for just one moment that he might strike her. That he might rage down the steps that led to his throne and grab her by the throat.

"Damn you for your impudence, Freyton," he said in a voice made all the more powerful for its quiet. The next words, however, he bellowed out in a voice that rivalled the herald's. "I am king here, in a line that traces back to Caltus and beyond. I do not recognise the authority of this council. Abaram's Pact is ancient history. It is no more valid than the laws against harbouring droos!"

He paused long enough to sit back down and leant forward, resting an arm on one knee. "I have permitted this little performance so far. It benefits the crown to demonstrate how traitors like yourself will be dealt with. Your mummery is at an end, Freyton. Know that an accounting awaits you."

"Threats, My Lord King?" Selena gave in to the drama of the moment. "Will you punish me? Do you intend to torture me as you did Lord Raysh?" She smiled sweetly at him as she saw the words hit home. "Did you think him vanished into thin air, your majesty?"

Selena turned to the lords once more. "Lord Raysh, would you come forward please?" She didn't need to turn to sense Pieter shift uncomfortably behind her as Raysh stood from a position almost lost in the shadows of the corner. He made his way slowly, leaning heavily on a cane.

"Thank you for doing this, Raysh," she murmured into his ear as he drew closer.

"I came to Celstwin seeking aid against the Bjornmen," she said, lifting her voice again for the chamber. "Baron Rentrew borders my lands and had travelled here for the same reasons. I'm sure Lord Raysh here is known to many of you. He was a stranger to me when I arrived but a close friend of Rentrew. When our king discovered he was privy to our discussions on how we might best convince him of the dangers our nation faces he took him."

She paused long enough to let the words sink in. "Raysh was abducted from his home, taken at knife point in the middle of the night. He was taken to a house in the poorest quarter of the slums, and there he was tortured. Our king, charged with the safety of the realm, kidnapped one of his own lords and did this."

Raysh ripped free the white cotton glove with his teeth, holding his hand high for all to see. The fingers were more like claws now, the flesh pared away from where the pad of each finger should have been and blackened from the coals that had seared the wounds closed.

Selena let the gasps and cries of revulsion die down before she spoke. "Was Raysh plotting treason he could have been arrested like any other traitor. Instead Raysh, like Rentrew and I, was simply asking what we could do to try and persuade the king to take action. Bjornmen have taken half of my duchy or more. They push through Baron Rentrew's lands and now, now they have set Celstwin herself to the flame. When would it have been enough for our king? He claims Abaram's Pact is dead and gone yet he claims the throne on the basis of an ages old bloodline. He demands we honour the tithe and yet refuses to defend the realm.

"This man," she said, turning to stab a finger at Pieter, "has proven himself unworthy of the throne on which he squats, toad-like in his inaction. I call upon this council to do its duty. Remove this man's crown and protect Anlan."

She fell silent as roars of outrage fought with cheers in the chamber. Pieter glared at her, hatred burning in his eyes. Though the chamber was in uproar he looked nowhere else and his fury shone.

Chapter Fourteen

"On the whole I'd say that went rather well," Salisbourne said, pouring whiskey into the crystal glasses.

Raysh shook his head. "We've torn a nation apart rather successfully, yes. I suppose you could say that."

"Don't be so dramatic, Raysh," Jantson told him, reaching for the glass Salisbourne offered. "We all knew this was never going to be an instant fix. The important thing is that Pieter is deposed."

"And so now we are a snake without a head, fighting the wolves." Raysh sneered. He glared at Salisbourne as the man made to bring the whiskey glass to him and stood with a grunt, leaning heavily on his cane.

Salisbourne frowned and sipped at the whiskey. "What would you rather, old man? That we left Pieter in place?"

"Don't be absurd," Raysh snorted. "I just feel that events have taken on a life of their own. We should never have entered into the Council without a clear plan for what happens next."

"You know what happens next," Jantson told him. "The Council will deliberate and a line will be invited to take the throne."

"And you plan to let just anyone take the throne do you?" Raysh asked. "If we'd planned for pure chance to rule we may as well have left Pieter on the throne. You know as well as I do that some of the noble houses are filled to the rafters with gibbering idiots. Take the Moorcroft's for example? They have a line going back past Caltus and not a one of them could match the intellect of an inbred sheep. Do you want one them on the throne? We may as well hand the kingdom to the Bjornmen now and have done with it!"

"Raysh, calm down," Salisbourne told him. "I never had any intention of leaving this to blind chance. The choice is an obvious one. I just wanted to discuss it with you first. That's why she isn't here yet."

"You can't mean?" Jantson blurted, bolting upright in his seat and slopping whiskey over his hand.

"Selena? A woman?" Raysh finished for him. "You can't be serious. I'll be the first to admit she is a rare specimen but come now, the nobles will never accept her."

Salisbourne smiled as he waited for them, sipping calmly at his drink. "Don't be so quick to judge, Raysh. The nobles are not as closed minded as all that. In any event, it doesn't matter what they think, it only matters what our syndicate thinks." He stepped away from the drinks cabinet and began to pace as he spoke. "Consider it, a woman on the throne. She is a remarkable woman, but still only a woman. She'd never manage without support. The southern duchies in particular will throw a merry fit. If, however, the syndicate stands with her, then we, ourselves, have the throne. Selena is just a figurehead. In one stroke we prevent the same sort of centralised idiocy that Pieter's reign embodied. The threat of empire is gone and the power of the throne dependent upon our cooperation."

Jantson nodded slowly. "So, in essence then, it takes us five steps closer to what Abaram had in mind with his pact."

"Exactly!" Salisbourne spun in place to point at him. "And without all that nonsense about a pact or written agreement. It was all stuff and nonsense if we're honest, anyway."

"I think this could be workable," Raysh muttered, easing himself back into the fine leather armchair. "This isn't something you've just cooked up though, is it? Admit it?"

Salisbourne gave a sly smile. "It's something I've had in mind for a time. If I'm honest I really had no idea who could fulfil the role until little Selena came along, but she does fit rather nicely."

"And the child?" Jantson queried. "What about that?"

Salisbourne shrugged. "The child is almost a boon. It's fatherless. Freyton is long dead. Succession is assured without any meddling consort seeking to syphon off his own power and authority. Not only that but we can mould and shape the boy as he grows. Assuming it is a boy, of course."

"You cunning old bastard." Raysh laughed.

Salisbourne raised his glass in mock salute. "You'll go along then?"

"I will." Raysh nodded. "There'll be time before any coronation to work out the finer details and get any reluctant members of the syndicate on side, but, yes, I think it's a workable plan."

"Jantson?" Salisbourne cocked an eyebrow.

"It's as good a plan as any I've heard," the Earl nodded. "I suspect Selena may prove to be more of a handful than you take her for though."

"You let me take care of Selena," Salisbourne said as he smiled. "She'll have the child to busy her mind before too long anyway."

Jantson pulled a pipe from his waistcoat and thumbed some stourweed into the bowl. "When do you propose we broach the subject with her?"

"She should be along any time now actually," Salisbourne said with a wink.

"You cut that a bit fine!" Raysh laughed.

"I had it all in hand, old friend." Salisbourne smiled. Conversation turned to other things as they waited, each casting frequent glances at the door until the servant finally knocked.

"The Duchess Freyton," the man announced.

"Hello, boys," Selena smiled. "Noses in whiskey? What a surprise!"

Salisbourne raised his eyebrows as he lowered his glass. "I'd say after the day we had yesterday that we'd earned it, wouldn't you?"

"I'd say that you'll always find an excuse, Uncle." Selena laughed.

"Can I tempt you?" Salisbourne cocked the decanter at her.

"Be serious, Uncle. It's barely past noon."

He shrugged. "Something lighter then? A wine, or perhaps a sherry?"

"Really, I'm fine." She sank down into an armchair close to the fire. "Now what's this all about?" She looked around at the three men. "You all have that conspiratorial look about you."

"I thought it was time we discussed our next steps," Salisbourne told her, settling into a chair.

"I would have thought that was rather obvious," Selena replied, giving him an odd look. "As soon as a new king has taken the throne, and order restored, I would expect our armies will march north. Even aside from their depredations in the Eastern Reaches we simply cannot allow for the attack on Celstwin to go unanswered."

"Yes, yes..." Salisbourne brushed that aside. "First, however, we need to decide who to place on the throne. This whole exercise becomes rather futile if we end up with another idiot like Pieter."

"Why do I get the feeling that I've rather blundered into something here?" Selena looked around at them.

"I wouldn't go that far." Jantson chuckled, resting the crystal tumbler on his paunch. "We're not going to insult your intelligence though, my dear. You know as well as anyone that whoever takes the throne is going to need the support of all the lords, with what's coming. We simply can't take the risk that some idiot will strike out on his own like Pieter did. You said it yourself. The invasion, the attack on Celstwin? They must be responded to."

"And so who did you have in mind?" She looked from Jantson to Raysh and settled on Salisbourne.

Salisbourne drained his glass, twisting to set it on the side table. "We were rather hoping you might take a crack at it, my dear."

"Please don't call me that, Uncle. It makes me sound about five years old." Selena pursed her lips, looking up at the ceiling. "Why me?" she asked finally. "There must be others more suitable? For that matter Pieter must have relatives, someone else in the line?"

"Second and third cousins." Salisbourne waved a hand. "Their claim would be weak at the best of times and, after what's happened, no one would bat an eye if we went another way."

"True enough." Selena nodded. "But you haven't really answered the question. Why me?"

"Forgotten Gods, Selena! Anyone would think you don't want the crown," Salisbourne burst out. He sighed, deflating as Selena levelled a look at him. "Stability, if nothing else. Our little consortium can almost guarantee you the throne. I think we need to put an end to the petty infighting before it really has a chance to take hold. We don't have time to squabble over the throne, we have a war to end."

"Yes, yes…" she said impatiently. "But why *me*? Anyone could do those things."

"Because you're a woman, Selena." Raysh told her, ignoring the sharp looks that Salisbourne and Jantson gave him. "We can sell the idea of you being the next best thing to a puppet to the consortium. At the very least you'd be considered a very friendly ear. Pieter came closer than anyone could have imagined to becoming an imperial power. It wasn't until you called the Council of Lords that most of us realised just how much power we'd lost. That thought terrifies most of the lords in Anlan, and I expect most would jump at the chance to have, what they would consider to be, a pliable monarch on the throne."

"I see." She sat back into the chair. "Do you know, Uncle? I think I will try a small glass of wine."

"Of course, my dear." He stood and went back to the drinks cabinet as Jantson stood.

"I think I might take my leave here, if that's all the same to you, your grace?" he nodded a small bow at Selena. "Someone has to bring Rentrew up to speed and I have other appointments."

"I'll come with you," Raysh said, levering himself up with the cane. "I have business of my own."

Selena sipped at the wine Salisbourne handed her, seeming not even to notice as the others left. "Well, that was interesting," she said as she sat up straight again, setting the wine down on the table. "Exactly what game are you playing, Uncle?"

His lips twitched as he winked at her. "It did go rather well didn't it?"

"I'm really not built to be anybody's puppet, Uncle," she told him with a grimace.

Salisbourne laughed. "I never imagined you would be."

"So this entire thing is a sham then?" she asked as she raised an eyebrow.

"Not entirely," he told her. "We do need stability, and I do think you're the best person to provide that. If the members of the consortium are foolish enough to think you'll be some weak little woman, unable to blow her nose without direction, then so be it."

"And Raysh?"

"He was the best," Salisbourne laughed, waving a hand at her as he grew red in the face. "The things he said to you, trying to convince you this will all be a front. He's terribly set in his ways sometimes. It'll take a good few months for him to realise that everything he said to you, thinking he was persuading you, were actually true."

"You're convinced then?" she asked. "That you have enough support in the Council to accomplish this?"

"I am," he said, suddenly all business. "Though I expect the notion will bring its own genuine supporters. You've impressed a number of people with the way you called for the Council."

Selena nodded, absorbing this. "So let me ask you again, Uncle, Why me? You've orchestrated this, why not take the throne yourself?"

"Honestly, my dear?" Salisbourne told her, leaning forward in his seat and meeting her gaze. "I'm too old for politics. Whoever takes the throne is going to have a rough ride of it and, frankly, I don't think I've ever met anyone who's as good a player as you."

A thought occurred to her and she narrowed her eyes as she spoke. "Just how long have you been planning all this, Uncle?"

"Well now, that would be telling wouldn't it, your majesty?"

"I'm not queen yet, Uncle. Let's get through the coronation first shall we?"

Salisbourne shook his head with an indelicate noise. "Coronations are for the commoners. You don't make a king or a queen with a coronation. Politics is a game played in the back rooms, everything else is just for show."

Selena didn't smile at the joke. "And Pieter?"

"Pieter." Salisbourne scratched at his cheek. "Yes, we do need to do something there I suppose. The Chaldragne springs to mind. I seem to recall he had plans to toss you in there."

"He did," Selena agreed. "I don't think so though. Putting the king in a prison for rapists and murderers rather sends the wrong message, I feel. Besides, there's always the slim chance he might get out. I was thinking something a little more public, and final."

Salisbourne's smile slipped. "Really? Do you really think that's necessary?"

"I don't like loose ends, Uncle."

"But executing him?" Salisbourne shook his head, looking uncomfortable. "You risk making him a martyr, you realise?"

Selena raised an eyebrow at him. "The thing with martyr's, my dear Earl Salisbourne, is that they tend never to be bothersome again."

"Forgotten gods, Selena! You're making me second guess myself here. I can't decide if you're going to be the greatest monarch Anlan has ever seen or a bloody tyrant."

"Isn't that the point, Uncle?" Selena purred. "Politics is a game and I never reveal my hand."

"People died, Selena," Salisbourne told her with a hint of reproach.

"I'm aware of that, Uncle," she answered. "Blood has always been the currency of politics. Gamblers play with coins but the game of power is played with lives."

PART THREE

Chapter Fifteen

"I would ask that you stay here," Aervern said, pointing to the grassy hillside behind them. "There is little point in placing you in danger and you would not find this that we do pleasant."

Miriam's head barely moved with the nod but Aervern seemed satisfied with that. Miriam turned her eyes from the distance city and gazed over the fae host. The gibbous moon was bright and the light made it easy to see even to the farthest edges of the force. Or it would have for someone with younger eyes than hers. It was both impressive and terrifying. Thousands of satyr mingled with hundreds of fae and faeborn, the latter's cyan eyes a brilliant contrast to the sea of amber. Above them all the Swarm spun lazy circles in the night sky, moonlight dancing on the wings of the fae'reeth and making the sight even more otherworldly.

Miriam stifled a laugh that was born of both humour and hysteria at the thought and Aervern glanced back at her. "Something amuses?"

Miriam shook her head and looked out over the sea of fae. The silver banners were pure glamour, the silver and blue standards glowing brighter than the eyes around them.

"Don't they worry about being seen?" she spoke without thinking. Aervern's eyes were a mystery as she regarded her before speaking. "This host you can see because you are afforded that luxury. The manlings behind their wall of stones? They see only the grass for now."

Miriam looked over the host again before looking back to the fae that waited with her. "So this is all glamour then? The banners, the armour?"

"Most is glamour. The armour? Perhaps not all of it. We, *Wildfae,*" Aervern said the word with a twist to her lips, "have long lost the knowledge of this art of fashioning, of creating armour like this. Those that endured in the Outside may have retained some. Still, more knowledge, I would expect, has been lost over the ages in that place. Most of these fae you see are wearing little more than pure glamour."

"So they're naked?" Miriam laughed but bit it back at a look from Aervern.

"Perhaps," she shrugged, unconcerned. "Though not all. We do not place such an emphasis on raiments as you humans might. We fae are not so affected by heat and cold as you. Ours is a warm world anyway and clothing is not truly necessary unless we wish it. Even so, Shaping is more strenuous than Seeming. There must be few with the patience to hoard enough of the Lady's Gift to create, even if they had the knowledge. Not when a simple spin of light has much the same result."

Miriam looked out over the fae again. The thought that most of them were naked didn't seem as funny as it ought to have. The breeze was light, but chill, and she pulled her robe tighter around her. Autumn was coming with winter fast on its heels.

"You almost sound like you feel sorry for them," she said softly.

Aervern sighed, sounding almost human for the moment. "It is a hard thing. These fae are thousands of your years older than I. Time is a strange creature and she runs at faster pace in the Outside, or so I am told. In this world, your world, time is a gentle brook idling along. My own realm is a merry stream, rushing over the pebbles and rocks. The Outside is a raging torrent. Thousands of your years must have passed whilst the *highfae*," again her lips turned in a minute grimace as she spoke and Miriam wondered if she realised she was doing it, "whilst they endured in that prison. I am no lover of this new order but I would not wish that torment on anyone." She paused as if realising something. "But then this is not new knowledge to you, is it, Miriam? You yourself endured the Outside. You know well the horrors of that place."

Miriam didn't speak but her expression must have said words her lips didn't shape and Aervern nodded once in response, looking out to the distant city.

"Why am I here?" Miriam asked.

Aervern didn't look at her as she spoke. "There are things I would have you see."

"There are always things you would have me see," Miriam muttered, though she knew the fae would hear her. The breeze was cutting through the thin fabric of her robe and her hips ached. She hunched down against the cold, trying to push the pain out of her mind.

Aervern's lips curled at the corners in a fleeting smile. "So it would seem." Her smile faded as something in the middle of the host caught her attention and she closed her eyes in concentration. A ripple passed over her form as she worked the glamour. The armour flowed down over her skin, flowing like water that shaped itself into breastplate and greaves. The plate was intricate, with delicate lines, and a shine brighter than any steel could hope to match.

"It will soon be time," she said, stepping close to Miriam. "Do not move." Aervern's hands began to glow gently as she held them over her eyes for a moment. She reached out repeating the motion but holding her hands over Miriam's eyes instead. She stepped back with a sigh and a satisfied nod. "It is done."

Miriam blinked and gave the fae an odd look. Her eyes felt strange, as if she were struggling to focus. "What is done? What have you done to me?"

Aervern gave her a confused look. "Did I not say, there are things I would have you see?"

Miriam shook her head. "I don't understand," she admitted.

"How could you see what I wish if you looked only through your own eyes?" Aervern asked her, frowning.

Miriam didn't answer that at all. Talking to the fae was confusing at the best of times and she'd found that, sometimes, the best strategy was just to remain silent and let the explanation come to her.

"You are not young, Miriam." Aervern told her. "You are untrained with blade and bow. I could not take you into battle without risk of injury to you. So I bring the sights of what I will do to your eyes myself. You will see what I see."

She felt herself gasp. "You can do that?"

Aervern shrugged Miriam's wonder aside. "It is a simple thing. No harder for any fae than it would be for you to jump into the air." She waved vaguely at the grassy rise behind them. "Remain here. The sight will come to you unbidden. I will return in time."

Miriam nodded but the fae had already turned and headed for the host. Army might have been a better word. The fae stretched farther than she could easily see, though she could easily make out Aelthen standing at the forefront. A sensation swept over her, as if a breeze had touched her for just a moment, and the army fell silent as all eyes looked to Aelthen. He raised one arm high and pointed at the distant city, and then the host surged forward.

Miriam watched as the fae rushed towards the city. There seemed no order to the host. Some raced towards the city with a speed that she still found shocking while others moved slowly, clearly in no hurry.

The strange sensation in her eyes increased as Aervern grew further away. It was painful pressure, almost like the beginnings of a headache. She eased herself down to the grass, rubbing at her eyes gently with the heels of her hands. A flash of colour in the darkness shocked her and she opened her eyes with a start, and then stiffened. The world around her was a welter of confusing images. It was as if two scenes had been laid over each other and she held her hand out before her, watching as the ghostly images of fae pushing past her ran through her flesh. Her stomach churned as the sensation of movement, and the certain knowledge she sat still on the grass warred with each other. With a lurch she fell forward onto her hands and knees and vomited into the grass.

She closed her eyes as her stomach heaved, and then her vision suddenly fell into focus. With the sight of the world around her gone, the vision she received from Aervern's magic became clear.

The fae's vision was like nothing Miriam had ever experienced. Aervern could see as well in the poor light shed by the moon and stars that peered between the clouds as Miriam could in the daytime. Not just that, but her sight was impossibly sharp. With little effort Miriam could pick out the texture of the moss growing on the stones at the base of the city wall.

It wasn't as simple as just seeing what Aervern saw, she noticed. She was restricted to the fae's field of vision but she could focus on whatever she wished. She shifted to the side, away from the stink of the mess on the grass and lay back, surrendering herself to the vision.

* * *

Miriam could pinpoint the precise moment that the glamour fell. The look of shock was clear on the Bjornman's face as he stood sentry on the wall. The glamour must have fallen in an instant, revealing the fae host that stretched out before the walls. The blood drained from his face as he stiffened, and then shook his head at the sight before him. His shouts were too far away for Miriam to hear on their own but they were joined by others, and within moments the alarm was raised. Men charged onto the walls in rushed, frantic movements, keeping low as they took up positions behind the battlements. Orders were screamed out and the confusion was obvious as men ran back and forth. Through it all the fae army stood in silence, a rock standing still in stormy seas whilst all around them the waves dashed themselves to frothy madness.

Arrows came then. Arcing high over the walls and hissing down into the host in great sheets, but they had little or no effect that Miriam could see. The fae shrugged them away like bothersome flies or simply ignored them as they bounced from their flesh.

The fae'reeth ceased their endless circling and rose high over the walls, the Swarm descending into the city beyond in a murderous cloud. The screams that followed were testament to the chaos and horror that they brought with them.

Aervern's vision shifted then as she turned her head, carrying Miriam with it while she focused on the stones beside the massive gates to the fortress. Small shoots were erupting from the earth and grasping the wall as the ivy snaked up out of the ground, heeding Aelthen's call. The horned creature stood at the forefront of the host, ignoring the arrows that shattered against him as he held his arms out to the gates, hands glowing softly as he worked his art.

The ivy grew, growing taller and thicker than any ivy vine had a right to. Tendrils burrowed themselves deep into the tiny cracks between the stones, forcing the stone itself apart as they wedged the cracks wider. A violent crack rang out as first one, and then another, jagged fissure appeared in the surface of the wall, extending out around the thick covering of ivy. A grim smile grew on Aelthen's face as the ivy grew thicker still, broader at the base than a strong man's thigh as it reached deeper into the fissure, tearing the wall apart.

Miriam found her gaze caught by a flurry of activity above the gatehouse. An old man in armour inlaid with gold was screaming orders at the men surrounding him, his white hair whipping in the wind. Large cauldrons of boiling oil and pitch were poured down to splash over the walls and ground where the ivy sprouted. Flaming torches and arrows followed and a thick oily smoke rose high as the flames shot skyward.

The damage was already done though and, as the flames subsided, Aelthen turned his attention from the cracked and soot-stained walls and looked to the gates themselves.

A green mist rose from the massed fae behind him as Aelthen raised an arm, pulling the power to him. His eyes glowed to rival the morning sun as the power flooded into him and his smile was broad as he reached for the gates. Where the ivy had grown slowly, making itself known over several minutes, the gates transformed immediately. The dark treated wood thrust roots down into the earth as the gates twisted and warped. A tortured groan came from the iron portcullis as the gates transformed, ripping the iron gate from its mountings. In moments the gateway stood empty, with only the strange tree-like remnants of the massive gates squatting low in the gap that was left. The thick branches thrust and heaved at the stone walls surrounding them and, with a tortured screech, the stone itself tore and collapsed, taking the gatehouse and much of the surrounding wall with it. Men tumbled with the stones and Miriam could easily pick out the old man as he fell, only to be crushed by the walls of the gatehouse as it collapsed over him.

There was a moment of stunned silence, replaced with the screams of those that had been caught in the collapse. The fae stood motionless as Aelthen turned to face the host. He held a broad-bladed spear in one hand and lifted it to point at the city and the defenders within. "Ciarlis'sur." He spoke the word softly but it carried to the farthest reaches of the host and Miriam shuddered at the cold despite in his voice. "Ciarlis'sur," she whispered to herself. "Cleanse them."

A great cry rose up in response and the fae rushed towards the ruined gate, surging through to crash against the line of defenders. They twisted past the swords and spears that thrust at them, reaching out to tear lives from flesh with spears or bone-bladed knives. The fae and satyr moved with the same deadly grace they always did, and few humans managed to land a strike on them. This was no battle, it was a slaughter. The Bjornmen reached and passed the point of panic, stumbling over each other in an effort to run from the carnage but the fae and satyr simply cut them down as they ran. Miriam found herself retching again at the sights Aervern sent her as she wished she could close her eyes against the vision.

Aervern's eyes carried Miriam along the streets, past bodies and screaming wounded that writhed in the light of the guttering torches. The fae didn't seem to be taking part in the fighting. It was almost as if she just wanted to show Miriam the worst of it. At least she hoped it was the worst of it.

A fae exploded into fire as an iron bolt slammed through its chest. Three satyr standing close to the fae's burning corpse fell in moments as more bolts followed, but then the fae were upon the hapless Bjornmen, tearing them to pieces as they fought to reload the massive crossbows they carried.

Her view lifted as Aervern looked up to the fae'reeth. The tiny creatures were no larger than the hummingbirds Miriam had fed sugar-water as a child but she knew each one was as deadly as they were beautiful. She watched as they swooped down, surrounding Bjornmen in a spinning maelstrom of knives and blood as their victims flailed at them in vain. Where they passed only torn and shredded bodies remained.

The Bjornmen city was more than just a fort, Miriam realised. Aervern had passed what were clearly shops and homes as she headed for the keep that thrust skyward at the centre of the city. Whilst the men outnumbered the women, Miriam saw more than one woman fighting beside the men and still more besides laying in the dirt.

A scream pulled at her and Aervern both and Miriam grimaced at the sound. She knew what she would see before it even came into sight. The Bjornman city was a fort first, but it still had homes and families. She felt the tears run from her eyes and down the sides of her face into the grass. People had homes here. They had lives. They had children.

The bodies were tiny broken things and Aervern seemed to stare down at them forever. Miriam was normally able to focus on other things within the fae's field of vision but Aervern moved to stand directly over the bodies, giving Miriam no choice but to look. Blood matted their hair and pooled under the small bodies. The boy could have been Devin's brother. He had the same hair, the same shape to his chin and nose. Even though death had taken the fear from their faces the sight tore at her heart and Miriam lay screaming in the grass until, finally, the fae moved on. Her screams may have ended but the tears lasted longer still.

Aervern came for her much later, placing a cool hand over her eyes and removing the magic she'd wrought. "You understand why this was done? Why I have shown these things to you?"

"No!" Miriam spat, anger robbing her of the caution she usually had around the fae. She no longer cared. Let the fae torture her, let her kill her. None of it mattered now. "I understand nothing, *fae!* For your cruel amusement? To see me broken? Why do you even keep me alive, Aervern? You treat me as an equal one minute, and then as a pet the next. What do you want with me? I'm of no use to you, you can't even breed me. Is it just my misery that you want?"

Aervern stood impassive as stone as Miriam screamed at her. The angry words were thick with her tears, and even in the depths of it she felt a thrill at having an emotion this strong. Living under the pressure of Ileriel's mind had left her numb for too long. Eventually she ran out of harsh words to hurl at the fae and sank down to the grass, hollow and spent.

Aervern glanced around her and crouched down beside Miriam, speaking in a voice little louder than a whisper. "Now you are ready. Now you have seen. Come, we should not speak here." She extended a hand to the old woman and lifted her to her feet with no visible effort. The moon was bright and the sparks of the Lady's Gift were clear under her skin as she closed her eyes. The glamour shrouded them slowly, making them part of the darkness that surrounded them.

Aervern moved smoothly, slow enough for Miriam to follow without taxing her, but fast enough to cover the ground with haste.

Shrouded in shadow they fled, away from the city and towards the darkness of the distant trees. Behind them Rimeheld crumbled. Thick vines worked to tear down the work of thousands as the city fell but no human eyes remained to see it. The laughter of the satyr filled the air as the fae'reeth turned lazy circles above the city and the first strains of the flute lifted in celebration above the ruin the city had become.

* * *

The darkness under the trees was almost complete, with only faint shafts of moonlight breaking through the gaps in the leaves. Miriam sat against the tree, as Aervern instructed her, and waited.

The fae seemed almost nervous, pacing back and forth in front of her. "You were the first," she began, stopping her pacing to look at her as she spoke. "I am told it was the taking of you that allowed Ileriel to pass through the Wyrde into the Land of Our Lady. You have spent more time in the Realm of Twilight than any other of your kind. What have you learned?"

Miriam frowned. It was an odd question, broad and unfocused. "I'm not sure—" she began but Aervern waved her to silence.

"I did not truly expect an answer," she told her. She squatted down in front of Miriam, fixing her with eyes that seemed to glow brighter with the intensity of the gaze. "You were the first. You alone have seen the changes in both this world and mine. You have seen what those at Tir Rhu'thin do, how they have taken your kind and used them."

"I have," Miriam said, fighting to keep her own voice level.

If Aervern caught the tone she didn't show it. "You have seen how they use your kind to breed from, keeping them like beasts in pens wrought of craft and glamour. That is as it is." She shrugged. "But now you have also seen of my home, my city, of Tira Scyon and what they have wrought there." She extended a long finger that shone in the light from her eyes, stabbing it at Miriam. "You witnessed how Aelthen and his *Highfae*," she spat the word with all the venom she had hinted at the last time she'd uttered it. "How they have enslaved my people with the promise of glyphlore and power. How they have broken tradition and peace by ending the gelding and returned the Great Revel to my home? How they ended Tauntha, a life that stretched back to the sundering."

"You want my pity?" Miriam asked, her words cold and hard. "You feel I should pity your lot when you fae have stolen my life? When I was taken? I was ripped from my own world and away from my son. My life has been an unceasing nightmare. I have been raped and used for years and had each child taken from me. I have laboured under an influence so heavy it sought to crush my very self until I barely knew who I was or what was happening around me. After all of that you expect me to feel pity for you? When all you have done is force me to see the things you insist I watch. The feast, your mother's death, the butchery of tonight?"

"I do not ask for your pity, *human*," Aervern spat back, matching her tone. "I ask you to see! All this time I have had you watching and still you have not seen."

"What are you talking about?" Miriam demanded.

"Think!" Aervern urged her. "Think back on what you have seen, what I have shown you. Your manling mind is as agile as any fae's. Since you passed into my care I have shown you what these ancient fae have done to my world. Now I show you what they do to your own."

Miriam narrowed her eyes and studied Aervern's face. It gave as many clues as rough-hewn stone. "Why?" she asked, finally.

The stone crumbled and revealed a flurry of emotion too complex for her to hope to understand. "Because the return of those from the Outside has brought nothing that is wanted," Aervern said softly. "Nothing that should remain. Even now I feel the touch of Our Lady. I feel the power that flows into me. This realm..." She shuddered, closing her eyes and taking a deep breath. "This realm is too much for any fae. The Lady's Gift is endless here. It must be locked away. Aelthen must be locked away."

Miriam gaped, and then shook herself. "How?"

"How were they forced to the Outside before?" Aervern shrugged. "The barrier your kind named the Wyrde. How is it that it fell?"

"How would I know?" Miriam sputtered.

"It is no matter," Aervern shrugged. "That which is broken can be remade."

"But how?"

"You wish this then? You will assist me in this?" The fae's eyes were intent and she placed a peculiar emphasis on the question.

Miriam shuddered, struggling free from the grip of the memory Aervern's words had brought with them. "Free me," she said.

The fae cocked her head, considering. "There will be no need. The Wyrde will set you free."

Miriam stood, pulling herself up on the rough bark of the tree. "How do you need me to help?"

"The Wyrde has fallen," Aervern repeated simply. "Who held it before it fell? Even knowing what little I do of the Wyrde I can remember the feel of its touch, of those that held it and worked it anew. Where are these Wyrdeweavers now? What befell them?"

"How would I know?" Miriam laughed at that, trying to stop herself as she heard the hysteria turning it into a cackle.

Aervern stared through the laugh until it faltered and died. "You will seek out these Wyrdeweavers, then we shall see what shall be done."

"Even if I could find them, even if I had any idea where to start, how would I find you?" Miriam protested.

"I will find you, Miriam," Aervern told her. "The power that carried us through the Worldtrails was mine, not Aelthen's. You carry the touch of it still. I could find you across field and seas. Have no fear of that."

Miriam paused at that. The notion of simply running away once Aervern had set her upon this task had only really half-formed in her mind but this put paid to that. She sighed and caught herself. A glance at Aervern, and the fae's small smile, told her that she had known exactly what Miriam had been thinking.

To find these wyrdeweavers though, to find one or two people in all the world. The notion was almost farcical. "Where would I even begin?"

Aervern nodded and began to lower herself to sit, inviting Miriam to follow suit. Miriam smiled and shook her head. "These old bones are too stiff for all this up and down. I'll stand." She bent and picked up a fallen branch, leaning on it with one hand as she propped herself back against the tree."

"I do not see this realm as you, Miriam," Aervern began. "To my eyes it is a place of wonder yet the scent of you manlings is heavy in the air. I smell foul *fehru* wherever I step, the manling city was rife with it. The power is thick here, and even with the Wyrde fallen I can still sense the echoes of it. The stains of it lay thick on the earth and there are places so thick with it that the very soil reeks. One such place we have both visited already, where Aelthen leads his hunt is where your search must begin, at the Withengate."

Miriam shook her head. "I'm an old woman, Aervern. I can't wander the world looking for people who might be dead for all we know. Even if they're alive somewhere how would I know who they are? Do you expect me to wander the world accosting strangers?" She laughed at the thought.

"You are not the withered crone you pretend, Miriam," Aervern said, ignoring the old woman's laughter. "I will take you as far as the Withengate. Your hunt can begin there." She paused with a small smile, as if she had told a clever joke and was waiting for the laughter. The smile faded and she frowned slightly. "You are right in what you say, however, even the satyr need some sign of their quarry. I could follow the stench of the Wyrde myself but the Lady will call me to my own realm soon enough. However, even were she not to, I somehow doubt these Wyrdeweavers would welcome my company."

She blinked in shock as Miriam burst into laughter, looking at her as if she'd gone mad, and then venturing a small, uncertain, smile before she went on. "Had I the knowledge of these glyphs I feel something could be fashioned. As it is I will simply have to place my sight upon you."

Miriam shook her head. "I can't walk around with your sight, Aervern, it's too much. It was all I could do to lay on the grass with it and not throw up."

"This would not be the same as giving you my vision, Miriam," Aervern explained. "I would merely allow your manling eyes to see that which stands in plain sight."

"I don't understand."

Aervern shook her head with a sigh. "It will be simpler to show you." She stepped out of the trees into the moonlight again, drinking in the power before beckoning to Miriam. "Stand close, I wish to move with haste. I do not believe Aelthen is taking note of us but Ileriel? That is one I do not trust."

She stared up at the moon as the sparkling swirls of light grew under her skin. "None should have power like this," she muttered and closed her eyes. "It is like the wind. With no limits or end."

When she opened her eyes again they blazed like twin suns and Miriam shrank back from her as the fae looked down to the ground beneath them, extending a hand and muttering as her brow creased in concentration.

The mist that came from her outstretched hand pooled down by their feet. It was a far smaller work than Aelthen had produced, barely wide enough for the two of them to stand upon, but it was enough. Miriam gaped in wonder as Aervern pulled her up onto the mist and it lifted them up into the air. Aervern made no pretence at running as Aelthen and the fae on the hunt had. Instead, she crouched low as the two of them rose, scarcely more than the height of a tall man above the grass that whipped flat in the wind of their passage.

Miriam leaned forward, bracing herself against the motion. Somehow flying so low to the ground was worse than being high in the sky. She gripped hard, sinking her fingers into Aervern's arm before she realised she'd even reached out to her. The fae seemed oblivious to it. Her face was a blank mask as she concentrated on whatever it was she did to maintain the mist underneath them.

They began to climb to crest the trees and Miriam hunched low against the wind that tore at them. The air was thick with moisture and it leeched the warmth from her flesh as bad as a winter rainstorm. She closed her eyes against the wind and the sight of the trees rushing underneath them in a moonlit green torrent. The journey seemed to go on and on, and when they finally sank down to the earth Miriam had to work to pull her hands out of the fists she'd clenched them into.

The Withengate was a trampled mess. A stone circle stood around a fallen arch with one stone still standing at the centre. The ground was churned from the passage of untold number of cloven hooves. Aervern flinched as she stepped into it, glaring at the oozing mud that sucked at their feet and hissing at it, cat-like, before she looked up at Miriam.

"*Fehru.*" She spat. "In the earth here the whole of the Withengate reeks of it. It is rare to come across it in the Realm of Twilight, save for the relics and ancient craftings. The Land of Our Lady seems riddled with it." She ignored Miriam's questioning look, crouching low and sniffing at the air with eyes half-closed. She took a step, and then another, moving towards the stones of the circle as Miriam watched on.

"Yes, here," the fae muttered. "I can sense it even without Our Lady's Grace." She straightened and beckoned Miriam. "Come, let us see what can be done with you."

Aervern's hand was cool as she laid it over Miriam's eyes again. There was a moment of intense heat and she would have pulled away had the fae not held her so tightly.

"There," Aervern said. "Now, look. See."

Miriam squinted. The world was suddenly too bright. Every image seemed too sharp, too focused. She followed Aervern's pointing finger and frowned at the spectacle, trying to make sense of what she saw. The circle was filled with traces of light, leading in odd patterns around the stones and the space between them.

"What is this—?"

"No," Aervern cut her off. "There is no time to speak of this. Now, close your eyes. Feel it too."

Miriam closed her eyes, feeling more than a bit foolish as she stood there in the darkness as she felt about for...something. She could almost feel the expectant stare of the fae boring into her but nothing more. She sighed and drew breath to speak and protest when she felt it. A vibration, an echo. There were no words to describe it. It was the sound of a bell as it fades to silence, the ringing so slight it hard to tell where the sound ended and the imagination began. It was more than a sound though, there was a vibration. A shimmer in the air that was more felt than heard.

"You feel it, do you not?" Aervern whispered, her breath hot on Miriam's ear.

She nodded.

"Now then, draw this sense back within you. Contain it, bury it deep down inside yourself." Aervern instructed and, without really pausing to consider what she meant, Miriam had done it. Coiling the power within herself, locking it away from the night.

Aervern leaned in close and looked into her eyes. She stood motionless and stared long enough that Miriam stifled an uncomfortable laugh.

"Good," she said, finally. "This gift will not remain long within you, Miriam. You manlings were never meant for the Lady's Grace and it will seek to leave you. Use it sparingly. I do not know how often I will be able to locate you to replenish it."

"What was it?" Miriam managed. "What was I seeing?"

"A remnant," Aervern told her. "Call it an echo if it makes it easier for you to grasp. This is the footprint of the Wyrde and the Weaver that worked it. Did you feel the path the Weaver has taken from here?"

Miriam closed her eyes and reached for the power, searching inside herself for it.

"No!" Aervern snapped, grabbing at her wrist. "You must use what you remember. The Grace will pass from you swiftly. It is not to be squandered.

Miriam nodded and concentrated, thinking back to the sensations that had rushed through her. The stones had been surrounded by the shimmering vibration, so strong it had almost smothered anything else. She turned to the south where she'd felt another, equally strong vibration. She frowned through the darkness at the confusing mass of shadows against the trees, the lines were too regular. She stepped closer and the images came together to reveal the ruin of what must have once been a cottage and outbuildings. They were torn apart now, threaded through with thick vines, with just the smallest section of wall still standing.

She glanced over at Aervern who watched her with an expectant expression. The vibration had stretched away from the circle and curious footsteps led her from the ruined cottage towards the other side of the clearing. The small path leading from the clearing was hard to see in the darkness but somehow she knew it was there. The faint echoes of the Wyrde led her on.

"Good," Aervern said, standing at her shoulder, though Miriam hadn't heard her take a step. "This is the path the Weavers took. Follow the trail and you shall find them."

"Aervern, it's not that simple," Miriam protested. The fae couldn't be that oblivious to her needs, surely? "What about supplies? I have no food, no tent or anything to shelter in at night..." She broke off and looked as the fae took a step back, glancing down at her swollen belly before looking at her, perplexed. "Are you creatures truly so frail?" She shook her head as Miriam started to speak. "It is no matter. I shall provide for you. I shall leave your supplies upon the path you travel."

Miriam gave a resigned nod but the fae still watched her with an expectant look. "Surely you don't mean for me to start now?"

Aervern looked at her in silence and smiled.

CHAPTER SIXTEEN

The air felt wet. The downpour had been finished for hours but the air was still filled with the smell that follows rain. The sun was doing little more than warm the rain-soaked robe she wore and Miriam trudged along the road, feeling more like she was wading through a humid soup than anything else.

It had been three days since she'd left Aervern and she was lucid enough to know she wasn't doing well. The simple fact of being back in her own world, and free to do as she wished, was almost overwhelming. She found it hard to stay on task. Several times she'd caught herself simply standing in the road, awed by the way the sun stayed in the sky for so long. Another time it had been the birdsong that had caught her attention and she'd stood for long moments before bursting into tears that grew to deep wracking sobs that hurt her chest and throat.

Her mind was flitting, drifting from place to place with nothing to hold it for long. She'd wondered for a time if it was being away from the fae that caused it or if she were simply going mad. Had Aervern's mind had still held her under some pressure, in spite of her efforts not to dominate her as Ileriel had?

Despite everything she had managed to keep moving, to take note of where she was and where she should be going. The fact she hadn't passed a single person, or even caught sight of anyone, hadn't escaped her notice and the isolation was beginning to take its own toll. She talked to herself for a while but found herself drifting from Anlish, to Islik, to Fae, and the sound of her own words stilled her to silence.

She reached for the small wineskin hanging at her belt and took a sip, grimacing at temperature and taste. Aervern had been leaving supplies for her. They were hidden in small caches just off the road, marked by small piles of pebbles like miniature cairns. How the fae knew how far she'd travel each day, was beyond her but she hadn't failed Miriam yet.

In a way it made a lot more sense for her to travel without carrying a full pack on her back. She was struggling enough as it was, and a heavy pack would only slow her further. She carried the wineskin though, and a few blankets rolled into the travel-pack. Aervern had left water for her with the supplies each night but still she worried that if she left the skin the next day would be the day there wasn't one there. Besides, it let her drink during the day without having to search for streams and that alone was worth the extra weight.

The nights were the worst. Aervern's caches were always next to a place for her to sleep. A bivouac formed of living saplings and bushes with the branches woven so tightly together that not a drop of rain had made it through. Despite the comfort Miriam had found it hard to sleep. She lay awake for hours in the darkness, listening to the sounds of animals in the undergrowth and staring at the moon as it shone through the clouds. The tears came then, too, slow and gentle. Not the panicked sobs of a mind broken and fearing to make itself whole but tears of anguish and pain for a lifetime that had been stolen from her.

Miriam caught herself. She was staring into space again, eyes locked on a shaft of sunlight slanting down between the leaves in the trees to her left. She shook her head and set off once more. Her foot slipped in the slick mud of the road and she staggered forward, catching herself on the stick she'd gathered up, wrenching her shoulder in the process.

She pulled herself up with a grunt, fighting back harsh words for half a second at the pain in her hand. A glance revealed the raw and torn skin on the webbing of her thumb, and she let loose with a string of curses that would have made a sailor blush. The nubs left behind by the twigs she'd stripped away had bitten into the flesh of her palm. It wasn't a serious wound by any means but Lords and Ladies it smarted.

A snap pulled her attention away from picking the splinters from her hand and she looked up to see a man emerging from the trees beside the road, some distance ahead of her. He looked more ragged than she did in some ways. His clothing was in a better state, but ill-cared for, and his hair and beard were unkempt. He met her gaze with a smile that sat awkwardly on his face as his spear dragged, unnoticed, in the mud behind him.

"Well then, Mother. What are you doing out here like this?"

She forced her own smile. "Just travelling the road, sir."

He laughed at that. "You don't have to 'sir' me, Mother. His smile didn't quite reach his eyes and they shifted over her in a way that made her pull her cloak tighter around herself. She'd seen eyes like that before, years past when she'd worked the taverns of Kavtrin, and they never led to anything good.

"I'll just be on my way then." She nodded a farewell at him.

He moved to block her path before she'd taken two steps, though he still stood some distance from her, and she stopped. Her hands grew tight around the walking staff as he came closer. "What are you doing all alone out here, Mother? The roads aren't safe to travel alone."

"I could ask you the same thing." She laughed, though the sound was forced and held no humour.

He shrugged. "I live here, my brothers and me. It's a cold life in the woods but there's ways to get by, if you know what I mean."

She nodded, not really listening.

He cocked his head to one side as he stared at her for a moment, and then nodded twice. "That's about enough of this," he muttered, more to himself than her it seemed. "Let's have a look at your stuff."

"What?" she drew back, clutching her cloak to herself.

"Your pack, Mother," he said, reaching for her.

She skittered back away from his hand. "What do you mean? I don't have anything."

He looked at her again, his eyes suddenly seeming oily and unfocused. "Don't be daft, Woman. No one walks the roads with no food or anything on their backs. Did you hear me coming and stash it?"

He moved forward, a sinuous movement that seemed almost fae-like for its sudden speed, and caught her robe as she shuffled away from him. "Are you holding out on me, Mother?"

Now that he was closer she caught the smell of him. The stink of stale sweat was overpowering and her nose wrinkled before she thought better of it.

"Where is it?" he demanded, oblivious to her expression. The mud-caked spear had appeared and his hand shook as he breathed ragged breaths into her face as he glared down at her.

"I don't have anything, I swear. Just this water, some blankets, and these." She held out a handful of crumbled oatcake she'd pulled from a pocket.

He flickered a look at her hand, dashing the food away with a sneer. "Well then let's see what else you've got." His eyes flicked to meet her gaze and darted away again as his hand slid from her wrist, making its way to her chest in a rough grope.

Miriam froze, locked in place as his hands ran over her body. His breath shuddered out of him in a staccato hiss of excitement, all nervous energy as he licked at his lips.

The anger seemed to come all at once. Fear giving way to indignation, which stepped aside for white hot anger all in the space of a heartbeat. A shove with one hand pushed him back half a step, just far enough for her to bring up the staff with the other, smashing it under his chin.

It wasn't a strong blow but it caught him unprepared and already off balance and sent him reeling backwards until he sprawled in the mud. An image lanced into her, of an unkempt spear-wielder, a bandit who in many ways had been the cause of everything that had gone wrong since Kavtrin. The man in front of her didn't look that similar but it was close enough. She screamed as she swept the staff up and drove it down into the man's head. It was a lucky strike and the tip of the staff smashed into the side of his face beside his eye. She barely noticed the shock of the impact running down the length of wood and she drew back for another blow, and then another.

Something dripped from her face and she reached for it absently as she panted, kneeling down over the dirt of the road. Blood coated her fingertip where she'd wiped at her face and she forced herself to turn her head to the figure laying in the corner of her vision.

"Lord preserve us, Woman. What have you done?" The voice was accusatory and she flinched away from the harsh words even as she looked for the speaker. The man stood at the edge of the trees, close to the road, and he flinched back as she locked eyes with him. In an instant she realised what she must look like. Hunched down low in the road beside the body, back cloak and robes ragged and torn, her white hair and face flecked with the man's blood. She was the witch from half a dozen children's tales.

She stood slowly, letting the fear show on her face as she stepped back away from the crumpled form of the man in the road, trying to control the trembling that was shaking her hands and legs.

His face softened immediately and he moved to check on the fallen man. "Frast, you poor stupid bastard." He looked back up at her. "You didn't have to kill him."

The accusation was still there but softer now, only half-hearted.

"I didn't mean to," she began. "It all happened so fast, and he was grabbing at me…" She trailed off into silence, looking down at her robes and picking at something stuck to the material.

"He din't deserve this," he muttered, and then looked at her, taking her appearance in. "Then again, maybe he did. He weren't right in the head. A dead-fall cracked his head a few years back, must've softened his brains or something 'cause he ain't been right since."

She nodded, not sure what to say.

"Any of that yours?" he nodded at her.

Miriam frowned at him.

"The blood," he explained, pointing. "Are you hurt?"

"Oh," she said, getting his meaning. "No, I don't think so."

He moved towards her, looking her over. It was amazing how two sets of eyes could be so different. Where Frast's eyes had been nervous and cold these held nothing but genuine concern.

"We'd best get you back to camp anyways," he told her. "A body needs something hot inside it after something like this. It's the least we can do."

She shook her head before he finished speaking. "No, really. I'm fine."

He grimaced. "You might just be at that but it's not as simple as all that. Frast was the boss's brother. I just let you go an it'll go bad for me."

She glanced up at the sky for a second. "I don't want any trouble, sir. I just want to be on my way."

"It'll be fine," he said. "Look, what's your name?"

"Miriam."

"I'm Redan," he told her. "There'll not be any trouble for you. Denn should never have let his brother wander like this anyhow. Come an' get a hot cup of somethin' inside you, get warm, get cleaned up. It looks like rain again later anyway."

He took her hesitation for agreement and moved to take her arm gently, leading her into the trees. He led her at an easy pace, supporting her as they climbed down ditches and over a small stream. The path was concealed where it approached the edge of the trees but soon became more obvious and easy to travel. It took no more than half an hour to reach the camp, long enough for the trembling to subside and for her to realise that this was probably a mistake.

The camp bordered on being a hamlet. A circle of shelters that had clearly once been little more than lean-tos had been built upon and worked until they were almost houses. A fire stood in the centre of the ragged circle, with a large boar roasting on a spit beside the crackling flames. Men sat idly beside the fire, tossing bones by the looks of things. Still others worked at various chores around the camp. It seemed a well-ordered place but the lack of women or children didn't escape her. Women would have made this place a home. Without them it was just a camp and she was in no doubt as to its purpose.

Redan held a hand high and waved at a man she hadn't seen, perched high in a tree with a bow resting on his knees. He caught her expression. "Can't be too careful, times bein' what they are."

"What's this? I know it's been a while for you, Redan, but you're not that desperate are you?"

Redan smiled weakly at the man who'd stood from his position beside the fire. "That's Denn," he managed to tell her in a low voice as the man approached.

"What have we here then?" Denn spoke down at them. He was a giant of a man. Big in height as well as in muscle, and his voice rumbled its way out of a chest it would have taken two women to encircle with their arms.

"It's awkward, Denn," Redan told him, keeping his voice low. "Frast found her on the road." His tone must have told the larger man something as his eyes flicked to Miriam with a guilty wince.

Denn nodded. "Not here then," he said and waved them into the trees, leading them a short way from the camp.

He looked Miriam over slowly, taking in the blood still staining her hair and flaking from her clothing. "What happened?"

"I found her by the road," Redan explained. "Looked like Frast had taken a liking to 'er. You know how he got sometimes?"

The past tense wasn't lost on Denn and he raised an eyebrow. "What'd she do?"

"Took a stick to him. I din't see much of it. He was in the mud by the time I got there."

"This little thing?" Denn didn't take his eyes from her. "He was my brother you understand?" he said, speaking directly to her for the first time.

Miriam nodded. "I'm sorry he's dead," she told him. "Not sorry I did what I did though."

Denn nodded again, narrowing his eyes as he thought. "I can't blame you for what you did, Mother. I don't have to like it though." He sighed then. "It's probably for the best. He was good to me when we were young, looked out for me when I needed him. He ain't been right though," he said, talking more to Redan than to her. "Not since the tree caught him, an' it's gotten worse these last years." He glanced over her again. "Did he hurt you?"

"Nothing that won't heal," Miriam replied, not quite meeting his eyes.

"We can get her cleaned up though," Redan said, giving Denn a serious look. "A hot meal wouldn't hurt either."

The dark haired man nodded. "That we can. Where did you leave Frast?"

Redan nodded back to the road. "I thought Miriam was more important."

Denn grunted. "We'll see her right. I'll send some men back to the road to take care of my brother."

They led her back into the camp. Redan pointed her towards a hut. "That one's mine. Go and get out of those clothes and I'll set some water outside the door for you when it's hot."

Miriam moved without thinking. The need to find the Wyrdeweavers paled in comparison to her need to get the blood out of her hair and off her skin. The hut was cleaner than she would have expected and she stripped out of the bloody robes, tossing them into a corner by the door.

A tap at the door was followed by Redan's muffled voice announcing the hot water. She eased the door open just wide enough to pull the bucket in, laughing at herself. "Is it still modesty if nobody would want to see you anyway?" she wondered in a whisper.

The water was steaming, fresh from the pot over the fire, but she wasted no time. A cloth, that was well on its way to being a rag, hung over the side of the bucket and she scrubbed at her skin until the water was pink with Frast's blood.

The camp was quiet as she eased the door open and stepped out of the hut, wrapped in the blankets she'd pulled from the straw-stuffed sacks Redan used as a bed. The reason for the silence became obvious as she glanced at the fire and saw it surrounded by men eating from wooden platters piled high with meat.

"Miriam!" Redan waved her over. "Come, eat."

She sat awkwardly on a section of log and took the offered plate as Redan took her wet clothes and hung them over a branch to dry. The conversation around the fire was quiet, with small groups of two and three. Miriam ate in silence, wishing she hadn't bothered washing the robe.

"So where were you heading to, Mother?" Redan asked her, his voice over-loud in the quiet.

She thought quickly. "Towards Druel," she said. "My brother has an inn over that way."

"That's a damned long way to go by foot," Denn said from the other side of Redan, speaking around a mouthful of meat.

Miriam picked at the boar on her plate, taking a small bite quickly to give herself time to think. She hadn't been prepared for questions and she felt exposed and off guard. Her eyes widened at the taste of the boar. Whoever had prepared the meat knew what they were about.

Denn laughed at her expression. "Not bad is it?" He nodded at a man sat across the fire. "Trent knows what he's doing. He was a cook with Rentrew's men before he came north."

"Rentrew?" she asked, before she thought better of it.

"Baron Rentrew," Denn clarified. "Most of us are from Freyton's men. Trent just ran farther and faster than us is all."

"Good thing for you I did," Trent muttered. "You lot can't cook for shit."

Rough laughter filled the circle around the fire and the stilted atmosphere was gone.

"So you're soldiers then?" Miriam asked.

"Well, some of us were. Nothing stops those bastards though, and damned if I was going to get cut to shreds for a handful of coppers." Redan gave her an odd look. "What did you think we were?"

The question left her flustered and grasping for words as Denn and Redan laughed at her reaction.

"She thought we was all bandits, didn't you, love?" The big man laughed. "Truth be told we're not far from it. I don't expect many here would cry foul at lifting a crown or two from a fat merchant if it came down to it. With the bastard Bjornmen though, there's nothing on the road but you an' a handful of stragglers running west."

The conversation was cut short as a short blonde-haired man emerged from a hut with a wooden bowl and a worried look. "He still won't take anything," he told Denn.

Denn shook his head. "It's been too long. A body needs to eat."

"Dravit," Redan explain, speaking to her in a low voice. "He came down with sickness. It looked like he'd licked it but he got worse again. He's not eaten in three days now."

"It's time we did something, Denn," the short man said in a low voice. "If it's catchin' it could take us all."

"It's not like that." Denn scowled down at his plate. "We'd all be sick already."

"You don't know that, Denn," the short man spat. "You're just guessing. Red fever took half my village when I were a lad. I saw men fine one day, and then pissing blood two days later. It'd cut through here like a new scythe through wheat."

"It's not the red fever, Bret," Denn said again, his voice rising.

"An' how would you know?" Bret demanded, his own voice rising to match Denn's.

"What have you given him?" Miriam asked, her calm voice cutting through the argument.

"Nothin'," Brett said, glaring at her. "He won't take nothing."

She looked over at the hut. "I could take a look at him."

"Do you know what you're doing?" Denn asked. "About tending the sick, I mean."

Miriam shrugged. "I know some. It won't hurt to look."

Denn looked at her for a minute as he chewed. Finally he shrugged. "He's not going to get worse for you poking at him."

The hut stank, stale sweat mingled with a musty smell and the faint smell of rot. Miriam sucked air in through her teeth, trying not to breathe through her nose as she knelt beside the low cot. The man lay still, on one side, his face covered in a sheen of sweat that shone in the light from the doorway. The heat poured off him in waves and she could feel it even without reaching to touch his head. She leaned in closer, peering at his face and the exposed skin of his neck before she nodded once and stood to step out.

Redan was waiting for her outside the hut. He peered past her through the doorway. "Is it...?"

"The red fever?" she finished for him. "No."

"You're sure? Brett has been on about it for days."

She snorted. "I doubt Brett has even seen red fever. The clue is in the name. If this man had red fever the skin on his face and neck would be covered in a red rash. Not only that but he'd be screaming the place down. The rash is supposed to feel like your skin is burning. There's no way he'd be laying quiet like that." She shook her head. "It's not red fever." Her words left no room for doubt.

Redan nodded, peering past her into the hut. "Can you help him?"

"I don't know," she admitted. "I can help with the fever at least. Do you know the yarrow plant? Get me some leaves and flower heads. Failing that, bring me some birch or willow bark but I'd rather have the yarrow."

"I'll see what I can find." He paused, frowning at her. "You're a strange person, Miriam. There aren't many who'd go out of their way to help a man, especially after what Frast did to you."

She scowled at him. "You don't know me, Redan. You don't know anything about me. But someone who leaves a man suffering when they know how to help they're not worth knowing."

He grunted at that and looked like he was about say more.

"Talk to me when you get back, Redan." She pointed at the trees. "Go and get me that yarrow."

He smiled at her tone. "Yes, Mother."

She scowled at his back as he loped into the trees before she turned back to the hut. It was well made but rough. Light came in through the open door and an attempt at a window, which wasn't much more than a hole in the side of the hut with a piece of fabric tacked over it. She tugged it loose and wedged the door to the hut open, feeling the air stir inside.

"Should help with the stink if nothing else," she muttered.

Five minutes and a terse conversation with Denn produced a bowl of water and a rag. She knelt beside Dravit, and wiped at his face with the cloth. He grimaced at the first touch and then lay still, apparently unable to muster the energy to care what she did to him.

"Can you hear me, Dravit?" she asked gently. "We need to get this fever down and get some water into you, do you understand?"

If he did he gave no answer.

She sighed and went to the door. "Denn!" she called out. As faces turned towards her she realised it was a barmaid's shout that she hadn't used in years.

"Get me someone to help get this shirt off him," she told him in a no-nonsense tone, as he approached.

He nodded. "I expect I can manage to give you a hand." Between the two of them they managed to strip the shirt away, tugging it over Dravit's head. The fabric was thick with his sweat and Miriam tried hard to ignore the greasy texture as she tossed it out through the doorway.

Denn hovered outside the doorway, watching her as she considered what to do next. "I hope you weren't planning to strip him entirely," he said with a smile that worked hard to turn the words into a joke.

It didn't work and her tone was flat as she spoke. "If it comes to it." She dipped the rag back into the bowl and set about wiping Dravit's chest and throat down, letting the water leech the heat away from him.

"At least he's getting a bath," Denn muttered. "He stinks!"

Miriam knelt up and fixed the big man with a stern gaze. "Don't you have anything you should be doing?"

He shrugged, unconcerned, and then shook his head. "Not really, no."

"Well then make yourself useful and put a pot on to boil," she said, looking back at Dravit and laying the wet cloth over his forehead. He reached weakly for it, trying to wipe it away but she stopped him with no real effort, shushing him absently.

With Denn gone she sat back, watching the man on the cot in silence. What was she doing here? She should be gone already. This man was not her problem. She knew the answer, of course. She'd already told Redan that. She wondered briefly what the reaction from Denn and the others would be if this man were to die whilst she tended him. She'd already killed Denn's brother.

The enormity of it hit her suddenly, as if she'd kept that truth locked away from herself, and her hands shook in the silence of the hut as she stared at the man laying on the rough cot.

Redan appeared then, rushing across the camp and thrusting a handful of yellow flowers at her. "Is this enough? I can get more if you need me to."

She picked over the yarrow and nodded approvingly. "It's more than I need for now."

"I got willow bark too," he said, glancing at her already full hands, and laying it down by the doorway.

"We'll start with the yarrow first," Miriam told him.

There was nothing like a pestle and mortar to be had so she settled for crushing up the leaves and flowers on a flat stone.

"Fetch me a cup of boiling water," she told Redan as she scraped the pulpy mess onto a square of sack-cloth and tied it up into a loose bundle.

"This isn't really ideal," she told him as he handed her the steaming cup and stirred the bundle around it in with a spoon. "This cloth isn't especially clean. Dried yarrow might have worked better too but we haven't time for that." She stood, arching her aching back as the tea steeped, and looked at him. "We'll let this cool for a bit, then try and get some into him."

"Brett hasn't had any luck getting him to drink," Redan warned her.

Miriam grunted. "Fetch me a thick stick. We'll have to force him if need be."

Brett's word proved prophetic as Dravit waved the offered spoonful away weakly, turning his head away from her.

"Get in behind him and hold him up, keep his head still," she told Redan.

Dravit moaned as she pulled him into a seated position, pushing at Redan's arms.

"Gerroff," he managed in a hoarse whisper. And then, "piss off!" when Redan wouldn't let go.

He managed to dash the first spoonful of the tea away, splashing it over the wall as he twisted and spat. The listlessness fell away from him as he fought and he clamped his lips tight when he wasn't screaming at them.

Miriam cursed under her breath and started as she realised the dim light was caused by the crowd outside the hut blocking the sun.

"You might as well get in here and help hold him then," she told them. It took three men in the end as she wedged the stick between with teeth and spooned the tea into his mouth.

Dravit screamed and roared at them to start with but the anger was hot and quick to burn out. Tears came as he coughed and choked on the steaming brew. Eventually she judged it enough and the men stepped out as Dravit collapsed down to the cot.

"He'll be easier to manage the next time," she told Denn, though she was far from as sure as she sounded. "Most of that was the fever. He should be able to reason with more in an hour or two."

"Is that it then?" Denn asked her. "Just some boiled leaves?"

"Where do you think healers get their medicines from?" she laughed, though the sound was tired and weak. "No, he's not out of danger yet. He's very weak and dry as hay that's sat out in the field all summer. The yarrow will make him sweat the fever out, so we'll need to force some water into him. It will help but most of this is down to him, and to luck. You could try some willowbark on him come morning but he'll need the yarrow probably three more times if it's to do any good."

"You're going then," Denn asked, prompting a confused look. "You said *I* could try the willowbark," he explained.

"I need to get moving, yes," she told him.

He walked her over to the fire and joined her on a log that had been set in place as a row of seats. "You should stay the night at least." He nodded at the sun, already touching the tree tops. "Not much point in blundering along in the dark."

She smiled her thanks. "That makes sense, thank you."

He snorted. "I should be thanking you! Brett means well but I don't think Dravit had long left. If you hadn't come along—"

She waved his words aside. "I didn't do all that much. After what happened with, well…"

"With Frast?" His gaze fell and he reached for a log to toss into the fire before he looked back at her with a sigh. "It wasn't the end I'd have chosen for him but," he sighed again, "he wasn't well. Anyone could see that. He didn't used to be this bad. He could look after himself. He'd help with hunting an' logging when we needed it. He was almost like an overgrown child a lot of the time."

"When…?" she left the rest unsaid.

"…Did it happen?" Denn asked, picking up the sentence. "Almost as soon as we left Freyton's men. We were posted at Tibbet's Shore. It's about as far east as Anlan gets," he explained in response to her blank look. "There was a watch beacon there. We were sent as a garrison to help defend it and light the beacon if any Bjornmen raiders came. Fat load of good we did." He spat into the fire. "They went through us like a child kicking at an anthill. Our corporal, useless piece of shit, was all for holding the line. Even after they'd smashed the tower down and were raining burning pitch down on us he wanted a slow retreat back to the tree line."

He met her eyes as he spoke. "I said, 'fuck that'. Grabbed Frast an' we was off." He paused, waiting for a comment that didn't come. "We headed west, fast as we could. Frast was a good hunter and that kept us fed. We settled in a few times, making camps a bit like this, but the Bjornmen kept pushing west. I couldn't tell you how many villages I've seem 'em torch.

"We met up with some others on the road. There's more men will chance the rope and run rather than face those savage bastard Bjornmen than you'd think."

"Face the rope?" she frowned.

"I'm a deserter," Denn said it with a simple honesty. "I know what that means. It's a hanging if I'm caught. I s'pose that's why we weren't bothered about robbing a fat merchant or two if it came down to it. Nothing to lose, see?"

He shifted over, making room for Redan as he knelt beside the fire and started chopping vegetable on a large wooden board. Hacking carrots, which looked like they were a couple of weeks past their best, into rough chunks.

Miriam watched for almost a full minute before she closed her eyes and shook her head. "For the love of all that's good and right, Redan. What did those carrots ever do to you?"

He glanced back in surprise and frowned. "What?"

"Oh, just shift over. Let me do it." She took the knife and began slicing the carrots, nodding at Denn who stifled a laugh. "Carry on."

"Hmm?" he grunted. "Oh, well, there's not much more to tell really. Frast got caught by the branch about two months before we got here. Damnedest thing really, just a dead tree. That branch could have fallen anytime but seems it just waited there for him. Caught him right on the top of the head too. Dropped him like a sack of wheat. We pulled him out from under it and patched him up as best we could. It didn't look that bad but he didn't wake up for three days. When he did he was, well, like how you saw him. Some days were worse than others. There were days when he didn't know anyone, thought we were all strangers. He went three whole weeks thinking Brett were his dad." He snorted a laugh at the memory but the smile faded quickly.

"Then there were days when he'd spend the whole time sat close to the road, just watching." He stood and went to a rain barrel, dipping out a cupful of water and drinking deeply. "He'd get this look on him, like his eyes couldn't sit still in his head. You'd look at him and he'd never meet your eyes for long, they'd just slip away. Almost like he was guilty about something." He shrugged and took his seat again. "Anyhow, you weren't the first woman he took a try with. We had to pull him back from a merchant's once." He glanced over at Redan. "Remember that one? They must've been running west. Had everything you can imagine packed into five big wagons, an' enough guards round it that we'd have never thought of going near it. He caught sight of a girl driving the third wagon, an' he was off. We got to him before he made it out of the trees, took three of us to hold him down though."

"He's my brother, an' I'll miss him, but I don't blame you, Mother." Denn looked up and met her eyes. "He's not been Frast for a long time now. Like I said, maybe it's better like this. I'm just sorry you had to get hurt as well."

Miriam reached up for the bruise on her cheek, without thinking. She brushed her fingertips over it, probing the pain, and let her hand fall. "You're not like…" she stopped, unsure how to finish.

"Like what you'd expect bandits to be?" Redan offered.

Miriam shrugged and nodded.

"We're all just people," Denn told her. "I've never met a bandit that I spoke to. Killed one or two when I was a caravan guard but only if I didn't have a choice. I suspect there's always something bad that drives a man to take to the woods. It's not the easiest of lives but it beats fighting those Bjornmen. I don't have many regrets."

Miriam busied herself preparing the meal, letting the conversation die. Denn's story had given her a lot to think about and she found herself drifting back to the spearman and the bandits who'd attacked Garret's caravan all those years ago. She'd spent years hating the man. Now, for the first time, she wondered what had driven him to that life.

She worked to fashion a thin stew. The boar was beautifully cooked but there was a limit she could do with the supplies that were on hand. As the sun sank behind the trees, and the smell from the pot drew others to the fire, she sank into a half-doze. Twice she tried to rouse herself to feed more yarrow to Dravit, and twice Redan pushed her gently back to her seat, telling her he'd see to it.

Conversation washed around her. She was the stone to its surf and though it touched her and swept past, she was never caught up in it. More than once she heard her name mentioned but she was too tired to care. Eventually Denn roused her. "You look done in, Mother. Take my hut for the night, there's a spare tent I can use." He waved off her protests, and, if the truth be told, she didn't argue too hard. He guided her through the camp, moving through the murk and shadows that danced in the firelight until he pointed her at his hut. She sank down onto the cot, not even minding the stale odour from the blankets, and slept.

A scream woke her. A cry of fear and pain that cut off with a despairing sob. Miriam rolled out of bed and crouched beside the door until the shouting and the sound of running feet drew her out into the moonlight. The fire was all but gone and the coals and tiny flames cast a ruddy glow over the centre of the camp as shadowy figures raced past with swords drawn. Fire flared as others thrust torches into the embers to light them and rushed past.

The sudden flare of light stabbed at her eyes and she squinted, trying to make sense of the scene.

Far to her right, steel met steel and a man screamed as another cried out. "Shit, Redan! I didn't mean it! Lord of the New Days, are you all right, man? Redan?"

Miriam followed the voices, not even considering the danger. Men circled a shadowy figure, crouched low with their swords ready. As the torchlight grew stronger Miriam caught the female form and her heart sank.

"Aervern! No!" She tried to shout, but her lungs had no strength and the shout was barely a whisper. The fae twisted, lashing out with impossible speed, and another man fell to the dirt, clutching at the gash that been torn in his thigh.

"Bitch!" a voice, she thought might be Denn, roared, and the swords and axes hacked at the figure. They may as well have been trying to stab the sky for all the good it did them. Aervern stepped past the swords with ease, moving no more than was necessary to avoid the blades, and stepping with the casual grace of a dancer.

Twice, swords found her, crashing away from her skin as if she were made of stone. Her eyes flared then, shining as bright as the torches held by her attackers. She crouched, baring her teeth and hissing like a feral cat as she launched herself at the men closest to her. Her bones knives flashed out twice, three times, and a man fell, unable even to cry out. The second staggered back, hand held high before his face as he gaped in horror at the missing fingers.

She moved like a flame in fury, leaping from one to another, dealing death wherever she touched. In moments it was over and the fae stood still surrounded by the dead and dying as she met Miriam's eyes calmly.

"Why?" Miriam whispered, feeling each and every one of her years.

Aervern was calm, relaxed as if nothing had happened. "You are bound to my purpose, manling. Mine alone. I will not stand by as others hold you captive or try to turn you from this path."

"You!" Denn's voice gasped out from the ground at Aervern's feet, the words thick with pain. "You brought this she-beast, this demon from the black among us? Why?"

Miriam tried to speak but had no words and managed nothing more than a small shake of her head as the tears pricked at her eyes.

"What manner of witch-woman are you?" Denn gasped. "What did we do to you that called for this?"

She had no time to answer as Aervern reached down with an almost tender touch and her knife parted his throat with a delicate motion.

Chapter Seventeen

Gavin sighed as he sat back, leaning his back against a tree. "I could get used to this."

Tristan paused, his spoon stopping halfway from bowl to mouth. "To sleeping on the ground?"

Gavin grunted in place of a laugh. "To easy food. This place is the best hunting I've ever seen."

Tristan gave the young man a long steady look. "Did you do much hunting, on the backstreets of Hesk?"

"I…err…" Gavin closed his mouth.

"Will you two stop it?" Klöss snapped, sitting up and glaring at them.

"Stop what?" Tristan asked

"This clever banter," Klöss told him. "It's like the two of you have to go out of your way to be funnier than each other all the time. This isn't a night out in a tavern. We're deserters. We're going to meet our enemy and betray our own people."

"We're going to find a way to fight these keiju, Klöss," Tristan said, his voice calm in the face of Klöss's irritation.

Klöss fell back with an explosive sigh. "I know, just lay off with the jokes for a bit, okay?"

Gavin looked back and forth between the two of them. "How far do you think we've come?" he asked finally.

"From Rimeheld?" Klöss replied. "It's hard to judge with all these damned trees. Sixty, seventy miles or more."

"Is that all? It feels farther."

Klöss shrugged. "It could be twice that, it could be less, I don't know."

"My feet say it is further," Tristan opined and gave a slow grin as Klöss smiled.

Klöss kicked his way out of the blankets. "Are you two about ready to move?" His only answer was a muttered grumble from Gavin but Tristan stood easily, arching his back to stretch out the kinks.

"These Anlish, I am hoping they do not make us sleep on the ground. Of this I have had enough." The big man knuckled at the small of his back with a wince.

The camp came down quickly, practice making it into a smooth procedure. Gavin kicked dirt over the remains of the fire and within moments they were on the move.

It was barely minutes to the road but the terrain had all been downhill to where they'd made their camp and, with the trees blocking the view, they'd barely needed to hide the fire.

"It should not be long now I am thinking," Tristan said, speaking to Klöss's back.

"Long for what?" Klöss replied, not turning his head.

"Until we meet these Anlish. We are far past our own lines now."

Klöss tilted his head, considering. "Could be any time now I suppose."

"So what's your plan, for when we meet them, I mean?" Gavin asked.

"Plan?"

"Don't do this to me, Klöss." Gavin groaned. "You weren't planning on just walking up to them and being taken prisoner were you?"

"That's assuming they take prisoners, isn't it?" Klöss's response had sounded funny in his own head. A dig meant to shock the thief to silence. Now that it was said though, it didn't sound so funny. He'd worked under a standing order of not taking prisoners. How many of the Anlish had he butchered? Was it really so far-fetched that they might do the same?

His mood darkened as he considered it and they continued on in silence. The road climbed up out of the trees and by mid-morning they emerged out onto a plain. Grass stretched out on both sides, extending towards rolling hills on their right whilst a blur in the distance on the left gave the promise of distant farms.

"It is not right," Tristan muttered after a while.

"Hmm?"

"I cannot see the sea," he explained, waving at the rolling hills. There have not been many times in my life when I could not see the waves, even far in the distance. There have been fewer still when I could not smell it."

Klöss nodded. It was a strange thing and not one he was enjoying. Idly he wondered just how large this land was. How much farther west it stretched.

They never stopped to eat. It was easier to keep moving and eat on the road.

Their pace was light but the condition of the road made up the difference and Klöss had reasoned that, even if they weren't pressing hard, they should be making fifteen miles a day or more.

"Horsemen." Gavin nodded at the horizon to the left of their path. They stopped, squinting until at last Klöss shrugged. "I can't see anything."

"There, look, on the ridgeline there." He pointed.

"Maybe," he conceded, shrugging at Tristan and receiving one in return. "We're getting closer if nothing else."

The road stretched on, the rutted surface taking them through the plains and towards the farmland they'd spotted in the distance. It was close to dark when they spotted the figure. A woman by the look of her, though she hunched low and leaned heavily on a thick staff.

"What do you want to do?" Gavin asked.

"We carry on," Klöss said after a moment. "We just ignore her."

She turned and stared back at them as they drew closer, stepping to the edge of the road to let them pass. Either she'd aged early or she'd had a long, hard life. Either way she must be stronger than she looked. The pack on her back barely seemed to slow her at all but the dark robe was wrapped around a body that looked to be little more than bones. Her white hair hung out from under her hood and surrounded a face heavily lined and a mouth pinched into a scowl.

Tristan nodded at her as they passed but neither side offered a word. They carried on, feeling her eyes on them as they walked.

"Think she knew?" Gavin asked in an unnecessary whisper as the woman fell further behind them.

"Does it matter if she did?" Klöss asked. "Who is she going to tell?"

They camped by the side of the road again that night, keeping their fire small. The night was clear and the waning moon was little more than sliver in the sky. Klöss leaned against a rock as he looked back at the road they'd travelled. The fire was as small as theirs but, in the black, he could easily pick out the glow of the woman's camp. Though he couldn't put a reason to it the sight made him uneasy.

The next day was bright and clear, the sun warm despite the chill air.

"We're going to have to stop and hunt again soon, we're getting low on supplies," Gavin said as he rummaged in his pack.

"We don't have time," Klöss told him. "A day or two on dried meat and fruit won't kill you."

"I might prefer it if it did," Gavin muttered.

Tristan grinned at him. "It is nobody's favourite," he told him, handing over a strip of dried meat.

Gavin ripped off a piece with his teeth and chewed slowly, grimacing.

"Oh it's not that bad." Klöss laughed. "Stop being such a baby."

Gavin hissed and reached for Klöss's arm, pointing wordlessly off to one side of them. The troops were easy to see, the horses they rode made it almost impossible for them to hide. They rode across the fields at an angle where they would cross the road slightly ahead of Klöss and the others.

"This is about as far as we go then," Klöss said, tensing despite himself. "If you two want to head back before they spot us…"

"I think it is too late for that." Tristan pointed. The horsemen had changed course, headed directly for them.

Klöss eased his sword out, laying it slowly down on the road in an obvious motion as he nodded at the others to follow. The horsemen fanned out, keeping their distance as some of the riders produced bows.

It hung there for a moment and Klöss looked from horse to horse until one rider eased forward.

The words were muffled behind the helm and Klöss looked blankly back at him.

"I don't speak your tongue," he said in what he hoped were calm tones.

The rider tried again, barking something unintelligible and stabbing a finger down at the ground.

"I think he wants us to get on our knees." Gavin hissed.

"Hells with that idea!" Klöss scoffed, glancing back at the thief.

The blow caught him on the helm, not hard enough to do any real damage, but enough to stagger him. Klöss spun in place, glaring up at the rider who'd struck him.

He sat back in his saddle, still holding the mace and stabbed at the ground again, roaring words out in his strange tongue.

"I don't speak your fucking language!" Klöss yelled back, his temper gone.

The rider edged forward, raising his weapon again.

* * *

Miriam chewed slowly. The oatcakes were stale and tasteless and, to be fair, she was sick of them. They stuck to her teeth and to the roof of her mouth, sucking all the moisture from her tongue until she was forced to swill water in from the wineskin and use that to her help chew. It was something that Caerl had done, taking a drink when his mouth was already full of food, and she'd always found it disgusting.

She glanced up at the sun. It was too bright to risk bringing Aervern's sight to check for the trail of the Wyrdeweavers. The fae had warned her about using the sight when the sun was out. She got to her feet, dusting the crumbs from her robe and packed quickly. The oatcakes she packed last, placing them on top of the blankets.

She counted them quickly, though she already knew the number. "It's make them last, or go hungry," she muttered to herself, as she hoisted the pack and picked up the staff.

It had been three days since she'd left Denn's camp. The first time Aervern had appeared, she'd refused to speak to her at all. Ignoring her until the fae had set down the supplies and left.

She'd come again the second night and stared until Miriam had relented. New moon was coming, she'd explained. The fae could not cross until the full moon returned. Until then, Miriam would need make her supplies last or fend for herself.

"It's a road, Miriam," she told herself, looking out at the trail that she knew lay ahead of her. "Unless they went out onto the fields then their trail's right there in front of you."

She set off. The walking worked slowly to ease the stiffness from sore muscles and she set a light pace until they were warmer. She could feel herself slowly growing stronger, fitter. Ileriel had kept her close, like a prized pet, when she hadn't shunned her and set her to working with the other women. A life spent picking terris berries and birthing fae-born hadn't made for legs that were accustomed to long journeys.

The walking wasn't so bad, it was the thinking that was the problem. The more time she spent in Haven, in her own world, the more her memories surfaced. She'd wondered for a time if it was the fae, or something about their realm, that affected the memories. Perhaps it was both. In any event, the longer she spent in Haven the clearer her mind became.

She'd spent three hours the previous night crying over children she barely remembered having. The fae-born had been taken from her almost as soon as they were born, given to other human women to feed and care for. It was the way of things in the breeding camps and being Ileriel's trophy had given her no protection.

A shout cut through her thoughts. She stopped dead, cocking her head to listen until she heard a second yell. The road curved ahead of her, blocking her view as it passed around a hill. For long minutes she stood, unsure what to do, before she shrugged and made her way around the corner.

The horses filled the road, spilling over onto the grass. Riders dressed in shining mail and plate armour faced into the centre of a rough circle they had formed. She approached slowly, being careful not to be too quiet. The last thing she wanted to do was spook these men. A rider wheeled his horse to face her.

"What do you want here, old woman?" he demanded in a deep voice.

She blinked at his tone. "Nothing, sir. I'm just following the road."

He stared at her, narrowing his eyes as if deciding if there was anything wrong with her response before directing her around them and onto the grass.

She went deliberately, taking time to set her feet. Though, if she were honest, it was curiosity slowing her feet far more than the slope of the grass. The men that had passed her on the road stood surrounded by horsemen. She'd paid more attention to their faces when they passed her before and hadn't paid attention to the odd black leather armour and strangely fashioned helmets they wore. As she watched a rider barked out a question again. "What do you do here, Bjornman? You're piss-poor spies. Are you deserters or have you come to surrender?"

The man looked back at the rider blankly as Miriam picked her way closer.

"Kneel in surrender, man," the rider ordered, pointing down at the road. When no movement was forthcoming, a rider behind the Bjornman nudged his horse forward and slammed a mace down, driving the Bjornman to his knees.

Horses shifted, blocking Miriam's view and drowning out the next words, but the shout of the Bjornman she heard clearly. "I don't speak your fucking language!"

She was moving before she could stop herself. "Lords love me for a fool," she muttered as she squeezed between two horses.

"He says he can't understand you, sir," she spoke up.

The rider's head shot round, shocked to see her there but refusing to show it. "What would you know of it, old woman? Do you speak this gibberish language?"

She nodded.

"Come closer, woman. Tell this man he must kneel in surrender or die where he stands."

"He wants you to surrender," she said to the men. The Islik felt odd on her tongue, the words rough and unrefined.

If the man was shocked she spoke his language he didn't show it. "What does he think we're doing? I thought it was bloody obvious when we put our weapons down."

"You have to kneel, apparently." She shrugged.

"Damned if I…" the man said but stopped as his larger companion reached for his arm. "It is easier, Klöss."

"They surrender," she told the rider simply as the Bjornmen knelt. She stepped back but stopped at a sharp look.

"Where do you think you're going, old woman?" the rider asked her.

Miriam cursed herself under her breath. "I'll just be on my way, sir. I want no trouble."

He shook his head. "I have questions that need answering, woman, as will Major Rhenkin. You'll have to come with us."

"But, sir!" she protested, thinking furiously. "I'm expected at my niece's. She's with child and I'm to help her with the birth."

His face might as well have been etched from stone. "I'm sorry, old woman, this is more important. Your niece will just have to muddle through on her own. You will have to come with us."

She bit back half a dozen responses before she realised she was angry about a niece that didn't exist.

"What's happening?" the Bjornman hissed at her.

"They want me to go with them," she muttered.

"What are you telling him?" the rider demanded.

"He asked what was going on," she told him. "I was merely telling him you wished me to accompany you."

He bristled at that. "Speak to them only when ordered to do so, do you understand me?"

Miriam nodded. The man was clearly overly impressed with his own authority. He had probably been a bully as a child, she decided.

The Bjornmen were bound with strong ropes and the four of them led to a line of extra horses.

"Tell them to get on," a horseman instructed her.

The Bjornman shook his head as she translated. "We can't ride. We don't use horses where we come from."

What manner of people didn't use horses? she wondered to herself. "They don't ride."

"They'd best learn quickly then, hadn't they?" came the uncaring response.

It had been years since Miriam had even seen a horse, and riding double with a man who had no idea what he was doing did not help. She managed to whisper some words of instruction to keep the man on the horse but, even so, she was soon sore from the motion. They fared better than the other Bjornmen though. It was barely five minutes before the first one, a giant of a man, fell crashing to the ground amid a flurry of curses.

He scrambled to his feet, face flushing at the laughter from the soldiers surrounding them.

"Grip with your legs," she called across to him. She didn't understand the word he called back at her, the tone was clear enough though.

They stopped in a gully that night, the soldiers setting camp with well-practised precision. She went where directed and perched on the blankets they gave her. She was so tired it took her ten minutes to realise they were her own. The food was bland but hot. After days surviving on oatcakes it was a feast and she devoured it, ignoring the amused looks of the soldiers closest to her.

It was fully dark before she attempted it. She'd never thought to ask if Aervern's Grace could be seen when she used it. The soldiers closest to her were already snoring softly and those on watch stood far enough away from her that, even if Aervern's sight were visible and showed on her somehow as she used it, they wouldn't see anything.

It took longer than expected. For one frantic moment she wondered if the power had been leeched from her by the sun and she was close to panic as she cast around within herself for the fae's power. It came to her in a rush and her head spun as her sight brightened to reveal every part of the camp. The light from the fires stabbed at her eyes and she looked away quickly, searching the darkness for the light she had seen at the Withengate. After minutes she gave up, closing her eyes. She'd taken too long, the power already felt weaker within her. Silently she told herself she'd been stupid to waste it.

The sound caught her by surprise. A shimmering sound so faint she thought she was imagining it until she truly focused on it. The echoes of the Wyrde. Though she couldn't see it for some reason she could still hear it. She could still sense it. She might be forced to continue with the soldiers for the time being but at least they were still travelling in the same direction as the trail of the Wyrdeweavers.

They rode for four days, riding harder each day as the prisoners grew more able to keep their seats. Though she wasn't quite treated as a prisoner she may as well have been. She was fed and treated well but largely ignored. The soldiers wouldn't speak to her and the snatches of conversation she managed to steal with the Bjornmen revealed little more than their names.

She took to eating alone when they stopped for the night, staring up at the growing moon and wondering what would happen when it grew full enough for Aervern to return.

The town came into sight on the morning of the fifth day, emerging from the line of the cliffs they followed as the road turned to the north. It seemed an odd place. It was not really large enough to be called a city but it was larger than a simple town ought to be and was heavily fortified. The buildings within the walls seemed grander than she remembered those of Kavtrin being. Even from this distance she could make out the decorative line of the roofs and what must be fountains and statues in the squares.

"Captain?" she called to the rider who'd forced her to come with him.

He glanced over at her and flushed, the first emotion other than irritation she'd seen from him. "Corporal," he corrected her.

"Sorry, corporal." She didn't quite manage to suppress the smile. "What town is that?"

"Druel," he said shortly and turned away from her.

Druel, that made sense then. The town was a bit of a contradiction from what she remembered, though she'd never actually been there herself. As the seat of the ducal palace it was the capital of the duchy. Despite this fact it was smaller than Kavtrin by probably half. As they drew closer it became obvious that the fortifications were a recent addition and great wooden scaffolds showed that more work was ongoing.

The corporal rode ahead of the double line of horsemen, dismounting to speak to men near the gates, and then waving them forward as another man mounted a horse and galloped into the town.

The line of riders passed through the gates ahead of them as other men rushed forward to take the bridles of their horses and pull Miriam and the Bjornmen to one side, motioning for them to dismount. A ring of spearmen moved to surround them. The spears were held low but the eyes of the men didn't waver. Miriam glanced at the Bjornmen but they stood easily, relaxed and seeming unconcerned. Her eyes darted left and right and with a sigh she settled in to wait.

The figure that emerged from the gates was flanked by guards. He was a tall man, his uniform impeccable with gold braiding on one shoulder, and he watched them as he approached. Other people might look at you but this man examined her. He studied everything from her eyes, to how she stood close to the wall. The intensity of his gaze left her feeling exposed and she reached to pull her robe more tightly around herself, avoiding his eyes until they moved on to the Bjornmen.

He stopped to have a brief, muttered conversation with the corporal and the man who'd met them at the gates, before drawing closer.

"I'm told you can speak their language?" His voice was like his eyes, direct and intense.

"Is that a question, captain?" she paused before the title, making the word itself a question.

He snorted, twisting his lips into a rough approximation of a smile. "Major, actually." The smile fell away, leaving her wondering if it had been false or if the stern expression that followed was the pretence. "Now answer the question. Can you speak their language?"

There was no point in denying it. "Yes," she told him simply.

He nodded to himself, looking off to one side for a moment. "I won't bother asking you how you learnt it. I would like you to stay and translate for me. There are many things we need to ask these men."

That was unexpected. "You're giving me a choice?" Miriam asked.

He winced. "I was attempting to be polite. To be honest..." he looked at her expectantly.

"Miriam," she supplied.

"To be honest, Miriam, this is too important to allow you to go free. For the short-term at least, I am afraid you must remain with us here at Druel."

* * *

Klöss shifted in the straw, making the chains on his wrists and legs clink. The chains were probably overkill anyway. There was no way they could have made it through the thick wooden door to escape. A single, barred window, set high on one wall let light slant down into the cell and he closed his eyes for a moment, listening to the distant sound of the wind. "What time do you think it is?"

Tristan grunted. "Early, I think. Not much past dawn. We would hear more noise from above otherwise."

Klöss nodded. It was a good point. He looked over at the man and the look on his face. "What is it?" he asked.

"Gavin," Tristan replied. "He has been gone a long time now."

"That doesn't mean anything, you know?" Klöss told him. "This is all games. More than likely they finished with him hours ago and just put him in another cell. They want us to worry. It gives them leverage when they speak to us."

Tristan grunted, falling silent for a while before he spoke again. "Well, we seem to have found the Anlish, Klöss," he said with a sidelong glance. "What was the rest of the plan?"

Klöss shot him a black look. It was a good question though, despite the joke. "We wait, I suppose. We don't have a lot of other options."

Tristan didn't answer that, shrugging and shifting in the straw as he leaned into the corner. Klöss watched him, envious. Though his hands were manacled they were at least chained in front of him rather than holding them up to the wall. The chain had enough give to allow him to lay down if he really wanted to but the position was awkward. The straw might be cleaner than he'd expected but he still didn't want it pressed to his face. Whether by design or a happy accident sleep had, so far, been denied him.

He stared at the door, letting his mind drift as Tristan's low snores rumbled from the corner. Where was Ylsriss now? He'd left it too long. He should have done something as soon as he received the message from his father. The thought brought a pang of guilt with it. He'd thought she'd just taken the child and gone. The child...

His son. He'd never even seen him. The thought piled the guilt higher and he shook his head. This was not the stuff to be thinking about right now.

The clank from the door woke him. He must have slept despite everything. He shook himself and glanced at Tristan to be sure the noise had woken him too.

Lantern light spilled into the cell, despite the light from the window, and a guard stepped in to crouch and fumble with his chains. In a smooth motion he removed the chain, leaving Klöss with just his hands manacled together. He stepped back and met Klöss's eyes, saying something Klöss couldn't understand but which he took to be an instruction for him not to do anything bloody stupid.

They hauled him to his feet, not ungently, and pulled him out into the hallway. The trip through the stone corridors was short but Klöss took the time to take note of the things he hadn't noticed on the way in. This was not a dungeon by any means. If he had to guess he'd have said they'd been placed in some manner of a military stockade. The walls looked fresher than he would have expected and part of this complex was new, if he was any judge.

The halls and corridors became a blur, punctuated with three flights of stairs until they stopped at a polished oak door and knocked before being called in.

The room was dominated by a large wooden desk, piled high with papers. Books lined one wall near the window but the majority of the walls were covered in maps and charts. Klöss absorbed the room in a moment and was struck by how much it reminded him of Frostbeard's study back in Rimeheld. Two men sat at the desk and they stood as the guards brought Klöss in.

The guards left him after a brief discussion and Klöss studied the men as they spoke together. *It was an odd language,* he thought, *nasal but yet somehow flowery.*

One of the men was clearly someone of importance. He hadn't had an opportunity to have a good look at him at the gates. The spearmen had kept them pressed to the wall as if they might overrun the town all on their own. He looked tired. Not the kind of tired that comes from missing a night's sleep but the kind that grows over weeks and months. A fatigue that has been shrugged aside so many times that it becomes almost a comfort, a norm.

He spoke, looking at Klöss, but then shifting his eyes to a corner behind him as he finished.

"He says his name is Major Rhenkin. He's in command here. He'd like to know your name." The voice took him by surprise and he looked back to see Miriam sat in a plain wooden chair in the corner. The woman looked small and frail. It was more than just that though, she looked trapped, like a caged animal eager for escape.

He took his lip between his teeth as he thought, then stopped himself. Nerves was not something he wanted to be displaying here. "Major is a name or a title?" he asked.

"A title," Miriam replied. "A rank in the army."

"So he would be someone of importance then?" Klöss pressed. "I need to speak to someone with some authority not just the commander of a local fort."

She nodded. "I would say that he is, yes."

"And the man with him?"

"His assistant, I think," Miriam told him. "A man named Kennick."

"Then tell him my name is Klöss. I am... I *was*, Shipmaster and Lord of Rimeheld."

Miriam relayed his words and listened to the response before asking him to sit.

"Your companion, the young man Gavin, has told us some fantastic tales," Rhenkin said, with Miriam translating.

"He's a young man," Klöss shrugged. "They're easily impressed."

Rhenkin smiled, a thin smile that was a nod towards politeness but little more. "You people have invaded this land, burned our villages, and driven off our people. You drove my forces back from the coast. Hell, you drove me out of the village of Widdengate myself. Is there any reason why I shouldn't just have you killed?"

"Because you're not an idiot," Klöss said, fighting down a smile at Miriam's startled reaction. "I hadn't realised it was you I'd faced. You're a skilled commander, the defence of that village was masterful." He shook his head. "I would never have thought of using logs in place of stone for the catapults. You're a man who can think on his feet and you must know there is more at stake here than a few villages. I didn't come here to talk about your lands. I came to talk about the keiju."

Miriam frowned at the last word. "Keiju, I don't know that word."

Klöss grimaced. "I don't know what you call them. The creatures with eyes like torchlight. The goat men."

She froze then, hissing a breath in between her teeth. "They call them the fae," she told him, and relayed his sentence.

Rhenkin paused, narrowing his eyes as he met Klöss's gaze and his assistant whispered into his ear. "And what would you know about this?"

Klöss shrugged. "We thought they were your troops to start with," he admitted. "Some sort of special unit. They appeared from nowhere, tore through my men like a reaver in calm seas."

"A reaver?" Miriam queried.

"A fast ship," Klöss explained, frowning at the interruption. "But then I saw them attack your forces in the middle of a battle. I saw them come down from the sky. I've tried lying to myself, pretending it didn't happen. That it didn't matter..." he paused, waiting for Miriam to catch up. "In the end I couldn't ignore it. They came too far through our lines, appearing miles behind our patrols. They emptied whole villages, leaving the bodies on stakes. I've seen things..." he fell silent and shook his head, waving at Miriam to pass it on.

Rhenkin and Kennick spoke then. A rushed, whispered conversation, before Rhenkin shook his head, obviously disagreeing with something.

"And so you came. You three, alone. No messenger, no parlay. The Lord of Rimeheld walked, alone, into Anlish territory and simply handed himself over." His expression made his meaning clear even if his voice hadn't been thick with sarcasm. "Why would you do this?"

"Because I have men I report to." Klöss sighed. "And those men are idiots."

Rhenkin raised an eyebrow and motioned for Klöss to continue.

Klöss shifted in the chair. "A village was attacked, behind our lines. I've told you this already but it wasn't the last. There is no way these attacks could possibly have been from Anlish troops but yet the sealord wouldn't accept this. He insisted, despite all the evidence, that this was an Anlish raid. The fact it was so far behind the lines just made him hungrier for revenge."

"And you disagree? You don't believe this?" The question was so close to a statement he barely lifted his voice.

"I told you, I've seen things..." Klöss said quietly.

Rhenkin absorbed that for a moment before continuing. "What is this 'sealord' planning?"

Klöss pursed his lips, considering. "I'm here to talk about the keiju. The fae, as you call them. I'm not here to give away my people."

"Your people have already butchered half their way across two duchies!" Kennick burst out.

Klöss gave the man a cold look and turned his attention back to Rhenkin. "I will tell you this much and no more. The sealord has taken direct control of this conflict. He has no true interest in taking a small portion of land. He was furious about the attack at Skelf, the first of the villages I mentioned. The last I saw he was sending the fleet south to burn."

"To burn what?" Kennick demanded.

Klöss shrugged. "Who could say?"

Kennick glowered at that but Klöss ignored him. His attention was fixed on Rhenkin, and the cold blue eyes that bore into him.

CHAPTER EIGHTEEN

"Grass," Joran said, barely bothering to glance at the strand Devin held.

"I know it's grass," Devin laughed from where he sat beside him on the gentle bank that sloped down to the water's edge. "That's an easy one. A *what* of grass though?"

That brought silence as the older man's brown creased. "A sword?" he offered finally.

"Close," Devin said with a smile. "A blade of grass."

Joran grunted and looked over his shoulder back towards the cottage. "They've been at it all day again."

Devin shrugged, careful not to knock the pole and scare off any fish. "Obair loses track of time. Keep your voice down or we'll never catch anything."

Joran looked from the surface of the lake to Devin's face. "You're sure you can catch fish with a stick like this?"

"Yes." Devin laughed. "You've never fished?"

"I only remember fishing with nets. Even that's a bit hazy," Joran said slowly. "Drowning worms seems an odd way to catch fish."

"The fish try to eat the worms." Devin laughed again. "That's how we catch them."

"Why would fish try and eat worms?" Joran asked. "How would a fish even know what a worm was? It's not as if there would be worms in the lake is it?"

"I…" Devin stopped, frowning. "You know, I never thought of it like that. I guess fish just aren't that clever." He looked at Joran as the man shuddered again. "Are you cold?"

"I'm cold a lot here," Joran admitted. "I can't get used to this place. It's cold, it's hot. You never know what it's going to be from one day to the next."

"You'll get used to it, I suppose you just have to give it time," Devin said. "The idea of a place where the sun is only in the sky for an hour a day is as strange to me as this world must be to you."

Joran nodded in silence and squinted up at the sky.

Devin watched his expression. "You miss it, don't you?"

Joran smiled, seeming almost embarrassed by the question. "I do. It's the only home I've ever really known. I mean, I know that this was where I was born but I can barely remember any of that." He shrugged. "Despite the fae, the Touch, despite all of it, it feels like home to me. I don't know how to act in this place. I don't know what to do." He looked down, avoiding Devin's eyes. "Ylsriss wanted to escape the fae to try and find Effan, her son. In the end though, it was me that pulled her through to this world. Not that we had much choice, you understand. The satyr were all around us. It was flee or die. The thing is, now that we're here, I realise how little I know this place. Ylsriss has people out there. They're probably looking for her. No matter how far away they are they're still out there. I was taken so long ago I don't even remember who my family is."

Devin looked at him long enough for Joran to glance up and meet his eyes. "I'm more or less alone too. I can't pretend to understand what it's like having been taken but I know what it's like to lose family. To lose a feeling of belonging somewhere."

The conversation fell silent for a minute and Devin stood to pull his line out of the water to check the hook before flicking it back in. "What are they really like?" he asked, looking over at Joran.

"Who?"

"The fae." He lowered himself down to the bank again, leaning his back against the smooth bark of a willow tree. "I just know them as something to fear, as the enemy. You lived with them for years. What are they actually like?"

Joran thought for a moment. "Different," he said. "Different to what you'd think." He smiled as Devin started to laugh.

"They are though," he began again. "And it's a mistake to think of them as all the same. A deer is a deer is a deer, right? They all look roughly the same and they'll all act more or less the same. The fae are more like us. They have their own personalities, their own wants. They're not like mindless animals hating us for hate's sake. They each have their own thoughts and feelings."

"You make them sound almost human."

"They are," Joran admitted. "And then at the same time they're not. They look at us like animals, probably because compared to them we're so small and weak. No human could ever hope to be as fast or strong as a fae. They live longer than us too. I've never seen one grow older. For all I know they might live forever. And then, of course, there is the Lady's Grace."

Devin blinked. "The what?"

"Their magic, I suppose is the best way to describe it." Joran forgot about fishing and set the pole down next to him in the grass. "They take power from the moonlight. They call that the Lady's Gift. Then they can use it to move faster, create glamours, visions of lights. I don't have the words to describe it."

"Illusions I think you mean," Devin said, then motioned for him to go on.

Joran gave a nod of thanks. "They all use it differently. Satyr use it to give them more strength and speed, though Aervern told me they use illusion to seduce as well."

"Aervern?"

"A...uh, fae that I met," he said, looking embarrassed.

Devin raised an eyebrow and gave him a sidelong glance. "It sounds like there's a story there."

Joran coughed and looked down to his hands, twisting inside each other. "Another time, maybe."

Devin got the hint. It was hard to miss after all. "Tell me more about the magic."

"There's not much more to tell," Joran said with a shrug. "They take the moonlight and use it to work their magic. Fae can do more with it than Satyr while Fae'reeth barely seem to use it at all. Then there's Aelthen, he can do things that I've never seen any of the others do."

"Aelthen?"

"Their leader. Well the leader of those at Tir Rhu'thin anyway." He shrugged. "I don't really know what he is. He doesn't really look like any of the others. He's a little like a satyr, I suppose, though he has antlers not small horns, and he has the body of a stag."

Devin nodded. "I've seen him," he said. "Twice now."

Joran went on, missing the grating tone in Devin's voice and the way he'd clenched his fists tight around the fishing pole. "Then of course there are the glyphs."

Devin's hands unclenched as he asked with genuine curiosity. "That's what Ylsriss and Obair are doing now?"

Joran nodded. "It's like a kind of writing, I suppose. That's the easiest way to describe it. A fae can sort of push their power into the inscriptions, and then anyone can use them. They were used for lamps and cooking with in the camps, but then in the city we found there were things there I've never seen anywhere else."

"Like the way you got home?" Devin put in.

"Yes." Joran nodded, eyes far away. "And those things didn't need the fae to power them at all. Ylsriss seems to think the people who made them had found a way to work glyphs completely independent of the fae. Even hundreds of years later most of them still worked perfectly, they just needed power."

"Hold on a minute," Devin said, eyes widening as he stopped in the middle of a nod and reached out for Joran's arm. "I thought you told me the city was ancient and abandoned?"

"It was," Joran said gently easing his arm from Devin's grip.

"Well then," Devin shook his head. "I mean, where did all the people go? Where did they come from in the first place?"

"I suppose the fae could have taken them from here. The fae didn't talk to us slaves much but they made it clear that we'd served them before," Joran said. "But then Aervern also sort of told me that we humans had come from somewhere else. This place," he waved an arm around vaguely, "was discovered by man and fae working together."

"Slow down a minute, this is too much." Devin pulled his knees up and turned to face Joran, shaking his head. "You're telling me that we, mankind, we don't even belong here?"

"No, not that." He waved his hands as if warding off the words. "Well, okay, maybe that is what I meant. It's just that we didn't start here. It might have all be lies for all I know, you can't tell with the fae, but that's what I've been told."

"You don't believe that though," Devin said, giving the man a serious look. "That it's lies, I mean."

Joran shook his head slowly. "No, you're right. I suppose I don't. The fae call this world The Land of Our Lady. Probably something to do with the way the moon stays in the sky for longer. The way Aervern spoke about it she made this place sound like the fae's heaven. They don't have gods or religion or anything like that but that's the best way I can think to describe it. Their promised land. As for where the people from that city went? Well, I think they came here."

Devin welcomed the silence that fell. It was too much to take in all at once. "And you've told Obair all this already?" He said eventually, looking back in the direction of the cottage.

"Yes, days ago. Why?" he replied, looking up as Devin scrambled to his feet.

"I just feel like I'm always playing catch up." Devin muttered as Joran pulled himself up. "I'm tired of being treated like a child, being the last to know things. He looks at me like a puzzle, something he can't understand. But there are things he's not telling me either. I can see it in his eyes." He sighed and glanced back towards the cottage again. "Let's go and see how they're getting along. We're not catching anything here anyway."

"I'm not that surprised. I wouldn't want to eat drowned worms either," Joran said quietly to the surface of the lake as he pulled his line in and set off after Devin.

* * *

There was something soothing about the sound of the pen scratching. It wasn't an intrusive noise, nothing so annoying as a branch brushing against a window pane or shutters banging in the wind. It was something she could just let wash over her and Ylsriss took comfort from it. She took the next page in the sequence. Obair had drawn the ritual out over several sheets of paper, laying them flat on the floor so the steps lined up.

"You see here," she said pointing the spiralling markings. "It's the first stages of an activation sequence. It couldn't be clearer." She waved the paper at Obair and moved closer. "This third glyph series is an odd choice. It seems to be drawing on energy that there is no conduit for but…" she stopped. "You can't understand a word I'm saying can you?"

Obair looked up from the paper with a blank look and smiled.

She sighed. It was intensely frustrating to be dependent on the one person she'd rather claw her own eyeballs out than talk to. She lowered her eyes to the paper again. It was strangely compelling. The ritual that Obair was sketching out wasn't immediately clear as glyphs. Obair dragged the pen in an almost constant flow of ink to trace the steps of his ritual. The glyphs, however, were distinct characters and it took time for her to puzzle out where each glyph started and the next began. Not for the first time she wished she still had access to the silvery books left behind in the Realm of Twilight. Transcribing the glyphs was one thing, understanding them would be far more difficult.

Already the complexity of the ritual astounded her. There were glyph series and partnerings that she'd never seen before. Some that seemed to completely contradict what she thought she knew.

"Get it written out first, Ylsriss," she muttered to herself. "Bang your head against it later." She picked up her own pen and dipped it into the ink to note down the next glyph in the sequence.

The voices stopped her hand with a sigh. It was so quiet in the cottage, and in the local area for that matter, that the sound of speech carried easily. Joran and Devin were returning from the lake. The spatter of ink drew her eyes to the paper and the spray she'd made as her hand clenched to a fist around the quill pen, snapping the cut tip against the paper.

She swore and reached for something to blot the ink away.

"Good, you're back," she said in flat, businesslike tones as the door opened and Joran and Devin came in. "I need you to translate."

Joran stopped with his hand still on the door he was closing, taken aback for a moment. "How have you been getting on?" he asked finally.

"Well enough, but now I need you to translate," she replied, allowing a touch of frustration to enter into her voice as Devin and Obair spoke quietly in their odd tongue.

"Fine," Joran sighed and looked to the old man. "Ylsriss wants me to translate for her. She has some more questions, I suppose."

"Good, good!" the old druid nodded and pushed his chair back from the desk. "Let's sit at the table. It's a bit cramped with us all pushed into this corner. Devin, do you suppose you could put the kettle on to boil? I'm suddenly very dry."

Ylsriss followed the others to the table, setting down her paper in front of her. "I'm working through the pattern and the individual glyphs are easy enough to find, well, most of the time," she told Obair. "What I can't understand is how the sequence draws power. If there were capture plates or something it would make more sense. As it is…" She shrugged as she shook her head. "You say this ritual of yours powered the Wyrde, or whatever you called it? Somehow kept the fae from coming into this world? I can't see how. The glyphs I might be able to puzzle out but without a fae to give their Gift, or capture plates to imbue this, I'm at a loss."

Obair nodded as Joran finished relaying the question and looked over Ylsriss as he spoke. "I was never told of any power source, as you call it. The ritual requires precise steps and concentration as it weaves around the stones but nothing like you've described when you told us of the way these glyphs function." He waited for a moment for Joran, before continuing. "That said, the more we're here the less I feel I know for sure. Lillith hints at things in her diary that I don't like to think about." He spoke the last words softly, dropping his gaze to the table.

"That's another thing," Ylsriss said, leaning forward to point at the paper. "Why the ritual at all? The glyphs would work no matter where they were inscribed. Moonorbs had the glyphs in the wooden base, runeplates had them carved into the rock. The only reason glyphs are inscribed into something is so they last. Why rely on footsteps? They're so tenuous they can barely be called a glyph at all."

Obair bit at his knuckle for a minute. "Safety, I suppose," he said finally. "The druids were hunted almost to extinction at one point. Having a huge carved stone inscription would make it hard to run. There's another element to it as well though," he explained to Joran. "The steps are only half of it. At the same time, as the ritual works around the stones, the steps must also be traced in the mind, forcing the sense of the moon along the path."

"Hold on, that doesn't make any sense at all," Ylsriss objected. "The mental bit, okay fine, I don't understand that, but why the stones? If the ritual was to replace written glyphs so you could flee then what about the stones? The stones have nothing to do with the glyphs. These series would work if they were written on a wall somewhere, provided you had the power source. Even if you didn't you could trace these steps in a cellar somewhere and no one would be the wiser. Why complicate things by trying to work the steps of this thing around a collection of stones?"

Hissing prompted Devin to rise and pull the kettle from the fire. "Maybe they have another use?" he called as he set about fetching cups. "You two arrived here at the stone. The fae came through the stones near Widdengate. Are the stones themselves the gateway?"

"I can't see that," Joran said, speaking quickly after translating what Devin had said. "If the stones were needed to pass through the Worldtrails then why not just smash them? That would keep the fae away forever."

"They're not exactly small," Devin said, handing steaming cups around. "The ones at Widdengate weren't as large as these but the ones in the centre were still bigger than any of us. I take your point though."

"There's more to this than just the stones," Obair said in a small voice. The quiet words cut through the conversation and left the tatters hanging as the others stopped to look at him. "Lillith mentioned another ritual, one I knew nothing about."

Devin was the first to speak. "Another one? What for?"

Obair shook his head in silence and for the first time Ylsriss noticed how haggard the man looked. He wasn't a young man by any means but it was more than just age that lined his face. It was a weariness etched deep, but overlaid with sorrow and what she fancied might be guilt. "Lillith left a diary, you've seen it. She talks about things. Things I could never have guessed at." He fell silent and the guilt that showed on his face kept company with such bitterness and self-loathing that Ylsriss almost moved away from Joran's whispered translation to put her arms around the man.

"She talks about a guardian," Obair explained. "A man tasked to work a ritual apart from the one that maintained the Wyrde and kept mankind safe from the fae. This ritual was so vile that the guardian was always kept ignorant of its true purpose. No one could have been trusted to keep up this task if they knew the truth of its real purpose. Lillith knew though, the knowledge was passed down from master to student until it had reached her. She wrote about it in her diary, a kind of confession, if you will. This ritual held a soul. A captive soul, trapped for eternity within the snare of the Wyrde and, I presume, providing the power for these glyphs that you've been seeking, Ylsriss."

"Lords of Blood, Sea, and Sky!" Ylsriss breathed as Joran fell silent.

Devin spoke slowly, looking slightly sick. "So Lillith was doing this? Keeping this soul trapped?"

"No, Devin," Obair replied. His voice was barely more than a whisper. "She worked the ritual to maintain the Wyrde."

"Well if not her...?" He looked confused for a moment, and then blood drained from his face as realisation took hold.

Obair nodded simply. "My whole life has been a lie, Devin. From boyhood I've been working a ritual that I thought kept the fae at bay. Instead I've been working to keep a soul imprisoned in the worst kind of hell, trapped for all eternity. Every wriggle I felt against my mind's grip on the Wyrde, every slight struggle I fought past, was a soul seeking release and I denied them all." He opened his mouth to speak again but words had failed him. It didn't matter. There were no words to match the horror in his eyes.

* * *

The stones were silent in the early morning light. Dew still beaded the grass and Devin's soft boots looked like they already soaked. A crunch of leaves turned his head towards the trail and Ylsriss and Joran as they approached.

"You're up early," he called in greeting.

"I could say the same of you," Joran replied with a faint smile.

"Obair?"

"Still sleeping," Joran replied as he drew close. "We thought we should leave, let him rest."

"For all the good that will do." Devin grunted. "What is she doing?"

Joran glanced at Ylsriss who was examining the hubstones closely.

"If you two must speak in that babble at least tell me what he's saying." Ylsriss said, without looking back at them.

Joran smiled briefly. "He asked about Obair, and now he's wondering what you're doing."

"These stones, they're different." She pointed from the stone arch at the hub of the circle to the stones surrounding them. "Tell him?"

Devin frowned and looked closely at where she pointed. "I don't see it," he admitted.

"The rock of these central stones, look at the colour, the lines in the stone. It's not the same type of stone as all these others," Ylsriss explained.

"So?" Joran asked for both of them.

Ylsriss sighed, looking at them both as if they were particularly dense children. "So that means that one or the other type was brought here intentionally. Or even both I suppose."

Devin shook his head. "I still don't see your point."

"I'm not sure I have a point," she admitted, hugging herself against the light breeze. "It's just odd that whoever built this place would use two different types of stone. It's not as if they were just random stones either. These outer ones are all uniform. You see the blue tint to the stone? These others are closer to granite or something." She walked over to the closest of the stones forming the circle. It was shorter than the hubstones but still taller than her. She traced her fingers over the stone lightly and her small size made the stone seem all the larger.

"Why move it at all?" she whispered. She turned to the others. "These things must have a purpose. The effort of moving them and shaping them must have been enormous. Why move them here at all if the ritual would work without them?"

Devin nodded at Joran and then her. "You're right, it doesn't make much sense. Okay, let's think about it. What do we know already? You both came out of the stones here, close to the hubstones, a bit like you were passing through a doorway. If those stones are the path to the fae world, or if they mark the place of gateway at least, then what are these others for?"

He went to another stone, motioning for Joran to go to a third. The stone was weathered and pitted with age, the tall grass cradling the base almost tenderly.

"What are we looking for?" Joran called.

"I have no idea," he replied back over one shoulder, resting a hand on the stone. His hand slipped gently down the surface, running in the pits and grooves under his fingers. "Just anything really. Like Ylsriss said, they have to be here for a reason." He moved around the stone, eyes searching the surface. It seemed smoother on the side facing into the circle or was that just his imagination?

He looked around him, trying to place himself in relation to the steps of the ritual, taking the steps in his mind almost by reflex. The flash was so slight that at first he wasn't even sure he'd seen it. A glimmer of quartz caught by the rising sun perhaps? He searched for a minute before giving up and thinking on the ritual again. Closing his eyes helped and he reached for the face of the stone to steady himself. The stone was cold, icy really and he could feel the heat leeching from his hand.

The stones would be facing in at the ritual, surrounding him, watching like sentinels. Watching, remembering. He traced the steps of the ritual as Obair had taught him and, just like that, the stone flared before him, a bright flash of brilliant light that was gone in an instant. Devin gave a shocked groan and toppled backwards into the grass, clutching at hands white with frost.

"Devin!" Ylsriss cried, and ran to him. "What's wrong? Joran! Ask him what's wrong?"

Wordlessly Joran turned Devin's hand, showing the thick frost on his fingers. He bent to feel for breath and Devin gasped, lurching back again as his eyes flew open and he looked about wildly. "What? What was that?"

"What happened?" Joran asked him in a shocked voice. "We just saw you fly back from the stone and found you like this."

"I don't know," Devin said, looking past them to the stone. His hands hurt and he flexed them, turning them this way and that to find the source of the pain.

Ylsriss prodded at Joran impatiently until he translated. "What were you doing right before it happened?" he asked.

"I was…" Devin stopped, thinking back. "I was stood at the stone, trying to think how the ritual would have me placed at this point."

"That's it? Just thinking?" Joran asked.

"Yes. No…" Devin shook his head. "Now that I think about it I was tracing the ritual in my mind too. The way Obair had taught me. The same way as when you arrived. I could feel something, something in the stone, sucking the heat out of me. It felt like it was sucking the very life out of me." He fell silent as Joran translated for Ylsriss and went to the stone, looking closely, though he was careful not to touch it. It looked different somehow, though it was nothing obvious. Nothing he could put a finger to.

Ylsriss appeared at his shoulder, reaching out to touch the stone before he could stop her. He gasped as her fingers made contact but she simply stood, silent for a moment before looking up at him with a raised eyebrow.

Devin reached out but the stone was just that, stone. Cold certainly, but nothing like the burning ice that he'd felt before.

Ylsriss looked to Joran. "Heat? Another form of energy I suppose."

Joran looked from her to the stone and back again. "What? There are no glyphs here, Ylsriss. I don't think that's what this is."

She pushed past him and crouched close, running her fingers over the face of the stone. After a moment she closed her eyes, hands questing, searching. She crouched for long minutes, running her hands over the rough stone, then pausing and peering closer. Her eyes opened to look at she moved her hand but there was nothing to see. She tried again, searching for long moments before she spoke.

"Glyphs," she murmured. "There are glyphs on this."

"What? Where?" Devin leaned close, peering at the stone as Joran translated.

"It's nothing you can see," Ylsriss told him. "It was so slight I almost missed it. They're too worn and weathered. I can only just feel them."

"But, there are no fae here. No capture plates." Joran looked around as if to confirm he hadn't missed them. "What I mean is, if there are glyphs where do they draw the power from?"

Devin's eyes widened as he listened to Joran and he crouched down beside her, placing his fingertips on the stone. After a moment he frowned at her and she reached for the stone with one hand, searching for where she'd found the glyph and pulling his hand to the spot.

"Here, you feel it?" she asked, knowing he wouldn't understand but speaking anyway.

His eyes widened as he found it and he grinned. They crouched around the base of the stones, taking one each, with hands tracing over the surface and calling out as they found more of the glyphs. They found them on each stone they searched, and though some were more eroded than others they seemed identical.

"I recognise one or two of these but there's nothing even close to an activation sequence," Ylsriss said, shaking her head as Joran relayed her words. "It's so hard not being able to see them."

"Perhaps we don't need to," Joran mused.

She stopped, giving him a curious look. "What do you mean?"

He chewed his lip for a moment, thinking. "Well, Devin managed to do something just by touching them. Maybe the activation isn't built around working the glyphs in a sequence. Maybe it's something else, like the way they do the ritual."

Devin looked at them both, gesturing impatiently. "Someone else here is going to have to learn Islik or Anlish," Joran grumbled before explaining the conversation.

Devin nodded thoughtfully and turned back to the stone, pressing both hands to the stone as his eyes closed.

"Devin, no!" Joran cried. "We don't even know what it does."

Ylsriss turned at the tone. She couldn't understand the words but the cry had been clear enough. Devin stood motionless, a faint frown of concentration on his brow. As she watched he stiffened and his breath fogged, white in the air between him. The stone cooled, and then turned icy. Frost formed on his fingers as his skin grew first pale, and then took on a bluish tinge. Long moments passed and Joran gasped in shock.

"Look at his face." He pointed with a hand that shook. "Stars above, look at him!"

His skin, so pale already, was withering in front of their eyes, the vitality and youth draining away. Faint lines grew into wrinkles, and then grew deeper in moments, the crow's feet lines by his eyes growing longer and reaching down to his cheeks. Hair, so dark before, grew grey at the temples and then whiter as the very colour leeched out of it. They stood, rooted by shock as the young man aged decades in moments.

The stone flared bright in front of him. Glyphs burning incandescent against the stone and Ylsriss saw that the entire stone was covered in them. Thousands of tiny, intricate carvings that the wind and rain had scoured from the surface. A burst of light turned her head as first one, then another of the stones burst into light, until the entire circle flared brilliant in the morning light.

* * *

Devin pushed forward through a darkness, somehow moving though he knew his body remained still, pressed to the stone. At the edges of his consciousness he could feel the stones drawing the strength from him, drinking it in hungrily and reaching for more. The ritual of the Wyrde surged through his mind, almost moving by itself as it turned faster and faster until the steps were a thunder that seemed to shake his very being. There was something, something indefinable that seemed just out of reach. He could feel it, tantalisingly close, and on some level he knew it would be the key to all of this.

He was already weakening, growing lightheaded as if he'd missed a meal, then worked hours in the fields. He could feel the strength leaving him but shouldered the worry of what damage he might be doing to himself aside. He needed to know. It was a compulsion now, a need strong enough that it overrode anything else and he threw himself deeper into the effort, forcing the steps of the Wyrde onwards.

It began almost like a light, somehow cold and filling his vision, dazzling him even though he knew his eyes were closed. The sensation of movement stopped abruptly as he found himself pressed to a barrier as smooth and cool as fine glass. The power of the Wyrde was still there, pushing him onwards, and the brief irrational thought that he might be crushed passed through him with a twinge of panic.

He pushed, testing the substance of the thing as it flexed against him. The pressure behind him was enormous, bearing down on him as it forced him against the wall before him. In an instant he understood, the power wasn't forcing him into the barrier. The energy was there, just waiting to be used. Without really considering how to do it he reached for the pressure building behind him, joining it with the steps of the ritual in his mind, and drove it into the barrier. The power tore through him, blasting through whatever force had stopped him, driving him onwards. The light grew brighter, searing at his mind as well as his eyes, and then knowledge filled him.

Chapter Nineteen

Obair threw the cottage door wide in response to the screams and Joran's shouts. His hair was wild and he had the wide-eyed look of someone who had pulled themselves from their bed at the noise.

"Help us with him!" Joran shouted as they staggered towards the cottage. Devin hung between them, feet dragging on the grass as Ylsriss and Joran clung to an arm each, thrown around their shoulders.

"Damnation and ruin, what's happened to him?" the old druid gasped taking in the sight. He took Ylsriss's place, ducking under the lad's arm and hissing at the touch of his skin. "He's as cold as ice!"

"He collapsed at the stones," Joran gasped between breaths. "We found something, glyphs, but then this happened."

They dragged him up the three steps and into the cottage, lowering him into the rocking chair close to the hearth. Obair pressed his face close to the boy's frost covered lips and sighed in relief as the faint breath stirred his whiskers. "Get that fire going!" He barked the order at Joran, peeling back one of Devin's eyelids and muttering at what he saw. He stepped back, looking down at the young man as he gnawed on a knuckle.

"What happened?" he demanded, rounding on the others.

"We were looking at the stones in the circle," Joran explained as Ylsriss ran in from the bedroom with blankets, laying them over Devin and tucking them in tight. "It just didn't make any sense for them to have no purpose. We searched over them and Ylsriss thought she'd found a glyph. It was worn, and you'd never have found it by just looking, but Devin managed to activate them somehow."

"Forgotten gods! Is that his hair? I thought it was frost!" Obair muttered as he looked at the young man. "So what happened," he demanded. "Tell me everything."

"There isn't much more to tell," Joran admitted. "Devin did something, somehow managed to activate the glyphs. The whole stone circle was blazing with them. He had his eyes closed, pressing his hands against the stone, but it's almost like it was feeding itself from him. First it was frost on his hands, and then this." He waved helplessly.

"And you two just stood there and watched?" Obair demanded of them.

Joran's mouth opened and closed as he searched for the words. "It just happened so fast," he managed in the end.

Obair muttered something in disgust and turned back Devin.

The small cottage warmed quickly as the fire stirred to life and ate hungrily as Ylsriss fed it first twigs, and then small logs until the flames blazed in the hearth. Through it all Devin lay motionless while Obair quizzed first one, then the other, repeating questions and demanding answers that neither could give him.

Finally there was nothing left to ask and they sat watching as the colour slowly returned to Devin's face and fingers. Joran prepared a small meal, though none of them felt like eating, and numb fingers moved tasteless food to disinterested mouths.

As the daylight began to fade they transferred him to a bed, piling the blankets high over him. Ylsriss perched on the other bed, watching him as the others left. The low murmur of conversation carried from the other room but she felt no urge to join them. Translation made the three-way conversation awkward at the best of times.

She awoke near dawn, eyes flickering in the half-light as she reached for her neck and muscles made stiff by sleeping in the awkward position. A cup sat near her foot, filled with tea long-since gone cold. She stood and stretched, reaching up towards the ceiling as she worked her shoulders and tilted her head from side to side to try and work the knot out.

The sound was little more than a hiss but it was enough and her head whipped round to the figure in the bed. "Devin?" She leaned closer. "Are you awake?"

He hissed again, lips parting just enough to let the sound escape. His eyes were open though, wide and alert as they looked back at her, tinged with panic.

She rushed into the other room. "He's awake!" she shouted as she lit a taper from the fire and carried it through to light the stub of candle set near the bed. Devin winced against the light, blinking until his eyes adjusted.

"Has he said anything?" Joran said, looking over her shoulder.

"Not yet," she replied. "Here, help me sit him up a little." They shoved at the pillows until he was propped up in the bed.

"Ylsriss," he managed finally. The word was barely more than a whisper, slipping past lips that seemed half-numb still.

She smiled down at him. "Ask him how he feels, if he wants something to drink?" she said to Joran.

Tea seemed to make a difference, though it took Ylsriss to pour it into a shallow bowl and guide his two hands as he struggled to drink it. The warm drink seemed to help and she followed up with a thin broth. The colour returned to his cheeks slowly and by mid-morning he was back in the main room, sat in the rocker pushed so close to the fire it was a wonder it didn't scorch.

"How much do you remember?" Obair asked him.

Devin frowned, pulling his gaze from the hands that he twisted and turned in his lap as he inspecting every new line and wrinkle. "I remember going to the stones with these two. I remember most of it, I think." He spoke slowly, as if reading from a book and unsure of his letters.

"Ylsriss found glyphs," he said, looking up and smiling at the old man, finding wonder where nobody else had thought to look.

"How much do you remember about the stones," Obair clarified. "About what happened?"

The smile slipped from Devin's face as he looked at the old man. "I don't know. Fragments. It's hard to make sense of it all." The words were coming more easily to him now and he looked at the old man with an intensity in his eyes. "I can remember touching them, the feel of the stone under my hands. I remember how it went so cold. It happened so fast it was like walking out into a winter storm. It was bitter, so cold that it burned my hands but, even so, I couldn't let go of it. There was a sensation, a bit like the pressure I felt when Ylsriss and Joran arrived, and when I pushed through it was like I was somewhere else. I hadn't moved. I could still feel the stone under my fingers but somehow that all felt so distant. It was almost like I was seeing with just my mind, without the need for eyes. Like I was dreaming, I suppose, but somehow different. The images were flooding into me. I saw the entire lifetimes of dozens, no, hundreds of people in moments, and then I could see it all."

"See what?" the old man asked in bafflement, glancing at the others.

"I can't describe it. My eyes were closed but it was like I was staring into a bright light. I could feel things, see things. I could focus on one area if I wanted. I could examine the colour of a man's eyes. Or I could rise up and watch it all unfold." He paused and the next words held none of the excitement of the last. "I think it was the histories, Obair. You keep telling me that they were all destroyed in the purges but I don't think they were ever written down. The true knowledge was here all along, safe within the stones."

Obair sat back, mouth flapping as he struggled for words. "Are you sure?"

The question was so ridiculous that Devin laughed, dry painful laughs that bent him over in the chair. "I could see things," he began again. "So much that it's hard to keep it all straight. It all flooded into me so fast that it's hard to understand what happened first.

"I saw the home of the fae, saw the red and gold trees under their twilight sky. I saw the first men and women pulled into their world through gates of light, bound and tied. I watched as the years passed and their cities spread out over their world. Mankind serving the fae as slaves and then, as time went on, working with them almost as equals. I saw silvery discs set down into stone, shining bright with power as they drank in the moonlight. I can't begin to describe half the things they created. There were men and women carving glyphs down into stone, glowing bright as the power filled them. Gateways created, ways through to other worlds. Towers so high they pierced the clouds." He looked up at them to the wonder in their eyes.

"And then there was war," he began again but shook his head as his voice rasped and caught in his throat. "Do you think I could have some water? I want to tell you all this before I forget it."

Obair fetched a cup quickly, letting Joran finish as he translated quickly for Ylsriss in a low voice. Devin drank in gulps, water running from the corners of his mouth before handing the cup back.

"I saw the war begin," he said. "Saw the towns and villages of mankind fall one after the other as the armies of the fae tore through them. They fought back, of course, using weapons I don't understand. Carved rods and staffs that sent fire and ribbons of light into the armies of the fae. Glyphs set into stone that exploded when a fae came near. Terrible things that were awful to see." The words drifted into silence as Devin stared into space, his expression pained. He shook himself and gave them a wan smile before he spoke again, missing the worried looks that Obair exchanged with the others.

"It was never enough and they were always driven back. The deaths were horrific, the sheer scale of it all, an entire people driven almost to extinction. The bodies were everywhere, I remember it like I was there, like I'd lived through it myself. Finally there was only one city remaining and mankind flocked to it, huddling together as the silver banners of the fae marched closer and closer. They broke through the walls, sending the trees themselves to rip the stones apart. The sky was filled with small purple creatures with wings, fae'reeth I think they're called. Thousands of them, swarming through the streets of the city and tearing us to shreds as we fled."

Obair caught the change in the mode of address and raised his eyebrows but said nothing.

"Finally we fled. The gateway was rough and thrown together in a matter of days. The glyphs weren't perfect and a lot of it involved things that had never even been considered before, let alone tried or tested. It opened though, a gateway as wide as barn doors, and mankind rushed through in panic as satyr butchered those who'd volunteered to hold the fae back.

"The Worldtrail was tattered and badly woven. It touched down in a thousand places, flinging mankind across this new world like seeds tossed into the wind. We were scattered but we fared better than those it left in the space between worlds, frozen in an instant and left to hang among the stars.

"The gate couldn't last long and there were still thousands pressing to get to it when it collapsed. Who knows what happened to them all when it did."

He sighed hard then. Filling his lungs and puffing it out all at once before falling silent. The silence was a welcome thing, surrounding them and holding them as the images played through each of their minds.

"We were safe then," Devin said, beginning again. "Safe and free in a world that had never known the touch of the fae. Though scattered, people managed to find each other and settlements were founded. Thousands more died within those first few months. Mankind had been dependent on the fae and the glyphs for so many things and this world was alien in so many ways." He looked over at Joran, still translating for Ylsriss. "Joran forgot most of what he knew of our world before the fae took him. He's still coming to terms with it now. Can you imagine an entire race of people who'd never known the change of seasons or had to fell trees for fires? We learned, though. We adjusted and slowly we began to grow and thrive.

"I couldn't tell you how long it was before the first fae found us." He admitted with a shrug. "Some things were easy to understand but just how much time had passed? That's really hard to judge. It could be a thousand years, it could have been only a hundred. I don't suppose it matters really," he said. "They found us. They must have searched thousands of worlds before they stumbled across us. Maybe they weren't searching for us at all, perhaps it was just bad luck. Maybe it was always going to be just a matter of time." He spread his hands helplessly. "The hunt began almost at once. They passed over to this world after every full moon, taking to the skies and hunting down mankind, taking delight in the chase.

"The Wyrde was born out of this, out of desperation. The glyphs were useless to us. With no way to power them they were nothing more than writing. The knowledge of the glyphs had been kept safe, hoarded by those that would become known as the druids. It was passed down from father to son, mother to daughter. As the fae began to hunt us they came together, bringing the stores of knowledge that had been painstakingly written out. Forming the Wyrde would be complex enough, a feat of glyphlore that would have challenged those even at the very peak of when man and fae worked together. Without the ability to harness the moon, and without the help of the fae to imbue them with their Grace, the glyphs were worthless."

He looked around at them as he drew a breath. They were clustered close to him like he and Erinn had pestered Samen for stories in Widdengate. The image brought a smile to his lips, despite everything.

"The hunt was a sporadic thing. The armies of the fae had worked united, to wipe out mankind, or at least cull them to manageable levels. I don't think they ever imagined we would fight back, or that we might manage to flee. The fae that first found us were far from united. It was a small group that first passed through the Worldtrails and stumbled across this world. I didn't understand this as I experienced it but now I realise that they were probably amazed at the way the moon stays in the sky all night. Joran explained it to me, this place, our world, it must seem like a heaven to them. So the Wild Hunt began, bursting from the Worldtrails and cutting down all that the fae could find. Some were taken back to the Realm of Twilight to serve as slaves again but most were simply slain.

"The druids worked at the notion of the Wyrde for years as mankind's numbers dwindled, and it was only desperation that led to the idea of using a soul. A soul trapped at the moment of death and tasked with protecting all mankind." He stopped, sinking back into the chair, suddenly too hot. The fire had made the room warm and under the blankets he was stifling. He pushed at them weakly, sending them tumbling down his legs.

"It is a little warm now isn't it?" Obair said, standing and making his way to the door. "I'll let some of this heat out if that's all right?" Ylsriss helped pull the rocker back from the fire as the old man stood at the doorway for a moment, savouring the cooler air and looking out over the lake in silence. "All of this was in the stones?" he asked finally, breaking the stillness.

Devin nodded wearily. "This and more. It's hard to focus on it all."

"The ritual of the Wyrde?" Obair pressed, coming back to join them.

Devin nodded. "I know the ritual now, how to lock the fae away from this world again. There was nothing about the other ritual though, nothing about how to power the glyphs."

"So then we're no better off than we were before!" Obair said as he threw his hands in the air.

"No," Devin said quickly. "You misunderstand. The knowledge of the keepers was placed into these stones, maybe into others too, but it was the knowledge of how to work the Wyrde. The knowledge of how to power the Wyrde was entrusted to the guardians."

"What?" Obair shook his head. "We've been over this. I know the ritual, Devin. I could maintain the Wyrde because it was in place but I haven't the faintest clue how to begin again. If my Master knew he never told me."

"He didn't need to, Obair." Devin said as he smiled weakly. "The knowledge is there. It's waiting in the stones at Widdengate."

"At Widdengate?" Obair repeated. "Surrounded by an army of Bjornmen."

* * *

"Caert," Ylsriss repeated, patting the side of the wagon.

"Cart," Devin corrected her. "Or Wagon."

She frowned up at him. The week they'd waited had done him some good. He'd never completely regain the look of youth but many of the lines had faded from his face. He looked more like a man in his mid-twenties now, though the white hair

266

would always raise eyebrows.

"Which is it then?" she asked Joran as he loaded another sack onto the cart behind Devin. "Wagon or cart?"

"It's both, or either," Joran replied with a shrug.

"What? Why have two words for the same thing?" Ylsriss demanded. "This language makes no sense!"

"Islik has more than one word for ships. Reavers, ferries, scows?" Joran shrugged.

Ylsriss shook her head, tossing blonde curls about her shoulders. "No, that's not the same thing at all. Those are types of ships. They don't look anything like each other. This language is ridiculous. It makes no sense!"

Joran laughed with a shrug. "She thinks your language is stupid," he explained to Devin.

"Do we have everything?" Obair called from the door to the cottage.

"I think so," Devin replied. "Let's go."

Obair climbed up beside Joran and clucked the horses onwards. The wagon had been a stroke of luck. Left in the barn and covered in a decade's worth of cobwebs he'd feared it would be useless when Joran first found it. Without the wagon the old man had worried they'd have had to wait another week or more before Devin was able to travel. As it was he still thought it was too soon. He watched the old man glance back over once shoulder at him with a concerned look.

"I'm fine, Obair," Devin told him. "If we don't leave now we'll be spending the winter here."

The druid muttered something that Devin didn't catch and turned his attention to the horses. It was slow going and the cart rattled and shook until they made it to the track. That had been another stroke of luck. Joran had found it when hunting. It was overgrown, barely visible in places, and probably hadn't been used in a decade or more, but it was wide enough for the cart and should lead them to the road in time.

He twisted to catch a last look at the lake before the trees blocked the view. It felt strange to leave now that it had finally come down to it. They'd come here seeking answers, not really believing that they were here to be found. Now that they had them, and more, it was time to leave. Rhenkin and the Duchess would be waiting for them but part of him could have stayed easily. The stones both fascinated and terrified him and, despite the ordeal, there was a small part of him that longed to touch them again.

He'd been right about the winter though. The last few mornings had carried the snap of frost in the air. It was nothing that was visible yet but autumn was definitely in its last gasps. Winter would not wait for them and the prospect of trying to pass over the mountainous trail in this rickety cart as the snows howled down was not a pleasant one.

The days soon fell into a routine. Obair or Joran drove the wagon, stopping every few hours to switch the horses with the other two that were hitched to the back of the cart. Devin and Ylsriss would sit in the back as she practised her Anlish. She was a quick study and the language was coming to her without issue, though it would be months before she had a firm grasp on it.

The nights had their own routine too as they set camp close to the road, actually on it during the second night. Obair had insisted on setting watches, though the full moon was over a week away. It was easier to give in than to argue. By the third night though, Devin had enough.

"We're stopping?" he called to Obair as the cart slowed, and then stopped. "Already?"

"It's going to get dark before much longer, Devin," the old man said back over his shoulder. "The horses need their sleep as much as you do."

Devin pulled himself upright from where he'd laid back against the sacks of supplies. "Obair," he began. "You've spent your life with nothing but goats and chickens. How much do you really know about horses?"

"Everything needs to sleep, Devin." Obair sighed as he stood up at the bench-seat and reached his arms skyward in a stretch.

"Every animal needs sleep, Obair, but not the same way as we do." Devin told him. "Horses are happy with about three hours a night so long as they get a break during the day. We can't do this forever but we should be travelling when it's not fae nights."

"I didn't know that," Obair admitted. "You want to push on then? In the dark?"

"It doesn't get *that* dark with the moonlight, Obair." Devin pointed out. "Besides, we've enough lanterns to keep us on the road. We can sleep in shifts just as easily on a cart as we can in a camp."

Obair gave him a look that sat midway between worried and irked and walked the horses back onto the road.

By the second week however, the routine of setting camp was set. The fire burned low in a pit dug out for that purpose and three slept as Joran or Devin kept watch from the wagon, bow and ironheads on their laps. It made for a miserable night and Devin often found he couldn't sleep even when Joran came to relieve him.

"What will you do?" he asked Joran in a low voice.

Joran looked down at him, his eyes reflecting the fading light of the coals in the fire. "Do? When?"

"Once we reach Rhenkin," Devin explained. "There's really no need for you to go to Widdengate, either you or Ylsriss. What will you do?"

"I hadn't thought that far ahead," Joran said softly, looking up at the stars above the trees. "If you'd been able to ask me before we came through the stones somehow I'd have said I would stay with Ylsriss. Now..." he spread his hands.

Devin looked over to where Ylsriss lay. "She hasn't forgiven you?"

"Would you have?" Joran asked him. "I took her away from her baby."

Devin grimaced. He was probably right. "There wasn't anything you could have done though. It was flee or die. Wasn't that what you told me?"

Joran nodded, meeting his eyes before looking away quickly. "I don't think she sees it that way. I don't think she ever will. She's pleasant enough when you're all around. When it's just us though, her eyes say it loud and clear. She blames me still. She *hates* me still."

"You and her though, you weren't...?"

Joran blinked. "What? No! No, nothing like that. I mean there was a time, after we'd run from Tir Rhu'thin when I thought maybe, but no. We were never anything more than friends. Then when she found me with Aervern everything changed."

"Aervern?" Devin asked, trying to make it sound nonchalant. "You've mentioned her twice now."

Joran looked away, muttering something to himself. "She was a fae who found us in the human city. When the Wyrde formed it created a barrier that locked the fae away from this world but it also locked some others away in an in-between place. Some hellish place halfway between our world and the Realm of Twilight. When it fell those fae were able to return to the Realm of Twilight. Those are the fae that kept Ylsriss and I at Tir Rhu'thin. Aervern wasn't from there. She said she was from a place called Tira Scyon."

"How is that any different?" Devin asked.

Joran climbed down from the cart and came to sit next to him, speaking in a low voice so as not to wake the others. "I only ever met Aervern but she was nothing like those from Tir Rhu'thin," Joran said. "She'd never met another human. She didn't even know about the Touch."

Devin looked at him, incredulous. "Oh, let me guess. She was different to the others?"

"You sound like Ylsriss," Joran said, bitterness twisting his face.

"Joran, these are the fae," Devin told him, striving to keep his voice level. "They took my mother when I was barely ten. They've killed the only father I've ever known and driven the woman I've come to call my mother to the point of madness. They took you so long ago you can't even remember your family. They've enslaved you, twisted your mind. They killed your brother for crying out loud! How could you think that she's any different to the rest of them?"

"Because she *is* different!" Joran snapped, glaring down at Devin. He shook his head and lowered his hands, aware now that he'd somehow stood and clenched his fists.

"These fae are different in a hundred little ways. It didn't even occur to her to see me as anything less than equal. She was as happy to teach me as she was to learn from me. They don't even have glyphs! The fae at Tir Rhu'thin have runeplates and moonorbs everywhere you look but Aervern had never even seen a working glyph. They don't know how to make them. They don't even have a written language. She was astonished at Ylsriss learning something from a book."

"So, what? You'd want to go back to her?"

The answer was too slow in coming. "No! No, of course not. But the things she talked about, that you talked about. When fae and human worked together…"

"I remember," Devin said softly. "But that was all a long time ago. There's nobody left who even remembers the glyphs. Even Obair only knew the glyphs of the Wyrde as a ritual."

"No, you're right," Joran muttered, almost too low to hear. "This world knows nothing of glyphs and fae."

Chapter Twenty

The fae nights were miserable and left them all short-tempered from lack of sleep. The trail had pulled them up out of the woods and taken them higher as it climbed into the rocky hills. The very wind seemed to rake at their skin with icy talons, lashing at them with rain that was closer to snow or hail than water. Despite the association that they all seemed to make between the forests and the threat of the fae all of them had been glad as the path began to descend again and they returned to the trees and the protection the woods offered from the elements.

"Why are you turning off?" Obair called from the back of the cart.

Devin glanced back at him. "You remember the road we took with the horses on the way here? It was barely more than a track in some places. We'd never get this cart through it. Even if we did it would take longer. We can head for Kavtrin until the roads meet, and then head back towards Druel."

"This is hardly a tour, Devin," the old man said testily.

Devin sighed in silence and thought better of half a dozen responses. "It will be faster this way, Obair. Trust me." He looked around again and met the old man's eyes. "Why don't you try and get some sleep?"

"Chance would be a fine thing!" Obair muttered, loud enough for Devin to hear and he snorted a laugh. It was a fair point. The cart was hardly ideal as a place to sleep and it rattled and creaked along the road. That would have been bad enough but it was the snoring Obair had been complaining about.

Ylsriss snored. Not the soft, feminine sighs that he might have expected but a grating rasp that mounted a determined assault on the ears. Obair had woken her twice and tried to move her head to stop the noise three times, but each time the snoring had begun again. Softly at first, and then louder until it was a wonder she didn't wake herself up.

She probably would have woken if she hadn't been so tired. They all were. The strain of keeping watches during the fae nights was wearing. They'd taken to watching in pairs. The prospect of sitting alone in the dark watching for the fae was terrifying and the practice of taking watches in pairs had evolved on its own, without the need for anyone to discuss it.

Sleep was elusive. It slipped through the camp and out the other side with ease, avoiding the feeble efforts of those that sought to snatch at it. It was rare for any of them to have more than three hours in a night. Sleeping on the wagon was not easy but the light of day made everyone feel safer.

"If you can't sleep why don't you come up here and talk to me?" Devin said.

A shaking of the wagon's bed was answer enough and Obair picked his way through the packs and supplies and clambered over the back of the seat to join him.

"How does one tiny person make so much noise?" he muttered as he tried to make himself comfortable.

"You're not all that quiet yourself, you know?" Devin said as he smiled into the face of indignation. Obair sputtered at him for a moment but neither of them had the energy for it. Still, it was easier to stay awake with someone else to talk to, and the wagon was making better progress on the wider road.

The rains had found them again by mid-afternoon and they huddled under cloaks and blankets as the winds shrieked down at them, hurling the rain with a vengeful spite despite the protection of the trees on either side of the trail. Devin eased the wagon off the road and onto the grass close to the woods. "We're not going to make much progress in this. The roads are already getting bad and the horses are struggling."

There was no protest from the others. Obair had water dripping from his nose and beard and Joran looked the very picture of misery. The trees offered some protection but not as much as Devin had hoped. Rain still managed to find them as the wind rose and tore at the canopy above them.

"Why don't you see if you can find some dry wood," he called over the noise of the wind. "I'll see to the horses." He set to work unhitching them from the wagon and rubbing them down as best he could. They were in fair condition despite everything they'd been through.

The fire they managed was pitifully small, fed from a small supply of wood. Wet sticks and small branches were piled close to the fire, in the hopes they would dry enough but Devin didn't hold out much hope. They'd not had to bother with the tents since the hills. They were small, awkward things. Hard to put up and not having the room to hold the four of them in any comfort anyway.

Devin fought with the thing for the best part of an hour until he managed to get it right. As it was, the best he'd managed to do was erect a tented sheet of canvas over ground already wet from the rain. The groundsheet would lock some of this away but not all of it, and the prospect of sleeping in the wet did not improve his mood. The others had tried to help but Joran and Obair were actually worse than useless and he was left to struggle with Ylsriss.

The rain eased off as it grew darker and they clustered close to the fire, trying to dry out. The woods were filled with the sounds of distant dripping as drizzle misted down onto the leaves above them. The conversation was muted, as miserable as they all felt. Finally, for want of something else to do, Devin crawled into the closest tent and slept.

A shaking woke him. A frantic shaking rather than the gentle rousing that came when it was time to switch watches. He blinked at the darkness but it was so absolute that there was nothing to see. "What is it?" he whispered, and then realised how foolish that was.

"I heard something," Obair told him in a tight, strained whisper.

Devin scrambled out of the tent, joining Obair and Joran as they crouched low beside the sullen glow of the fire. "What is it?" he began but Joran hissed him to silence.

The woods were quiet and the rains had fled leaving a cool moonlight to shine down from the cloudless sky. Devin had been hunting since he was small and knew well that woods never really grew truly quiet. There should have been birds and the faint rustle of distant animals in the undergrowth. Instead, the only noise was the whispered conversation of the leaves above them.

He stared into the darkness between the trees, trying to focus on using his ears rather than his eyes. The sound was distant but enough to raise the hairs on the back of his neck. It was childlike but there was no innocent joy in that noise. It was the laughter of a cruel and thoughtless child.

"Satyr," Devin whispered to Joran and saw him nod in the dim light of the coals. He thought quickly. If the creature knew they were there it would probably come straight for them. Its eyes would be better than his in the dark, he knew. Hiding would be futile unless it had no idea they were there.

The laughter came again, closer this time but from another direction. Devin looked into the trees, following the sound. "More than one." He grunted. "They're playing games with us. They already know there's someone here."

"What do we do?" Joran hissed.

Devin smiled slowly. The expression stole what little warmth remained from a face already made pale by his hair that shone like frost in the moonlight. He turned his eyes to the darkness, "We play games of our own."

* * *

The fire was easy enough to stir back to life. The wet wood they'd stacked beside the coals had dried well and, before long, a large fire was crackling and tossing sparks skyward. Obair sat beside the fire, poking idly at the flames.

Devin waited, crouched low between the first tent and a broad horse chestnut tree. The bowstring felt good against his fingers as he held the ironhead to the string. Joran was positioned on the other side of the camp and they both had a clear view of Obair at the fire.

The druid had put up remarkably little protest, all things considered. He would be in the most danger, and that was assuming things all went to plan. If not… Devin was trying hard not to think about 'if not.'

The long minutes passed. Twice Devin had to shift to ease the cramping muscles in his legs and he'd had to settle for dropping to his knees. Joran was still, a patch of darker shadow pressed to the trunk of the tree. Even knowing he was there Devin had trouble making him out.

Doubt began slowly. A small question that grew steadily until he gnawed at one knuckle. Had he been wrong? Had the sound just been a bird? What if the satyr attacked as he gave up and stepped out from hiding? Indecision joined with doubt as, together, they whispered into his ear.

The leaves rustled softly, as light as the stroke of the breeze, but it was enough to freeze Devin. He stared past the fire into the bushes as Obair stiffened.

A man emerged from the woods, moving cautiously towards the fire. Devin eyed him curiously. A tall man in a simple white shirt, with dark trousers tucked into polished black boots. He moved slowly, making no sound as he passed over the dry leaves and twigs. Devin scanned the trees for signs of movement but the trees were silent.

Obair jumped visibly as he spotted the man and opened his mouth to speak. An arrow hissed past him and the man screamed as it buried itself in his shoulder, close to the collarbone. The image shattered as the satyr fell to the ground, the familiar blue fire spurting from his chest. It wouldn't be a killing shot, Devin knew. The arrow had skittered along bone before finding flesh and hadn't gone deep enough, though the fire might play its own role. He sighted quickly and let fly, taking the satyr in the side of the neck and the flicker of blue fire became a torrent as the creature exploded into flame.

"Just what was th—" Obair began but turned as figures exploded out of the bushes. Devin fired again, dropping a satyr as Obair staggered back towards the tents and fell hard, tripping over his own staff. Joran fired true this time and within seconds the camp was silent again.

"Is that all of them?" the old man's voice was shaky as he picked himself up.

"I don't know," Devin said softly. "I think so." He picked his way over to the charred remains of the closest satyr, working the shaft of the arrow back and forth to free it. It snapped before it came loose, the fire had eaten away at the shaft until it was little more than a charred stick.

He moved on to the next body and pulled the shaft free. The sensation hit him all at once and washed over him, taking him back to his childhood, back to the tatters of memory he had about Garret and fleeing into the trees. It was an intense feeling of being watched, coupled with the desire to cower down, to run and hide. He raised his head slowly, already knowing what he would see. The fae stood at the very edge of the trees, watching him calmly with its glowing eyes.

"Three satyr gone at the hands of a manling," the fae mused with a cruel, half-smile."

Devin froze as thought left him, feeling as exposed as a hare before the hounds. The fae watched him for a moment, seeming to take pleasure from his growing panic. It darted forward. Just two quick steps as it crouched low but even this had Devin scrambling backwards with a cry of panic. The fae's musical laughter followed him, carrying through the trees, mocking and belittling.

"Joran!" he heard Obair call out. "Joran, shoot it!"

The fae cocked his head curiously and looked at the tree Joran had pressed himself to. "Well, manling?" His words were simple but malice hung heavy in each one.

Devin watched as Joran stepped into the light, bow held ready with the string pulled to his lips. The fae regarded him with calm contempt, a faint smile curving his lips as Joran's hands began to shake. He raised one perfect eyebrow and Joran dropped to his knees in the dirt, sobbing in terror.

"Damn you, Joran!" Devin spat. "You should have shot him."

"Yes, Joran," the fae mocked him. "You should have shot me."

The fae took three more steps, each one slow and deliberate as he surveyed the clearing. "You have managed to slay my satyr. Though not true fae. They are far more than the measure of you pitiful creatures. This will not stand." He reached behind his back and pulled knives free with a casual motion. A blur of movement behind Joran stopped the fae cold as Ylsriss snatched up the fallen bow. Her hands shook as badly, or worse, than Joran's had and the fae gave her an incredulous look before bursting into laughter.

The arrow was close. Ylsriss was obviously unused to a bow but, despite that, the arrow still buried itself in the ground less than two feet from where the fae stood. His laughter followed his smile as both fled into the darkness and he froze in place as Ylsriss reached for another of the ironheads thrust into the ground at the base of the tree. She nocked it smoothly with hands now steady and assured.

"Maehro, fae!" she hissed in a voice as bitter as it was hateful.

The phrase rocked him. Shock stood out clear on the fae's face at the words. His pulled lips back in a snarl and then, moving so fast it was almost a blur, he darted to the side and retreated back to the edge of the trees before Ylsriss had time to settle the bow on him. He paused, looking back into the camp and the whisper was as clear as if he'd spoken in a normal voice. "You should have shot me, Joran." Laughter trailed behind him as he vanished into the trees.

"You damned fool!" Obair raged as he rounded on the young man. "You could have killed us all!" Joran ignored him, rubbing his eyes with his sleeve.

"It's not his fault…" Devin began, but he fell silent. It was Joran's fault. The shot would have been an easy one. He may have had his reasons but the blame was all his.

He looked to Ylsriss, still staring after the vanished fae "What was that you said there, right at the end?"

"The words, I speak?" she queried in broken Anlish.

Devin nodded.

"I say, 'die, fae.' The casual shrug made the words that much more chilling. He sank down beside the fire, hands shaking gently as he buried them under his arms.

The sound of a hunting horn cut through the woods just as the others joined him. A clarion call as clear as any general's charge.

"Shit!" Joran gasped as Obair turned frantic eyes on Devin.

"What do we do?" the old man whispered.

"We run!" he said flatly.

"But our things! The tents, the horses—?"

"...Are no use to us if we're dead," Devin told him. He snatched up the bow and pulled the ironheads from the ground. "Grab some things quickly, I'll see to the horses." He stood with arrow held ready as the others scrambled for the packs. Would they be better with the horses? Obair could barely ride on the best of days and Ylsriss and Joran seemed to know nothing of horses at all. He watched the others loading the packs as he thought, making his way over to the horses. A rustle in the trees made the decision for them and he stripped off the bridles, letting the horses go free before he turned and led the others out towards the road at a run.

They ran at a panic-driven sprint, packs bouncing on their backs until Obair called out in a breathless gasp as he began to lag behind. Devin called the others back as he stopped beside the old man. Obair was bent double, chest heaving as he leaned on his knees. Devin put one of the precious ironheads to the bowstring and felt in the quiver, counting with his fingers. He swore viciously as he counted only four more.

"What?" gasped Obair, turning his head to look at him.

Devin pointed at the nearly empty quiver. "They must have fallen out on the road." He looked over to where Joran and Ylsriss approached. "How many arrows do you have, Joran?"

He checked and, even in the darkness, Devin could tell it wasn't good. "Just three."

"Shit!" Devin spat. "This was his plan, to make us panic. This is all a game to him and we're playing right into his hands. We left the tents, the horses. Now he'll drive us before him until he's ready to finish us."

A shrill, whinnying scream carried to them, chilling despite the distance. Ylsriss looked back towards the camp and then to Devin with wide, scared eyes. Frightened but not panicked, Devin realised. He glanced as Joran and saw a different story entirely.

He spoke softly as the others gathered round. "Okay, let's not be stupid about this. We have the ironheads, Obair's staff, and even the knives if it comes right down to it. We are not helpless, that's what just what he wants us to think. We keep moving but we'll stay close together and be ready to stop if need be." They nodded, even Ylsriss who'd probably only caught three words.

They set off at a trot, packs jingling and bouncing on their backs. Not for the first time Devin wished they'd gone back for the horses. The scream of the animals had been harrowing, worse still because it was so needless. It had been an effort to strike fear into them. An act of demonstrating cruelty for cruelty's sake. It put him in mind of what Obair had told him of the satyr and his goat.

They ran in cycles. A gasping walk became a jog, which then grew into a run. When Obair couldn't go on they fell back to a walk. The night was still, save for the leaves in the treetops, but somehow the silence behind them seemed to spur them on even more and they never slowed for long.

Shadows danced in the trees on either side of the road, shifting in the pale moonlight and the breeze-tossed branches, drawing the eye. By the third hour Obair was suffering. His run had become a juddering stagger as his feet sought to find the ground in front of him in time to keep him from falling.

Their walks had grown longer, the runs so short they barely began, yet they pushed on. All of them had glimpsed the eyes glowing in the darkness behind them. They never drew any closer but seemed to dance around them in the darkness. Sometimes to one side of them, sometimes appearing up ahead for a moment, only to vanish in a blur of movement.

The light grew slowly. It was a glacial lifting of the gloom that turned the moon-pierced darkness into shades of grey. It paled further still, to the strange light of pre-dawn as the first blush of pink stained the sky. Obair cried out when, at last, the first glimpse of the sun stabbed at them between the trees. He stopped, pointing at the light as if it were something new and wondrous. Devin grinned and sank down onto the packed earth of the road on legs that trembled with the effort. Not even bothering to make a camp they slept, lying beside the road like the abandoned victims of bandits.

* * *

The horn came as soon as the moon rose. Each night, for the past three nights, it had come. A hunter's call, haunting, and somehow mournful, but also filled with a hunger that pushed them into a run.

After that first night they'd taken to sleeping at sunrise, rising after mid-day and setting off once more. Obair had managed well, despite his age, but Devin knew it wouldn't be enough. They were being toyed with. He'd realised that on the second night when the horn sounded. Even with Obair's slow pace they'd covered at least fifteen miles from the point when the sun rose the previous morning yet the horn sounded as if it were less than half a mile away.

He glanced at the others as they ran. He'd not said anything about his realisation yet, it wouldn't help anything if he did. He'd guessed that Obair probably knew anyway, possibly Ylsriss too, but Joran seemed oblivious to it. He greeted each sunrise with a look of triumph and was the first to suggest they set off as they rose from their camp after noon.

The horn had been closer this time. It sounded as if the hunter had been close enough to watch them from the trees. They were being goaded, driven on for the amusement of the creature that hunted them. Another horn sounded, off to the left of them this time and the sound of crashing branches had him shrugging the bow off his back and scrambling for an ironhead. Joran held his own bow ready as Ylsriss and Obair stood close behind them, iron daggers at the ready.

Devin stood with the bowstring to his lips. His arm was already trembling with the effort and, with a grimace, he let the tension relax in the bow. "It's nothing," he told Joran. "He's just playing with us."

"What if it's not though?" Joran said, his words tight and just one frightened step from panic. His hand shook as he held the bow and he looked about wildly.

"Joran." Ylsriss made the word a sentence all its own. Calming, soothing. She laid a hand on his shoulder and he relaxed the string. "You say it's only one fae, Devin," he said, as the panic faded from his eyes. "What if you're wrong? What if there are others? Or satyr and fae'reeth?"

Devin looked at Obair and Ylsriss, taking the measure of them before he met Joran's eyes. "It wouldn't matter. They could have us any time they wanted, Joran."

The confused expression stood in place of Joran's reply and Devin sighed. "We probably cover the best part of twenty miles during the daylight, Joran. If this thing can find us again to sound that horn at us as the moon rises then what hope do we have of running from it?"

The panic returned again as the words sank in. "Why run at all then? What's the point?" His voice rose as he spoke, the fear riding high and clear.

He was close to breaking. Devin grabbed him by the arms, just below his shoulders, and shook him as he spoke. "Because every mile we cover is another mile closer to Druel. We're not running from this fae, Joran. We're running to Druel."

"What if it attacks us, stops playing games?"

Devin looked him in the eyes and spoke softly. "Then we'll kill the bastard."

Joran looked at him, disbelieving. Devin might as well have told him he could fly from the look on his face. "I hope you're right, Devin," Joran said after a moment. "That it is just the one. I really do." He didn't wait for a response and set off down the road, running in an easy trot.

Devin watched him go and, as the others set off after him, he looked around at the bushes lining the edge of the trees beside the road. "So do I," he whispered.

That night passed more peacefully than most. The woods were far from silent, even over the sound of their packs jostling around on their backs, the hoots of owls and rustle of creature darting to cover in the brush were clear. It was a natural sound and Devin was glad for it.

The fae seemed to bring a silence when they entered the woods. The birds hushed and animals huddled in their burrows. Tonight the woods were alive with noise and Devin took comfort from it, though Obair twitched and started with each noise. They were making good time, though it was hard to judge how much ground they'd truly covered. Obair was adjusting to the routine and seemed to stop less often. The fact their packs were growing lighter was definitely a factor and Devin tried hard not to think about it. Normally, there would have been time to set snares or to try and hunt but now they had to rely on what supplies they had and those were dwindling far too quickly.

A faint sound tore him from his thoughts. Something at odds with the rest of the sounds of the night. He reached for Obair's arm and slowed, trusting to the druid to pass the signal on. An owl screeched a hunting call behind them and, for a moment, he relaxed until he caught the sound again. It was the faint strain of music and laughter.

He opened his mouth to speak but Ylsriss's pale face caught at him, fear mixed with despair and something that might have even been guilt. He frowned at her but she shook her head.

"Did you hear that?" he whispered at Obair.

The old man nodded. Shadows hid his face but Devin didn't need to see the expression. "It could as easily be the same as the hunting horn. More games."

There was something in the man's voice though. "You don't believe that though, do you?" Devin asked.

The shadowed figure shook his head. "No. I can't tell you why but no, I don't."

They wasted no more time talking and fell into a trot, shifting into a run as soon as they were all moving. Laugher followed them along the road and the trill of flutes grew closer with every passing mile.

"Devin!" Ylsriss cried out, grabbing at his arm and pointing behind them.

He lurched to a stop, twisting to see what she meant. The figure was clear in the moonlight. A satyr stood in the centre of the road behind them, at the very limits of their vision. It stood still, watching them with eyes that were visible even at this distance. Devin pulled one of the precious ironheads from the quiver, spilling the strips of torn cloak he'd stuffed into it to keep them from falling, out onto the road.

"What do we do?" Obair asked, deferring to him again.

He said nothing for a while, staring as the fae creature watched him. "Nothing," he said at last. "Nothing for now. We keep going."

They set off again, fear pushing them into a faster pace. Devin glanced back once as they set off but the satyr had vanished. It was different somehow, knowing for certain that they were back there. Before, the fear had almost been an abstract thing. Despite the horns and glimpses of movement it had been fear more of the unknown than anything else. The suspicion that everything they'd seen and heard could be a trick of the fae had given the fear an unreal quality.

He heard the snarl before he heard the footsteps and turned mid-step, staggering sideways for a moment before he came to a stop. The satyr threw themselves after them with an abandon that only a child could match. Devin nocked the arrow he'd already held as they ran and released smoothly. The fear was gone now. All he felt was the icy calm that had surrounded him when he'd shot the Bjornman in the eye.

The arrow took the first satyr in the chest, burying itself deep. The iron tasted the fae blood, filled with the grace the moonlight had given it, and the creature exploded into blue flame, falling without even the time to scream.

Devin reached for another arrow and let fly before Joran had loosed his first. His second shot was as true as the first and within moments it was over.

"Lords and Ladies, Devin!" he heard Obair gasp but the words were muffled, like he was hearing them from a great distance. He ignored them and ran to the first of the satyr, ripping the arrow free before the fire could ruin the shaft. He dashed to the second, burning his hands as he worked the arrow free from the creature's throat. Then Ylsriss was there, pulling him backward away from the flaming corpse.

"Your hands, Devin!"

He looked down at them and the pain came with the sight. His hands were already an angry red where they weren't covered in black and gore.

"Stupid man," Ylsriss told him as she soaked bandages in water and wrapped them. It wasn't ideal but they couldn't spare the water to soak his hands properly. Devin grinned despite himself. It was one of the first phrases she'd asked him for. She seemed to be putting it to good use.

"Stars above, Devin, have you lost your mind?" Obair puffed at him as he came to stop. "What were you thinking?"

He shrugged. "We need the arrows, Obair."

The old man muttered to himself. The simple fact was they both knew he was right. The arrows were their only real weapon against the fae. The knives would mean a hand to hand fight and that didn't even bear thinking about.

"Can you stand?" Obair asked him finally.

Devin nodded. "I'll be fine." Movement behind the old man drew his eye and the others followed his gaze. The fae watched them calmly, surrounded by a pack of satyr. They were too far for Devin to make out numbers but the sound of their voices carried easily on the breeze as the tall figure turned and vanished into the trees, the satyr glaring at them before they too were swallowed by the woods.

It was less than three hours before they came at them again and the satyr came rushing out from the trees beside the road. The creatures were among them almost before anyone had a chance to put an arrow to bowstring, and the bone knives flashed in the moonlight. Joran fell quickly, grasping at his thigh as the blood ran through his fingers. Devin fired an arrow into the mess but it struck only ground as the satyr skipped aside. Things would have turned badly had Obair not acted. He struck out with the iron staff, slamming it into the side of a satyr's head and throwing the creature to one side, where it crashed to the ground twitching as tiny blue flames licked at the blood oozing from the crater in its head.

The blow seemed to shock both human and satyr alike and the fight paused long enough for them all to take in the spectacle. Ylsriss didn't slow however and her iron dagger slammed into a satyr, thrusting up into the beast's side and up between the ribs. She tore the blade free and stepped back as the flames erupted from the wound and fountained from its mouth.

The sheer savagery of their attack seemed to confuse the satyr and the remaining two fell back for a second, long enough for Devin to find his arrow and put it into one of their legs. The last creature gave a snarl of rage before breaking free and rushing into the trees.

Ylsriss dashed to Joran, kneeling over him and speaking quickly in their language. The blood was pooling under his leg and, even if he hadn't seen that, the look on the man's face was enough to tell Devin it was bad.

She turned to him, snapping her fingers as she motioned for him to come closer, then tugging at his cloak until Devin handed it to her. Three quick slashes and a tug had a thick section torn from the bottom, which she twisted and thrust under Joran's thigh, pulling it tight and looking up at them.

"Get me a wood," she ordered.

"A wood?" Devin repeated. "You mean a stick?"

"Yes, stick," Ylsriss snapped. "Go!"

He returned with a thick stick quickly and watched as she tied it into the knot and twisted it, drawing the tourniquet tighter. Joran screamed as it grew tighter and Devin and Obair exchanged awkward glances before looking away.

It took two of them but they managed to get Joran to his feet. He leant heavily on Obair's staff with one hand and stood with his other arm around Ylsriss, white faced and shaking.

"What are they doing?" Devin burst out. "There's no thought to these attacks. They don't seem to care if they live or die!"

"Possibly they don't." Obair shrugged. "I don't know much about the satyr. They're nowhere as intelligent as the fae, I know that much. Maybe it doesn't occur to them that we might be able to hurt them."

"It's not that," Joran managed in a strained voice. "They don't expect the iron, that much is true, but they're not as stupid as you might think. They're not used to battle. This is more of a hunt to them. They tried the direct approach when they charged at us. Then they tried rushing us from the trees. I don't know what they'll do next but they're testing us, learning our responses."

Their progress was slow and painful over the next few hours. Joran hobbled between him and Obair, making as best a pace as he could with his arms around their shoulders. His face was pale and it was probably only the pain that kept him conscious. The night showed no sign of ending and Devin travelled in silence, not trusting himself to speak.

"What's that?" Ylsriss called out, pointing ahead of them into the darkness. Devin stopped with the others, squinting into the gloom.

He shook his head. "I don't see any—"

"There, look!"

He glanced at her face before looking again. A flicker of light from between the trees, so brief he almost lost it. It came again as the breeze shifted the branches gently.

"Fire!" he breathed the word, almost with reverence, and urged Joran onwards.

"Devin…" Obair's voice was low and urgent and Devin was already groaning as he turned. The glow of the eyes filled the road behind them in the distance, shifting around in the darkness. It was hard to judge the distance but it was close enough.

"Ylsriss, get his feet," Devin ordered as he lifted Joran up higher. She reached to grab Joran's ankles, bending his knees back towards her and they began an awkward run. It wasn't much faster than a trot and Joran grimaced with each step, fighting to keep the cries in.

The firelight was clearer now, a large campfire shining through the trees.

Ylsriss twisted to look back over one shoulder "They're coming!"

Obair pulled them into a run and they lurched unevenly as Joran screamed in pain between them.

"It's no good!" Devin shouted as he slowed, lowering Joran down to the road. He snatched up the bow, drawing and releasing before the image before him really registered. Another ironhead left his fingers and the scene drew into focus. A seething mass of satyr surged towards them, knives bare in the moonlight.

Devin froze with the arrow in his hand. There were so many they couldn't hope to stand against them. He looked to Obair and saw the same thought mirrored in the old man's face.

Arrows erupted from the woods to either side of them with yet more arcing overhead. The satyr exploded into flame as Devin looked behind him with mouth agape as figures rushed forward to help with Joran

"We can't hold them here," one told him. "Come on!"

Devin allowed the strangers to pull them back as they fired arrows in a retreating line back towards the light of the fire. Whoever they were they had ironheads and the line of satyr was scattering, breaking for the trees to either side of the road as the arrows brought fire wherever they fell.

The camp was larger than it had looked through the trees and Joran was rushed off to a row of tents to have his leg tended. Silence fell as the satyr melted into the woods and men quickly took up positions around the camp. Devin found himself watching the trees as he snatched up the quiver of ironheads that had been dumped at his feet. This had all been too easy. A quick glance at some of the men told him he wasn't alone in thinking this. A man on the far side of the camp fell with a gurgling scream, and then the satyr boiled out of the trees, rushing into the camp from all directions.

Arrows flew and blue fire flared. Devin froze for a moment, taken by the chaos that raged all about them. The satyr surged into the camp and it seemed that for every one that fell, another two pressed on, darting past the swords that sought to find them.

Devin buried an arrow into the back of a satyr fighting in front of him and moved on, seeking another target. The camp seethed with the creatures and he fired again, reaching for his quiver before the arrow had even struck.

The air seemed suddenly to be full of a gritty sand and he coughed and spat before the taste of the iron registered with him. Around him satyr clawed at their eyes as tiny pinpricks of blue fire flared and were gone. Another grasped at its throat, lurching with panic-ridden eyes as flame burst from its mouth with each breath.

None wasted the moment, and swords rose and fell in an orgy of butchery. As the beasts fell Devin caught sight of the fae. He stood in the centre of the fray, bone daggers whistling around it as he danced between the swords striking at him. A man fell as the fae laid open his throat with a casual stroke and thrust both knives deep into the side of a second man as he moved past. The creature moved like a cat, making his way through the camp with a grace as beautiful as it was deadly.

Devin released the arrow without thinking. He was barely aware he'd drawn the bow. The fae moved in a blur, batting the shaft out of the air with one knife as he shifted out of path of its flight. Devin's hand scrabbled at the quiver as the creature turned its burning eyes on him, stalking unhurried through the chaos towards him.

A frantic glance told him what his hand already knew, the quiver was empty. He backed away, feet catching at unseen obstacles as his hands reached for the knife he knew would be useless. The fury on the face of the fae was the sea at storm and it leapt the last ten feet, landing without a sound and sinking into a fighting stance.

Devin flailed with the dagger, lashing out in a desperate attempt to keep the fae's blades from his skin. It didn't even bother to block the strike, leaning back away from the iron blade, and then shifting in toward him.

A figure in a long cloak stepped past him as the fae lunged in and coolly hurled a handful of dust into his face. Blue sparks erupted from the fae's eyes as he screamed, the lunge forgotten as he pawed at his face. The figure didn't pause but moved in low and rammed a dagger into the fae's chest, reaching for Devin's arm to pull him back away from the creature as it fell.

The flames that erupted around the wound were far fiercer than anything Devin had encountered from satyr and he staggered further back with a cry, shielding his face with his arms. It was only as the fire began to subside that he realised the hand holding his arm still belonged to a woman. He looked up to her face and the shock of recognition mirrored his own. "Erinn? Is that you?"

CHAPTER TWENTY-ONE

Caerl spat, his vomiting had long since stopped bringing anything up and now the heaves were dry and painful as his stomach spasmed. He shook his head blearily and crawled back away from the spattered mess he'd left on the broken flagstones of the alleyway. He felt his way up a wall, leaning heavily as he found his feet.

Staggering steps took him out to the street and, by the time he made it through the winding roads and alleyways to the docks, he almost felt close to human again. It wasn't the first time he'd woken in an alleyway. It probably wouldn't be the last either. He caught the disgusted look of a man passing him. Rich, a merchant or something, by the looks of him.

Caerl glanced down at his clothes. There was some mess, that was to be expected, but it wasn't that bad. "What?" he shouted after the merchant. "You're think you're so bloody high and mighty do ya?"

The merchant looked back at him, though he didn't slow, and shook his head, grimacing.

"Bloody rich bastards," Caerl muttered. "Think they own the fucking world."

He spat again, wiping his mouth on his sleeve and his hand turned over, the fingertips coming up to probe at his temple unbidden, tracing the scarred indent in the side of his face.

He scowled as he caught what he was doing and snatched his hand away. "Bloody bitch," he whispered.

The sun was well on its way down already, gracing the rooftops of the buildings in the distance. Caerl noted it sourly. Vetram would be cross at the day's work missed. He might piss and whine about it but he'd still be good for some coin tomorrow. For now he needed something in his belly to settle it. Stew or bread, something to soak up the sket his retching had missed.

It had taken a long time before he'd grown desperate enough to try the stuff. Wine was water to him these days and ale had never really been enough. It was a month or two after the bitch and her brat had walked out that he'd tried it. He smirked, laughing as he remembered the way it had burnt his lips that first time. The sign of a virgin sket-drinker.

Sket was brewed up or distilled, he really had no idea, in the back streets of Kavtrin. You'd never find it sold in taverns, not the ones that hung signs outside their doors, anyway. It was hard and pure, burning all the way down and immediately taking him to a place that it would normally take five or six large cups of strong wine to reach.

His steps grew stronger as he went, the stagger becoming a slow walk as one hand reached for the stones of the buildings that he passed. The smell of grease and warm bread reached out to him and he knew he was nearly there. Elsa's Kitchen, home to the best food in Kavtrin, or at least the best food he was likely to get.

He pushed his way through the door and down the steps. The room was dark with grease-stained windows and lamps were already lit on the walls.

"Caerl?" The woman's voice carried over the low rumble of conversation and the sounds of eating. "Lords and Ladies, man, you look like you've just been scraped off a nobleman's boot!"

He smiled, that rakish smile he'd always found so useful with women. "Elsa, you say the sweetest things. That's why I love you."

She *humphed* and pointed him to a table in the corner. "You love me because I put food in your wine soaked belly and put up with your stink." She sniffed at him as she drew closer. "What is that? Sket? That stuff'll make you go blind, you daft bastard."

He shrugged, sinking into the chair and wishing she'd shut up and just bring him some food. "What do you have on?"

"Some stew," she told him. "It's been there for a while though. I might be able to do you some eggs and bread if you fancy that instead?"

"Eggs sounds nice. Don't eat stew these days."

"No." She gave a small nod and he watched her gaze shift to the side of his face and back to his eyes again.

"Eggs'll be good," he said again.

She stood watching him, not moving. "Come on, Caerl. I ain't so stupid as all that!" she told him.

He huffed, reaching for his purse. Hands scrabbled for a moment until he realised the truth and sighed.

"Lost it again?" she asked, guessing the truth. "If you weren't out of your mind on sket you'd noticed being robbed, Caerl, or at the very least you'd remember it."

He reached down to pull off his shoe, pouring the coppers out into his hand. "Don't use purses, is all, Elsa. Too easy for the thieves, like you said."

"Is that it?" she muttered, not convinced.

"Will this cover it?" he held out the coppers. It was barely more than the price of an apple but he already knew her answer.

"It'll do." She sighed. "Put your shoe back on, you're stinking up the place."

The food was quick, or maybe she just wanted him gone. Either way it was fast and getting it inside him worked to end the shaking in his hands he hadn't noticed was there until it stopped.

Elsa made him drink some sweet tea too, full of honey and too sweet for his taste, but he knew she wouldn't stop nagging until he did. Nobody looked at him as he stood. This wasn't a place where people spoke or made friends. Deep down he knew what it was. It was a refuge for scum and lowlifes. The people half a step from the gutter. Elsa fed them partly out of kindness, partly because she knew no one else would.

The sun was almost gone by the time he made it back outside. It hid behind the rooftops, lurking until it leapt out between buildings, blinding him and bringing curses at the pain.

He should go and see Vetram. He knew he should go and make some apology but he couldn't face it. He still felt dry. The tea had left a sour taste in his mouth and, despite the fact Elsa had done her best to make it leak from his ears, he was thirsty. Tea was never going to do the job and the idea of Sket was almost enough to make him lose his eggs. He could have something light though, an ale maybe. That might help.

The docks were quiet, or as quiet as they got. Most of those who worked the wharves would be soaking their innards now. Drinking while they tried to dry wet feet. It was a simple matter to steal a prybar. The dockers were famous for leaving them lying around. He stuffed it as far into his sleeve as he could, palming the end as it stuck out.

The key to this was not to pick anyone too rich or important. If you went after someone whose purse was heavy with gold crowns then it was as good as asking for trouble. He wandered the streets, keeping away from the better areas of town and the watchmen that would be patrolling soon.

It didn't take long. The mark was young for a merchant. Maybe a merchant's son or a pampered apprentice. Caerl staggered towards him, feigning a drunkenness that he was more than familiar with. He lurched into the man's side, driving them both into an alleyway.

"Drunken fool!" the young merchant raged, his face twisted in righteous indignation. "Watch where you're—"

Caerl didn't let him finish, whipping the prybar out and tapping the man expertly on the side of the head. A tap was all it really took. Much more and the man wouldn't wake up with his purse missing, he wouldn't wake up at all. The merchant's son fell like a sack of wheat and Caerl wasted no time dragging him deeper into the shadows. Moments later and he was hefting the purse, judging the contents by feel.

The first ale felt like water. He peered into the tankard, tilting it to the light to see the colour. It wasn't the type of place where you could ask if the ale was watered though, so he'd suffered it, and then the three that followed it.

He moved on after the fifth. People tended to watch you when you drank quickly and the ale wasn't doing much for him. He tried whiskey at the next tavern. The purse he'd snatched was heavier than he'd thought and it had been a good while since he'd been able to stump up the coin for a good whiskey. It went down smooth but with barely a bite to it. Sket might be cooked up in the backstreets but it had more of a taste to it than the whiskey just had. Somewhere in the back of his mind a voice pointed out that his sense of taste had probably been dulled by the spirits but he ignored it. The things that voice told him were never things he wanted to hear.

It was four taverns later before he came up with the idea to climb the wall. Kavtrin was walled on all sides but the view over the harbour was considered the best. Caerl didn't want to watch the water. Water meant docks and that would just remind him of Vetram so he'd staggered his way to the north side.

He stumbled up the steps, catching his feet on something or other he didn't see, and made his way up to the battlements. The guardsmen wouldn't mind so long as he didn't get in their way. The moon was rising, fat and heavy as it rose over the fields. The figures emerged from the darkness, almost seeming to dance as the sparkling mist rose around them. He stared for a moment, wondering if it was just a trick of the light, or something worse. Sket did things to you. It wouldn't be the first time he'd seen something that wasn't real but not like this.

The moonlight shone on the tiny figures as they spun and danced around each other. Caerl watched, mouth open as they drew closer. The wings took a while for him to make out but the sense of wonder he felt when he did was better than a bellyful of Sket.

"S'beautiful," he murmured to himself, looking around for someone to share it with.

The figures moved closer and he picked out more and more of them in the moonlight. Tiny purple-hued women, seemingly as naked as babes and as perfect as any man could wish. What he'd taken for a handful quickly became a legion as they spun and danced in the air before the walls.

The others took him completely by surprise. He'd been so focused on the spectacle of the dancing figures that he hadn't even noticed their approach and the field of sunset eyes almost shocked him sober.

The change came all at once, rippling over the sea of shadowy figures like a breeze passing over a field of wheat. Where it passed, the figures lit up, bearing bright shining standards of blue and silver or sheathed in amour that was so polished it almost seemed to glow itself.

They came, not in a rush but as a surge. A wave, the child of the worst of storms, and made up of creatures escaped from children's fables. They charged towards the walls with a scream that matched his own as he stumbled down the steps.

The cries that rose from the sentries on the walls as they called out in warning turned to screams as the diminutive winged creatures shrieked over the walls like leaves in a hurricane.

Feet that suddenly felt half-asleep carried him down the street. He staggered, crashing into a wall and careening across the street towards the other until a wave of nausea stopped him.

The crash from behind him spun him around and he stood, dumbstruck as the first section of wall collapsed, torn down by vines that were thicker than oaken branches, thrusting out of the ground and grasping at the stones.

"Caerl!"

He turned, seeking the source of the cry and spotted Elsa, waving at him through a street suddenly filled with screaming people.

"Caerl, run! You daft, drunk bastard!" she screamed, pointing behind him.

He turned slowly, alcohol making his every movement over-complicated and deliberate. The creature stood before him, as tall as him and more beautiful than any woman he'd known. Dimly he was aware of others rushing past him but he seemed frozen by her gaze and the eyes shining like a winter's sunset.

The smile was cold, as cruel as it was beautiful, and it didn't waver as she reached behind herself and produced long bone knives. He barely felt the first cut but she made sure that he felt the second. If there was a beauty to be found in his pain she was intent on finding every aspect of it and, as she cut him, she took delight in his every scream.

Kavtrin fell. Not in a way that its defenders would ever have imagined, but in every way that mattered. The fae and satyr poured through the streets, fae'reeth howling through the air above them as they delighted in the slaughter. Soldiers fought alone as terror tore their units apart. They fled, running through the streets until they died alone. Fear stripped away all loyalty, all oaths, and the only fellowship that remained was born of blood and pain.

* * *

Klöss blinked hard, wishing he could rub his eyes as the guards rushed him through the halls. He'd been dead asleep when Gavin kicked him but the guards had moved so fast there was barely a point to the thief's warning.

Unlike the last meeting when he'd been walked through the halls, this time they moved so fast they nearly dragged him. He took the treatment in silence. Whatever the cause he'd find out soon enough. Even if he knew the language of these men they'd be as unlikely to tell him anything as they would be to know the reason for the urgency.

Rhenkin looked like hell. His jacket was unbuttoned and he was unshaven. The sleeplessness was etched clear in the lines of his face but it was nothing to the fury that burned in his eyes.

"You lied to me," he spat. His anger didn't need translating, though Miriam spoke the words anyway.

Klöss thought back over their last conversation. He'd concealed things, of course. But he didn't remember actively lying. "I have told no lies. What are you talking about?"

"You told me your forces had gone south with your fleet," Miriam translated for Rhenkin. "That this 'sealord' had sent them to burn."

Klöss nodded. "I did, and I told you that I wouldn't talk about my men. I came to talk about the fae."

"I received word just this morning that Kavtrin has been overrun." Rhenkin said, his voice cold and quiet.

"Kavtrin?" Klöss shrugged. The name meant nothing to him.

Rhenkin stood and stabbed his finger at a map on the wall. "Here!"

Klöss tried to stand, then sighed up at the guard who had pushed him roughly back into the seat.

Rhenkin snapped something at the man and he stepped back, eyes flashing as Klöss gave him a small smile as he stood. The map was covered in notations in an odd flowing script that seemed more loops and dots than real writing. He looked questioningly at Rhenkin until the man pointed again.

"It seems too close to my thinking. Our fleet would have passed this place weeks ago." He shrugged. "As far as I know we didn't even know this place was here. Our lines don't extend this far."

"You're saying it wasn't your men?" Rhenkin scoffed, his derision was so clear, Klöss barely needed to wait for Miriam.

"This is a larger place? A bigger town than these villages over here?" He waved to the east, towards where Rimeheld stood.

Rhenkin nodded.

"Where are we now? On this map I mean?" Klöss asked, waving around him.

Rhenkin paused, thinking for moment before indicating a position to the north and west of Kavtrin.

"I don't know how far we are here from this Kavtrin," Klöss began. "I would have thought you'd be able to see some of the smoke from here if my fleet had razed it."

Rhenkin turned as Kennick whispered furiously into his ear and the two muttered a low conversation while Klöss looked on.

"Why would you burn a city that large? I thought you people were more interested in plunder," Rhenkin asked.

"This is not a reaving," Klöss began. "This is no raid for plunder, as you put it. You're not a fool, Rhenkin. Don't think me one. If we captured this place we would have thousands of your people behind our lines. Thousands of eyes and mouths that we could never really control. We have no need of your cities or the people that live within them. Our goal was always to seize lands for our own people to settle. If we'd attacked this 'Kavtrin' of yours we'd have burnt it to the ground."

"And all the people with it," Rhenkin replied.

"In battle, people die." Klöss shrugged.

Rhenkin ignored that. "So what are you suggesting? That some other force did this? Or are you telling me that my reports are wrong and Kavtrin is untouched."

Klöss met the scathing look with a shrug. "I don't know. It's not my business to know. I will tell you this though, we both know there's another force capable of attacking your city."

"The fae?" Rhenkin raised an eyebrow. "I've seen these creatures fight, I've lost good men to them and I won't argue that they're a threat, but an entire city?" He shook his head. "I can't see it. They don't have the numbers, surely?"

Klöss glanced back at Miriam as she translated. There was catch in her voice as she spoke. It was easy to forget she was there, despite the fact she was translating. He frowned at her but her old face was blank, expressionless, as she looked back at him.

"If you believe that, major, then you are a damned fool and I've wasted my life for nothing," Klöss said. He turned his back on the man, walking back to the desk and throwing himself down into the chair. "These things attacked us after a battle, attacked our camp. They came out of the night, going through my men like they were nothing. I lost the greatest swordsman I have ever known to one of these fae and yes, they have the numbers." He realised he was almost shouting and drew a deep shuddering breath, forcing himself to calm down as Miriam caught up.

"I told you what happened at Skelf," he said, in a calmer voice. "How these fae emptied an entire village, piling the bodies on stakes driven into the ground. Those they didn't kill they took north with them. We followed the trail from Skelf. I took a group of trackers into the woods myself and we headed after them. It took some time but we found them. They were in a sort of valley in the forest. I'm telling you this, Rhenkin, because I don't think you realise the numbers of the fae. The goat-men, these satyr, they *filled* that valley. There must have been ten thousand at least, possibly double that. Not fae, not the things that look like men. Just these goat-men. So yes, Major bloody Rhenkin, they have the numbers to take your city."

Rhenkin studied him as Miriam talked. The man wasn't stupid despite what he'd said and Klöss knew it. "There's more to this isn't there? Something personal. A man doesn't give up his life and walk into the hands of his enemy even if his commander is ten times a fool. What is it you're not telling me?"

Klöss looked down at his hands and felt the edges of surprise that they'd curled into fists. The man irritated him for some reason. His cold control, his insistence in baiting him.

"You know the answer already, I'm sure," Klöss said, working to keep his voice level. "You didn't spend all those hours talking to Gavin about his favourite ales. There are fae in the Barren Isles, in my home. They're involved with the Church of New Days somehow. They have my wife…" he faltered, voice cracking as he dug his fingernails into his palms. "They have my son."

CHAPTER TWENTY-TWO

Kennick knocked. After a minute he leaned his head in towards the door and frowned at the silence, knocking again. Nothing. The door creaked slightly as he eased it open.

Rhenkin sat in his chair, bent low over the desk with his forehead resting on the report.

"Sir?" Kennick called softly, trying to decide the best course of action. He took a single step towards the major and stopped. Rhenkin's breathing was slow and rhythmic and Kennick froze with a wince. Another hour wouldn't hurt anything more than it was already. He'd barely moved, just the shifting of weight in preparation for the step, when Rhenkin spoke.

"What is it, Kennick?" He hadn't lifted his head from the report and his voice took on a hollow dimension, overlaid by the fluttering sound of the edges of the paper made by his breath.

"Sorry to disturb, sir. Didn't realise you were sleeping."

"I'm not. I wasn't. What would make you think that?" Rhenkin sat up, there was ink on his forehead where he'd rested it on fresh writing. Kennick coughed into his fist and tried to focus on the man's eyes. "My mistake, sir."

"Was there something, Kennick?" Rhenkin asked.

"Scout report from Kavtrin, Sir," Kennick replied, reaching to put the papers on the desk.

Rhenkin ignored it and his eyes narrowed as his lips shaped unspoken words. "Too soon," he said after a minute.

"Sir?"

"It's too soon for them to have made it there and back already," Rhenkin explained.

Kennick nodded, impressed. "Yes, sir. They encountered refugees on the way there and sent a man back by horse with the report."

"Survivors?" Rhenkin, asked in mild surprise.

"No, Sir," Kennick said as he shook his head. "A caravan. It arrived in Kavtrin after the attack and met our men half way here."

"And?"

"Sir?" Kennick frowned at the Major.

"Damn it, Kennick." Rhenkin slammed a hand down on the desk. "Do I have to drag this out of you? Give me some details!"

"No, sir," Kennick apologized. "The scouts report that the city is devastated, not a man found alive."

Rhenkin absorbed the news in silence. "Burned?"

Kennick shook his head. "No, it doesn't appear so, sir. The bodies are heavily mutilated, 'torn to shreds' was the term used, I believe. There is also some mention of the walls having been pulled down by some manner of plant."

"Oh, come now, Kennick," Rhenkin burst out. "I asked for a report not the deranged ramblings of idiot peasants."

"I'm just forwarding the report, sir," Kennick said mildly. "The report did say the man was an ex-corporal, not normally the type to make things up."

Rhenkin's eyes flicked from Kennick's face to the window and to the map on the wall. He gnawed at his bottom lip "Those scouts should be back in a day or so. We'll get confirmation then." He looked up at the lieutenant. "There's more, isn't there?"

"Yes, sir," Kennick said with a nod. "Confirmation may not be necessary. We've just had word from Carik's Fort. Survivors report the fort suffered a devastating attack. Only a handful made it out but they report the fae swept through there like a plague."

Rhenkin's face turned the colour of ashes as he looked at the lieutenant with haunted eyes. "How many survivors?"

Kennick grimaced. "They're still coming in, sir, but it's peasants and townsfolk. Not a man in colours among them. It seems the old man, Obair, and the lad that went with him, stumbled across them on their way here."

Rhenkin reached into a cupboard, pouring the whiskey with a steady hand despite the shock on his face. "Settle them somewhere comfortable. Send them up once they're in."

"I'm afraid that's not all, sir," Kennick said with a wince.

"What the hell else can there be?" Rhenkin asked. "Has Feldane decided to invade too?"

Kennick drew a deep breath. "Celstwin reports an attack from a Bjornmen fleet."

"They what?" Rhenkin stormed to his feet.

Kennick carried on, unmoved. "Apparently the fleet was driven off but the city suffered heavy damage and a large portion was caught in the fire."

Rhenkin sank back down, reaching for the glass. "Fire!" he breathed, stretching the word out. "Lords and Ladies, I never imagined Celstwin would be threatened. Still, I suppose even Pieter will be hard pressed to ignore this."

Kennick said nothing, but reached out and presented a letter, embossed and sealed.

Rhenkin raised an eyebrow and cracked the seal.

Kennick carried on as he older man read. "The word from the messenger was that Pieter has fallen, sir," Kennick said. "He reports that Duchess Freyton had called a Council of Lords and that she now holds the throne."

He read in silence, lips moving occasionally until the message fell from his fingertips. "About bloody time..." he whispered.

"Sir?"

Rhenkin looked up, seeming surprised to find the lieutenant still there. "It seems the messenger's gossip wasn't far from the truth. Our duchess now holds the throne as queen and, more importantly, as lord commander of the crown's armies. From the sounds of things she's gutted every garrison within easy reach of Celstwin and sent orders on to others. We're to expect the entire force from Savarel, as well as the rest of Baron Rentrew's men within days. Her forces will march north as fast as they are able."

Kennick looked over at the map. "That will certainly present a few options, sir. Did you want some time before I send Obair in?"

Rhenkin looked up from the letter. "Hmm? Oh, no, send him in as soon as he's able."

"Very good, sir," Kennick said, but Rhenkin didn't seem to be listening. He let himself out, leaving the man with his thoughts.

* * *

Rhenkin fingered the letter. Selena, queen, barring the pomp of a coronation. He shook his head and snorted a laugh at the situation. She'd always held the power, even when Freyton was still alive but damn, this was on another level.

The child! Rhenkin pinched at the flesh between his eyes as the thought struck. He hadn't had time to decide how he felt about her passing off the child as someone else's. "Liar," he breathed to himself. He'd had plenty of time. He'd just avoided it, telling himself the war was too important. This time he really didn't have time to think about this. Selena was a distraction at the best of times. He drained his glass, trying not to think about the feel of her skin, how that red hair had looked against the pale flesh of her shoulder.

She'd picked him like a ripe plum. Oh, he'd never admit that to anyone who asked. He snorted at the thought. *Who would ask?* She had though. He shook his head, smiling at how she'd had to tell him to stop calling her by her title as she'd wrapped her legs around him.

A tap at the door brought him back to reality and Kennick stepped in, ushering Obair inside. The man looked, if possible, older still. His journey had aged him but it was more than just that. Rhenkin looked at him as he waved him into a chair. There was a sorrow there that he hadn't carried before. A trace of what might have been guilt perhaps.

"Obair," he said, coming around the desk to clasp the old man's hand. "It's good to see you." Even his handshake was weak, he noticed. "Did you…?"

"Find anything?" Obair finished for him. "Oh yes, as many questions as answers though. We found Lillith's cottage, just as I remembered it. She's dead," he said, getting the words out before Rhenkin could ask the question.

Rhenkin winced. The lost opportunities there were endless. "So you found nothing?"

Obair laughed. It was a hollow sound, tired and empty. "No, not nothing. More than we could have thought possible. We found a way to possibly rebuild the Wyrde, to lock the fae out of Haven again."

"Then that's good news, isn't it?" Rhenkin frowned, the man was talking in riddles and circles. His tone didn't match his news. He had too much going on to play games like this.

"I suppose it is, in a way." Obair nodded. "Do you think I could have some of that?" He nodded at the whiskey Rhenkin had left it out on the desk.

Rhenkin flushed. The whiskey wasn't exactly a secret. Every officer he'd ever known past the rank of lieutenant had kept some in a similar place. At the same time it seemed an admission of weakness somehow and he'd always kept it out of sight. He reached for another glass, pouring for the druid.

The first drink barely covered their arrival at the cottage. By the time Obair recounted the arrival of Ylsriss and Joran and their time in the Realm of Twilight it was Rhenkin reaching to fill his own glass.

"So many months we went with no way to communicate with these Bjornmen and now I have six within my own walls."

"Six?" Obair blinked owlishly at him, the whiskey obviously taking effect.

"Three Bjornmen surrendered just this week." Rhenkin told him. "Just walked into a patrol and handed themselves over."

Obair shook his head. "You said six. Even with these three and Ylsriss and Joran, I count five?"

Rhenkin nodded with a grunt. "The old woman, Miriam. She was following along behind the Bjornmen, travelling the same road. She can speak their language."

Obair frowned at that. "From what I'd understood there'd been no real contact with the Bjornmen, other than their raids I mean. No trading or anything like that?"

"That's true," Rhenkin told him. "We know they come from the east but, so far as I know, no vessel has ever managed to pass the ice currents."

"Where did she manage to learn it then?" Obair wondered.

Rhenkin's only response was a shrug. "I've too many other things to worry about, to be honest. What the Bjornmen have said is interesting though. Hells it's downright terrifying if you believe it all."

Obair raised a bushy eyebrow and waved the glass in his hand for Rhenkin to go on.

"This 'Klöss' claims to be lord of the city they've built in eastern Anlan. He says he sought us out because of the attacks his forces have suffered at the hands of the fae. Says there are satyr beyond count coming for us. Not only that," he bulled on before Obair could interrupt, "he says the fae have been in their lands too, across the sea. In these 'Barren Isles' of theirs."

Obair sat back at that. "That makes sense I suppose. I'd never really thought about it but the world the fae inhabit might touch on our own in any number of different places. My master and I always focused on the Withengate because that's

FAE - THE SINS OF THE WYRDE

where the Wild Hunt was supposed to come from. That doesn't mean it's the only place they could cross through. I'd be interested to speak to this man if that could be arranged."

Rhenkin nodded. "I can't think of a reason why not. I can have Miriam translate for us, unless you'd rather use Joran?"

Obair tapped the glass against his lips for a moment, then shook his head. "No, let's use Miriam. Joran's Anlish is good but he's still rusty. I don't want to risk any misunderstandings if we can avoid it."

Rhenkin went to the door and had a brief conversation with one of the men in the adjoining room. "Shouldn't be too long," he said, retaking his seat. "I'll admit, Obair, I'm having a hard time with a lot of this. The Bjornmen I can cope with. I can even cope with the fae to a degree. But these things you're telling me about glyphs and rituals, it sounds like something out of a storybook."

Obair sighed. "I know. There was a time when I'd have said there was a good reason for that. That the truth of the fae was buried in fables. These days, I'm not even sure what the truth is. If what Joran told me is true Haven isn't even our own world. The fae plucked us from some other place, using us for their own purpose and then we escaped here after the rebellion."

Rhenkin shrugged. "Does it matter? How many forgotten religions have given their own versions of where we all come from? I'd rather deal with the life I have than worry about where it came from."

"Well, I'd say it matters," Obair replied leaning forward. "If Joran's right then we live in a world that must be very close to paradise for the fae. If we truly did come here from the Realm of Twilight then mankind first rebelled against them, and then fled to this world, locking them out with the Wyrde. To intents and purposes we have first stolen their heaven, and then locked them in a hell between worlds for thousands of years."

Rhenkin shrugged. "I make a point of not looking for the common ground with my enemy. Understanding their motives is all well and good and has its place. Sympathy for them, however? That doesn't sit well with me, as a man or as a soldier."

Obair nodded and raised a finger to make a point when a knock at the door stopped him.

"The translator, sir," the soldier announced.

301

Obair stood and looked at the woman curiously as she entered and Rhenkin dismissed the man who had escorted them. The woman was probably older than he was, white hair surrounding a face that had suffered more than its fair measure of pain and loss by the looks of it. She glanced up at Obair once, frowning as if she recognised him.

The change was fast, so quick that Rhenkin might have missed it had he not been looking directly at her. Her eyes seemed to slip out of focus, and then flashed, obscuring her eyes for the time it takes to blink as a blaze of amber shot across them. She staggered back, as if stumbling, and reached blindly for the doorframe as she pulled herself upright.

"Wyrdeweaver!" she gasped.

* * *

"What did you call me?" The old man demanded through lips pinched tight with shock. He'd almost staggered when she spoke.

Miriam shook her head, her vision still swimming as the effects of Aervern's sight faded. "The Wyrde, you wove it didn't you? You worked the ritual. I can see it on you. I can smell it."

Obair's mouth worked, trying to form words. "I did, but—"

"Just who are you, woman?" Rhenkin demanded, interrupting.

Miriam pressed a hand to her forehead. This was suddenly all too much. "I need to talk to you about the Wyrde," she said in a weak voice.

The old man seemed to recover himself and looked at Rhenkin. "Why don't you sit down? It seems we have a lot to talk about."

She eased into the chair gratefully. "Thank you, my hips aren't what they once were."

"I know the feeling," Obair said as he smiled. He glanced back at Rhenkin and Miriam followed his gaze but the major made no move to stop him and seemed content to let the old man take the lead for now.

"You're right, of course," Obair told her. "I worked the ritual of the Wyrde for most of my life but what do you know of this?"

"My name is Miriam, but I imagine the major told you this already." She nodded at the man as he looked on. "I was sent to find the Wyrdeweavers. I've been searching for you since I left the Withengate, I followed the trail here."

"The Withengate? What trail?" Obair shook his head in confusion before the realisation took hold and he looked up at her sharply. "Just who is it that sent you?"

Miriam took a deep breath. "Aervern of the fae," she said.

"What?" Rhenkin burst out. "And you just think to mention this now?"

"Rhenkin, please," Obair said, holding a hand up to the man, though his eyes never left Miriam's face. "Why don't you start at the beginning?"

"I barely know how to start," she murmured. "I've been with the fae most of my life. I was taken, stolen really, when the Wyrde still stood. Ileriel, the one that took me, used to taunt me by explaining just how it was that I was responsible for allowing the fae back into this world and the false religion she'd created through me.

"For years I lived," she stopped, shaking her head. "No, I don't suppose it was really living, enduring comes closer but even that's too generous. I've been slave, trophy, and breeding stock. I've been the key the fae used to pass through the Wyrde. My mind has been crushed so many times there are days when I doubt my own senses but I remember the lies and myths they used me to spread. The church they created to serve their own ends."

She fell silent, staring into space for a moment. "I'm sorry," she said finally. "I'm not doing a very good job of this am I?"

Obair smiled with a shrug. "It's not easy to put a life into a few sentences. We'll piece it all together. Carry on."

"I saw the beginning," she said. "I saw Aelthen cross into this world and lift his fae into the air for the Wild Hunt."

"I did too," Obair told her. He nodded at Rhenkin, "We were all in the glade as the fae burst through. Aelthen, is that the name of the creature that leads them?"

Miriam nodded and her voice dropped to a whisper as she began again, a dark confession as her gaze fell to the floor. "I've been dragged along with them as they gather heads like trophies and drag women and babies back to the Realm of Twilight. And now I've seen the beginnings of their purge."

"Purge?" Rhenkin interjected. "Make yourself clear, woman."

"Aelthen isn't content with just the Hunt," Miriam told him. "He wants to reclaim this world for the fae and he intends to wipe it clean of its human infestation."

"Ambitious," grunted Rhenkin. "I've seen these creatures fight, they're nasty bastards, but even with that they'd struggle with an entire world. They've greater numbers than I'd first thought but not that many, surely?"

"You have no idea, Rhenkin," Miriam said with a shake of the head. "Aervern made me watch as the armies of the fae attacked the Bjornman city. I saw them call plants from the ground to tear the walls down. I watched as the fae'reeth swarmed through the streets, tearing men to shreds. The Swarm alone could have taken the city. He..." she stopped, held by the look on his face. "What?"

"Did you say they called plants?" Rhenkin turned, rifling through the papers on his desk for the report. He read without turning, grunting sourly, and then tossed it down onto the desk. "This is all very interesting, I suppose," he began again, "but it's not the reason you're here. You're here because you were sent by the fae. Tell me, Miriam, what does this Aervern want with us?"

She glanced at Obair before she spoke. "I can't pretend to know what she plans but I know she wants to speak with you."

* * *

Selena shifted in the seat, keeping her face neutral at the stab of pain. She allowed herself a frown as she glanced out at the sky. "Hanris, we can't be stopping already can we?"

The chamberlain glanced at the trees through the window to the carriage. "It would appear so, your majesty."

"I've asked you not to call me that." She sighed. "Not until things are formalized anyway, and certainly not when we're alone."

"It hardly seems proper, your grace," the stuffy man objected. He seemed to have grown old over the last months, as if age had suddenly reached out from a dark corner to claim him. Secretly Selena worried about him. Losing Hanris was something she wasn't prepared to accept just now.

"Would you call over that nice young man and see just why we seem to be stopping?" she said, pushing at the seat with one hand and easing herself over again.

"Captain Coulson, your grace?"

"Coulson!" she snapped her fingers. "Why can I never remember the man's name?"

Hanris's lips quivered in an approximation of a smile and he worked the glass window down, speaking to the man who had been riding close to the side of the carriage.

"Your grace?" Coulson said, failing to conceal the sigh within the question.

"Coulson." Selena beamed. The man was worse than Rhenkin had ever been it seemed. He simply had no idea how to cope with a woman who wasn't content to sit and wash pots. "I can't help but notice that we seem to have stopped."

"Indeed, your grace." Coulson nodded. "The light is beginning to fade and I'd like to have a secure camp established before dusk."

Selena squinted up at the sun. "Coulson, it can't be much past four of the clock. I expected to reach Druel today."

"We're not that far off, in truth, your grace," Coulson admitted with another nod. "We wouldn't arrive before dark however and we're not so strong a company that I'd be comfortable with the risks of travelling in the dark."

Selena nodded soberly, unconsciously mimicking the man. "Exactly how far from Druel would you say we are, captain?"

He winced before he spoke. It was slight but it was there. "We should be able to arrive by mid-morning comfortably, your grace."

"That's not really what I asked now, is it?" Selena pointed out with a smile. "Specifics, captain. How far?"

"Three to four hours if we pushed the horses," Coulson said.

Selena tapped her lips with one finger while she pretended to consider this. "We push on then. The horses would rather be tired and in a warm stable than rested and out in the cold, I'm sure." The thought of sleeping in a camp for another night was not something she was willing to endure, not with Druel so close."

"Of course, your grace," Coulson said. "I had just thought…"

She raised an eyebrow. "Yes?"

"Well, in your condition… The baby and all."

"Captain Coulson," Selena said, drawing herself up and fixing him with a stern look. "I rather think that I am the better judge of my fitness to travel, don't you?"

"Yes, your grace." Coulson wilted until his pride couldn't shrink further, then gave an awkward bow in the saddle and wheeled his horse, barking orders.

"Damn that hurt," Selena muttered, sinking back into the seat and shifting gingerly.

"You have just had a baby, your grace," Hanris chided her.

"I had a baby almost a month ago and I've spent the best part of the time since being coddled and mothered. Neither the Bjornmen, or these fae that Rhenkin has produced, will wait for us."

Hanris gave her a look that clearly said that, whilst he might find merit in her arguments, he was not about to admit it.

Coulson had the column moving again in a surprisingly short space of time. They weren't travelling in any great numbers. Coulson had flatly refused to let her and Hanris travel unescorted and she'd had to haggle the numbers down to the size of the company. Even then he hadn't been happy about it. It seemed she was doomed to be coddled for the near future. The thought was not an appealing one and she sat back into the seat of the carriage, slouching as much as she could as she stared unseeing out of the window. Hanris was wise enough to leave her alone and her thoughts ran from the baby, to Rhenkin's expected reaction, to the war.

The near sacking of Celstwin had been a close thing. Too close by far. Anlan had never really been a seafaring nation. Its trading partners were all easily accessible by land and, in many cases, journey by sea was simply not worth the risks. The Bjornmen had been within sight of the city before anyone had the faintest idea they were close. If the river had been that little bit wider, or if there had been fewer bridges, Celstwin may well have been burnt to the ground.

She chewed her lip and scowled at the thought. Pieter may have been dealt with but she had done little more than inherit the problems he'd been ignoring. Removing him from power had done nothing to present her with solutions.

Not for the first time she wondered about the wisdom of sending troops northeast. Though the Bjornmen seemed to have concentrated their efforts there, if Celstwin had taught her anything, it had taught her that the Bjornmen could be anywhere.

Guilt caught her completely unaware as a stray thought of the baby drifted through her worries. She hadn't thought of him in hours. Wasn't she supposed to be consumed with thoughts about him by now? She'd spent the last month having her ears filled with advice and the mouthings of women who'd done nothing with their lives but birth children and produce their own squalling brats. They undoubtedly knew more about child-rearing than she did but it was doubtful they knew anything about saving a nation.

She wasn't like them, she'd realised. She was never going to be a doting mother.

This baby had been a means to an end, at best a happy accident. And yet she felt guilty that she hadn't thought of him. If she didn't care at all wouldn't she not feel that?

The baby was a safe as she could make him. She was under no illusions over the plots some of Pieter's supporters still hatched. She could never have left him in the palace, a knife in the dark and her line would end with her. Bringing him north was out of the question and so she'd laid trails all over Anlan as to where he was. Raysh would guard him like nobody else could. Not because he felt a sense of loyalty but because he owed her. Jantson would have dithered and Salisbourne would never have thought to employ a thief to find their friend. Raysh owed her his freedom and probably his life.

Druel crept into sight like a clumsy thief, the pinpricks of light distracting her from her thoughts and providing a sketchy outline of her home as they drew closer. Her guard swelled as Rhenkin's men rushed out of the town and attached themselves as escort. She'd just travelled for days with her small contingent but now she was within the walls of Druel more protection was clearly warranted. She smiled to herself at the foolishness of it all.

The town was an odd place. It had never been large, and whilst Freyton's decision to make it his ducal seat had added its own prestige, it hadn't had a major impact on Druel's population. There had been many who had drifted out to the smaller villages, or headed east into the Reaches, but they had been offset by the influx of affluent merchants, hosteliers, and toadies seeking to benefit from Freyton's presence. The result had been an odd town, not even half the size of Kavtrin but somehow missing the cross-section of society that one expected to find in a town of any real size.

She glanced over at Hanris as the carriage clattered through the streets. He was asleep, head hanging down to his chest. Quite how he managed it with the carriage bouncing them around she wasn't sure but it was good to see the man taking some rest for a change.

His eyes flickered open as they passed through the gates to the ducal palace and the wheel crunched over the fine white gravel Freyton had insisted be spread. She looked toward the entrance and the figures stood waiting for them. She didn't need to see his face. She could tell Rhenkin just by the way he stood.

He waved the footman away and reached to open the door himself. "Your majesty." His eyes gave away nothing as he nodded in place of a bow. "It's good to have you back. We weren't expecting you quite this soon."

She eased herself out of the carriage and down the small step before she spoke. "The roads were good to us, Rhenkin. And thank you, it's good to be back."

"Celstwin seems to have been productive," he said. His eyes flicked to her stomach and back to her face. It had been quick but the meaning was unmistakable. "We can discuss things inside, Rhenkin," she told him. "I'm sure there are many things you have to report."

"Indeed, your majesty." He gave another short bow and extended an arm, ushering her to the entrance.

Selena headed inside. The sound of the gravel didn't quite mask the sound of Hanris being roused from his sleep and she flashed a quick smile at Rhenkin. The look he returned was carefully neutral, giving nothing away, and she pressed her lips tight together as she sighed and led the way to her study ushering him inside.

"It's late Rhenkin," she told him as she leaned back against the wall beside the closed door. "I don't want to get into all of this now. You can give me a full report in the morning."

"Where is my child, Selena?" He sounded strained, drawn, but his voice was nothing to his eyes.

She blinked "As far as I'm aware you don't have any children, Rhenkin. My son, however, is safe and well."

The mask had cracked and she pressed back against the door as his anger shone through and he bit each word off. "That is my child, Selena. Don't play games with me. Now where is he?"

"Don't be a damned fool, Rhenkin," she hissed in an urgent whisper. "This child is Freyton's. Without that fact I was not still a duchess, not able to call the Council of Lords, and this nation would have no queen. You know damned well this is bigger than your wants, now stop acting like a petulant child!"

He glared at her and she could see her words fighting to push through his rage.

"We're not done here," he snapped and moved to wrench the door open, stepping past her as it slammed back into the wall. She stood frozen for a moment and it wasn't until she sighed that she realised she'd been holding her breath. He would keep, she decided. There were more important issues to deal with at the moment but Rhenkin would need to be managed. The only question was how?

* * *

The knock at the door was followed by both Rhenkin and Hanris as they made their way in. Selena ignored Hanris's bows and formality as she studied Rhenkin's expression. The rage was gone. Today the man was all business and his eyes gave away nothing as they approached.

"Your majesty, Major Rhenkin has some rather pressing news to report," Hanris said with a nod at Rhenkin.

Selena raised an eyebrow. "So pressing it requires you both to deliver it?" she mused with an arch smile. "It must be important."

"I merely thought to…" Hanris began but stopped as he caught her smile.

Selena gave a delighted laugh and sat up at straighter at the desk. "You know me better than most by now, Hanris. Please, both of you, continue."

"We have a Bjornman in custody," Rhenkin told her. "We have had for a number of weeks. He claims to be one of the leaders of their forces."

"And you managed to capture him?" Selena asked. "How in the world did you manage that?"

"We didn't," Rhenkin told her with a shrug. "He and two others walked here on their own. He says he wants to discuss the fae."

"Wait a minute." She held a finger up with a frown as she thought. "How are you managing to speak with him? You've told me before that any men you've captured or taken from the battlefield haven't been able to speak Anlish."

"That's true, your grace," Rhenkin admitted, ignoring the look Hanris gave him at the title he'd used. "The patrol that found them encountered a woman travelling behind them. She is able to speak their language."

Selena raised an eyebrow at that. "That's awfully convenient, don't you think?"

Rhenkin nodded and reached for the back of the chair set at her desk in front of him with a questioning look.

"I'm sorry. Please, do sit," she told them.

"Thank you, your majesty," Rhenkin said, seemingly unable to stop his sidelong glance at Hanris as he did so. "Normally I'd agree with you, it's just too convenient to have much faith in it. However, there have been other developments as well that have put her in a different light."

"Go on." Selena told them. She set aside her playful teasing, now was not the time.

"It's come to light that the translator has spent some time in the realm of the fae. Indeed, it would seem that a fae herself tasked her to locate Obair for some purpose."

Selena's eyes widened and she nodded, thinking quickly. "And do we know for what purpose?"

Rhenkin shook his head. "Not as of yet, though Obair could probably tell you more than I could."

"They're back then? Obair and the boy?" She picked a pen from the holder on the desk and toyed with it.

"They are." Rhenkin nodded. "They arrived two days ago but, again, I feel he could give you a better report than I."

"You seem to be dancing around the edge of something, Rhenkin," she told him. "It's really rather irritating. I do wish you'd just come out and say it."

His eyes flashed then, a hint of the anger from the previous night. It was gone in a moment but it was there. "Very well, your majesty. We've had word that the fae have attacked and razed Carik's Fort and a large portion of Kavtrin." He glanced up at her expression and bulled on. "We don't have full details of Kavtrin yet but some of the survivors from Carik's Fort have managed to make it here. I suspect that this woman, Miriam, the translator, would have something to tell us about this. Despite all of this, I would urge you most strongly, to speak to the Bjornmen we have here first."

"And why is that, Rhenkin?" she asked with a dangerous lilt to her voice.

If her tone bothered him he didn't show it. "There are a number of reasons, your majesty. First and foremost would be the fact that the Bjornmen are a present and permanent threat. The fae seem able to vanish at will, or at least move faster than we can effectively counter. The Bjornmen are more easily dealt with. If we must face two enemies at once I'd rather deal with the one we can find first."

"And the other reasons?"

"If I can be candid for a moment?" He waited for her nod. "The fact we have these Bjornmen here presents us with an opportunity. From what they are telling us the fae have a presence in their own lands too. Not just the lands they've taken from us but their homeland. It's taken some time but I'm coming to the realisation that they may be a larger threat to us than the Bjornmen could ever be. This is more than simply a hunt, picking off the peasants that the fae can find in the open. They're going further than that. Kavtrin alone shows us that. If we could find a way to reach an accommodation with these Bjornmen then I believe we should explore that."

"And you think I should speak with them first?" Selena asked him.

"I do," Rhenkin stated firmly. "Obair doesn't live in a world with firm numbers and facts, he works on suspicions and best guesses. I can't blame him for that but I'd rather deal with something solid first before finding a way to deal with Obair's best guess."

"That sounds reasonable," Selena conceded. "I think before I speak to these Bjornmen though, I'd like to talk to this woman. It may be she has more to tell us than anyone else."

"I'll have her sent in directly, Your Majesty," Hanris said with an odd, seated bow.

"Before you do, there is something I'd like to discuss with the both of you," she told them speaking slowly as she thought it through. "I find myself in a rather tenuous position. I may hold the throne but I have been manoeuvred there by various machinations and I have no intention of being anyone's marionette. I occurs that I have two rather strong allies under my nose, if the right appointments were to be made."

"Appointments?" Rhenkin raised an eyebrow.

Selena nodded, and looked up at the ceiling. "Within weeks most of the armies of Anlan will be mustering under my banner. Whilst I am sure the general staff have exemplary credentials I've yet to meet a single one of them that I could say I truly trust. Now is not the time to begin a campaign under untested officers, wouldn't you say?"

Rhenkin said nothing, frowning slightly.

"I can't have someone else in command, Rhenkin. You've shown you can achieve results. You've proven your skill and loyalty time and again. I want you to lead the armies."

"That's…generous, your majesty," Rhenkin replied. "But I'm afraid that would never work. The men would never follow a simple major."

Selena nodded. "Yes that's why I'm appointing you Lord High Marshal."

Rhenkin gaped, seemingly lost for words.

"Your majesty," Hanris said, leaning into the desk. "You are aware the position of Lord High Marshal is usually an honorary one? It is not one usually associated with officers actually in the field, so to speak."

Selena allowed herself a tight smile. "I am, Hanris, thank you. It does, however grant a military rank and an authority over and above any other save my own, I believe."

Hanris coughed. "It does indeed. The rank was historically reserved for the crown prince and, on occasion, the prince consort."

"Well now," Selena said, glancing at Rhenkin. "Isn't that interesting? I do take it you'd be willing to work under me in that…position?"

Rhenkin flushed, and then coughed as Selena smiled at him.

"The general staff would throw a merry fit," he managed finally.

"I'm sorry?" Selena said, in mock confusion. "Who's queen?"

Rhenkin laughed as he shook his head. "I would be willing to consider it, your majesty."

"Excellent. As for you, Hanris," she said, turning to the small man, "I believe I will have need of a Lord Chancellor. If you'd be willing to consider the post."

"I would be honoured, your majesty." Hanris said, looking shocked. "Though I feel I ought to give the matter some thought."

"Do," Selena said, staring at the wall behind them as she thought. "I believe that will be all, gentlemen. You have things to consider and I believe I have a woman to meet." She barely noticed them leave and was still staring into space when a guardsman tapped at the door and escorted the old woman in.

Selena studied the woman as she approached. She was old, certainly. Her eyes and face carried more than their fair share of pain and struggle. At the same time though, she had a youthful look about her eyes, as if she hadn't really lived her years.

She grimaced as the old woman winced her way through a curtsy. "Please, don't," Selena told her. "I get more than enough bowing and scraping from the servants. I've no need to make a woman's life harder than it needs to be." She motioned her into the chair. "Sit, please. I have a number of things I'd like to talk to you about."

"Thank you, your majesty," Miriam smiled as she eased herself into the chair with a soft grunt of pain.

Selena gave her own wince. "Let's dispense with that, as well, for now. I've only held the crown for a little more than a month and I still look behind me whenever someone uses that title."

"As you wish," Miriam murmured.

"Major Rhenkin informs me you can speak the language of the Bjornmen and that you learned this in the world of the fae?" the question sounded fantastical even to her and she shook her head at herself.

Miriam frowned for a moment before she spoke. "That's correct, your..." she stopped herself with a grimace. "That's true, my lady."

Selena looked at her for a moment. The woman was nervous, that much was obvious. She looked as though she might bolt at any moment. "I think, perhaps, that we might have an awful lot to talk about," Selena told her. "I'm suddenly very dry. How would you like a nice cup of tea?"

Miriam smiled with a sigh that took much of her tension out with it. "I'd like that, my lady."

Selena reached for the bell-pull she'd had installed and looked up in expectation at the door. "Servants can be annoying," she confided, "but they do have their uses."

"I think we'd both like some tea," she told the servant when he arrived.

The wait wasn't long and Selena waved both the servant and Miriam away as she poured for both of them. "Now," she said, settling back into her seat and sipping at her cup. "Why don't you start at the beginning?"

Miriam closed her eyes for a moment. "I suppose, in a way, it all started with Caerl," she began.

Selena sipped her tea as the old woman told her story. There was something about it that nagged at her but she ignored it as the tale passed from Miriam's flight from her abusive husband, into the world of the fae, and then, finally, to her time at Tira Scyon. It would have been easy to pity the woman, her life had been torturous, but pity was a luxury she hadn't the time for.

"Tell me more about these Wildfae," she asked as Miriam paused to sip her tea. "Do you think there is a division there?"

"A division?" Miriam tapped at her cup as she thought. "Possibly, but it's not as simple as that. If Aelthen had lorded the powers of the Highfae over them from the start, if he'd withheld the knowledge that they have of glyphs and the things they can do with them, then perhaps things would be different. As it is they are rediscovering things that have been lost to them for centuries. Their world has been turned upside down by the changes Aelthen has brought but this has been tempered by these discoveries. He's destroying their society and everything they know with one hand yet offering them wonders with the other."

Selena nodded. "And what about the people there, the humans I mean?"

"There aren't many in Tira Scyon," Miriam told her. "Just the few that the highfae brought with them from Tir Rhu'thin. Humans are probably as much creatures of myth to the wildfae as the glyphs themselves."

"That's not the case at Tir..." Selena gave up. "At this other place?"

"No." Miriam shook her head, apparently unaware of the expression she pulled as she spoke. "No, the humans at Tir Rhu'thin are either kept as slaves or used for breeding. The fae don't reproduce quickly and there's more chance of them breeding satyr or fae'reeth than a true fae. By interbreeding with humans they can change all of that. Their numbers have grown steadily since I was taken, and even more so since the Wyrde fell. This religion they created, this Church of the New Days, has resulted in hundreds, if not thousands of children passing into the world of the fae. Time passes more there than in this world and they will all have grown to be used as breeding stock."

"The fae are behind the church?" Selena gasped.

Miriam nodded, guilt plain on her face. "The fae that took me used me as a way to pass through into our world, piercing the Wyrde. It was depressingly easy for them to dupe men with glamours and the religion grew from there. I am sure there are honest people in the church, that most have no idea, but there must be some who know what it is they are doing with the orphans and street children."

Selena shook her head. "Lords and Ladies this is too much." She took a deep breath. "Okay we can talk about that later. Tell me about this Aervern. What does she want?"

"If there is a division, Aervern lies at the centre of it," Miriam told her. "She spent the last month I was with her in Tira Scyon showing me how Aelthen was bringing these changes with him. From his allowing the satyr to rejoin the fae, to his claiming of the Ivy Throne, his actions have all been calculated and she knows that. She has her own agenda though. There has been nothing selfless about her efforts. The fae don't place as much emphasis on family that we do but it was her mother that Aelthen killed to gain the Ivy Throne. It's her world he's disrupting."

"So why show you?"

"Because she didn't just show me the impact he's had there in Tira Scyon," Miriam explained. "Aelthen has brought the fae together with a common purpose that they probably haven't had for thousands of years. He's offering our entire world to them, their promised land. I watched as the armies of the fae swept through the city the Bjornmen have built in the Eastern Reaches. I saw the Great Revel, the horde of satyr that he's unleashed, and the swarm of fae'reeth that tore through the streets of that place. Not a thing was left living in that city. He plans to march this scourge across all of Haven until this world is all like Tir Rhu'thin."

"And so she showed you in order to enlist your help in contacting us," Selena nodded. "I suppose that makes sense. And what do you suppose she wants with us?"

"I don't know, my lady," Miriam admitted. "But she will wish to meet you and your Wyrdeweavers, and soon. I've had no contact with her at all since I arrived here and the new moon fell soon after. The moon will be full again in another few days. My hope is that she will reach out to me then."

Selena reached for the bell-pull again. "I don't like repeating things," she told Miriam. "It's probably best if I bring the others in at this point."

"Of course, my lady," Miriam said as Selena rose to her feet and went to meet the servant at the door, giving instructions in a low voice.

"I've asked Rhenkin and Obair to join us," she said as she settled back into her seat, wincing slightly at the pain.

Miriam nodded. "If I can ask, my lady, how old is your baby now?"

Selena's shock must have shown on her face as the old woman smiled at her expression. "How did you know?"

"It's been the talk of every servant here, your majesty," Miriam told her. "And even if it wasn't I'm an old woman. I can see the signs."

Selena managed a small smile. "He'll be five weeks this Setday."

"You're still in pain," Miriam told her. It wasn't really a question. "He wasn't a small baby was he?" Her smile was a shade away from a laugh as Selena shook her head with a grimace of remembered pain.

"Salt baths will help," Miriam told her. "Witch hazel won't hurt either. You just need to give it time, I'm afraid."

Selena nodded, frowning at this other side of the woman.

"I was the first taken," Miriam told her in response to the unspoken question.

"The first human the fae stole from this world. I've helped so many women after they've had their fae-born children I couldn't even count them."

The door saved Selena from having to think of a response as a servant announced Obair.

"Your majesty," the old man said with the briefest nod. "I thought it might be best to bring Devin along. I hope you don't mind?"

His words were lost on her as she turned at Miriam's gasp. The blood had drained from the old woman's face and her eyes were full of tears. Selena followed her gaze as the question worked its way to her lips but the words were forgotten as she saw the young man.

His hair was shocking enough, somehow turned white as if the colour had simply dripped out of the ends, but it was his face that had silenced her. The recognition was clear as he took half a step forward, frowning as if he couldn't quite believe what he was seeing.

"Oh my stars, Devin!" Miriam gasped. Her hand reached out blindly, clutching at the back of a chair to keep herself from falling.

"What's going on here?" Obair demanded, confusion disguising itself as frustration in his voice.

Devin's face twisted and the years fell away from him as he spoke. His voice didn't belong to a man almost full grown but somehow reached back through the years to the child that had been lost and scared in the woods. "Ma?"

Miriam went to him slowly, one hand reaching out in wonder to touch his face, and then she pulled him gently into her arms.

"She took you!" Devin began and then their tears stole what words remained as they clung to each other in an embrace that was almost visceral.

CHAPTER TWENTY-THREE

"Now then, shall we get started?" Selena told them as she closed the door Devin and his mother had just left through. The morning was getting away from them and she could feel her frustration rising. "Obair, why don't you bring me up to speed on your trip?"

Obair nodded, though his gaze was still on the door as Selena settled down behind the desk again. "Yes, your grace. Or perhaps your majesty is more appropriate?"

Selena gave a wry smile. "A man recently told me titles are like a warm cloak, a comfort in some places but awfully bothersome in others. Why don't we dispense with the majesties for now?"

"Very well…" he floundered.

"Selena?" she offered.

"…Selena," Obair finished, looking profoundly uncomfortable.

"Rhenkin tells me your journey met with some success?" she prompted him.

He nodded, his fingers twisting the folds of his robe in his lap. "It did, though it may be that it provided more questions than answers. Lillith's cottage was exactly where I remembered it, though she was long dead when we found her." A flash of something that might have been pain passed over his face and she gave a brief smile of sympathy.

"She did, however, leave a diary," Obair explained. "Lillith made it clear that the Wyrde was much more complex than I ever imagined. She had been performing her own ritual, just as I was working my own. As it turns out it was Lillith maintaining the Wyrde, I merely helped to provide her with the power to do this.

There was something he wasn't telling her and she fought back a spike of irritation as she motioned for him to continue. His story twisted away from whatever it was he'd been concealing, becoming so fantastical that she might have scoffed if it hadn't been for recent events. A faerie creature that could melt through iron bars to effect its own escape, did a lot to eradicate any scepticism she might have had.

Obair continued his tale, taking her through his efforts to teach Devin the steps of the ritual, the arrival of the two Bjornmen that had somehow passed between the worlds, and Ylsriss's stunning discovery.

"One moment," she said, stopping him with an upraised hand as she pinched at her forehead with another. "Are you telling me that this ritual you've been performing is somehow related to these fae markings? To their magic?"

"They call them glyphs, apparently," Obair told her. "And yes, that would seem to be the case. As surprising as that is it's the least of our discoveries."

"I hardly see what more there could be!" Selena muttered to Rhenkin but he returned her look with a blank expression that gave nothing away. *That was another conversation to be had today,* she thought.

"It would seem that what I'd always been told about the knowledge and records of the druids was not entirely correct," Obair explained. "My master had always told me that they'd been destroyed during the purges, lost as the druids fled from the men Caltus sent out to hunt us down. Devin, Ylsriss, and the other Bjornman, Joran, managed to locate a series of glyphs. They were etched into the stones themselves at the circle near Lillith's cottage. Somehow Devin was able to activate their power and access the records and histories."

"Is that how?" she left the question hanging

"How his hair turned white?" Obair finished for her. "That and more. It was almost as if the stones sucked the very life from him. He had ice on him when they carried him into the cottage. Ylsriss and I have spoken about it a few times but the best we have is guesses."

"Guesses are often a good place to start when you have nothing else to go on." Rhenkin put in.

"Guesses, Rhenkin?" Selena said with an arch look. "That doesn't sound very professional at all!"

"We dress them up and use terms like 'force predictions' and 'logistical estimates.'" He shrugged. "They're guesses all the same."

Obair looked back and forth between them, *probably sensing the undercurrents,* Selena thought.

"Our best guess is that the glyphs were designed to work differently," the old man continued. "Ylsriss tells me that the glyphs created by the fae function with the power they can draw from the moon. The glyphs Devin activated seem to draw on our life-force itself. I suppose, in a strange way, that makes sense. The Wyrde worked on much the same…" he stopped, clamping his lips shut and glancing at both of them in a panic.

"On much the same what, Obair?" Selena asked. She'd barely beaten Rhenkin to it and he examined the druid intently as he started to speak.

"I wasn't going to tell you this," the old man said, sighing the words out in a confessional whisper. "It was something I never knew. From what I gather none of us ever knew." He shook his head, ignoring them for a moment before he began again. "Lillith's diaries made it clear there were two sects of druids, the keepers and the guardians. The keepers, like her, were responsible for maintaining the barrier of the Wyrde. They also kept the knowledge of the truth of the Wyrde, the truth of what it was that provided the power for the barrier.

"The guardians worked a ritual to provide that power. You see, the ritual I performed was keeping a soul captive, trapped between this world and whatever place it is that we go on to after death." He sucked in a breath, shaking his head. "This doesn't get any easier to tell the second time around," he said. "I'd struggled to hold the Wyrde for decades, never realising that every time it tried to escape the hold I had it was a soul trying to escape its torment. I suppose, in a way, it all makes sense. If the Wyrde is a magic based upon the glyphs of the fae then it wouldn't have their ability to draw power from the moon to rely upon. Our souls are all we have to offer. It's hardly surprising that Devin's hair turned white. He's lucky to be alive at all!"

Selena glanced at Rhenkin but the major was staring at Obair. His mask had slipped for once and the stark horror was clear on his face for just the briefest moment before he caught himself. Someone else might have missed it but she knew that face too well.

"What did Devin discover?" Rhenkin asked.

"Everything and nothing," Obair told him. "We talked about it on the journey back to Druel. The stones held the records of the druids but it was nothing like we could ever have imagined. The souls of dozens, if not hundreds, of druids had passed into those stones, given freely at the point of death, carrying their knowledge with them."

Obair shook his head with a bitter laugh. "My master would talk of the lost histories when I was a child. It was the closest I ever got to bedtime stories. This was far more than the collection of dusty books I'd always imagined though. For the moments that Devin managed to reach the histories he touched the lives of those who'd lived there. In that moment he shared years, decades maybe, of their lives. He touched their memories, their lives, everything they'd known. The knowledge came like a flood, overwhelming him, and threw him from the stones."

"He must have discovered something we can use?" Rhenkin pressed.

Obair gave a helpless shrug. "He learned how to maintain the Wyrde, a glimpse at the history of mankind and the fae, but nothing of any true use."

"Then it was for nothing?" Selena murmured the question.

"No," Obair shook his head. "The stones only held so much but they did point us in the right direction."

Rhenkin frowned. "How's that?"

"Those were not the only stones," Obair reminded him. "The histories pointed him very clearly to Widdengate." He laughed then, a hard sound touched with bitterness. "I left the glade looking for help, hoping to warn mankind. As it turns out the answers lay in the very stones I'd spent my life with. The knowledge, and probably the help I'd sought, was right there with me if I'd only known how to access it."

"Widdengate!" Selena said with a wince. "How far beyond our lines is that now?"

Rhenkin sighed as he shook his head. "At this point it's hard to say who holds what. The fae destroyed Carik's Fort before the Bjornmen ever reached it."

"So you have no idea what we'd be heading into?" Selena burst out. Rhenkin looked at her calmly, a raised eyebrow asking if the words had been question or statement.

"We do have scouts out there, your majesty," he reminded her.

Selena nodded at him as she pushed the chair back and went to the map hung on the wall. She'd had it commissioned shortly after the Bjornmen invasion and the detail was something she appreciated every time she examined it. "We have troops en route from Savarel, Celstwin, and what's left of Rentrew's forces. Surely it's just a matter of pushing east?" she asked.

Rhenkin joined her at the map. "Against a normal enemy I'd agree with you, your majesty. These fae don't appear to wish to play by the rules, however."

"Explain," she said in a curt voice.

Rhenkin glanced at the map again, perhaps collecting his thoughts. "If it were simply the Bjornmen we faced your proposal would make perfect sense, a push east with these troops might well drive the Bjornmen from our shores. These fae though, we've yet to find a way to fight them effectively. I'm not sure how well we'd fare against both the fae and the Bjornmen."

"The Bjornmen may well be less of a threat than you think, Rhenkin," she said, peering closely at the map. "From what the woman, Miriam, tells me, their stronghold in the Eastern Reaches has been levelled by the fae. The ships they have returning from Celstwin are likely to find little but rubble."

"Interesting," Rhenkin mused. "Though it doesn't change the situation all that much. If the fae can take Carik's Fort, Kavtrin, and Rimeheld in this short time…"

"Rimeheld?" Selena interrupted.

"The name of their fallen city," Rhenkin explained.

"Then they are a significant force and moving around at will," Selena finished for him. "Damn it, Rhenkin, how do we counter an army we can't hurt?"

Rhenkin frowned as he looked at Obair. "We hurt them at your glade. Some of us did anyway."

Obair grunted his agreement. "Those that weren't overwhelmed by them, yes."

"We know iron will hurt the fae…" Rhenkin stopped, staring into space.

"And?" Selena prompted him.

"Sorry, your grace." He grimaced. "Your majesty," he corrected himself. "The girl from Widdengate, the one who concocted the notion of trapping the satyr we captured. She managed to lead a group of survivors from Carik's Fort to here. Apparently they were attacked numerous times by the fae and gave quite the accounting of themselves. I only have half the story, but…" He shrugged. "I believe it would be worth speaking to her."

"Do," Selena told him.

"Me, your majesty?"

Selena raised her eyebrows. "The last I looked, Rhenkin, you were the one wearing the uniform."

"I merely thought—"

She tapped her lips with one finger, thinking. "No, Rhenkin," she told him. "I'm not convinced of that at all. I still have your captive Bjornmen to speak with. Surely you can manage to speak to a peasant girl."

"As you wish, your majesty." Rhenkin agreed.

"My majesty does," Selena said with a broad smile. "As to the other matter concerning you and I, I believe it is something we should discuss at length but now is not the time."

"I rather thought you had made your feelings clear," Rhenkin told her stiffly, ignoring the perplexed expression Obair was failing to conceal as he looked back and forth between them.

"I don't believe so, Rhenkin, no," she replied with a toss of her head. "I don't believe you understand my feelings on the matter at all."

"If I may, your majesty," Obair butted in. "If you plan to speak with Rhenkin's Bjornmen you may find it useful to take Ylsriss and Joran along."

She looked at him blankly.

"The two Bjornmen who escaped from the Realm of Twilight," Obair explained. "Devin and I brought them here with us. Joran will be able to translate for you easily enough."

Selena sucked on her lip. "Do you think they could be trusted?"

"I think they recognise the fae are far more important that the childish squabbles of two nations, your majesty," Obair told her, meeting her eyes.

"Why do I get the impression I've just been told off?" She asked the room.

"I only meant, your majesty…"

Selena stopped him with a shake of the head. "If it was a scolding then it was probably deserved. If not, then it shows I probably needed one. I'll take them with me, Obair."

* * *

The night air was cool. It was closer to cold, if he was honest, but it was good to have a moment to himself. There had just been so much going on it was hard to process it all.

"Devin? Is that you?"

The sound of the footstep had him turning before his name was called but his groan at being disturbed cut off as he caught sight of her.

"Erinn?"

She ran to him, five darting steps that pulled up short as if she were suddenly unsure of herself. "I wasn't sure it was you. I'm not used to your hair yet. You never really did tell me what happened?"

His fingers reached for it without him thinking. It had grown coarse over the weeks, almost wiry in texture. He shrugged. "It's a long story." She looked different somehow, older perhaps. No, now he looked at her it wasn't really age, it was more something about the way she carried herself.

"You never really told me what happened at Carik's Fort either, you know?"

"Carik's Fort was attacked." She gave him a curious look. "Didn't you hear about that?"

He shook his head. "I've been away, from just about everyone actually. I'm still catching up." He looked out over the wall again, turning only halfway so his position was an invitation. "They won't be able to push much further. I hear that the king's armies are finally on the move."

"It wasn't the Bjornmen, Devin," Erinn said in a soft voice as she joined him at the wall. She didn't look at him as she spoke but stared out into the darkness beyond the lights of the town."

Devin stiffened "The fae? Against an entire fortress? What happened?"

She glanced at him and her expression made him regret the question before she started to speak. "They did what they always do. They tore down the walls and slaughtered us until the streets ran red. I only survived because of someone brave enough to shove me under one of the huts. Even then I don't know how they didn't find us."

He probably shouldn't ask the question, knowing it would be better to stop. He asked it anyway. "Us?"

She shrugged "A girl, Kel. She was the first I found anyway. After that I found Samen, and then Fornn and Jarik joined us once Samen stopped them robbing us. The others drifted in as we made our way here."

"It sounds like I've just been robbed of one hell of a story," he said with a crooked smile.

She shrugged and gave a small smile of her own. "You get nothing for nothing. You tell me what happened to you and I'll tell you my story."

He pushed back from the wall. "Telling stories can be thirsty work, Samen taught us both that. Why don't we go and find something to drink?" He hefted his purse meaningfully.

She raised he eyebrows at the clinking sound. "Where did you get that lot?"

"Rhenkin's man, Kennick, gave it to me." He grinned. "I don't think they really know what to do me at the moment."

"More fool them," she said with a look that had Devin wondering which meaning she'd intended.

He coughed and looked into the night breeze to cool hot cheeks, hoping she hadn't noticed the blush. "Shall we then?"

She gave him another look, a smile that said she was laughing as much at herself as she was at him. It was a look he remembered from Widdengate. He'd seen it on her face whenever she been flirting with one of the boys from the village or trying to get something she wanted. He extended an arm and she took it easily and they made their way out of the palace and down into the town. She chatted lightly, filling the holes in the conversation that he left as he tried to decide which one it was. Did she just want the story or was she flirting?

The Half Moon was possibly the finest inn in Druel, catering to the elite and the toadies that clustered around the palace. Devin weighed his chances as they approached, and the large man on the door looked at him appraisingly. Erinn was busy looking at a tavern on the other side of the road. Devin cocked his head with a raised eyebrow, making the motion a silent question. The doorman's eyes flicked to the purse tied to his belt and a smile bloomed on his lips as he shrugged. Druel was too small a town to turn down custom by the looks of things. He waved them inside as Erinn looked at him in surprise.

"Here?"

"Why not?" Devin shrugged, enjoying the look on her face. "My coin is as good as any other."

They were settled in at a table set in a bay window. Secluded enough for private conversation but close enough to benefit from the fire. Devin ordered a bottle of wine at random, hoping it wouldn't be foul. He watched as Erinn sampled it. She was acting the part as much as he was, at least he hoped she was. She couldn't know much more about wine than he did and that wasn't much. He watched as she swirled the wine in the glass, admiring the colour before she sniffed at it, and then tasted.

Devin's anxiety was mounting until she gave a smile of approval and the serving man poured for them both; leaving the bottle, and the responsibility with Devin.

"How did you learn so much about wine?" he asked, as soon as the man was out of earshot. "I was just hoping it didn't taste awful."

"I don't." She shrugged with one shoulder, letting her red hair tumble down her neck. "I was playing along as much as you were."

"What was all this about then?" he asked, swirling the wine in his glass.

"I copied the couple behind you, in the corner." She nodded towards the bar and laughed at his expression as he glanced back and raised his glass to her in mock salute.

"Not bad for a couple of hayseeds, are we?"

"We, sir, are the finest Widdengate has to offer," she corrected him with an arch look and touched his glass with her own before taking a sip. "Now, before you fuddle me with this wine, I believe you promised me a story."

She was a good listener, prompting him when it was needed at the beginning, and coaxing the details out of him when he faltered, but then sitting wide-eyed as the tale unfolded around them. She gasped when he spoke of Ylsriss and Joran but yet had been sober and calm when he'd talked about his hunting the satyr.

"And this?" she asked, reaching out to touch his hair. Her fingertips brushed his face as they drifted down to the table and he stumbled over his words as she smiled at him with mischief dancing in her eyes.

"The stones at Lillith's cottage," Devin explained. "When I reached for the histories, they took something from me. It was like they were sucking the heat, the very life out of me."

"The histories of the Droos," Erinn breathed. "We're lost in a fairytale you realise?"

Devin nodded. Her words had been light, meant as a joke, but that didn't hide the truth in them. "I know, and we're searching for a happy ending." He shook his head and took a deep drink before topping up their glasses. "Still, we're here. We've had better luck than most. Your father must be in his element working with Rhenkin's smiths."

Her face fell. "He's not..." she faltered.

"I'm sorry," Devin said with a frown. "I just assumed he'd be working with them."

Her gaze sank to the table as she spoke in small voice. "He's not here, Devin. He fell when the fae came to Carik's Fort."

Devin closed his eyes, cursing himself for the worst kind of idiot. "I'm sorry, Erinn. I didn't think."

She nodded. "It's okay." She still looked down at the table. The mood was broken. They'd been dancing on the ice that held them from the reality of their lives and now he'd come blundering in, stamping about in hobnail boots. Harlen had been more than just her father, though that alone was bad enough. In a way he represented all of Widdengate. They'd avoided talking about it until his mention had brought it all home to them both. Widdengate, their families and friends, it was all gone.

"I found my mother," he said, trying to shift the conversation.

She frowned at him, confused by the shift in conversation and the statement. "Hannah?"

"No," he shook his head. "My real mother, Miriam."

She blinked. "What? How?"

"She was here when we arrived apparently," he told her. "She came in with some Bjornmen they'd captured."

"So she just wandered in out of nowhere? Where has she been your whole life?" Her anger rose from nowhere and she leaned forward with palms pressed to the table.

"The fae had her, Erinn," he told her. "If I try hard enough I can almost remember it. The creature in the woods, the stone circle. Miriam was taken by the first of the fae in this world in thousands of years. In a way, I suppose, all of this began with that."

"I hate them," she said quietly. There was a venom in her voice that made him sit back but she carried on before he could speak. "They've taken so much from us. They're evil in a way I don't even have words for."

Devin nodded, reaching for his drink. There wasn't much he could say to that.

"I hate what they do to us too," she told him, ignoring him as he offered her the bottle. "We're so convinced that we can't beat them, that they're better than us, that most of us don't even try. We cower down like mice in a field, hoping the owl won't spot us."

"What else can we do?" Devin asked her. "I've killed satyr but a true fae… Well you heard what happened at Obair's glade. Most of the men with us wouldn't even fire their arrows."

"I've fought them too, you've seen me fight them," she said, looking up at him from where she'd tipped her face towards the table. "They can be killed the same as anything else, we just need to realise that. That's the thing with the fae. We're so convinced they're so powerful that we couldn't hope to challenge them. The truth is, with a handful of this," she reached for the string around her neck that ran to the pouch she wore, "they're nothing."

"You've changed," he told her, smiling into the face of her angry green eyes.

She wrapped a lock of hair around her finger, "Says you."

That brought a smile to both of them.

"You have though," he insisted. "You're not the girl I knew at Widdengate."

She sniffed. "That girl was a fool."

"She was," he agreed. "She had lousy taste in men too."

She laughed then, a genuine laugh that stole the tension away from the table. "Yes, well, that seems to be improving."

He blinked. "Is that so?"

"Pour me another drink and we'll see," she said, her eyes dancing.

* * *

Klöss watched as Tristan paced. Three steps to the wall, turn, and then another ten until he turned again, doing a slow circuit of the cell.

"If you're trying to make me dizzy you're going to have to walk faster," Klöss muttered, drawing a snort from Gavin who sat in the straw beside him.

"You are not funny, Klöss," Tristan told him, sagging down to the floor. "When you suggested speaking to the Anlish about the keiju this is not what I was expecting."

"I wasn't exactly expecting a feast in our honour myself," Klöss told him, "but I take your point. Being locked up like this wasn't what I'd hoped for but I can't really blame them. What would we have done to them if they'd come walking into Rimeheld?"

Tristan grunted. "At least you are being taken out and spoken to. We have been caged for weeks."

"At least we're not chained to the walls." Klöss shrugged.

Tristan didn't bother to comment.

"Have they even spoken to you about the trels?" Gavin asked him.

"Some," Klöss said with a glance at the thick wooden door. "Not enough. I don't know how much their man, Rhenkin, believes. I don't think he trusts me or trusts that this isn't some ploy. I can't blame him, I suppose."

"They think this is a trick of some kind?" Gavin scoffed. "So first we get ourselves taken captive, and then we conquer them from inside their own cells?"

Klöss gave the man a wry smile. "I think that's the plan, yes."

Gavin grinned back. "Let's get started then. This cell is beginning to bore me."

Klöss glanced over at Tristan but the man was ignoring them, watching the door with his head tilted to one side, listening.

"What…" Klöss began but stopped at a muffled clang from the iron grates that lay in the hallways beyond the door. He raised an eyebrow at Tristan but the expression was lost in the dim light and his eyes turned back to the door as a grating came from the lock.

The men didn't speak as they came in. One reached for him and put the chains on his wrists as the other held a club ready. It was the same thing they'd done every time they'd come for him lately and Klöss shook his head in silent amusement. Where was he going to go, even if he could overpower them?

Tristan and Gavin watched in silence as he was led away. He managed to meet Gavin's eyes once but the brief nod said everything there was to say.

It was only moments before he realised they were taking him somewhere new. He was pushed roughly into an empty cell before a bucketful of shockingly cold water was tossed over him, followed by another. His angry question must have shown on his face as one of the guards muttered something to him before holding his nose and grimacing in a pantomime of disgust whilst pointing at him.

Apparently he stank. Klöss could believe that easily enough. They'd been in the same clothes for weeks, rough sackcloth that had been crudely stitched into shape. It was so ingrained with dirt and sweat now that it had stopped scratching.

They marched him on, passing through passages that turned and twisted until he had no idea of the path they took, except that it was new to him. Finally they passed through a series of metal grates and into another passage. The light was brighter here with lamps on the walls here instead of the smoky torches. Wherever they were taking him it was outside of the cells and not to Rhenkin.

They passed up a staircases and into a richly appointed hallway. Twice startled servants skipped out of the way to let them through, staring after them with scandalised looks. They finally stopped at a door guarded by two men in armour.

The men themselves were not large but one look at them told Klöss everything he needed to know. These men were not here to look imposing. They were here because they knew their jobs.

He shook the remains of water from his hair as his escorts had a brief, whispered conversation with the guards, the shorter guard glaring at him as the droplets spattered on his face as the other knocked. Klöss grinned at him once and they pushed him into the room.

A woman sat waiting for him. She sipped from a porcelain cup as she watched him come in, her fine gown at odds with the rough wooden table. Armed men stood behind her, almost hidden in the shadows as they stood against the wall. A glance at one face told him they were ready, and close enough, to prevent him doing any harm to her. Still, they were further away than they would have liked, that much was obvious. She was someone of importance then.

The room was mostly bare. Disused he decided as he looked around. The woman motioned for him to take a seat and he stepped towards the chair, looking around for Miriam. A figure peeled itself away from the wall, rushing towards him before being held back by a guard. She struggled and kicked at him, producing a muffled grunt as she twisted away.

Blonde hair flew as she shook her head and then looked at him with a smile. "Hello, rich boy."

"Ylsriss!" he gasped, his poise gone. "What in the hells are you doing here?"

"Not the hells, Klöss." She gave a sad smile as she shook her head. "Though it might as well have been."

She glanced at the chains on his wrists and turned to the woman at the table, speaking quickly in Anlish before shaking her head violently and stabbing a finger at him. The guards took a step towards her as she slammed a hand down onto the table, her voice rising.

Through it all the red-haired woman remained calm and in control, speaking in a soft voice as Ylsriss raged at her. Klöss couldn't understand the words but he'd seen her angry enough times to know that she was close to losing control completely. The woman peered around Ylsriss at him once and shrugged before looking back to her.

The guard wrestled with the lock on his manacles briefly and they fell clanking to the ground. Klöss rolled his shoulders and rubbed at the skin of his wrists as he looked at the tiny blonde woman. "Were you planning on telling me what the hell is going on?"

"This is Selena, queen of the Anlish," Ylsriss said as she waved at the woman at the table. "I've had you freed, on the condition that you help us."

He gaped at her for a moment "Us? How did you…?" he gave up as Ylsriss burst into laughter, pointing at his expression.

"It's very simple, rich boy. They need me and I told her I wouldn't help unless they free you. In a way you're my price."

"Was that price or prize?" Klöss muttered, trying to catch up.

She gave him a look that he'd missed for far too long. "Maybe both."

PART FOUR

CHAPTER TWENTY-FOUR

"Why am I doomed to be surrounded by an endless reunion?" Selena sighed to herself as the two Bjornmen babbled away at each other. She knew enough of their story to know this could go on for hours.

"Just tell him the bare bones, Ylsriss," she said, interrupting them. "I need to talk to him."

The blonde woman gave her a look that seemed to carry any number of curse words with it, but then nodded.

Selena sighed and turned around to one of the men behind her. "It's Picking, isn't it?"

"Pickering, your majesty," the soldier said with a faint grimace.

She nodded, filing the name away. "Do you think you could send one of your men to fetch Rhenkin and the druid?"

He raised his eyebrows. "Here, your majesty?"

She looked around in mock surprise, as if just noticing the state of the room. "Oh, do you suppose we ought to clean it up for him first?" she asked, wide eyed. "Yes, here! If I can stomach it I'm sure they can find a way to manage!"

He set off at a run as she sipped at the tea,

"Does he know who I am?" Selena asked as Ylsriss turned to face her. She grunted her acknowledgement of the woman's nod. "Rhenkin tells me that he is some kind of commander?"

"His name is Klöss," Ylsriss grated, not bothering to soften her tone.

Selena sighed. This was clearly not going to be as easy as she'd thought. "Would you please ask Klöss exactly what his position is?"

Ylsriss narrowed her eyes and then, apparently unable to find anything wrong with the request, turned for a brief conversation.

"My name is, Klöss, Lord of Rimeheld and Shipmaster of the Thane of the Barren Isles," Klöss told her through Ylsriss. "But then I'm sure your man, Rhenkin, already told you this."

Selena nodded, smiling as Ylsriss relayed the message to her. "He did. As your wife?" she paused on the word, lifting her tone to make it a question before carrying on. "As Ylsriss informed you I now rule here in Anlan. It would seem to me that we have been given an opportunity here, one that is perhaps too great to pass over."

"I don't negotiate standing up," Klöss told her, though Ylsriss failed to completely hide the smile as she spoke for him.

Selena didn't bother to hide her own and turned to a guard, "Run along and fetch some more chairs would you?"

Klöss settled down into the plain wooden chair when it arrived and smiled. "You mentioned an opportunity?"

Selena shook her head. "I'm not a great one for playing games. I excel at it when the situation demands but I've rather come to believe that the time has come for some plain speaking, wouldn't you agree?"

Klöss's only response was a guarded nod.

"I'll begin then," Selena told him. "We could sit here for hours and talk about the Bjornmen invasion of my lands but that's not why you came here. Frankly you're no threat to me now. As a mere duchess I was unable to repel your people but as queen, with all the armies of Anlan behind me, I could drive your forces into the seas and burn your villages behind you."

She waited as Ylsriss relayed that and held her hand up as his eyes widened and he started to speak. "I think though, that the fae pose a greater threat to both our nations than we could ever pose to each other. I've no intention of keeping you imprisoned or executing you. You're far more use to me alive than dead. It is the threat from the fae that I wish to speak about. What would you say to a temporary truce? An accord by which we agree to work together against these creatures?"

Klöss leaned in, clasping his hands on the table that stood between them. Selena sensed, rather than saw, the hands that tightened around sword hilts behind her and she took a deep breath as the man began to speak. "You're right, Queen, I didn't come to talk about our battles. I do not know how much authority I still have," Klöss admitted. "As I told your man Rhenkin the sealord has taken direct control of this conflict but I think your plan is a good one. With as much authority as I have left I will support you against these creatures. The issues we have between our peoples we can discuss later. These keiju… These…*fae*, as you call them. I think you are right, they are the greater enemy…" he broke off, shaking his head.

"It began as skirmishes, attacks that came out of nowhere and left too few behind to bring the news. Then they began attacking our villages, emptying entire settlements and leaving the bodies behind to rot. I've seen these creatures, seen a horde large enough to give an entire fleet of men pause." He stopped as the doors opened and Rhenkin and Obair filed in, followed by men bringing more chairs and servants with refreshments.

"Your majesty," the druid gave a passable bow. "I thought it might be an idea to bring Joran along. We have a great deal to discuss and neither Ylsriss nor Joran would be able to contribute much if they're constantly translating."

The man, she'd noticed, was possessed of uncommonly good sense at times. "Very well." She looked around at the faces about them. "Shall we discuss what we can do against the fae?"

* * *

The woods were close to the walls of Druel, reaching out towards the town from the edges of the hills. Selena glanced up at the moon and glanced over at Obair with a raised eyebrow.

He shrugged in response to her unasked question. "All we can do is wait, I'm afraid." Behind him Rhenkin muttered instructions to his men and fingered his own bared sword.

The breeze was light but carried the bitter promise of winter with it. It cut through Selena's cloak and clothes as easily as any knife might and she shivered, pulling the cloak tighter around herself as she glanced around at the others. Nerves showed on their faces and in the way they fidgeted. Of them all, only Miriam and Joran seemed unconcerned.

Rhenkin had picked the place well. Whilst the trees would provide cover for the creature should she try to flee they were positioned some distance from the edge of the trees and Rhenkin's men all carried ironhead arrows for their bows.

Devin sniffed and stiffened, turning to point out the figure that stepped out from the darkness between the moonlit elms. Selena followed his finger to the shadow making its way out of the woods. She moved with the casual grace so common to dancers and acrobats yet there was something feline about her. There was a beauty to her that went beyond her features and her form. She was a thing of wonder, a myth made flesh. She was glorious.

Selena shook her head, biting hard on her tongue as she fought to chase away the sense of wonder. Even though she'd been warned about this it was one thing to hear about it and quite another to experience it.

Dimly Selena was aware of the men behind her drawing bowstrings back as the creature stopped, cocking her head to one side as she looked at them curiously for a moment before searching the group with her odd eyes.

"I would speak with you, Wyrdeweaver," she said to Obair, her accent alien but yet somehow formal. "Have your manlings put away their *fehru*. You have no threat from me."

Obair cleared his throat as he came to stand beside Selena. "I find that hard to believe."

She shrugged, a picture of indifference. "Believe what you will, manling. If I wished you harm your arrows and blades would be of little use, *fehru* or no."

He glanced back at Selena and Rhenkin with a worried frown. "Ahh…"

Miriam pushed past him with a frustrated sigh. "You set me on this path, Aervern. You sent me to find these Wyrdeweavers. Let's not waste time posturing, I'm too old for this foolishness."

The fae nodded soberly. "There is a wisdom in your words."

Selena pushed forward, clearly if anything was to be achieved here, she would have to do it herself. "What do you want with us?" She cringed inwardly as the creature's glowing eyes turned to her, appraising her for a moment before it spoke.

"The Wyrde has stood for untold ages, locking those that would hunt away from both this land and my own. Their return has not proven to be all I would have wished," Aervern told her.

"Your kind has slaughtered thousands of my people," Selena grated, "forgive me if I find it hard to sympathise with you."

"Your people?" The fae put a peculiar emphasis on the words, cocking her head. "Can a manling own others of its own kind?"

"I am queen here in Anlan," Selena replied, unabashed. "The people of Kavtrin and Carik's Fort that you fae slaughtered for your amusement were my people."

"You are manlings, we fae." Aervern shrugged. "Tales tell that the hunt was ever the way of things." She pushed on before Selena could speak. "Those that have returned, however, would move beyond the hunt. They seek to take this world for their own. Understand, Queen, that this land belongs to the fae far more than it ever has to your people. Your kind fled here, stealing that which was promised us. Aelthen would punish you for this. He would drive each and every one of you before him with a lash until you collapsed to the dirt if he could. He no longer is content with a mere hunt but has raised banners that have not been seen in countless ages. He would set the fae to war, to purge this world of your kind until only a handful remain."

"And you just want to help us out of the kindness of your heart?" Devin called out.

The fae glanced at him, a dismissive look that said far more than words could hope to. Her gaze lingered though, and she frowned at him for a moment before turning her gaze back to Selena. "You know nothing of my kind, of my world. My reasons are my own, take my aid or spurn it at your peril."

"What exactly is it you propose?" Selena asked.

"The Wyrde held our worlds apart for thousands of years," Aervern said, speaking softly. "Now that it has fallen our worlds touch once more. Better that it had never fallen." She looked past Selena, pausing for a moment on Devin as she sought out Obair's eyes. "Better that it was remade."

Selena followed her gaze. "Can you do that, Obair?"

"Perhaps," the old man said, looking troubled. "The knowledge is locked in the stones at the Withengate, though it nearly killed Devin the last time he reached for it."

"Aervern!" Joran blurted out.

Aervern smiled at the young man. "Yes, my sweet?"

He flushed as all eyes turned to him, frowns asking questions. "No, I mean Aervern could power the glyphs. It would be just like giving power to a moonorb, there would be no need for Devin to do anything."

"I think you're forgetting the small matter of an army of fae between here and Widdengate," Selena put in. "It's not a simple matter of strolling across open country."

"The girl, Erinn, had some ideas about that, your majesty." Rhenkin put in. "Things I'd rather not go into in present company but that should make our forces more effective."

Selena pursed her lips. "Even so we're looking at some time before we have enough men to put into the field. Where else will this Aelthen have razed by then?"

Obair cleared his throat. "If I may, your majesty? There is a rather obvious solution to this."

"Oh?"

"Widdengate is behind Bjornmen lines, is it not?" he asked Rhenkin.

The man grunted his agreement with a confused frown.

"In fact, from what I remember from your maps, Widdengate is no closer to us here than it is from the coast and the Bjornmen city is it?" Obair persisted.

"What are you suggesting, old man?" Selena asked.

"Isn't it obvious?" Obair asked with a broad grin. "You need more men. Didn't you say that there was an entire Bjornmen fleet headed for home to the city that the fae have just destroyed?"

"Ally with the Bjornmen?" Selena said, aghast. "My rule would be the shortest in history!" She shook her head hard enough to make her hair fly. "I just deposed a king on the basis of his inaction against the Bjornmen, now you would have me ally with them? No, the notion is ridiculous," she insisted. "Even if I were open to the idea it would take months to broker an agreement."

"I don't think it would take nearly that long," Obair disagreed. "I imagine Klöss could be convinced to come on side reasonably easily."

"Klöss?" Selena scoffed. "The man is a deserter in their eyes. Exactly how much authority do you imagine he'd have?"

"But this Rimeheld of theirs has been razed, your majesty," Obair reminded her. "The commanders there are dead, at least that's what Miriam told us?" He looked to the woman for confirmation. She nodded, her frown mirroring those of the others.

"And from what you've told me, Rhenkin, Klöss claims to have left after the fleet had already sailed? So those on the fleet would have no idea he'd deserted would they?"

Selena sighed. "This is all very interesting, Obair. And yes, you're right, Klöss would probably be able to take charge of the men returning on their fleet. That is if it weren't for the tiny matter of him being here, not there."

"Ah hah!" The old man grinned, the smile looking out of place on his usually sad, tired, face.

"What now?" Selena demanded, losing her patience.

"You're overlooking something. The fae can move from place to place far faster than our forces are capable of, isn't that right?"

"Well, yes?" she shook her head as she spoke, unsure what he was driving at.

"Then Aervern could take Klöss to his men, couldn't you?" he looked to the fae who stood watching them.

"I am not here to act as your servant, Wyrdeweaver. There are dangers you have not yet considered. Aelthen will know of your coming. The stench of the Wyrde is still thick on you both and he will know of your presence long before any other fae might detect it. If you attempt to battle your way through to the Withengate he will know of your presence. He will seek you out and lay you low." That gave Obair pause and he tugged at his beard as he looked to Selena.

"A distraction then," Rhenkin said, speaking before Selena could. "If you believe you can recreate this Wyrde and banish these beasts by reaching Widdengate then our job is simple. We must provide a threat sufficient enough to keep Aelthen and his forces occupied whilst you do. If the Bjornmen can strike from the east as we move our forces in from the west then so much the better."

Selena nodded in a distracted fashion, looking at the fae. "Why do I feel I'm being toyed with here? We're busily making plans to rebuild the Wyrde, as I understand it, to banish you and your people from a place you admit is close to a paradise for you. What I don't understand is why you would do this? We seem to be taking all the risks here. Even meeting with you was a risk. What exactly is it that you stand to gain?"

Aervern hissed through her teeth, sinking down slightly as she shifted unconsciously towards a fighting stance. "You think I risk less than you? In doing this I betray my race, my entire people. You speak truly, I would snatch their promised land, their paradise, from within their clutching fingers. The response, when I am discovered, will be hot with fury. There will be no flight or hiding from Aelthen. I cannot huddle down inside my burrow and hope the shade-cat will pass. Our Lady pulls at me the same as it does he. Here, in her land, or in the Realm of Twilight he will find me. This is a slave we speak of, granted untold Grace and power and grown to king and tyrant. His vengeance will know no limits. I can be denied my death for a thousand years as he imagines torments to inflict upon me. My life will not end swiftly. Do not tell me I risk nothing, little queen. I am the one laying with the jaws tight about my throat."

Selena raised an eyebrow. The fae's obvious anger was interesting and she remained carefully composed as she wondered how best to use it. "If this is true then why would you do this? What do you stand to gain?"

"She gets a legend." Joran stepped out from the press of men. "There was a time when we achieved wonders, when mankind and fae walked together between worlds. The Realm of Twilight has thousands of us still there, thousands of us who would never know this world as their home even if they were returned here." He lowered his eyes as his voice fell, "There are some who never could."

Selena narrowed her eyes, noting others giving the young man the same questioning looks. She shook her head. It was hardly the most pressing thing at the moment. "I don't like the idea of abandoning them…"

"I don't see any realistic alternative, your majesty," Obair told her, though his eyes drifted to Joran as he spoke.

Selena grunted, there wasn't much she could say to that. "Will you agree then?" she asked Aervern. "If what you say is true we will need the Bjornmen's numbers to be a credible threat to the armies of the fae. Will you take Klöss to find the fleet?"

Aervern met her gaze and regarded her in silence for a moment, obviously thinking. She touched her hand to her lips, chest, and forehead as she stepped back into a bow. "I will do this thing."

* * *

The trees flew past her, silvered trunks shone as they were caught in a flash of moonlight that filtered down through the trees. The hand reached for her again and she lashed out savagely as she twisted away from its grasp. Fingernails that were closer to claws than anything else caught at her hair, slowing her as the other hand reached out for her.

The forest floor rushed up to meet her and her hands skidded painfully through leaves and twigs as she fell. Ylsriss screamed, a breathless sound robbed of any force as the wind was driven from her. Terror gave her the strength to roll over, kicking out at the face of the horned creature. The satyr avoided her flailing easily, grinning through its lust as it lowered itself down, crawling towards her.

She lashed out again, stamping out with her heel.

"Oh shit!" The groan of pain was followed by a muffled thud as a body rolled over in the bed and fell to the floor, dragging the blankets with it. She sat up in the bed, curling herself tight and hugging her knees against the cold of the night air.

"Klöss?" her voice sounded small, even to herself.

He groaned again. "Kicked me in the bloody balls," he trailed off, his words more than halfway to being a whimper.

She rubbed at her eyes, grinding the heels of her palms into them to drive away the sleep. A faint glow still came from the embers of the fire and she crouched down beside it, blowing gently to coax a flame onto the taper before lighting the lamp and moving on to the others.

"Lord of the bloody seas," Klöss whimpered, curled into a ball beside the bed with his hands between his legs. The laugh burst out of her before she could stop it and she clapped a hand over her mouth to hold in those that followed it. "Oh, Klöss, I'm sorry."

"Mmph," he managed, curling tighter against the pain.

Ylsriss, staggered to the edge of the bed, laughing harder. "I was dreaming, I…"

He pulled himself up, falling onto the bed as he curled up again. "Some bloody dream."

"Oh, come on," she chided. "It can't be that bad."

He stopped long enough to give her a black look, and then snapped his eyes shut against the pain.

"I was dreaming," she told him again, her laughter fleeing in the face of the memories. "I was being chased, a satyr."

He sat up then, still bent against the pain, but listening. "A nightmare?" He grimaced at the stupidity of his own question but she ignored it.

"I hate them." There was a venom in her voice that surprised even her. "I hate them, Klöss. I hate what they've done to me, to us…to the whole fucking world."

He nodded, seeing she wasn't finished.

"The things they did to me," she whispered. "To everyone in that place. We're worse than cattle to them but what's worse than that is that they make us feel like that's right. That that's the way it should be, you know? They lay the Touch on thick, sometimes without even seeming to notice, and all we do is adore them, worship them. People like the girl I told you about, Tia. You remember?" She looked at him for a moment but was more focused on his eyes than if he agreed with her or not.

"She reached out for the Touch. She *wanted* it. She saw the fae as gods, or something like it. If Aelthen's war succeeds the whole world will be filled with people like her."

"It won't," he said.

She was crying now. The tears hadn't fallen but they hung there in her voice. "It will, Klöss. You don't know, you didn't see."

"We'll stop them," he told her, reaching for her.

She pushed away from his touch. "And what about Effan? What about our baby?"

He took a deep breath, hand still outstretched towards her. "I don't know, Ylsriss. I don't know what to say. What can we do?"

She shook her head, hiding from the question.

"You told me that the time passes differently. That a week or a year here would be far longer in this Realm of Twilight? How old would he be now? Even if we could find him, would he even know you? Would you know him"

She turned on him then, eyes flashing. "This isn't just about me! This is your son!"

"I know that," he shot back. "A son I never even got to see before he was taken."

"That's not my fault."

"It isn't mine either!"

Silence fell then, thick and heavy between them, swallowing their words and smothering them.

"If we do this thing…" he looked at her, leaning in and lifting her eyes with his gaze.

"I know." It was barely more than a whisper. She closed her eyes as she took a breath. "I want to go home. Back to Hesk, back to a place that's ours. I want to be me again."

"We will," he promised. He reached for her again and this time she didn't resist.

"And now you're leaving me again. You've only been out of their cells for a couple of weeks, we've only just found each other, and you're abandoning me." She smiled up at him, softening the accusation.

He smiled back. "Someone has to go and take charge. If the sealord really is dead…" he sighed. "We have to try and salvage something from this mess."

"I know," she murmured, nestling closer, drawing comfort from him.

"I'm more worried about you than me," he told her. "Why do you even need to go? Surely this Joran can find these glips for you?"

"Glyphs," she corrected him. "And no, Joran might be able find them but he couldn't read them well or understand anything much. If they're any different to the ones we found at that cottage, well, this whole thing falls apart."

"I don't like you going near those things, those trels." He squeezed his arm tighter around for a moment.

"I don't want to." She shrugged. "Someone has to… Don't worry, rich boy, you're not getting away that easily. Besides, you'll be closer to them than I will. I don't like the idea of you travelling with that fae woman one little bit.

"You don't trust her?"

"I don't trust any of them." Her anger and hate bubbled to the surface again for just the barest moment before she pushed it back down.

"At least take Tristan and Gavin with you," he suggested.

"Okay."

"Maybe we need to think about something else," he suggested with a smile.

"Maybe we do…" She tilted her head up to meet his kiss and the shreds of the dream fled, at least for a time.

* * *

Ileriel stood in silence as her eyes closed and she reached out around her, searching with her senses. The grass was cool on her feet and the wind soft as it brushed her face but she felt it still. The Lady still pulled at her, even as her Gift filled her. It was a gentle touch now, little more than a reminder of the power that would drag her back to the Realm of Twilight but it was there, ever-present, nagging.

A satyr snarled out, breaking her concentration, and Ileriel snapped her eyes open, glaring at the foolish creatures. The Great Revel was restless. Riahl, their supposed leader, barely had even nominal control. He was the feral leader of a pack of rock wolves. He might be leader of the pack but that did nothing to make the members less wild.

These satyr were nothing like those that had been imprisoned with her in the Outside. Those had a dignity about them, a sophistication that was lacking in these others. Their isolation and banishment from Tira Scyon and the wildfae had made them wilder and more savage. In many ways they were little more than animals. They were ignorant of much of the power the Lady gave them. Their control and use of the Lady's Grace was limited at best, driven mostly by instinct.

The Great Revel spread out before her, filling the valley they had stopped in. This was the first night they hadn't run, following the setting of the sun in search of the next manling stronghold. Controlling them was not easy. Might as well try and control the wind. She could direct them, force them in the right direction, but beyond that her influence mattered for little.

The faeborn were no help. Her gaze followed the thought over to where the trio sat under a willow. They spoke little but were always together, their sapphire eyes shining faintly as the Lady blessed them. Aelthen had sent them with her to help control the Revel. So far they had been of little use.

She looked over towards the source of the snarl. Two satyr crouched low as they circled each other, surrounded by a crowd of spectators. The knives flashed as one hurled itself toward the other, blades slicing through the air in a flurry of motion. There was a beauty to the fight of these satyr but it never lasted for long. The grace and elegance of a fae was there but overlaid with something far more savage. For a time the two were able to combine into something quite wondrous but the savagery always won out. In the end the fight would devolve into little more than a brawl.

Ileriel watched them for a moment, channelling the Lady's Gift towards her eyes and enhancing her vision. The two were well matched in size and strength, it seemed, but the similarities ended there. One fought with all of the grace and beauty of a true fae, the other with a bestial brutality. His blade may as well have been a rock, or a club snatched from the dirt, for all the elegance he showed.

She pursed her lips, appreciating the movement of the first as he stepped outside of the line of attack, shifting behind the satyr's back and slashing with his blades before breaking off, creating space with which to control the next clash. The response was a roar as base as an enraged shade-cat as the second satyr flew at him, crashing into his body and bearing him to the ground where they rolled in the dirt.

Her lip curled in disgust and she turned back to the curiosity. It lay in a bare patch of earth, scuffed clear of plant and grass. The arrowhead was roughly fashioned, nothing like the precise crafting of her own bone-headed arrows. The metal was dull and barely reflected the moonlight. How odd that something so simple could steal her Grace or set her to burning. How odd that here, in the Land of the Lady, this substance was so common. She reached out, not quite touching the thing.

"They spoil for the battle."

The voice shocked her, both because of how close it was, and because she hadn't heard the speaker approach. She shifted, a casual movement that dropped her own arrows neatly over the thing as she looked up at Riahl.

"They are satyr. Your kind is never far from hunt or blade." She didn't bother to hide the disdain in her voice and his face wrinkled in the briefest of snarls at her response.

"The huntmaster will soon be nearing his destination," he told her, keeping his tone level despite the anger that must be raging inside him. "When the sun falls again we will move on."

She shrugged, the picture of indifference. "We will move when Aelthen wishes it."

He shook his head, the long hair on his head billowing out like some great shaggy mane. "This thing of moving together, waiting for others to be in position, it has a strangeness to it. It does not feel right to me. It would be simpler, I think, to just loose my revel upon the manlings and gut them as they flee."

She grimaced, her disgust showing at the idea. "This is not some mere hunt, Riahl. The manlings have an arrogance born of ignorance, they know not their place. They seek to stand against us, to defy us with blade and fire. Aelthen's Purge will cull them. It will grant us this land, the land that was promised us. *If* you can keep your animals under control, that is."

He glared at her then, his anger bright enough to make her rise to a half-crouch as his hands strayed to the knives in his looping harness. "I and my kind are not mere beasts, Ileriel. The Lady blesses us as she does you. We are all fae."

"You are satyr," she hissed at him. "I am fae. You *will* do as you are bid. Now go!" She flicked a dismissive hand before her, shooing him away.

It hung there for the length of an angry breath until he gave a small bow and turned away, but it wasn't until he'd taken twelve steps that she let go of the knife strapped to her back.

The iron arrowhead lay waiting under her quiver. She crouched slowly, watching the satyr around her. Were any close enough to see? To wonder? She moved quickly, extending a hand again, reaching out with flesh and mind. The light flared under her fingertip, sparked by the barest contact and with a light bright enough to blind. Pain shot through her, numbing her arm and leaving her with an odd feeling of emptiness, of being drained and she clenched her teeth together to contain the scream that sought to escape. She glanced around her quickly, catching the odd looks from the satyr closest to where she crouched.

A glare turned the eyes from her and she reached to retrieve the thing, covering it in a fold of fabric to keep it from her skin. It had drained the Grace from her. Not so much that she would suffer, but that in itself was interesting. She twisted to look behind her to where she knew the sun would rise, draining the Lady's Gift with its touch. She'd huddled in the dark of the woods to avoid it this far whilst the satyr milled about, ignoring of the power it stole from them. Perhaps that was a mistake. She narrowed her eyes, thinking.

CHAPTER TWENTY-FIVE

"Rhenkin?"

Kennick turned to the speaker. A red-faced man sat astride a horse that looked almost as miserable as he did. The man was well past his fighting years yet here he was, dressed in armour that was probably too tight and had most likely spent the last twenty years decorating a hallway in his mansion, if Kennick was any judge.

"No, my lord." He gave a nod in place of a bow. "I am Lieutenant Kennick, the major's second. If I can be of assistance?"

The man tugged off his gauntlet and pulled a handkerchief from his belt, mopping at the sweat running freely from his face. "A bit of direction wouldn't go amiss," he muttered. "I have five thousand lancers here, lad. It would be nice to know where he'd like us."

"I'm sorry, my lord...?"

"Salisbourne, Earl of Westermark," the man told him. "I'm here with the Celstwin garrison. Those of it that managed to keep up anyway. The rest will be along in a day or so, I imagine."

Kennick took a deep breath through his nose. Bloody fops were worse than useless most of the time. "I'm afraid the lord high marshal is..."

"The marshal is what, Kennick?"

The lieutenant turned. "Ah. sir, his Lordship, the Earl Salisbourne..."

"Has five thousand horse and wants to know where the hell you want them," Salisbourne snapped over Kennick's head.

Rhenkin gave the man a flat stare until he shifted his weight in the saddle. "Good to have you with us, my lord," Rhenkin said with a nod. He looked to Kennick. "How are we doing?"

The younger man looked skyward for a moment, mentally checking things off. "I would say we're slightly behind, sir." He shrugged. "All things considered it could be a lot worse."

Rhenkin grunted. "Numbers man, give me some numbers."

"The Savarel contingent arrived last night with General Ackerson, but we've had columns trickling in for the past week. With Lord Salisbourne's lancers," he nodded towards Salisbourne as he clambered down from his horse, "we have something in the region of sixty thousand on foot and twenty thousand horse. I'll have a more definite figure for you later in the day. Ackerson has requested to meet you at the earliest opportunity as well, sir."

Rhenkin waved that off. "Supplies?"

"Well in hand, sir," Kennick said. "We have wagons already rolling to supply dumps and more ready to move with us. I can give you specifics if—"

"No, that's fine. Send runners. I want to begin the march as soon as possible." He looked to Salisbourne. "I trust your men will be able to manage that?"

Salisbourne nodded. "I dare say they'll be ready. They're in far better shape than I am and we all knew this march was coming. An army this size won't take a step in the next few hours anyway, long enough to give the nags a break eh?" He patted his grey affectionately. "They do the hard work, after all."

"They do, though this won't be an easy ride for any of us." Rhenkin gave the man a meaningful look.

Salisbourne chuckled. "I'm not as useless as I look, Rhenkin. I may not be twenty-five anymore, and it took me a good hour to squeeze into this armour, but I can still swing a sword if need be." He glanced down at his figure and back with a wry smile. "I know my limits, marshal. I'll leave the bone-cracking to younger men with less sense and more muscle, unless it comes down to it, of course. I can help you lead and organise though, not that I'd want your job, and not that I'll be getting in your way. An army needs one leader not five."

Rhenkin nodded in thanks and smiled despite himself. The man, for all his bluster and ridiculous armour, had an easy smile and it was hard not to like him. "I'll leave you to take what rest you can and ready your men then, my lord. Kennick will get you settled until the runners send word."

"I suspect there'll be enough titles to trip over, Rhenkin. Call me Salisbourne, or Thomas if you've a mind to."

Rhenkin gave tight smile and nodded a farewell, stepping past the pair and into the command tent where he knew reports would be waiting for him.

The army moved ponderously. Flowing out of the regions surrounding Druel like a great slug and swallowing the fields and countryside to either side of the road. It took hours for them to begin moving, and longer still to form up into a decent marching order. The first day seemed to finish almost before it had begun and, though Rhenkin knew they would cover more ground in the days ahead, the fact that Druel was only just out of sight as they made camp grated.

By the week's end the army was making better progress. Rhenkin dealt with the reports and subordinates as he rode, though he managed to pass a great deal off on Kennick. It hurt to admit it but the man might be more competent that Larson had been.

"How long do you imagine it will take us?" Obair asked, nudging his horse up alongside the major.

"Hmm?" Rhenkin looked up from the paper he'd been reading as he rode.

"To Widdengate?"

"Four or five weeks at least," Rhenkin told him. "Though I don't expect we'll get that far." The druid frowned and Rhenkin folded the report, tucking it into his belt. "We've talked through this twice already, Obair. What's the problem?"

Obair sighed and looked over one shoulder to Devin, riding behind them as he chatted with Ylsriss. "It's all too tenuous, Rhenkin. I don't know, you're a military man, I suppose I expected firm plans that were set in stone."

Rhenkin laughed, a genuine laugh that was devoid of mocking. "Plans aren't often worth the paper they waste. They've usually changed before the ink's dry," he told him. "We're pushing eastwards. I have scouts out there already but most of this is in the hands of the fae." He shrugged and spoke in a lower voice, "It's not something I'd toss around, Obair, but I don't honestly know what to expect. This isn't an army of men we're marching towards. They don't think like us, don't act like us. There are too many unknowns here for us to plan." He met the old man's eyes and, for the first time, his frustration showed. "Will they even form ranks like a human army? Will they group together? Or will they fight like a wild mob? For that matter will they even be in one group?"

Obair opened his mouth to respond but Rhenkin stopped him with a shake of the head. "There's no point in guessing. We've been through this and you've already told both me and the queen what you know of these fae. The best we can do is head east and wait for the scouts."

Obair winced. "That's really all we can do?"

"Unless you have a better idea." Rhenkin raised an eyebrow.

"Hold on." Obair frowned back at him. "What do you mean you don't expect to get that far?"

"To Widdengate?" Rhenkin shook his head. "I doubt we'll get anywhere close to it. If what the Bjornman told us was true then the fae are here in force. They'll meet us long before we ever get near Widdengate."

"Then how…?"

"You'll have to leave, strike out on your own, or with a small force at best." Rhenkin frowned himself. "This can't be news to you, Obair. Devin has spoken to both the queen and myself about this at length."

"He what?"

"His memories of the fae." Rhenkin shrugged. "Maybe memories is the wrong word, but I mean the knowledge he gained through the stones. The visions he had of the fae armies."

"I hadn't realised he'd been speaking to you about them," Obair admitted with a glance back at the boy.

"As soon as we engage… Even before that, really. At first contact you'll break for the stones at Widdengate with Ylsriss, Devin, and the others. I can send troops with you but I rather suspect you'll be better off without them."

"How does that make sense?" the old man demanded.

"Think, old man." Rhenkin told him, shaking his head. "Once the fae engage it will be too late for you to go anywhere and escape their notice. For us to fight through all the way to those stones of yours could take months. That's assuming we last that long."

He glanced around at those closest to him and lowered his voice. "Your group will have to move before we have any real contact, and it'll have to be small enough to either escape notice or be overlooked. Sending you off with five hundred men is no use. You might as well be waving flags and blowing trumpets as you ride along. This whole plan is a distraction. This army, and whatever the Bjornmen send west, are there to keep the fae busy, keep them focused on us whilst you get to those stones and do what you have to do."

"That's…"

"Incredibly noble?" Rhenkin said with a snort. "Don't flatter yourself, Obair. It's what we'd be doing anyway. If the fae are coming in strength, as an army rather than a hunting raid, then we have no choice but to meet them."

"I was going to say, that's the stupidest idea I've ever heard." Obair laughed. "But you're right, we don't have a choice. I don't think keeping their attention will be as difficult as you might think though."

"Oh?" Rhenkin raised an eyebrow. "How's that then?"

"It's a guess more than anything," Obair admitted, patting his horse's neck absently. "Something I've picked out of the stories Ylsriss and Miriam have told me. There seems to be an incredible arrogance about the fae. Some of that is warranted, of course. Toe to toe I don't imagine any human is a match for a fae. But still, there is an arrogance about them." He gave a grim smile. "I expect the notion of a human army marching to meet them is something that they could never have imagined. Even Devin's tales of the fae wars tell of mankind retreating, fleeing. The idea of us actually marching to meet them might just be enough to shock them."

"You may be right," Rhenkin said. "Getting their attention may be easier than I'd thought then. Let's hope the iron holds out then."

"There is that." Obair sighed, looking around at the army. He looked to Rhenkin, and then glanced back at the black-robed figure of Miriam as she rode behind them. "If you'll excuse me?" he said to Rhenkin but the man was already frowning at the papers in his hand.

"I hope you don't mind if I join you?" Obair said with a smile as he dropped back beside Miriam.

She shook her head with a small smile. "Some company would be nice."

He looked at her expecting more but she looked away, gazing blankly ahead of them as the horse plodded behind those in front. They rode in silence for a few minutes as Obair cast glances at her with a frown.

"I was a bit surprised to see you'd come along," he said, trying again. "I thought you'd have stayed in Druel. By all accounts you've had enough travel for three lifetimes lately."

She looked at him with an odd expression he couldn't decipher. "I need to see this done."

He tilted his head at that. He'd not really thought about it before but what was she doing here? This was hardly a gentle ride in the country. "See *what* done?" he asked with a frown. "What are you even doing here, Miriam? You should be back in Druel."

She laughed then, a bitter sound that somehow didn't fit. It had a tone to it, something that wavered between the wild and the not-quite-right. He shivered at the sound of it and almost missed what she said as she spoke again. "So much of this is my fault. I let them into this world. I started all of this."

"I don't really think you can blame yourself, Miriam." He spoke carefully, using the soothing tones he'd once used on his livestock.

"But I can." She looked at him again and he saw himself reflected in her eyes.

"The Wyrde was already failing, Miriam," he told her gently. The rituals Lillith and I performed may have been a part of it but there's so much more we don't know about the Wyrde itself. It was much more than just a simple ritual. It was bigger than anything we two were doing. My master once told me that the Wyrde was something that all mankind was a part of. It was helped along in a thousand little ways. Even traditions like hanging horseshoes and morris dancing probably played their part." He scratched at his beard, thinking for a moment before he carried on.

"I do wonder how much impact this religion, the Church of New Days, really had on things. The way they worked to stamp out the old traditions certainly didn't help but I suspect that the Wyrde would have failed anyway."

"You can't know that," Miriam told him. Her eyes were hard and voice had a brittle edge to it.

"I can, Miriam," he insisted. "I felt the Wyrde failing for decades. It was a slow thing, like the beginning of a winter's thaw, but little by little I felt it. Every year it grew just a touch harder. It was barely noticeable sometimes." He snorted a laugh but it was more noise than true humour. "For a while I thought it was just me getting older, getting tired."

He fell silent, lost in his own thoughts. The horse plodded on without his direction and when he finally looked up her eyes were still on him, questioning and somehow forgiving.

* * *

The stones were silent and cold. Klöss reached out to the tumbled blocks that had once formed the gatehouse with hands that still shook. He drew in another breath, running his fingertips along the coarse stone as he fought down the nausea and shook his head.

This had been a home as much as it had been a fortress. Not just for him but for the thousands of men and women who'd lived here. The wind tossed at his cloak, rustling the leaves that grew from the roots and vines that looked to have thrust out of the earth and made wreckage of the walls.

"This is how you make war then?" he called out to the figure standing high on the broken stones of the wall. "With plants striking from the earth and creatures from the skies?"

Aervern turned her gaze to him slowly, her burning eyes bright in the shadows. "Are your kind any better, manling? Do you not hurl fire and rain arrows down on your foes? We are not that different, manling."

"Don't call me that," Klöss muttered but there was no force in his words. He picked his way over the stones, moving into the city itself as Aervern watched him. The place was quiet, a silence somehow intensified by the soft sound of leaves blowing through the wrecked streets. The city was dead. He'd known that when it first came into sight. He'd searched it, of course, calling out whilst the fae stood and watched on with unreadable eyes.

A glint called to him for a second before it was gone. Something golden flashing from the rubble as the moon peered out from behind the clouds that scudded across the skies. It had only been visible for the barest moment before it vanished but it was the colour of it that called to him.

Klöss frowned, crouching down and poring over the stones as he looked for the source. He grunted, shoving at a heavy stone until it toppled to the side, taking a small avalanche of pebbles and fragments with it. Questing fingers found cold metal and he pulled at the rocks, clearing a space until the moonlight stopped him. The armour was ornate, steel plates inlaid with gold in a complex scrollwork. "Larren," he breathed. "You poor, stupid, bloody bastard."

He stood slowly, walking away and letting his feet take him. There was nothing he could do for the man and he deserved no better than the thousands of other bodies that lay in the streets or under the rubble. Rimeheld was dead and Larren had killed her with an arrogance deadlier than any knife.

The thought came to him unbidden. The sealord was dead. With Frostbeard gone then he himself was probably the ranking Bjornman in all of Anlan. To all intents and purposes he *was* the sealord, at least until the fleet returned to the Barren Isles. The thought gave him pause. With their warleader dead what did this mean for his people?

He looked over to the fae, silent on her rooftop. "What will you do?"

She cocked her head on one side as she looked at him, the question clear but unspoken.

"If this magic is successful," Klöss explained, "what will you do when the barrier that locks this world away from you is remade?"

"Yours is not the only world that has been ravaged, Klöss," she told him. Her accent altered his name, putting the emphasis in the wrong place and he shivered at the sound of it. "You did not like to hear it when I told you that we were not so different but it is the truth I speak. We both have betrayed our people for what we believe to be the best path. You sought aid from this Selena. I, from the Wyrdeweavers. Our goal is the same, to rid our worlds of Aelthen and his followers."

Klöss struggled with that, frowning. "But if this magic, this Wyrde, works. What happens to you?"

"I plan to be in my homeland when the Wyrde falls," Aervern told him. "I hold a hope, a small hope, but a hope all the same, that a great thing can be achieved." She sighed at his questioning glance and made her way down to him, stepping easily over the shifting rubble.

"Listen then and I will speak of it," she told him. "Legends tell of a time when we were not foes. Ancient tales so lost in time that none thought there was a truth in them, but they tell of a time when manling and fae were as one. Together we wove the gifts of our Lady about us, weaving glyphs and crafting wonders that bridged worlds. This is not the only world we touched. Ours is a fallen people, Klöss, the Wyrde locked Aelthen and his host in the Outside, a horror that hangs between worlds, but still other parts of my race are scattered across the stars. The Carnath fled, taking their own path through the Worldtrails as their quest for the Ivy Throne failed. They were not the first to leave my Realm. The people of Tir Riviel had already left, seeking another path to the ancient home of your own people."

"So that's your plan then?" Klöss said, contempt clear in his curled lip. "To lock Aelthen away behind the Wyrde and dominate yourself?"

Aervern shook her head at him. "Your mind is not so simple, manling. Do not act the blind fool with me." She ignored him as he glowered. "Through fate, or some scheme of the Lady herself, my kind and your own are bound. Together we might thrive if only given the chance. Tales tell of the wonders your people can work with glyphs but these glyphs are powerless without the gift of Our Lady that only a fae can bring." She held a finger up, stopping him before he could speak. "My own people are slow to breed. A coupling brings about a fae'reeth or satyr far more often than a true fae. Manling blood mixed with my own could change all of this. Manlings make us more than we can be alone. This is what Aelthen cannot understand. He has fixed his sight so strongly on hate that he cannot look beyond it. I seek to build a world, manling, I seek to reclaim a legend. Even with the thousands of my people who have flocked to Aelthen's banner there are enough that remain in my realm to begin again."

"With the humans left behind, trapped in your world," he added not bothering to conceal his disgust.

"These are people that do not even remember your land, manling," Aervern told him. "Joran tells me that most were stolen from this world as babes or children too young to even remember being taken. It would be no kindness to return them."

"You stole my son, fae." The words grated as they left his lips.

"I took no child," she replied, calm as a still pond. "Do not hold me for what Aelthen has done. This child of yours, Joran has spoken of this. He was a babe, yes?" She stared at him until he nodded. "Time passes at different rates between your world and mine, our offspring grow differently also. I would return your child to you if it were possible but time grows short. How would we find him among all the children in the Realm of Twilight? It may have been many years since you saw him, would you recognize him even if he could be found? Would your *she*?"

Klöss stared at her wordlessly until he finally shook his head.

She turned away before he could speak, walking in smooth strides through the ruined streets as he gaped at her. Klöss muttered to himself and followed. The fae was like nothing he would have thought, complex and layered. Frankly he'd preferred it when he could just think of them as monsters.

357

He hurried after her as best he could, picking his way over the fallen walls and buildings. The rear of the city was mostly intact. The defenders of Rimeheld would have flooded out to meet the attacking fae and, by the time any enemy stepped foot in this part of the city, the battle would have been over.

The wind was stronger here and he clutched his cloak around him as he picked his way up the stone steps to the city wall. The moonlight may have been enough to see by but he'd have given a lot for a torch or lantern.

"Your people," Aervern said. She spoke without turning, pointing out over the harbour to the dark seas.

Klöss followed her finger, squinting. "I don't see anything."

Aervern shrugged. "That is no surprise. They approach still, however. The vessels will reach you this night." She gave him an appraising look. "I could take you to them, if you desire it."

Klöss shook his head, hoping the darkness was enough to cover his expression. The trip to Rimeheld had been a thing of nightmares and his stomach lurched at the memory of all that empty air gaping beneath him. The thought of willingly letting the fae woman lift them into the air again, and then over water... "No, Aervern, I'll wait here."

"You are certain?"

The words were innocent but he wasn't sure there wasn't a sly smile hidden amongst them. He nodded.

"I will leave you then. I would return to Joran before the Wyrde falls."

He looked at her, for the first time seeing past the glowing eyes and the alien cast to her skin. Perhaps she was right, perhaps they weren't so different.

"Would you wait?" he asked her. "Kieron can lead the men west as well as anyone. I'd like to be there, with Ylsriss, when it happens."

She nodded gravely and turned to face the darkness of the ocean. Klöss stood beside her staring into the darkness as they waited for the fleet.

* * *

"You want me to do what?" Kieron demanded, slamming the tankard down onto the table. Rimeheld had changed in the daylight, revealing damage that had been hidden by the darkness and exposing large sections of the city that seemed untouched by the attack. The docks had escaped unscathed and the fleet rocked gently at anchor as Klöss met with Kieron in an abandoned tavern on the edge of the harbour.

"I want you to march west," Klöss repeated. "Unload any supplies from the fleet and head inland as fast as possible."

"Why in the name of the frozen hells would we want to do that?" Kieron burst out. "In case you hadn't noticed there's a little mess here to clear up."

"I can see that," Klöss said, pitching his voice deliberately low. "I'm telling you to form the men up and march west. Rimeheld is chock full of extra supplies but if we don't move soon it'll be too late."

"Too late for what? The Anlish will be long gone by now," the grizzled shipmaster said, taking a long pull on his ale without waiting for Klöss to speak.

"It's not the Anlish," Klöss told him. "And you'll do it because I order it."

Kieron raised an eyebrow at that. "Oh aye? I will, will I? And just what is it gives you authority over me Klöss? Rimeheld has fallen. You're lord of a pile of rubble here not seamaster. We may as well be at sea at this point which gives you no more say over me than any other shipmaster."

"Rimeheld wasn't the only thing that fell, Kieron," Klöss told him, reaching into a sack beside him. The gauntlet thudded onto the table, the ugly sound at odds with the quality of craftsmanship that must have gone into the gold-inlaid piece.

"The sealord?" Kieron muttered. "Not that surprising I suppose."

Klöss nodded. "And as Seamaster of Rimeheld, in a time of war, I claim the rank of sealord until the thane himself orders otherwise."

"Damn you've a weighty pair, lad." Kieron grunted. He held a hand up as Klöss's face darkened. "Hear me out, I won't dispute your claim but you're going to need some support. You won't take command of the fleet with nothing more than a shiny glove. If you want us to march west then you're going to have to give us a reason. The Anlish won't be hanging around, we're way beyond their lines. This was a raid. It must have been a damned big one, I'll grant you, but still a raid."

"It wasn't the Anlish, Kieron," Klöss told him again.

The old shipmaster's face creased in confusion. "Don't be daft, lad, who else?"

"The fae," Aervern said, dropping the glamour that had wreathed her in the shadows of the corner.

"Lords of the bloody frosts!" Kieron spat, lurching back out of his chair so it landed with a crash. He scrambled back, crab-like, across the floor.

"Don't worry," Klöss managed between laughs. "She's not here to eat your soul, she's here to prove a point."

Kieron looked at him incredulously, glancing back and forth between him and the fae.

"This is what attacked Rimeheld, Kieron. Fae like Aervern here, and there are more coming. We have one chance to stop them, us and the Anlish together."

"What?" the man's face was ashes, fear wrestling with confusion.

"They're already in Hesk, Kieron, already in our homes," Klöss told him, boring in. "They took my wife and still have my son. And if the bastard that leads them has his way they'll drive an army over Haven, killing everything in their path. So that's why I'm taking command as sealord, and that's why you are going to take our men west, to meet the fuckers and feed them some iron bolts from the arbelests."

Kieron blinked, seeming to realise he was still crouched low, and stood slowly. "And this one?" He shook his head. "Hold on. What do you mean *I'm* going to lead the men west?"

"I'm going with Aervern," Klöss told him. "If I stay here I'll be bogged down in endless conversations with shipmasters, all with their own ideas. You're better off with me gone. Just take the orders and go."

Kieron nodded, still frowning as he took it all in. "And the iron?"

"Fehru, what you call 'iron,' is the most effective weapon you have against my kind, manling," Aervern told him, speaking in a low menacing tone. "Blade or arrow, it matters little if you use this foul thing."

The shipmaster swallowed hard, looking back to Klöss "West? That's a bit vague, Klöss... I mean, Sealord," he added with a weak smile.

Klöss nodded, reaching for the sack again to retrieve a chart. "Head for this village," he told Kieron, unrolling the map to stab a thick finger onto the mark. "You should find them here, probably already in battle with the Anlish. They call it Widdengate."

* * *

The scouts came in, riding hard on horses that were foam-flecked and close to panic. Rhenkin climbed down from his own mount and rushed to the first scout, reaching for the bridle of the horse and patting its sweat-soaked neck as the scout climbed out of the saddle. It was less of a climb and more of a fall but the man managed to keep his feet, clinging to the pommel as if he didn't quite trust his legs.

Rhenkin winced as he looked at the man. A latticework of tiny slashes covered his face and neck. His leather scout's armour was probably the only thing that had kept him alive and even that was slashed half to ribbons.

"Report, lad," Rhenkin said in a gentle voice, pitched too low for anyone else to hear. "Keep it simple, you're barely on your feet."

"The fae, sir," the scout managed between gasped breaths. "No more than thirty miles from us, possibly less by now."

"Numbers?"

"Couldn't tell, sir," the scout said, white-faced. "They filled the skies...covered the land as far as I could see."

Rhenkin nodded, his eyes going distant as he juggled distances and the time necessary for formations and defences. "Kennick!" he roared over one shoulder as he reached for the waterskin from his own horse and handed it to the scout.

The Lieutenant arrived quickly. "Sir?"

"Take these men and get a full report, and get them patched up too," Rhenkin ordered.

"Where shall I find you, sir?"

Rhenkin glanced back at him from where he'd been scanning the closest ranks. "I'll not be long. I think we've reached a point here. We're not going to get much farther. It's time to get the old man and his company going."

Kennick nodded. "If we can crest this rise, sir, I believe it would give us a better position."

Rhenkin looked and grunted. The man wasn't half bad. Thinking ahead and not getting caught up in the smaller details. "Agreed. Send runners and get the officers up to speed, I don't want to waste any time."

Kennick nodded but Rhenkin was already moving, pulling himself back into the saddle and searching for the druid. It didn't take long. He'd had them attached to a unit close to the front lines for this very reason. The lad seemed to have a firm grip on things but, in many ways, dealing with Obair was like talking to a child.

"We're sending you out," Rhenkin announced as he drew close. "I don't know how long we have and we can't run the risk of you getting caught here when this battle starts."

Obair looked about in alarm, eyes wide as if the fae were moments away. "Already? Are you sure?"

The old man looked close to panic. Rhenkin shook his head with gritted teeth. "What did you think this was, old man?" he demanded. "A little country walk? Those men are cut half to ribbons. Tiny slashes all over them, it's a miracle they even made it to us. You heard Erinn's story the same as I did, this is the fae'reeth. You need to move, now!"

Devin pushed closer as Obair gaped. "We're ready, marshal," he said in firm voice. Rhenkin looked him over and nodded, liking what he saw. "Good man. Riddal will lead you out. He's a good scout, a good man, and he has experience fighting the fae with Erinn. I'm sending ten men with you. You'll have the Bjornmen too. Any more than that and you'll be too visible."

"If the fae find us with any real numbers then a hundred wouldn't be much help anyway," Devin told him, sounding calmer than he probably felt.

"Is there anything you need? Anything other than the obvious?" Rhenkin asked.

"Ironheads, some bags of the filings." Devin shrugged. "If that's not enough then nothing will be."

"Good man. Riddal will be along shortly. Grab your gear and anything else you need for supplies. I want you gone within the half hour."

Devin reached for his hand, grasping it firmly. "Good luck, marshal."

"And to you, lad. Try and keep the old man in one piece." Rhenkin turned away and headed back for the front lines. Wishing luck wasn't the done thing. It was something only the newest of recruits would do, none wanted to invite disaster, but he had the feeling they'd all need it before long.

Kennick was waiting for him as he emerged from the waiting ranks. "Why are we still standing here?" Rhenkin demanded.

"I've sent runners, sir. We're simply awaiting your order."

Rhenkin bit down half a dozen responses. The man was just doing his job. "Signal the troops then, we move."

Kennick nodded and snapped off a salute before turning to the flagmen behind him. The army surged forward, reaching the crest of the low hill in short order.

It wasn't ideal by any stretch. Rhenkin grumbled to himself as he considered the terrain but it was more than he'd hoped for. Woods lay a few miles to their north but the immediate terrain was grassland. They were lucky for what they had. The rise was actually the southernmost of two low hills, sloping down to form a small gully between them. It wouldn't be enough to influence any human army but, perhaps… He squinted up at the sun, already more than halfway down to the horizon and around again at the terrain.

"Get the men to it. I want stakes and trenches on both these slopes, as many rows as we can get done. Archers to the front and get those engines ready. If those bastards come in the rush I expect them to we're not going to have the time to piss about. Send some men with axes to those woods, we'll need the firewood."

The army deployed as fast as possible for a force of that size, as units formed into ranks and set to work creating the field fortifications. Within the space of an hour the hillside had been transformed as rows of trenches were carved into the soft green grass and stakes rammed into the mix. Here and there the sun caught on an iron spike mixed in with the wood.

He watched the men work as runners came and went, bringing reports to Kennick. Only occasionally did the man need to bring the issues to him and so Rhenkin watched, and waited, and worried. Any man that tells you they are not nervous on the eve of battle is a liar and Rhenkin had told this lie a thousand times. A commander is a living flag. He hadn't the luxury of allowing his emotions to play over his face. Instead he scowled at the men and the field fortifications as he watched, grunting at the readiness reports that Kennick delivered.

The clouds rolled in, taking the warmth of the autumn sun and painting the skies in drab greys. Rain wasn't too much of a threat, the clouds were too pale for that, but the light faltered early and evening came too soon.

They waited. Men were still working, building huge stacks of logs and dousing them with lamp oil, but most simply waited. Rhenkin sighed explosively and looked to Kennick. "Scout reports?"

"Due any moment, sir," the man told him. "The last three had nothing to report. It's as if they were never there."

"Or that they're not advancing," Rhenkin suggested, chewing on his lip. "How far are we ranging?"

"Two hour's hard ride, at last reports," Kennick told him with a wince.

Rhenkin shook his head. "And there's no sign? That's past where the scouts were attacked."

Kennick shrugged. "As I said, sir, it's as if they vanished."

The wind had picked up as darkness fell and the night was full of the snap of canvas as it tugged at the tents. Rhenkin picked his way through to the perimeter, squinting against the darkness as he headed for the closest of the men on watch.

"Anything?" he asked.

The man didn't stop his inspection of the night. "Not a bloody thing." He glanced at Rhenkin and stepped back half a step in shock. "Um, sir," he added.

Rhenkin snorted a laugh at the man's discomfort, "Don't worry about it, son."

The horn sounded as he finished speaking. It sang out long and low, a mournful sound that would have had the men twitching even if it hadn't come from nowhere. Rhenkin turned his head, trying to pinpoint the source but the sound had seemed to come from more than one direction. Another joined it, calling from a different direction, and then still others sounded, until the noise was loud enough that he felt it in his chest. The men closest to him looked about in all directions, as panic reached for them.

"The hell with this!" Rhenkin muttered and pushed his way back to the command post.

"Lord Marshal!" Kennick rushed to meet him. "We have reports of movement at the eastern perimeter."

"You think?" Rhenkin muttered dryly. "They're playing games with us and I'm not in the mood. Get those fires lit and let's see if we can spot the bastards."

Fire arrows were touched to braziers and lofted high into the darkness before they fell on the mounds of oil-soaked wood. The bonfires were as large as haystacks and the flames tore through the lamp oil before eating away at the logs.

Within moments the gloom of the night was lifted as the flames of thirty fires reached up to the heavens. The air shimmered with the heat as men squinted past them and still the horns sounded. Whatever illusion the fae had employed fell like a dropped sheet and the banners of the fae blazed blue and silver as they were revealed.

"Archers!" came the call from a dozen mouths but men were already moving. The fae had appeared only fifty yards from Rhenkin's front lines, a sea of shining silver armour and glowing eyes that extended as far as anyone could see. The rushed shots of the Anlish archers were panicked and rough. Blue fire exploded among the fae as ironheads stuck home but far more were lost in the darkness.

The fae paused, almost seeming to recoil for a moment, like a great shining wave reaching its limit, and then a great howl rose from the host and they charged.

Anlish archers exacted a terrible toll and sheets of ironheads carved a broad channel through the fae. The range was such that the arrows almost couldn't help but hit something and, unlike human armies, the fae carried no shields. Wherever the ironheads tasted blood, fire raged, and the arrows rained down upon the fae leaving a river of blue fire behind them. And then the fae closed.

The battle was chaos. The fae didn't fight like a human army and the Anlish troops splintered and faltered as fae and satyr leapt over whole units to attack from within their own lines.

Rhenkin watched in silence. His men knew their jobs and there was little point in screaming orders at those already on the front lines.

"Sir?" Kennick said in an anxious tone.

"Yes, Kennick?" Rhenkin's voice was flat.

"Orders, sir?"

Rhenkin glanced at the lieutenant, the man's fear tinged with panic. "Calm down, lieutenant. Let's let them arrive at the party before we pour them drinks."

Kennick gave him an odd look, "Sir?"

"Fine," Rhenkin sighed. "Send runners to Salisbourne and have him ready the lancers."

Rhenkin barely noticed the man leave. The front rippled and surged as the fae slammed into the Anlish army and the air was thick with screams and the sickening crunch of weapons on bone. They were more evenly matched than he could have imagined. The incredible speed of the fae was offset by his own men's iron weapons and often the smallest scratch was enough to send a satyr screaming to the earth as flames erupted from the wound.

White arrows came screaming in from the fae host. Some trick of the fletching Rhenkin assumed, but the keening sound was unnerving. Despite the fletching their power was undeniable. The arrows tore through the Anlish, often passing through shield, armour and body before they erupted from their victim's backs.

Entire companies fell in moments and Rhenkin grimaced as he looked to the north for the lancers.

He did not have to wait long and the ranks of horses thundered towards the fae flank, dull, iron-tipped lances lowering as they rode. The first fae to meet the lancers simply darted out of the way. Satyr and fae both, taking the single step or two needed to avoid the iron tip, and then the horse was past them. As they penetrated however, the weapons found flesh and the creatures screamed as the heavily armoured lancers tore through the flank of the host.

The sound of a thousand hungry bees announced the fae'reeth before the swarm even came into sight. "Ready the catapults," Rhenkin told Kennick. "Red flag." The man had managed to retain control this far but so much depended upon this. The iron weapons were proving that they could shift the balance back from the huge advantage the fae held over human troops. The fae'reeth, however, were another matter.

The swarm moved slowly, perhaps enjoying the panic they caused as they drifted over the ranks of the fae host and drew closer to the Anlish lines. The fires had lit the skies but Rhenkin couldn't even guess at their numbers. It was as the scouts had said, they filled the skies. They passed over the Anlish ranks and hung, a mere fifty feet above the heads of those that fought and died below them, and then on some silent signal the cloud disintegrated and the fae'reeth fell upon the hapless Anlish like wolves upon sheep.

"Sir?" Kennick said, plucking at Rhenkin's sleeve. The Marshal ignored him, watching the scene as the diminutive creatures howled through the foremost elements of his army. They passed like a black wind, leaving nothing but the dead and screaming in their wake.

"Sir!" Kennick said, with more urgency.

Rhenkin nodded to himself slowly. "Now!" he roared.

The signal passed through the army, long red flags that fluttered in the breeze signalled others in a relay until the message reached the catapults. The contraptions rocked forward against the thick ropes staking them down as they hurled their payloads skyward. Massive balls of cloth shot towards the fae'reeth, unfurling as they flew, and releasing a smoke-like substance that drifted gently downward like a dark cloud.

The fae'reeth tore through the Anlish ranks causing death and chaos. Where they passed order simply ceased to exist and the fae and satyr took full advantage of this, carving through entire companies in moments.

"Archers," called Rhenkin, pointing.

The gesture prompted a sharp look from Kennick. "Our men, sir?"

"Are already dead, Kennick," Rhenkin told him. "Let's take some of the satyr with them."

Kennick shook himself and gave the order.

The iron filings misted down, hanging in the air just long enough for the fae'reeth to enter the cloud. The result was shocking. Tens of thousands of blue sparks erupted above the battlefield as iron found wings or flesh and the tiny creatures burst into flames. The fae host faltered and fell back and then, as the Anlish began to press forward, they vanished.

Chapter Twenty-Six

The very ground was scorched. What had he really expected? Devin spat into the long grass and looked back to Halther. The scout nodded at him, though Devin had no idea what that was supposed to mean. He was already looking back to the remains of the village.

Widdengate was a charred ruin. Most of the buildings were nothing more than scorched sections of earth but here and there blackened beams thrust up from the tumbled stones and reached, claw-like, to scratch at the sky.

Against all odds a single house seemed completely untouched in the middle of the wreckage. Devin frowned at it, trying to remember who had lived there, but with the village burned around it he couldn't place the building and the failure grated at him.

"Shouldn't stand on a hill like that, lad," Halther told him. "Makes you too easy to spot." He reached up to touch at his hair, nodding at him.

Devin nodded, swearing at himself silently at the rebuke. He knew better than that. "That was my home," he told the man in a low voice, reaching for his hood to cover his bone-white hair.

Halther glanced down at the village and looked back to him with an unreadable expression. "Time to move," he told him. "I'll lead off."

Devin followed the scout, hunched down into a crouching walk as they made their way down the hillside and towards the trees where the others waited.

"No sign of anything," Halther announced as they drew closer. "Doesn't look like anyone or anything has been here in months."

Riddal nodded, still looking out at the remains. "Judging by the map your home was a good bit north of the road anyway," he told Obair. "It'll take longer but I'm not daft enough to walk the road in Bjornmen territory."

"They are supposed to be working with us, you know?" The druid replied with a glance back at Tristan.

Riddal snorted and curled his lip. "Them as sit at the top might be. Your men on the line though? That's another matter. You argue your point all you like, crossbow bolts don't tend to listen too well in my experience."

It was hard to argue with that and Obair let it go. Riddal and the scouts led them off, north of the village itself, and into the woods.

Devin walked in silence, though any conversation was a hissed whisper anyway. Obair and Miriam walked together as usual, heads leaning close as they spoke. Devin had avoided speaking to anyone much as they had approached the village. Every clearing and tree stump seemed to be familiar, each telling a tale of the childhood he'd spent here. Having Miriam with him made his memories seem surreal.

The boy who'd fled into the trees with his mother as they hid from bandits seemed a very different person to the one who'd grown up in the village. Miriam's presence forced him to admit that they were one and the same and that was not something he could cope with especially well. He'd avoided her mostly, keeping to Ylsriss and Joran or ranging ahead with the scouts.

For her part she'd left him mostly alone. There had been the occasional time when he'd felt her gaze on him and looked up to find her watching him with a strange look in her eyes, a mix of sorrow and guilt.

"Do you want to speak of it?" the voice was hushed but full of concern.

Devin turned to see Ylsriss watching him. He shrugged, "I wouldn't know what to say."

"I never really knew my mother," Ylsriss said then. "Sickness took her while I was too young to understand it."

Devin winced. "I'm sorry. Some kind of fever?"

"Not a sickness here," she said, touching her chest. "A sickness of the thoughts." She grimaced, touched her forehead. "I don't have the words."

"Of the mind?" he guessed.

"Yes, good. The mind." She shook her head, falling silent for a moment. "Your mother was taken from you? By the fae?"

Devin nodded but she was already speaking again.

"My mother was taken, too, by this sickness." She looked away from him, speaking more to the woods around them than to him. "It began as a small thing. She would forget things. Names, places… you understand? Soon, though, she was forgetting to feed us or getting lost. Then one day she left us, my small brother and me, to fetch food from the markets. She never came back. I was five."

Devin looked at her. "What happened?"

"To her?" she shrugged. "I do not know. There are many things in the darker places of Hesk that can take a life. I cared for Egham as best I could but he was not a strong child. The winter took him from me."

He closed his eyes in a grimace. The message was clear enough. "You think I'm being foolish?"

She looked at him, smiling sadly. "I think the fae have taken enough lives. Your mother has been given back to you, do not waste that gift."

"I don't know her, it's—"

"It is not easy for you?" she asked and he nodded gratefully.

Her eyes hardened. "Then try harder."

He looked ahead to where Miriam picked her way through the trees.

"Go, foolish boy!" Ylsriss pushed at him and watched him leave.

"You don't change, you know?" Gavin told her.

She looked back at him. "How do you mean?"

He smiled. "Even after all this time you're still the little mother of Hesk looking after the lost ones. You probably couldn't stop if you tried"

She looked back to Devin as he approached his mother, watching as she smiled at him. "Shut up, Gavin."

* * *

Water still dripped from the trees, though the rain seemed to have stopped for now. The sun peered warily through the clouds, shining from a dozen directions at once as the wet leaves reflected the light.

Riddal's hand shot up, clenched into a fist, signalling them for silence. Devin froze, fingering the arrow he held ready as he frowned at the scout. It began as a feeling, but there was nothing he could see or hear. The woods were as still as they had been all day, silent without even a breath of a breeze. The quiet was odd but he'd almost grown accustomed to it. Gradually he became aware of it though, the prickling sensation of being watched. He peered ahead of them, scanning over the trees and bushes, trying not to let his vision settle on anything. A flash of amber caught him but, by then, it was too late.

The arrow slammed into Riddal and tore its way through his chest, bursting free in a shower of gore as it slammed into a tree with more force than any shaft had a right to. The scout toppled, sinking to his knees without a sound and collapsing to the dirt as blood rushed out to embrace the dried leaves under him.

Ylsriss was the first to move, grabbing Miriam and dragging her down behind the cover of a stand of birch. The others were quick to follow her lead, seeking shelter from something unseen that had killed without uttering a sound.

The laughter carried through the trees easily, cutting the silence to tatters. Devin looked to Halther, the closest of the scouts he could put a name to. He reaching for his quiver from where he lay in the dirt he pulled the ironhead free, making sure the scout saw the red marking on the shaft.

The laughter carried again, a childlike sound this time, and from another direction. An arrow flew from one of the scouts and crashed into the bushes as he swore.

"Up, and move," called Halther. "We sit here we're dead."

Devin got a foot under himself and surged forward, passing the scout and racing in the direction the arrow that had killed Riddal had come from.

"Shit! Not that way, lad," Halther called in a tight whisper. It was far too late and Devin was past him, darting around the edges of a holly bush as he ran. He didn't look back but could hear the others following as he ran. The heavy footsteps of the large Bjornman, Tristan, crunching after him. The fae would have moved. Only a fool would have staying in the same place after a kill like that. Devin hoped fervently that the fae who'd fired on them was no fool.

The sound of the others following behind was thunderous and Devin sank down behind the torn stump of a tree, setting arrow to string and waiting. Halther reached him in moments but saw the plan for what it was and kept going. The others passed him, Obair and Ylsriss giving him worried looks as they fled. Miriam gave only a small smile and what looked like an approving nod as Joran and Tristan helped her along. They had no chance of running. Even if it had been a Bjornman that killed Riddal they would have not been able to outdistance them. Miriam and Obair were simply not able to move at any speed. Against a fae they may as well have stayed put.

Devin looked back along the path he'd carved into the woods. He held the ironhead in place but without a full draw on the bow, that would just lead to aching muscles and missed chances. The woods were silent again with not a breath of breeze and only the sound of his companion's passage behind him. The leaves above him rustled in the breeze and he took slow and deliberate breaths as he sought to slow his racing heartbeat. Satyr were one thing but a true fae was something quite different. Ambushing it was tantamount to suicide but then, that was the idea.

The leaves rustled again and in a moment Devin realised his mistake. He was still thinking like a human. A man hunting quarry would only ever pass over the ground a fae though, with all its grace and power, wouldn't know that restriction.

He lifted his head slowly. Nothing draws the eyes so much as movement. The leaves danced gently in the branches ahead of him, sending shafts of sunlight down to the forest floor. He let his eyes wander slowly, scanning the resting canopy. In a flash he understood there was no breeze, and the arrow left his bow barely a second after his eyes shot back to the dancing leaves.

Blue light exploded in the canopy and the fae trailed flames down as it fell screaming to the dirt. The arrow had taken the creature in the thigh and it clawed at the shaft in a panic, trying to tear it free as the flames spread. The shaft was buried deep though, and in moments the fire consumed it, leaving only a blackened husk that collapsed in upon itself like a burnt out building.

Devin crouched down behind the stump, listening as his legs shook. If there were others he would be lucky to live through the next few minutes. Arrogance had killed the fae as much as Devin's arrow. It had probably never even occurred to it that one of them might lay in wait as the others fled. They were humans, quarry, *manlings*. They weren't supposed to think like this. The next fae, or satyr, wouldn't make the same mistake.

He waited until his legs gave up their shaking and peered out around the stump again. The body of the fae had all but vanished, ashes turning to dust and sinking into the leaves. The faint sound of birdsong drifted through the trees and Devin stood with a sigh, leaning gently on his bow as he closed his eyes.

The others had stopped in a dry stream bed, tucked in under a mass of roots that reached down from a tree growing on the bank. Devin walked openly, being sure to step into the spaces between the trees so as to be seen. Being shot by his own companions was not something he had in mind.

"Devin!" Ylsriss called out as he approached.

Obair clambered out to meet him, grasping his arm as the others clustered around. "I thought we'd lost you, boy," the old man told him.

"I'm fine, Obair."

"You're a damned fool is what you are!" His lips were pinched and his eyes flashed as he glared at him.

Devin blinked. "What?"

"Why do you think Rhenkin sent men with us?" the druid demanded. "It's because we needed protection. They're here to do the fighting, and the dying if need be, because we are too valuable to risk." He glanced over at the scouts. "Better one, or even all of them, fall than you. You are the only one of us who has an inkling of how to work the stones. How dare you put yourself in danger like that? Don't you ever do something so stupid again!"

Devin gaped. The old man was genuinely furious. He stepped back, pulling his arm from where Obair gripped it, his fingers biting painfully into his flesh.

"He's right, lad," Halther told him in a soft voice. "Yours was a good plan and I'm guessing it worked but that's what the boys and I are here for. We're only a few hours from this clearing of yours. Leave it to us."

Devin looked from face to face but the same admonishment was clear in their eyes. He shook his head in frustration.

* * *

Rhenkin pulled the tent flap aside as he looked up at the sky. How could it be this close to dusk again? The days had blurred for a time as they'd pushed eastwards but the full moon would return this night and inwardly he wondered if they would be ready.

"Nerves, Rhenkin?" Salisbourne asked from the camp table with a tight grin. His voice was pitched low enough not to carry but Rhenkin looked around anyway before he spoke.

"Any man who claims not to feel nerves before a battle is a liar," Rhenkin said.

The smile faded from the earl's face. "That's true enough. To be honest you look more worried than nervous."

"Damn," Rhenkin said, dropping the flap and going back to the table, resting his hand on the back of the chair. "I thought I was hiding it better than that."

Salisbourne snorted a laugh. "I've spent too many years in politics not to see things like that, Lord High Marshal."

Rhenkin grimaced. "Let's dispense with all that shall we? It's a hell of a mouthful and I'm not about to stumble through 'my lord' every time I need to speak to you."

Salisbourne pushed his way to his feet. "Quite right. I don't hold with titles on a battlefield anyway. Rank is good and well but titles stick in my mouth."

Rhenkin gave the man a look and managed a polite smile.

"What are you worried about, Rhenkin? Your plan seems as sound as any other."

"It's not so much a worry as it is this not knowing," Rhenkin admitted. "I feel blind here. Any other enemy and I'd have scout reports, force estimates, a march path. We don't have any of those things with these damned fae. All we know is that they can return to Haven tonight but where?" He shrugged and walked across the tent to refill his cup. "For all we know," he said, speaking back over his shoulder, "the blasted creatures might pass us by completely and head straight for Celstwin or Savarel."

Salisbourne grunted, reaching inside his jacket. "If there's one thing I've learned over the years, Rhenkin, it's that there's not much point in worry. Trouble will find you if it comes looking you don't need to show it the way with worry." He worked the stopper open on the hip-flask, taking a sip and tossing a wink at Rhenkin. "You should have a nip or two of this. Water's not going to help you."

Rhenkin nodded, ignoring the whiskey. "I'd give a lot to know where those damned Bjornmen are too. This will be short and ugly if they don't pull their weight."

"You're expecting a major battle then?" Salisbourne asked.

Rhenkin sighed. "The hell with it," he said, reaching for the flask and taking a sip. "Not bad, not bad at all." He sniffed, scratching at one cheek. "Honestly, Salisbourne? I expect them to hit us with everything they can muster. We had one brief encounter with them and they fled. The arrogance of these creatures is endless. We're the runt that's just kicked the street tough in the shins and slammed the door in his face. As soon as they can get through from wherever hell they come from I expect them to come at us in a giant storm of shit and hate."

"You paint a pretty picture, Rhenkin," Salisbourne joked but his face was solemn.

"You asked." Rhenkin shrugged.

The tent flap flew open then as Kennick stepped in. "You asked that I inform you when the moon rises, sir."

Salisbourne gave Rhenkin a grim smile. "I suppose now we'll see, eh?"

Rhenkin grunted and followed Kennick out of the tent. It wasn't especially dark and the moonlight worked with the fires to make it brighter still. "How do things stand?"

"As you ordered, sir," Kennick said. "Scouts are rotating in every half hour and the men are at half-rest."

Rhenkin nodded. Half-rest would ensure the men all had weapons to hand and were able to move at a moment's notice. None would be sleeping and company commanders would be keeping a close eye on their men. "Keep me updated. I'm going to take a look at the men," he told the lieutenant.

"I believe General Ackerson wished to speak with you, sir," Kennick said, stopping him.

Rhenkin grimaced. "Again?"

"I'm afraid so, sir." Kennick told him, his face gave nothing away. He's better at hiding it than me, Rhenkin realised.

"Well it can wait." Rhenkin sighed. "I'm going to look at the men."

"Where shall I find you, sir?"

Rhenkin looked back at him. "Use your initiative, son. There aren't many marshals here."

He wandered aimlessly, picking his way through the camp. The army stretched out much farther than he could hope to circle but he felt a need to see the men. Talking to them would be a waste of time. Every soldier picks themselves up when speaking to an officer. What he needed was to taste the mood.

The men were nervous, that much was obvious. It could be seen in the over-loud laughter from the three he passed playing dice just as easily as it could in the silence of the others who ran whetstones over their weapons or checked their armour. The officers were feeling the nerves too, barking orders at their sergeant and corporals. Oddly, what sergeants Rhenkin saw seemed to be taking things in stride. Experience, he supposed. There weren't many sergeants who made officer rank. Most stayed sergeants for the duration. Officers were likely to be new to their company or their rank, a sergeant though, they were the bedrock of any army and familiarity probably gave them something firmer to cling to.

He shook his head at himself. There was nothing familiar about any part of the situation. The coming battle would be huge, somehow he knew that. The small clashes they'd had with the fae before the new moon had been small. They'd been tasting his men, testing their responses. Now that the full moon had returned, the full fury of the fae host would descend upon them and a small part of him wondered if they were really ready.

It wasn't just the tactics, though they were novel enough. It was the fact that he would have to relinquish control. This army was simply too large a force for him to manage everything. He would need to trust in his men and his officers to do what needed to be done and pray to any gods that might exist that they'd do it well. "Time to loose the reins, old man," he whispered to himself.

The report, when it came, was delivered with more calm than it ever had previously. The runner that found him pointed him back in the direction of the command tent but the mood of the army had already changed. It was almost possible to see the point that orders reached units as men shovelled down the last few mouthfuls or rushed off for a last piss.

"Tell me," Rhenkin called out to Kennick as he approached the tent. Salisbourne stood already half into his armour, surrounded by majors, and not a few colonels, as he pointed at the map in the lieutenant's hand.

Kennick snapped off a salute. "Lord High Marshal, scouts report contact to the east, no more than an hour away at best."

Rhenkin chewed his lower lip as he squinted up at the sky. "The sun will still be up then. Are they on the march?" he frowned at the nod from the lieutenant. "Seems out of character but I suppose that's what we get for making assumptions isn't it, Kennick?"

"It is indeed, sir," the lieutenant told him but he was already turning to the others. "Gentlemen, it would seem that the fae have come along to play. They've even arrived in daylight, isn't that accommodating of them?" He gave a thin smile at the chorus of responses.

"You all have your orders. I don't see that anything has changed overly and so I intend to stick to the plan as much as we can. The fae are far too fast for us to control a battle if we try and advance towards them so we'll fight a defensive position and let them come stick themselves on our iron. Objections?"

Kennick cleared his throat from behind him and Rhenkin turned with raised eyebrows as the more senior officers muttered complaints. "Something to add, lieutenant?"

"A suggestion, sir," Kennick said. "A retreating line of archers to harry them as they approach?"

"I don't think so, no." Rhenkin shook his head. "Normally I'd agree with you but with the little presents we're going to be leaving for them, I don't want to give them any reason to speed up. If that's all then, gentlemen? I believe you all know your jobs." He made his way back into the tent as the others left, reaching for his own armour.

The catapults were already launching by the time he had the gambeson on and he smiled a grim smile to himself as he shrugged his way into the mail. The plate could stay where it was, he decided. His armour was only for show anyway. If the fae made it deep enough through the ranks to fight him then the battle was lost anyway.

"No sign of the Bjornmen?" he asked Kennick in a low voice as he stepped out of the tent.

"Nothing so far, sir," Kennick told him, apologizing as if it were his fault.

Rhenkin muttered darkly and looked eastwards, past the foremost ranks of his army. The command tents had been erected on a small hill, with the army arrayed around him. The hill wasn't large enough to make any kind of defensive position but it would afford him a decent view of the battle. Not for the first time he wondered if he'd been right to settle in this location. There were more defensible positions to both the north and west, but none that allowed for the same range of movement and visibility over the battlefield.

"Rhenkin!" the voice was loud enough to cut through the noise and Rhenkin groaned as he looked to the source.

"I told your man I wanted to talk to you an hour ago. Where have you been man?" Ackerson bulled his way through to the tents, thick white moustache standing out against the red of his face.

"General, I really don't think this is the time for a discussion," Rhenkin told him as he approached. "The enemy have been sighted. We could have less than an hour."

"Listen to me, Rhenkin," Ackerson told him in a quiet voice. "We can do this here, or in your tent. Either way this shouldn't take long."

"Fine," Rhenkin sighed, leading the way into the command tent. "Give us a few minutes," he told the men poring over the large map spread over the tables.

Ackerson waited, watching the men leave until the flap fell closed behind them. "Rhenkin, do you know what I've learned over the years as I rose through the ranks?" Ackerson said, turning to him. "I've learned that it's impossible to do everything yourself. There is a world of difference between being a major in command of a few companies and being a general with an entire army under you. There's no shame in accepting help from someone more experienced."

"Thank you, Ackerson," Rhenkin told him. "As I've said before I appreciate the offer but I am quite comfortable with the command. Now, if you'll excuse me?"

"Damn it all, Rhenkin," Ackerson snapped. "You're a country major with no real battlefield experience. How well do you really think you're going to do when the lines buckle and men start falling over each other and pissing themselves?"

"I think that's about enough, Ackerson," Rhenkin told him quietly.

"I really am going to have to insist, major." Ackerson snapped. "Go and play with the maps and let someone who knows what he's doing take care of things."

"I said, that will be enough!" Rhenkin snapped out the last word like a whip. "I am Lord High Marshal and you will do as ordered, Ackerson."

"Don't be ridiculous, boy." Ackerson sneered. "It's an honorary rank from a girl who's not even been queen long enough for her arse to warm the seat of the throne. If I'm forced to have you removed I will do so."

"General Ackerson," Rhenkin told him in a dreadfully quiet voice. "I am in command here and your insubordination will not stand. I will give you this one, final chance to return to your men and carry out the orders I give you or I will have you put in irons and chained to the supply wagons, do you understand me?"

That actually seemed to puncture the pomposity and the man gaped at him for a second before collecting himself. "You wouldn't dare!"

Rhenkin pulled open the tent flap. "Kennick!" he roared.

"Sir?"

"General Ackerson will be returning to his company now. If he finds any cause to delay he will become a colonel. If he countermands my order he will become a major."

Ackerson's mouth dropped. "Now see here, Rhenkin. I don't need to stand for this…"

"Ackerson, if you don't leave this tent right this moment I'll have you digging latrines and watering horses before the day's out," Rhenkin warned him.

"I..."

"Now!" Rhenkin roared.

"I think we'd better leave, sir." Kennick told Ackerson, holding the tent flap open for him.

An hour passes very quickly when you're counting the minutes and Rhenkin stood in silence as Kennick dealt with the readiness reports that came and went. Finally even the catapults fell silent and a hush drifted across the army as men were left with little to do but wait and think.

The dark stain that was the fae host seemed to appear in moments, passing over the horizon and pooling out over the ground like a scribe's mistake. Rhenkin watched as the fae host drew closer and frowned at the dark clouds that seemed to follow them.

"Another illusion, sir?" Kennick nodded at the clouds.

Rhenkin glanced at his second. "We'd better hope so, lad. If those bastards can control the weather then we're going to be in for a shit time of it."

"I think we all knew we'd be in for a shit time when we left Druel, sir," Kennick replied.

Rhenkin snorted, laughing through his nose. "Keep an eye on that toffee-nosed bastard, Ackerson. If he so much as farts out of turn I want to know about it."

"Understood, sir." Kennick's face was carefully blank.

The fae moved slowly. If they were a human army Rhenkin would have assumed they were using the time to make sure units were in position but these creatures didn't seem to work in the same way. The previous battle, and the few small skirmishes they'd had since, had shown a different way of thinking. Though the fae were banded together in a host they almost seemed to work independently, rushing into battle in a mob that placed little or no reliance on individuals working together. It was something that should work to give him a decided advantage. Men fighting as a unit were always more effective than men fighting alone, or so he hoped.

The armies of the fae approached until they were at the limits of catapult range, and there they stopped. Aelthen was clearly visible in the vanguard as they drew to a halt, surrounded by fae riding some form of massive cat. Horrors were visible among the fae, creatures formed of flame or raging storms of ice. Still others seemed to be formed of writhing smoke or things fresh from nightmares.

Darkness fell steadily and the huge fires that dotted the field were lit by torch and flaming arrows. Still the fae stood, silent as they waited. Rhenkin felt the mood of his men shift as surely as he heard the mutters.

"What are the bastards waiting for?" Kennick spoke up in a low voice.

"The moon I expect," Rhenkin replied, not taking his eyes from the massive figure of Aelthen at their head. "From what the druid tells me so much of their power comes from the moonlight."

"And you're just going to wait and let them have it, sir?" Kennick asked as politely as he could manage.

Rhenkin fought the grin back as far as he could, glancing over at him. "It's in hand, lieutenant. It's in hand."

There was no signal, no horn or trumpet. Between one breath and the next the fae charged. They ran in silence, moving so swiftly that for a moment Rhenkin froze, and then the first catapult fired, lofting a cloth bundle that unfurled as the air tugged at it and loosing a cloud of iron filings into the path of the oncoming fae.

The fae faltered for a moment, but then barrelled on, pushing through the clouds that grew thicker as more catapults hurled the iron into their path. Rhenkin glanced up to the horizon and a small smile grew as he saw the first sliver of the moon. Sparks were visible even from this distance as the moonlight worked with the iron filings misting down out of the air and landing on exposed skin.

The satyrs raced ahead of the fae, rushing in a dark torrent as they passed the first of the bonfires. They were still far beyond arrow range and Kennick gaped at Rhenkin as the first of the fae faltered, and then fell to the ground howling as they burst into blue flames. The charge faltered in moments as the host bunched up behind the satyrs writhing on the ground in agony as the flames consumed them.

Rhenkin narrowed his eyes and he watched the forward elements of the fae host bunch up. It was too good an opportunity to waste and he opened his mouth to give the order. The first of the catapults fired again before he could speak and he nodded approvingly.

"Good man," Rhenkin breathed as he watched the fresh explosions among the fae. "Loose iron arrowheads," he explained to Kennick who frowned in confusion.

Kennick nodded. "A good idea, sir. But what made them falter in the first place."

Rhenkin grinned then, in genuine pleasure. "Caltrops," he told the younger man. "An idea of that smith's daughter, Erinn. Three long iron nails worked together so a point is face upwards no matter how they lay. Easy to make and damned effective by the looks of things. The catapults have been littering the field all afternoon.

"Damned clever," Kennick grunted. "It won't hold them though."

"No." Rhenkin nodded as his smile faded. "No, it won't."

CHAPTER TWENTY-SEVEN

The clearing had changed from the last time they'd seen it. The once-peaceful glade had been ravaged and the ground was churned to ruin by the passage of thousands of hoofed footsteps. Obair's cottage had been torn to pieces where thick tree roots had thrust out from the ground and burrowed into the sides of the building to rip it apart.

Tristan turned to Ylsriss, muttering something in his deep voice.

"What did he say?" Devin asked, curious.

"He said it doesn't really look anything special and asked if we were sure about this place," she told him.

"Forgotten Gods, you'd better be!" Halther said, looking over to the stones. "This place gives me the creeps."

"Do we need to wait for the moon?" Obair wondered, raising an eyebrow at Joran and Ylsriss.

"I don't think so. It doesn't seem to work the same way as the glyphs the fae use," Ylsriss told him with a shrug. "That's just my best guess, of course."

Halther worked his way around the others, leaning in close to Obair. "How long do you think you need?" he asked.

"I really have no idea," the old druid admitted.

Halther muttered something to one of the scouts near him and shook his head darkly. "You'd best be getting on with it then. I really don't want to be here when the moon rises, not if we can help it."

Miriam pushed past them, making her way out to the circle of stones and wandering through them with a bemused expression as her fingertips brushed over those she passed.

Devin followed her, glancing up at the sky almost without thinking. The sun hadn't shown itself all day. The sky had been blanketed in pale while clouds, making it hard to guess at the time of day. Halther was right though, time wouldn't wait for them.

"Let's get started." He stepped into the circle reaching for the first of the stones as he crouched, feeling for the glyphs. Dimly he was aware of the others fanning out around him and searching the stones.

"There's nothing here!" Joran called out.

"Try another one," Devin shouted back. The edges of panic were already reaching for him. Joran was right, these stones were different to the ones at Lillith's cottage. Not just the height, though these were far shorter, the stone was not the same. The stones at Lillith's cottage had been pitted with age but there had been a grain to the rock that had made the glyphs easier to find as they broke with the stone's natural pattern. These stones were nothing like that. They were ancient and pitted from ages exposed to the elements but other than that they were featureless. Devin looked around at the others and panic sought and found him. There was not a glyph to be found.

"Try the hubstones," Obair suggested. He had probably intended his voice to sound calm. It wasn't, and the tinge of panic only served to make his own worse.

"Here!" Joran cried out, crouched beside the fallen hubstone. It lay to one side of the monolith making a shape with its fallen companion that was close to forming a T.

Devin rushed over, crouching down beside him and searching with his hands. There was definitely something there, a series of lines that were too regular to be anything natural.

"It doesn't feel like the others," he said with a frown at the younger man.

"How do you mean?"

"The other glyphs were more curves and loops. This is more angular."

Joran looked at him for a second and barked out an incredulous laugh. "That's your expert opinion is it? Not enough curves?"

"If you two have quite finished?" Ylsriss stood behind them, arms folded over her chest with a raised eyebrow.

She crouched into the gap they made for her, tracing the glyphs lightly. After a moment she closed her eyes, frowning.

"They are different," she said at last, sitting back. "At the other circle I couldn't read them but I was closer to it than this. This is almost like reading a different language."

"Nothing?" Devin pressed. "Nothing at all?" He looked over to Obair, sharing a worried look as the druid drew closer.

She shook her head. "Not really. There are a few things that are close. Characters that sort of remind me of others but they're really not that similar. It could just be coincidence."

"What about this?" Devin asked, pointing at a small hole in the stone. "I thought it was just a chip in the stone to start with but look, it's too regular."

Ylsriss leaned forward to peer at it, running her hands over the stone around it. "I don't know. I can make out glyphs around it but…" She shrugged.

"Does it matter?" Joran asked?

Devin cocked his head, frowning at him, but Obair got there first.

"I'd say it matters!" he snapped. "What do you think we travelled all this way for? If Ylsriss can't work these glyphs then this has all been for nothing!"

"Easy…" Devin told the old man, pushing his arm down from where he'd stabbed it at the air in front of the Bjornman.

Joran was unruffled though. "Except that Ylsriss didn't work the glyphs at the other circle, did she?" He looked to Devin. "Don't you remember? She couldn't find anything close to an activation sequence, you did it all yourself."

"That's true, isn't it?" Obair mused. "Can you remember how you did it?"

Devin flushed as the faces turned to him and looked down at the ground. "It was the same way I felt the moon," he spoke slowly, dredging through a memory that was jumbled and confused. "The same as when Ylsriss and Joran came through—"

"Wait, what about Aervern?" Joran stopped him. "I thought we were going to wait for her to power the glyphs?"

Devin glanced around the clearing and looked back to the Bjornmen. "I don't see her, do you? Face it," he said as Joran's face fell, "this is about fighting the fae, about shutting them out of our world. How much did you think we could really trust her?"

He stopped then, ignoring Joran's response and reaching for the stone. There was a feel to this, a sensation of movement, though he himself never took a step. He closed his eyes and grasped the stone.

For long minutes nothing happened. Obair exchanged worried looks with the others and tried to ignore the muttered conversation of the scouts at the edges of the clearing.

"Look!" Ylsriss hissed urgently, pointing at the stone. Where Devin gripped at the stone, a faint covering of frost was forming.

"Is it…" Obair began, but stopped himself. Devin's eyes were blank, staring into nothing as he frowned in concentration. The frost grew thicker, climbing over his fingernails as the skin on his hands grew paler and took on a blueish tinge.

"Is there no way we can help him?" Joran asked. "This nearly killed him the last time."

Ylsriss shook her head. "I don't even know what he's doing. Though…" She paused, looking at Devin again. "Maybe it's not that complicated."

She reached out, grasping the hand that hung loose at his side. The cold was instant and immediate, sucking the heat from her body so swiftly that it robbed the strength from her gasp. She stiffened, throwing her head back as the shiver took hold, shaking her in tremors so strong it was a wonder she stayed upright.

"Ylsriss!" Joran gasped, reaching for her other hand.

"Don't!" Obair stopped him. "For all we know she's not helping him at all. Don't blunder in."

Joran glared at him for a moment, and then peered at the stone. "Look." He pointed. "The frost is lessening. It's doing something." He met Obair's eyes with a defiant look. "By this time at the cottage there were lines growing on his face and his hair colour had gone."

Obair grunted. It was true, the frost did seem lessened, though both wore painful grimaces.

"This I can help with better than you, I think," Tristan rumbled. His hand looked huge as he reached for Ylsriss's small one but the effect was no less pronounced and he gasped and stiffened. Joran watched him for a second and reached out, followed by Gavin.

Obair looked on in silence, after long moments a cold hand reached timidly for his own. Miriam's worry mirrored his own. They were not so very different, he realised. Both their lives had been taken up by duty and suffering and neither of them had ever been given a choice. He returned her worried smile and, together, they watched on and waited while the scouts held a nervous vigil around them. Miriam nodded as Obair gave her a questioning look. The old man gave her a small smile and reached for Gavin's hand. Where the others had gasped, Obair barely stiffened. Miriam's eyes closed but his eyes simply grew blank as his brow furrowed in concentration.

* * *

The skies grew darker as afternoon headed for evening. Halther and the others gathered wood and set to work building fires around the clearing. If the fae were to make an appearance they wouldn't remain hidden for lack of light.

One of the scouts settled down beside a fire and set to work rummaging through the packs. He glanced up at the strange look from the others. "We may as well get a hot meal going. We still need to eat and it's not as if any fae close enough to see us would miss these fires is it?"

Halther shrugged and glanced at the others. "He has a point, I suppose."

They gathered around one of the fires set close to the ruins of the cottage. Clumps of iron still jutted from the ground. It was unlikely to be of much help but it was better than nothing.

The conversation was hushed and stilted and frequent looks drifted over to the figures clustered around the stone. A small fire had been set beside them where they knelt, but if they drew comfort from it they gave no sign.

It was well after night had truly fallen that Joran gave a long, pained, groan and fell to the earth. After hours of silence from the stones the sound cut through the hushed conversation of those sat around the fire and Halther jerked upright, spilling the bowl he'd cradled on his lap and sending it spinning to the dirt.

Tristan blinked and stood slowly as the scouts rushed over to the seven of them. He shook his head at the barrage of questions, none of which he could understand. After a moment he reached for Ylsriss, grasping her by the shoulder. As if something passed between them she let Devin's hand drop and collapsed into Tristan's arms.

Obair barely noticed as Devin sat back. His hand trailed down the side of the stone until it touched the earth.

"I know," he managed, his voice so soft it bordered on being a whisper.

Obair sank to the ground beside him, reaching for his shoulders to keep the young man from falling. "Are you okay?"

The look Devin gave him was murderous. "I know. I know what the Wyrde is, what it always was. I know what we will have to do. And you knew all along, didn't you?"

"I'd guessed at it," Obair admitted. "Lillith left enough in her diaries to hint at it. It was nothing more than hints, mind you."

"What are you talking about?" Ylsriss asked. Her voice was weak and she still clung to Tristan but she was awake and alert.

"Somebody has to die," Devin told her. "The Wyrde is a soul, a human soul holding the fae back. The druids use its power to form the Wyrde. I can rebuild the barrier but to do it one of us has to die."

Ylsriss reached for the steaming cup Halther offered her, taking a sip and waiting while another was offered to Devin. He smiled his thanks, wrapping both hands around it and seeking to pull the warmth directly into his hands. "It needs a soul, someone Wyrde-touched. It was always one of the druids in the past. The master gave a part of himself to the stones and to the Wyrde as the apprentice took over but it doesn't need to be. You, Joran, even Obair or I, any one of us could do it."

Her face was stricken as she looked from him to Obair. "How do we choose?"

"The choice is already made," Miriam told her softly. "You're so young, all of you. You all have long lives to live. Mine was stolen from me by the fae long ago. I've had years of torment but I haven't really lived a life. What years remain to me are mine to use as I see fit and I can't think of a better way to live, or die."

Devin's head shot round, horrified. "Ma... No!"

Her hand reached for him, stroking his cheek. "It's okay, baby boy. You've a whole life ahead of you," her voice grew thick and almost fierce as she forced the words through the tears that threatened, "and I am just so very proud!"

"Miriam, you don't need to..." Obair cut off. "I'd planned..."

She shook her head. "I know, Obair. Devin can't do this alone though. You'll be needed here. He'll need someone to guide him."

He paused at her words, eyes narrowing in thought for just a second as something struck him. He nodded slowly, turning to Devin. "Are you ready?"

"No." Devin shook his head as he pulled himself to his feet. "No, I'll never be ready."

"I know," Obair gripped his shoulder. "I'm not either but who knows how much time we have?"

Miriam moved past them both, climbing up onto the stone laying at the centre of the circle. It was only as she lay upon it that Devin realised that this stone had never been resting upon the others, this had always been its purpose. She smiled at him once and lay her head back, closing her eyes.

The moon was clear through the clouds as they began, stepping in concert as they moved through their different rituals. Obair had begun at one side of the circle with Devin facing him from the other. The rituals brought them close together and twisted them apart again. There was an odd symmetry to it as they moved, something that pulled at the edges of Ylsriss's mind, crying out to be understood yet eluding her. Their steps traced glyphs across the churned mud of the ground, forming sequences that made even the gateway she and Joran had used to escape the Realm of Twilight seem simple. The rituals wound on, moving in spirals around each other in a dance so complex it was unnerving.

Miriam gasped as it began, her face etched with pain as the frost climbed up over her clothes and skin. Fern-shaped fingers of ice reached up over her cheeks as the stones drew on her strength and her body's heat. Though the woman made no sound and barely moved, the agony she suffered was clear. Ylsriss gripped Tristan's hand tight as she watched, biting at her own lip until finally, unable to take it any longer, she turned away.

"Ylsriss!" Gavin grabbed at her arm, finger pointing upwards. "Lords of the Seas, look! Look at the moon!"

"What about it?" she looked from the sky to his face.

"It was full before, look now!"

She followed his finger with a frown. Where the moon had hung full it was fading, drifting into darkness as if a veil were being drawn across it. She looked back to the pair moving through the steps of their rituals. Were they doing this? Was this even possible?

Footsteps turned her head even as Halther's men snatched up weapons.

"I offer no threat, manlings." The voice was soft and somehow familiar.

"Aervern?" Joran wondered as she stepped into the circle of light from the fire. "You came!"

She smiled at him as she came closer. "I go where I will, sweetling, did I not once tell you this?"

He shook his head, nonplussed. "I…"

She went to him, reaching out to press a finger to his lips. "I come for reasons of my own, but also this one desired to be here." She stepped aside with a graceful sweep of the arm.

"Klöss!" Ylsriss ran to him, hurling herself at him as he emerged from the gloom. "What? Why?"

"Isn't it obvious?" he told her as he stepped back and looked at her. "I had to come as soon as I knew Aervern was coming here. I couldn't risk not coming."

"What do you mean?"

"You belong here with me, Ylsriss," he told her. "If these two succeed there will be no way back here from the world of the fae."

"You thought?" She shook her head. "You thought I might go back?"

"I know you would," Klöss told her. "If you could find a way to pass over I know you would."

He stopped her as she started to speak. "Let me finish, okay? Effan was stolen from us, he was taken. He's my son and I never even got to hold him but he's gone from us as surely as if he'd never taken breath. Aervern explained it all to me, the way that time passes differently between our worlds. Our baby could be three summers or more by now. He's probably walking and speaking."

"I know all of that, Klöss," she said, looking away from him. There was an edge to her voice, an angry hurt waiting to lash out.

Klöss smiled, looking past her anger as he moved to meet her gaze. "I can't lose you, Ylsriss. If these two succeed there will be no coming back. If you were to pass over you'd be trapped there forever and who's to say you would ever find Effan?"

She frowned, shaking her head. "How would I even get there, Klöss? If there was a way I might have but…" she stopped, looking at Aervern.

"You!"

"I would assist if I could," the fae told her. "The loss of a youngling is something I would not wish upon anyone, fae or manling. I can well imagine your torment." She looked at Joran as she spoke and a slight smile curved her lips.

"Wait…how?" he began

Aervern took three swift steps and reached to rest her fingertips on Joran's chest. "We do not place such an importance on these things as you manlings," she told him. "Yet ties of blood are not unimportant to us. Our child will wish to know its sire. This is not your world, Joran. There is nothing for you here. If these Wyrdeweavers succeed then all that is fae in this realm will be torn free and cast to the Outside. I would have you return with me before the veil is drawn between us."

He looked over at Ylsriss and the frown caught up with him as his head whipped back to the fae. "Hold on, what do you mean, 'its sire?'"

Her smile was all the answer she gave and all the answer he needed.

"We have a child?" he asked.

She nodded, her eyes a mystery. "There is not much time, sweetling. Will you return with me?"

"Joran, you can't be serious!" Ylsriss blurted as she turned to look at him.

He shrugged with a sad smile. "You left the Realm of Twilight to come home, Ylsriss. I have no home to here to find. You told me that yourself, remember?"

Ylsriss shook her head. "I was angry, Joran. I didn't mean for you to do this…"

He smiled at her, "But I can make a home there, something to belong to."

She shook her head again, confusion making her face hard and angry. "What about the touch? You're making a slave of yourself!"

Aervern shook her head. "The touch is a thing of the highfae, of Aelthen and his kin. I would never do this thing. This smothering and crushing of self, it is a thing only a creature that needs endless assurance of their own superiority would do. I seek Joran as my life-mate. I have no need of a mindless pet." She bared her teeth slightly in a smile that was stepping closer to being a snarl as she laid a possessive hand on Joran's arm.

Ylsriss ignored the veiled threat, shaking her head again as she denied everything. "Don't do this, Joran," she insisted in a voice thick with tears. "You've only been here such a short time. Don't give up on our world, don't give up on us."

"Don't you see, Ylsriss?" he asked gently. "This isn't our world, it never was. I'm not giving up on it, I'm just choosing something else. The Realm of Twilight will change with Aelthen gone. There will be no camps, no breeding pens. You were there in the ruins of that city, you saw the things that man and fae can do together. We could rebuild that. I want to be a part of that."

"You're sure?"

He nodded.

"Well come here, you dumb ox." She sniffed, wiping her eyes with the back of her hand as he came to her. She wrapped arms around him, holding him fiercely. "I will never forget you."

Aervern stiffened, looking out over the darkened trees and sniffing at the air. "We must hurry. Our time here grows short."

Joran frowned and seemed about to speak but stopped as Aervern met his eyes. "Maybe you're right."

She led him over to the standing stone, stepping past Obair and Devin as they moved in their dance around Miriam. All three seemed oblivious to their presence, lost in the ritual of the Wyrde.

"Find my son, Joran," Ylsriss told him. "Find Effan."

He nodded once into the silence between them. There were no words. There was no need.

Aervern reached for the monolith, gazing into the distance behind them with an odd expression. and then the fae was reaching for him, and they passed out of the world in search of a new one.

* * *

Rhenkin found himself reaching for his sword as the fae crashed into the line. It was odd, both being removed from the lines but also the manner of the clash. Human armies would smash into each other, meeting blade with shield. The fae were nothing like that and more of them stepped smoothly past the iron blades of Rhenkin's men than sought to parry the strike.

The fae and satyr were not so much as driving the lines back as they were fracturing them. Units disintegrated and crumbled back in upon themselves, seeking to kill the fae that raged in their midst.

White arrows hissed out of the fae host, driving completely through men and showering others in gore. They passed through bodies without slowing, slamming into other men before coming to a halt. Iron arrows flew back in return, spreading blue fire wherever they struck home. Up and down the line the battle raged and Rhenkin watched on. There was little to do and entirely too much time to think. Reports came and went and Kennick issued small orders for small details in a steady stream.

His eyes were drawn to Aelthen. The huge creature was always where the fighting was thickest, laying about him with a massive broad-bladed spear. Huge roots suddenly burst from the earth as the creature held his hands forth. They whipped out, grasping up men by arm and leg and tearing them slowly in two as they screamed. The line shrank back from the spectacle as the blood spattered across the ranks and, as another hail of white arrows struck, the line simply dissolved.

"Hold it, Ackerson," Rhenkin muttered to himself as he watched the men stagger backwards. "Damn it, hold the line!"

Satyrs surged forward with a bestial roar that reached even to Rhenkin's ears and the flank buckled, and then broke. Men turned and fled as satyrs drove into their midst, bone knives flashing. The charge, when it came, was textbook perfect. Neat orderly cavalry rows arranged perpendicular to the front line and flowing down from the edges of the flank. Rhenkin nodded to himself in satisfaction as he saw the sabres flashing in the moonlight as the men charged. And then the realisation hit.

"Kennick," he grabbed the man's arm. "Send reserves to the right flank. Send them now!"

"Sabres," he breathed. "You bloody fool, Ackerson." The sabres were the preferred weapon of the Savarel cavalry, a swift slashing weapon. In many ways they epitomised the way the men were trained to fight. A lightning quick strike on a fast horse, sabres flashing, and then away before the enemy had a chance to gather themselves.

The problem was not the men, or the tactic Ackerson was employing, it was the sabres the men carried. Ackerson had dismissed the warning that steel weapons were useless against the fae. The weapons Rhenkin's men carried were pure iron. Ugly, quick-forged weapons that had none of the grace of the steel swords they were used to. Iron was simply too brittle to forge into a sabre worth having and it certainly didn't shine in the moonlight like that.

The charge faltered as it punched into the fae, the sabres slashing into fae and satyr and rebounding with little or no effect. Horses screamed as the bone knives of the satyr slashed into flanks and eyes, and then the men themselves were torn from their mounts.

"Sir!" Kennick cried out as Rhenkin rushed for the horses picketed beside the command tents.

Rhenkin ignored him and threw himself into the saddle, driving his boots into the startled beast's flanks as he urged it towards Ackerson's flank. "Stupid, stupid, stupid." He growled as he crouched low over the horse.

The captain staggered back as Rhenkin hurled himself out of the saddle. "You there, get those archers firing. Four sections in a constant volley, right into the breach."

"Are you mad?" The captain burst out. "Those are our men out there! Who the hell are you anyway?"

Rhenkin grabbed the man by his mail shirt, hauling him close until their noses almost touched. "I am Lord High Marshal Rhenkin, now get those fucking archers moving!"

The captain paled, and then flushed before turning and barking orders. The men moved swiftly but Rhenkin knew it was too late. The fae were already deep into the ranks and the cavalry had been butchered. Arrows streaked overhead as the first of the volleys were lofted and blue fire exploded along the lines but Rhenkin winced at the screams. Some of them would be his own men.

The flank stabilized over time, forcing the fae back with sword and arrow but the losses were horrendous. Over half the reserves had already been committed and the lines had buckled twice more at the centre and the left flank. The moon was high in the sky now and the fires were barely necessary as the bright light shone over the battlefield.

A low moan of terror rose from the foremost elements of the army as Aelthen stepped up onto the mist that surrounded him, waving the fae behind him into the air. The hunt rose up in the same spiral that Rhenkin had first seen in Obair's glade when the fae had burst free from the stones. He winced as they charged up and over heads of the foremost lines and plunged down into the ranks, hacking left and right before rising up into the skies again.

Arrows streaked after them but most fell short. Those than did make it close enough to threaten, exploded into splinters before they ever found flesh. Snarling in frustration Rhenkin turned his face away as Kennick pulled at his arm.

"Sir, look!" Rhenkin stifled a groan as he followed the lieutenant's pointing finger and frowned. The fae host stretched out before him, extending so far that there were elements that hadn't even entered the battle yet. On their flank though, something seemed to be happening. It was too far to make out any detail but the flashes of blue fire told their own tale.

"The Bjornmen?" Kennick asked.

Rhenkin shrugged and glanced up at the sky. The sight stole the words from his mouth and he gasped as he pointed himself. The moon had risen high over the horizon now but where it had been full, a dark stain now spread over the face of it. The most easterly edge was already as dark as the skies behind it and the darkness was increasing.

"What the…" Kennick managed but his words were lost in a roar of fury. Aelthen stood still in the air, glaring up at the moon. He raised his great spear high and screamed out his anger again. His eyes glowed, growing in intensity until they shone brighter than the bonfires. Then, with a thunderous inrushing of air, he vanished.

CHAPTER TWENTY-EIGHT

The clearing had fallen oddly silent. The rituals of the Wyrde were performed in silence and the only sounds were the faint footfalls of the two druids as they wove their steps about the stones. Ylsriss let Klöss take her hand and lead her to where Tristan, Gavin, and the scouts waited.

The wind was picking up, whipping leaves from the treetops and tossing them up into the moonlight.

"You managed to keep her in one piece then?" Klöss said as he grinned at the big man.

"What could harm her?" Tristan smiled but turned, frowning at a faint noise behind him.

"Problem?" Gavin asked but the man didn't answer.

The spear came out of the air, emerging from nothing as it passed into reality and thrust savagely at the Bjornman. Tristan was already moving, twisting one the side on instinct but the broad blade cut through leathers and flesh with ease until it skidded along his ribs.

Aelthen stepped forward, flinging Tristan aside as the air shimmered, falling from him like water as he emerged from the illusion.

"You pitiful creatures dare to attempt this?" he demanded in a powerful voice.

Tristan was the first to answer, picking himself up with rage burning in his eyes as he tore the axe from his back and rushed at the fae creature with a roar. Blood ran freely from the wound along his side but the man didn't seem to feel it. His eyes were wide and the scream unending as he struck at the creature in a savage fury.

Aelthen shifted away from the berserker, pushed back by the sheer fury of the assault. His spear moved with ease to block strikes that were little more than a blur but which left little time for a return stroke.

Gavin was the first to move in a battle that had lasted only moments, pulling daggers free and darting in behind the fight, crouching low and waiting for an opening. He moved smoothly, blades flashing as he struck but he may as well have been fighting smoke. Aelthen shifted out of his reach with ease, barely seeming to take his attention from Tristan and the axe.

The blow came from nowhere as Aelthen's rear hoof lashed out and caught the thief in the side of the head, hurling him across the clearing. The satyri lunged forward against the axe-wielder, becoming a blur of motion as his eyes flared. The spear caught Tristan squarely in the ribs, bursting through his chest as if his flesh offered no real resistance. Blood spattered over Klöss as Ylsriss screamed and they staggered back away from the sight.

"And is that all you offer?" Aelthen sneered, tearing the spear free of Tristan's body as the man dropped to the dirt.

The only answer was the hiss of an arrow as Halther let fly an ironhead. Aelthen barely seemed to notice as one hand came up and snatched the shaft out of the air. He turned his gaze to the scouts as they readied their own arrows and a cold smile spread over his face. The arrow splintered in his hand as his eyes flared, bathing his face in amber. Along the line men cried out as their bows shattered, thrusting jagged shards of wood into unprotected hands and wrists.

"This abomination ends here," Aelthen declared, lifting the spear once more as he stepped towards the circle where Obair and Devin worked on.

The sword hissed as Klöss pulled it free of the sheath, the sound itself calling out a challenge. Aelthen turned his head at the sound. "You also?" he asked in surprise. "You would pit yourself against me? Are you so eager to die, manling?" The satyri seemed almost incredulous, the shock reaching out to him from some place beyond his arrogance.

Klöss gave no answer, stepping away from Ylsriss and sinking back into the fighting stance Verig had spent so many years schooling him in. He raised the blackened blade of the sword above his head in a two handed grip and met the creature's eyes in defiance. "Come then, *fae.*"

Aelthen inclined his antlered head in a nod as formal as any bow and raised the great spear again, shifting into a guard position. The strike was fast as Aelthen uncoiled like a whip, seeming to move from a relaxed posture into the strike without passing through any of the movements that should have been involved in between.

Klöss barely moved, adjusting the great sword less an inch and shifting his line so the strike slid down along the blade and extended out behind him. His slash was savage, passing under the spear and lashing out at a foreleg. Aelthen stepped aside, letting the blade pass him. The shock on his face made way for a grudging respect, and then the blades lashed out again.

Ylsriss ran past the pair as spear crashed into blade. Klöss moved with a grace she'd never seen from him as he flowed from stance to stance, his great black sword a blur in front of him. Aelthen held the spear as a staff, whistling the blade and haft about him with one hand and striking and blocking with both.

"Help him!" she screamed as she raced to Halther.

He looked past her, unseeing as he gazed at the creature in awe, eyes wide with adoration. She kicked at him but he didn't even seem to feel it as he staggered to the side. Light flared behind her and she spun in shock as the stones of the circle burst into life. Glyphs that had been worn out of sight by aeons of rain and wind burned brighter than any flame as they flared along the length of the stones.

She shook her herself violently as Klöss grunted in pain, bringing her back to herself, as a slash caught him high on the arm, biting through his leathers. Halther didn't react as she shoved at him, turning him around to reach for his quiver.

Aelthen thrust a palm forward into the air and Klöss suddenly rocketed away as if struck a hammer blow. The creature's eyes glowed brightly as a faint green mist began to rise from him, torn free in the glow of the stones.

Ylsriss screamed out Klöss's name but he ignored her, heaving himself to his feet and edging closer to the stones as he sank back down into his stance.

"Impudent." Aelthen sneered as contempt flowed over his features. He raised the spear again, ran ahead of her, and charged.

There was no way to block the strike. Aelthen was easily three times Klöss's weight and the blow would pass through him without even slowing. He ducked and rolled to one side, gasping in the green mist that seemed to surround the satyri as Aelthen passed him with less than an inch to spare.

The power rocked into him and Klöss gasped in shock as a flash of understanding hit. He breathed the mist in deeply, eyes flaring amber as he spun to block the blow he had somehow felt coming. His blow was slight, a backstroke that had been robbed of any real force by the strike he had parried. It caught Aelthen a glancing blow on the ribs below one great arm but the bellow of pain from the beast was deafening.

The satyri staggered back, clutching at the wound with one hand as he stared at Klöss in shock and dismay. The shipmaster raised the black sword with a smile and Aelthen's eyes widened as he looked from Klöss's glowing eyes to the blade, seeming to truly see it for the first time.

Klöss surged forward with a flurry of blows, drawing on the power that coursed through him. The blade felt like nothing in his hand and he wove it in combinations that he would never have even attempted normally. Aelthen staggered away from him, fear and confusion robbing his movements of any grace as he desperately fought to keep the black-iron blade from him.

Ylsriss didn't hesitate. Hesitation would just have made her movements more obvious as she circled behind the creature. She raised the ironhead in one hand, grasping the shaft like the hilt of a dagger. Three quick racing steps brought her close enough and she rammed the arrow down, thrusting it deep between the ribs of the stag body beneath Aelthen's human torso and feeling the shaft snap in her hand. "That's for my baby, you bastard!"

Blue fire gouted from the wound and Aelthen screamed, a shockingly human sound, as he turned and slammed the length of the spear against her, crashing her aside like a discarded toy. He ripped at the wound, ignoring Klöss, as he strove to tear the ironhead from his flesh.

It was almost too easy. This was no longer a fight, it was slaughter. Klöss raised the black-iron blade high and hacked. The sword sheared through flesh and bone, tasting blood, and then the iron blade met the Lady's Gift.

The explosion tore through the glade, throwing Klöss through the air to crash into the stone circle, blasting the air from him as he slumped to the ground and lay still.

* * *

Devin worked in silence but it was a silence that was ignored. The ritual took his all, took his entire self, dulling his emotions as it stole him away from the world. Dimly he was aware of the surge of power that was rushing into the stones from Miriam, powering the ritual and opening the histories of the druids to him.

The steps of the ritual were almost second nature to him, implanted in his very consciousness by the knowledge buried in the stones. As he moved, forming glyphs with his steps, he mirrored his movements within his thoughts, forcing the sensations and his awareness of the moon through the channels he carved in his mind. Screams and shouts nagged at him from the edges of the clearing but it was a half-heard babble, unimportant and easy to ignore. Instead, the knowledge of the druids filled him, reaching out from the stones that surrounded him and pouring into him.

The histories of the druids stretched out before him, the lives and experiences of hundreds, if not thousands, of men and women passed into the stones at the moment they gave their lives to the Wyrde. He knew now that the Wyrde had always been a single soul, but that soul had never been trapped and held for all the ages. It had served, waiting until the next master was ready to pass on the task of the ritual to their apprentice. Death had never been an ending for these druids. It was merely the next stage in a task that only ended as their soul was released from the Wyrde, passing on to whatever lay beyond the veil as another took their place.

He could feel Obair, feel the ritual he wove about him, but it was powerless. It was like the old man was painting with water, the strokes sure and certain but holding no colour. What was the difference between them? Why could he feel this power and not the old man? He reached back through the histories, passing through lives in an instant as he sought answers.

The histories ended with the purges. Devin's mind shot back to childhood memories of Samen's tales at the first mention of King Caltus. His purges had succeeded in ways that that mad king could never have imagined. Though the druids had lived on the knowledge buried in the stones, of the hidden glyphs and how to access them, had been lost. The druids themselves had been reduced to simple caretakers, going through the motions of a ritual that none of them truly understood.

Devin flew back through lives, passing generations in an instant while his feet led him through the ritual, back to the very beginnings of the Wyrde, when mankind was fresh from the war with the fae and the desperate flight through the Worldtrails. The answer was right there, simple in its truth. The knowledge filled him with horror. Mankind was never meant to touch the power of the fae, mankind never could. Fae blood was needed to touch that power and it was the fae blood within him that worked them now.

Centuries of interbreeding with the fae had resulted in fae-born that were little different from mankind. For some, the fae heritage had thinned over countless generations. For others it ran true. That was why he had been able to feel the moon so easily. That was why he had been able to feel Miriam and the fae host as they passed between the worlds. He hadn't been feeling the Wyrde at all. He had felt the passage of the fae through the Worldtrails. Obair must have a touch of fae blood, enough for him to push his ritual onwards but nothing close to what was needed to relight the fire that was the Wyrde. That would come from him.

He felt him then. As the realisation of what he was came to him he felt Obair moving through the histories. It was as if the rituals had themselves merged and formed a bridge allowing the old man to see what he himself had already discovered. He felt the shock of discovery and the old man moved with purpose, driving back through to the very forging of the Wyrde with a desperation that startled Devin even through his numbness.

Devin's mind fled then, pushing away the histories and rushing through the halls of his consciousness until his eyes snapped open and he saw the glade once more. His step faltered for the briefest moment as he saw the burning corpse of Aelthen and the crumpled forms scattered around the glade but he moved onward. The strands of power he wove were hollow, he saw that now. In many ways, little different to those woven by Obair. It was a vessel they created, needing only to be filled.

Obair lifted his head then, glancing at Devin as they reached the culmination. His steps wove glyphs ever closer to Miriam until he stopped beside the stone, waiting as Devin moved on.

He knelt then, reaching inside his robe. "You won't be alone, Miriam," he said softly. "I understand it now. There's no need for you to be alone in this."

Her eyes were wet as she reached to touch his face with her fingertips. "You're sure?

Obair nodded as he gathered Miriam to him, embracing her and placing the long iron blade against her back. She kissed him then and the surprise in his eyes softened as his smile grew.

"It was never intended to be a single soul, Devin," he called out. "The forgers of the Wyrde were close but they never truly grasped it. One soul alone was enough to power the Wyrde as they intended, trapped and directed by the living druids working the ritual. But with two it is a power unending. The ritual would never be needed, the Wyrde would be maintained from within. One soul to power and one to guide."

Devin froze at the words, struggling to free his mind from the strands of the ritual that bound him as he fought to understand what the old man meant. And then it was too late. Obair thrust his body forward as he drove the blade through Miriam and into his own chest.

There was a moment of utter silence, and then the stones exploded in light as the glyphs flared brighter than a noon-sun. Devin staggered back, shielding his eyes as he stumbled from the circle, stumbling over Klöss who groaned beneath him. His mind burned as the steps of the ritual seemed to repeat themselves, coursing on and flowing ever faster until it was one blinding blur.

He heard screams, though at least one was his own as he lay in the grass. A force seemed to snatch at him, tugging but somehow unable to get a firm grasp. Above him them the veil grew stronger, passing over the moon until nothing remained and the skies fell into utter darkness as the light of the stones guttered and died. Devin lay in the darkness. In the stillness that followed he felt it, the first stirrings of the Wyrde.

* * *

Ileriel spat curses as Aelthen vanished and allowed the flow of the battle to carry her back away from the manlings. The stench of fehru was everywhere and the foul taste of it covered her tongue with every breath she took. Manling arrows rose high above the host, bringing crude slivers of the stuff down towards her and she reached out with her Grace, slashing the shaft that would have taken her in the throat.

"Variska!" she called out, lending strength to her cry with what reserves she had. The sight of the Lady, half-obscured by some black taint, filled her with dread and she tried to keep her gaze away from the sky.

The fae'reeth had ceased their attack as soon as Aelthen vanished and the Swarm turned in lazy circles above the battlefield. Variska shone at its heart, easily visible to both fae and manling. She turned her burning gaze to Ileriel for the barest moment before looking away, unconcerned with whatever the fae might wish of her. Ileriel spat a curse. The manling impudence knew no bounds and their use of fehru was taking a toll that she doubted Aelthen had ever imagined.

The satyrs were hurling themselves against the manlings. Riahl's horde of beasts were mad with bloodlust and barely seemed to notice that they were being cut down with each surge they made against the line of fehru facing them. She could easily pick out Riahl himself, more than half lost to the blood-rage as he stood and ordered his horde onwards.

This was not a fae battle. Fae did not line up in these neat rows and crash together in an endless succession of screams. This ebb and flow was reaping as much fae blood as manling.

As she watched the satyrs gave up their endless clashing against the manling lines. Instead, they hurled themselves high into the air with shining eyes as they employed what Grace they could. The beasts crashed down, deep into the manling lines, laying about them with blade and fist. The humans fell into chaos for a moment, but then flares of sapphire exploded within their ranks. The tactic was useless.

Riahl seemed to ignore the losses, sending more and more of his Great Revel leaping to their deaths as two fae sought to stop him. The creature was a liability, too far gone to the wilds to respect the order of things. She had been right about him from the beginning.

The sensation built slowly, a thin shard of pain that wrapped her fear around itself and bore through her until it was buried deep into the core of her. Ileriel looked up at the moon in terror. The black hole in the sky told her as much as the thick green mist that rose from the fae around her, whipping away in a wind that seemed to have come from nowhere.

Pain took her and she staggered further from the front lines until her terror overcame the agony and she fled, stumbling past fae and satyr who held their hands before them in wonder as the Lady's Gift poured from them, surrounding them in green torrents that seemed to rush about, tugging at them, pulling.

The manlings seemed to have stopped their attack, looking on in wonder as the armies of the fae fell about in panic and dismay. Ileriel scrabbled at her quiver, dumping the fine white arrows out onto the ground until the bundle of cloth fell free. Desperation robbed her of any grace as she fell to the ground, scrabbling at the cloth in panic. Already she could feel it tugging at her. Already the foulness of it pulled at her, seeking to drive her from this world.

Blue fire flared between her hands as she grasped the arrowhead and Ileriel screamed bitter agony as she fled through the fae host, burning what Grace she had by forcing more speed from her legs until she left the battle behind her and reached the trees. The fire burned away at her hands, flaring bright between the wreckage of her fingers but already the flames were lessening, no longer the raging furnace they had been.

The fae stopped, leaning against a tree as she glanced back at the battle. The mist was thicker somehow, filled with motes of something darker. Flecks of black sand tossed about in the wind-driven mist. The screams reached her easily, cries of panic and despair as the specks grew larger until they looked like ashes tossed up from a fire.

Ileriel glanced at the fehru in her hand. The fire had gone but never had she felt so utterly drained. The tugging of the Wyrde was still there but somehow it was slipping past her, unable to find purchase.

A howling reached her from the satyr on the fringes of the host and she looked over in time to see the closest of them dissolve into fragments, blown like ash in the wind as the Wyrde tore them from the world. Hundreds of satyr fell in moments and a keening wail pulled her gaze to the Swarm and the glowing fae'reeth at its centre. Variska screamed and all about her the fae'reeth exploded into fragments.

Panic spoke to her in a voice that was too quiet for her ears. Her legs listened and she fled through the trees, deeper into the forest. The cave had the scent of beast about it, damp fur and musk, but Ileriel barely noticed. She retreated to the darkest corner, hidden far from the reach of the Lady or her jealous sibling. As she curled into a ball around the fehru arrowhead still clasped to her breast she smiled. The Wyrde had no hold on her. What the sun or moon might bring she did not know but for now she was free.

* * *

Devin came to slowly, blinking at the light. There was something between his lips, a cold texture on his teeth and he probed at it with his tongue. His mind was slow, his thoughts struggling over each other as he fought to make sense of it all. The taste hit him first and he spat, mud and grass mixed with the blood from his split lip. There were noises around him, voices that sounded familiar. Slowly he pushed himself onto all fours, dizziness threatening to pull him back down to the mud as he fought his way up to his knees.

"Devin?" The voice seemed over-loud, everything was too bright. He waved a hand, not really knowing himself what he meant by it as he pushed the sound away.

"Halther?" he said, frowning at the sound of the name.

"Here, lad. Get this inside you." A flask was pressed to his hands and made its way to his lips. He coughed and sputtered at the brandy, pushing it away.

"Are you all right, lad? Are you hurt?"

"No." He shook his head, then regretted it as a wave of dizziness hit. "Just a bit groggy." He looked around the clearing, eyes registering but not quite understanding the scene before him. A small crater had been driven into the soft earth at the edge of the stone circle and the grass that surrounded it was blackened and scorched. Halther's scouts were huddled around a small fire, tending to their own wounded.

"What happened to the others?" he asked Halther.

"The Bjornmen?" Halther pointed, not waiting for the answer.

Klöss lay in a tangled mess, half-curled around one of the stones at the edge of the circle. Ylsriss had slumped down beside him.

"They're all right, just out cold by the looks of things," Halther confirmed. "Come and let me get a look at you. You could use something to eat if nothing else."

"Obair!" Devin gasped as the memory hit him. "Miriam!"

"Don't, lad. They're gone," Halther warned him but Devin was already moving. The figures were bound together in an embrace with the knife driven through both of them. Whatever force the ritual had let loose had stripped the life from them. Their skin had an odd grey tone and stretched over hollows left by sunken cheeks and wasted muscles. He reached out gingerly.

"Don't," Halther whispered but it was too late. The flesh crumbled where Devin reached for Obair, tumbling down in a cascade of fragments, closer to ashes than skin and bone. The fragments tore others free until the bodies collapsed in on themselves with a soft sigh.

Devin staggered back with a horrified expression.

"I told you, they're gone," Halther said gently. "Don't beat yourself up over that, there was nothing left there but a shell." He led Devin over to the fire and sat him on a section of log, spooning stew out of the pot for him.

The food was almost tasteless but it was hot and Devin found that the more he ate the more he came back to himself. "How long?"

"Were you out?" Halther finished for him. He shook his head with a shrug. "It's about mid-afternoon by my reckoning, so throughout the night and most of this day. Most of us didn't move until morning. I checked you over and left you be until you started moving."

Devin grunted and poked at the stew with a spoon. He sat for a while, soaking up the heat from the fire and trying to coax the stew into tasting better than it did. Klöss and Ylsriss came to after another hour and the group around the fire grew.

The silence that surrounded them was thick and decorated with the frequent glances cast toward the stones as each of them wrestled with memories that felt closer to being dreams.

"Is it done?" Ylsriss asked finally.

"I don't know…" Devin began but stopped himself, letting his eyes drift out of focus as he concentrated. The Wyrde was there, as strong as it had been during the ritual but far easier for him to feel. It was almost as clear as the pain he'd felt from the passage of the fae through the worldtrails but subtly different, somehow familiar.

He nodded. "It is, I can feel the Wyrde."

Ylsriss stared at him for a moment and buried her face in her hands for a moment before rushing away from to the fire for the solitude of the trees. Klöss stared after her, reaching for Gavin's arm and shaking his head when the wiry man made to follow.

It was only as Klöss turned and looked at him expectantly that Devin realised they had no way of communicating without Miriam or Joran. Ylsriss was obviously not going to be of much help right at the moment. Devin frowned at the Bjornman and shrugged helplessly as the man sighed and pointed first at the axe, then the trees, and finally the fire. He nodded as a smile of understanding showed on Devin's face and made his way over to where the body of Tristan lay.

The remains of the cottage provided some easy lumber but even with everyone helping it still took time. It was growing dark by the time Klöss judged the pyre to be ready. It towered above them and the Bjornman refused any offers to help as he worked to light the bundle of twigs and tinder at its base. Klöss stepped away from the heat as the flames rose, seeming surprised to find the others gathered around the pyre as Ylsriss reached for his arm.

They did not speak. There were no words even if they had been able to understand each other. Devin thought back, remembering a different pyre formed from the ruins of another cottage. So much had changed since Artor's death but it yet seemed he had come full circle. The conflict between Anlish and Bjornman would be settled by wiser men than he. For now it was enough that the threat of the fae was over.

He looked up, following the sparks of the fire as they rose into the skies. The moon was bright, just rising above the trees and Devin gazed at it with wonder. He closed his eyes for a moment and forced himself to concentrate, to feel. The Wyrde coursed onward, and through it he felt that same familiar presence. His could feel his mother. Miriam was out there with Obair as he guided her steps in a ritual that would never end. She always would be. Devin looked up at the moon and smiled.

EPILOGUE

Ylsriss burrowed deeper into the furs piled thick on the bed. "Burning hells, what possessed me to come back here?" she muttered to herself.

Hesk was freezing. Winter had come early and wrapped the city in an icy embrace. She hadn't been able to get warm since they'd arrived. Anlan had been cold but Hesk was bitter. It was a cold that crept in past the thick walls and warm fires and leeched away at you until your bones ached. Perhaps some tea would help. She needed something hot inside her.

A low crawl took her to the edge of the bed, moving carefully so as not to let the chill under the blankets. She reached out blindly for the slippers and worked them onto her feet before wrapping herself in the furs and braving the cold air in search of clothes that would go on quickly.

She should have lit the fire in the bedroom when Klöss left that morning. "Daft idea, woman." she muttered. "He should have lit it himself."

A shuffling walk, trailing the furs, took her down the stairs and through into the kitchen. The stove was lit at least, that was something, and the warmth of the kitchen was a blessed relief. She sloshed the kettle experimentally and set it onto the stove to boil.

Snow was falling heavily outside. She peered out through the window and shuddered at the sight. The snow lay thick on the rooftops and was filling the streets. Winter was here in earnest and in Hesk it would be no fleeting visit. The city would be cloaked in snow for the best part of three months now, and even then it would only be tempered by the driving rains of early spring.

The Realm of Twilight had been a warm land. Winter was unknown there, and for the first time she found herself almost envying Joran. Just thinking of the name brought a host of memories and feelings with it, tumbling over each other as they fought for her attention. She pushed them aside as thinking of Joran would only lead to thoughts of Effan and that just led to tears.

She been inconsolable for much of the trip back to the Barren Isles, avoiding most conversation and spending as much time as she could alone by the stern as she looked out over the water. "I hope you're happy, Joran," she whispered.

She reached out with one finger, drawing idly in the condensation on the window, and then stopped herself. The glyphs stared back at her, a simple series that would have worked to activate a runeplate. The water droplets were already running from the bottom of her finger strokes, ruining the image, but for a moment she wondered at it. The glyphs almost looked like the Dernish script that she'd often seen on the precious casks of keft that Klöss so loved. She'd never noticed the similarities before.

The hiss of the kettle brought her back to the stove and her hands worked automatically, producing cup, leaves and honey. She filled the pot and poured. The tea needed to steep but she needed something hot to hold. "Flavour can wait for the second cup," she told herself as she cupped her hands around the mug.

The knocking was insistent, less of a request than a demand, and Ylsriss hurried to the door.

"Gavin!" She flinched back from the snowflakes and the cold wind that burrowed through her furs, seeking exposed flesh.

"I thought I'd see how you're getting on," he said.

She stepped back. "Come in, you look half frozen. Oh, for all that's good and right, you don't even have a cloak! Kick the snow off your boots and get in here."

She pulled him through into the kitchen and poured him hot tea as he stood near the woodstove warming his hands.

"What brings you here?" she said, passing him the cup and setting two chairs close to the stove.

He took it gratefully, hunching over it and blowing at the steam. "Nothing really. It's just been a week or so and I wanted to see how you're doing."

She gave him a look. "Klöss sent you didn't he?"

Gavin blew on his tea.

"Oh, Lord of the Frosts, I'm fine!" she said. "I don't need checking up on."

"If you say so." Gavin sipped at the tea as she glared at him.

"If anything, you need more checking on than I do," she told him. "What have you done since we got back? Where are you even living? Back in that cellar?"

"I'm still finding my feet," he said with a shrug.

That gave her pause. They were more alike than she really liked to admit. "It hasn't been easy," she muttered. "The cold doesn't help."

He glanced over to the window. The snow settled in the frame and stuck to the glass. "It was a lot milder in Anlan."

Hmm." Ylsriss nodded. "Do you think about them?"

"Who?"

"Devin, Obair, all the others." She waved vaguely.

Gavin shrugged, sipping at the tea again. "Sometimes. It's more Tristan for me than anyone else. Though I suspect Devin is going to have his hands full with that red-headed girl."

"Erinn." Ylsriss nodded.

"That's the one." Gavin smiled. "Still, the boy got his happy ending."

Ylsriss looked down at the cup she nestled in her lap. "Happy endings only happen in faerie tales, Gavin. In life you need to work for any ending you can get. The happy ones always seem to take their price in tears. Yours or those of another, the price must always be paid."

He looked at her for a moment. "We didn't have to come back so soon you know? We could have stayed for the coronation at least. Part of me wanted to see their queen get her man too. Rhenkin is as clueless as any man I've known."

"I don't have any interest in foreign queens." Ylsriss sniffed. "Besides, this is my home."

"True." Gavin stood and made his way to the window. "Hesk is home, snow and all." He looked back at her. "What do you think the Keepers will do? With the trade offer I mean?"

She sucked on her bottom lip for a moment. "I don't know. It would change everything, if we had something to trade. The reavings, the whole make-up of who we are would shift. I can't see them doing it though. If we trade our reavers then how long would it take before the Anlish were making their own?"

"I don't think that was the idea," Gavin said. "I got the impression it was more that the Anlish would pay for cargo space on our vessels."

Ylsriss shrugged. "I suppose. I don't really care so long as it gets Klöss's head out of the noose." She'd tried to sound relaxed. She failed.

Gavin went to her, crouching down and taking her hands. "You can't think they blame him for the sealord? For everything?"

"Who else is there to blame?" She gave a sad smile. "Klöss puts on a brave face but he's never been that great at hiding things."

"Klöss will be fine," Gavin told her. "He's already told me they're focusing on the sealord. This whole war has been a disaster from the beginning. The Chamber will need to place blame somewhere and the best place to put it is with a man who can't argue. The sealord sponsored this effort from the start."

Ylsriss stood, turning away from him quickly. "This tea is closer to being just warm water than anything else." She sniffed, wiping at her eyes with her sleeve. "You want another?"

Gavin shook his head and watched as she busied herself at the stove. "You're right though, you know that?" she told him over one shoulder. "They'll spend a month talking but it will work itself out. I..." she broke off as she fumbled the cup and it fell to the ground shattering on the unforgiving floor, splashing the hot liquid everywhere. "Shit!"

Gavin was out of his seat and rushing to her as she stepped back from the mess. "Are you okay?"

"I'm a clumsy fool is what I am," Ylsriss muttered as she fetched a cloth from the sink.

"Well that much is obvious," Gavin said with a grin. "But are you hurt?"

She shot him a black look from where she was crouching over the mess but her smile wouldn't be held back. "I'm fine. Just a bit wet and stupid. I haven't been this clumsy since..." she broke off.

He helped her pick up the pieces of the clay cup and sat back as he watched her make another, stepping awkwardly over the wet floor. The butter dish was set back on the counter, away from the edge but as her foot slipped it was the first thing her flailing hand caught. It shattered as easily as the mug had, sending butter and shards of pottery flying.

"Ylsriss!" Gavin cried as she landed heavily.

She looked up at him, and then back to the butter and the tears began. Flowing hot and fierce with the shock and joy that fuelled them. "I was wrong, Gavin. Maybe it doesn't need to be a faerie tale."

THE END

ABOUT THE AUTHOR

Graham began writing with children's books for his own kids. Fantasy is the genre he has always read himself though, and this is why he started The Riven Wyrde Saga, a fantasy series beginning with *Fae - The Wild Hunt*.

Visit his blog at grahamak.blogspot.co.uk where you can sign up for e-mail updates and be the first to hear about new releases.

Find Graham on Facebook at on.fb.me/1pMyWmK.
He loves to chat with readers.

Follow him on Twitter at www.Twitter.com/Grayaustin

Graham can be contacted at
GrahamAustin-King@Hotmail.co.uk or through his website:
www.GrahamAustin-King.com.

Acknowledgements

And so here it is, the end. In the last few months I've wondered if this book would ever happen. To be honest, it came very close to not happening, and so I owe a massive debt of thanks to a long list of people. This book, in fact this series, wouldn't have happened without the support of my family and my amazing wife. I also need to thank Claire "The Smurf" Frank and Clare Davidson for stepping in at the last second to help with edits and formatting. A big thanks to Steve Drew for my endless blacksmithing questions, and endless gratitude goes out to Tim Marqitz for his amazing work editing and helping to produce this final draft. Finally the biggest thanks goes to everyone who has read and enjoyed my books and taken the time to leave a review or who got in touch to tell me.

It's been fun everyone, I hope you enjoyed the journey.
—GRAHAM AUSTIN-KING